THROW AWAY THE SCABBARD

The Chancellorsville Chronicles

Volume One

C. L. Gray

ISBN 978-1-60145-740-0

Printed in the United States of America

www.chancellorsvillechronicles.blogspot.com
2009

For Stefan and Susanne, who wouldn’t let me quit.

On May 2, 1863, during the Battle of Chancellorsville, Confederate General Thomas "Stonewall" Jackson was accidentally shot by his own men. After his death, the Army of Northern Virginia, commanded by Robert E. Lee, wouldn't see another victory. This is why many historians point to Jackson's death as the turning point of the war in the east and the death knell of the Confederacy. But what if Jackson hadn't been wounded on that lonely stretch of road in the Virginia wilderness? Would the skill and daring of Lee's brilliant lieutenant have changed the outcome of the war? What if...

"Soldiers make short speeches, and, as for myself, I am no hand at speaking anyhow. The time for war has not yet come, but it will come soon, and when it does come, my advice is to draw the sword and throw away the scabbard."

Thomas Jackson
April 13, 1861

Chapter One

Virginia Wilderness
Near Chancellor's Crossing
May 2, 1863 – Night

Lieutenant General Thomas Jackson, commanding the Second Corps of the Confederate Army of Northern Virginia, raised his hand. His party of eight staff members halted on the Mountain Road, a half-mile in front of the corps' skirmishers. Jackson was inching his way down the heavily-rutted path, cut through an impenetrable terrain of pines, shrubs, and hardwood trees, trying to spy out whether the Union army was going to run all the way back to Washington or make a stand in the wilderness. Since he heard nothing but tree limbs rasping in the cool evening breeze, Jackson nudged Little Sorrel, his small red horse, and continued down the road.

The moon escaped from its cloudy shroud and illuminated the thickets on both sides of the road. Jackson scanned them; they were empty. A flurry of activity, 200, no, maybe 300 yards in front of him, caught his attention. He flung up his hand. His aides pulled up, not making a sound. Jackson leaned forward in his saddle, listening. The sounds were recognizable: the sharp ring of axes on trees, shovels scraping against the rocky ground, shouts, and commands. All the sounds associated with the hasty construction of breastworks.

Jackson took out his watch and tilted it until he could read the thin black hands in the faint moonlight. It was nine o'clock. Four hours ago, the Second Corps came screaming out of the woods and smashed into the Union's right flank. The surprised and overwhelmed Yankees ran. Jackson ordered his men to give chase until fatigue, darkness, and the thick undergrowth unraveled his assault. He instructed his three division commanders to reorganize the men as quickly as possible. Not satisfied with routing the Yankees, Jackson was determined to cut them off from the fords along the Rapidan and Rappahannock Rivers. While his men hastened into formation, he pressed ahead to see if he could determine what the Yankees planned to do. A tree crashed to the ground. Jackson had his answer. They were going to fight.

"Let's go," he said, turning Little Sorrel around and heading back toward the Confederate line, back to the battle, and back to the two-year war for Southern Independence.

He followed his aides onto the Bullock Road where he had left the 18th North Carolina Infantry Regiment holding the Confederate forward position. Suddenly, the woods exploded with the thunder of hundreds of guns. Musket flashes pierced the darkness, lighting up the blooming dogwoods. Bullets ricocheted off trees, whistled through the underbrush, and slammed into the dirt. A branch crashed to the ground on Jackson's left. His aides stampeded to avoid the deadly fire.

Before Jackson could flee, someone knocked him out of his saddle. He flew through the air and landed on an exposed tree root. He stifled a groan. A body fell on top of him and pinned him down. Bullets smashed into the tree above his head.

"Lie still, General!"

Jackson recognized the terrified voice of his brother-in-law, Joseph Morrison.

Another volley pierced the night. Jackson tried to get up, but Morrison shoved him back down to the ground. The root dug into his ribs. Overhead, his men yelled for the Tarheels to cease firing. Slowly, the gunfire abated like the end of a rainstorm.

Jackson shifted impatiently. "You can get off me now, Lieutenant. The shooting has stopped."

Morrison released his grip and rose to his knees. Jackson sat up, leaned against the tree, and felt his ribs. He winced in pain.

"Are you bad hurt?" Morrison asked.

"It's nothing. Providence has been kind to us this evening."

More horses poured down the road, this time from the direction of the Confederate line. In the moonlight, Jackson saw the red-shirted Ambrose Powell Hill, commander of the Light Division, jump off his horse.

"General, are you hurt?" Hill asked.

"Just a couple of bruised ribs," Jackson replied after completing a very thorough search of his person. He stood and plucked his weather-stained kepi from the ground. He shook the dust from it. "Tell me, Hill, have you managed to find your way to the Rappahannock?" Jackson drew the kepi down over his blue-gray eyes.

"Yes, sir, but the men are exhausted. I think we should hold off the attack until morning."

"No, sir. No! Press them!" Jackson stabbed his finger into Hill's chest. "Don't let them escape. Cut them off from the United States Ford."

Hill remounted and disappeared into the night.

"Lieutenant Morrison, I want you to return to General Lee. Tell him to press forward immediately." Jackson swung up on Little Sorrel and rode in the direction of the army. His aides scrambled to catch up.

Chapter Two

Fairfield Plantation
Guinea Station, Virginia
May 9, 1863

Jackson stood on the steps of the Chandler House waiting for General Stuart to arrive for a staff meeting. The Yankees were gone. They had retreated to Washington to lick their wounds. When that was done, conscripts would refill their depleted ranks, new weapons would be distributed, the cavalry would be mounted on fresh horses, and the Army of the Potomac, twice the size and strength of the Army of Northern Virginia, would march, once more, down the highways to Richmond.

Jackson knew time was not on the South's side. An opinion shared by General Lee. That's why the moment the Yankees lit out for home, Lee, accompanied by his senior staff, left Chancellor's Crossing for Richmond and a meeting with President Jefferson Davis. Lee stated that he wanted to take advantage of his army's victory before those people – as he called his northern opponent – had a chance to regroup and return to Virginia.

After an exchange of pleasantries and congratulations, Jackson opened his battered portfolio and proposed an immediate invasion of the North. His goal was to impede the Union war machine by destroying the railroads and canals that brought Pennsylvania coal east. A Confederate presence north of the Mason-Dixon Line would force Lincoln to send the Army of the Potomac before it could refit and rearm from its latest defeat. "We pick good ground and destroy their army," he told the attentive Davis. "Once we do, the Eastern Seaboard will be open to us. We can winter in Harrisburg or Philadelphia. In the spring, we can march on New York or Washington. We'll force the Yankees to understand the price they'll have to pay to hold the South in the Union at bayonet's point."

Davis and the Cabinet approved the plan. Jackson immediately left Richmond to prepare his corps for the journey.

Now came the difficult part; saying goodbye. He crept into the nursery and leaned over his daughter's crib. Julia was awake. She recognized him in the morning light and smiled. He swept her into his arms and held her close. She grasped his finger in her tiny fist. Tears stung his eyes. Since her birth, less than six months ago, he had only been with her a handful of days, and, if all went according to plan, a year or more would pass before he held her again. In that year, she would take her first step and say her first word. He kissed her forehead. "My sweet little girl, your Papa has to go away. But I want you to know that I love you very much, and I'll think about you every moment I'm away." With another kiss on her forehead, he laid her back in her crib. "But I'll come home. I promise."

Anna filled their last moments with loving admonishments for him to take care of himself. When she ran out of advice, he gathered his wife close. "*Set me as a seal upon thine heart,*" he quoted from the Song of Songs. "*For love is strong as death...*"

"*Many waters cannot quench love, neither can the floods drown it,*" she whispered.

The clock on the mantle struck the hour. He had to go. One final kiss; one lingering glance at the door.

Tears spilled from Anna's eyes. "I'll expect you home."

"Then I best come home." It took all his strength to walk down the hall and out the front door. The way back to his family was to perform his duty and defeat the Yankees.

The sound of hard riding turned his mind from the heartbreaking scene in the parlor to the more practical matters pressing him. General James Ewell Brown Stuart, called Jeb, pulled up with his typical flourish: the yellow fringe of his sash dancing, black ostrich plumes bobbing in his hat, gold spurs jangling, and red silk-lined cape swirling about him like a matador's cape.

"Good morning, General Jackson." Stuart threw himself off his mare and came to stand at the bottom of the steps.

"General Stuart." The early morning sun reflected off something shiny on Stuart's jacket. Jackson pointed to a small gold shield. Attached to the shield was a chain, and at the end of the chain was attached a small stiletto. The blade was stuck in the coat's buttonholes. "That's new."

Stuart gazed at the shield fondly. "I think it lends me certain panache, don't you think?"

Jackson laughed. Stuart and his love for fancy uniforms! He was the South's Beau Brummell. The more gold braid a uniform had, the better he liked it. He imbued the role of the knight errant, the dashing cavalier he had read about when he was a boy. The romantic portrayal of Stuart as the Beau Saber sold newspapers, but Stuart was more than the dandified caricature the editors portrayed. He was the best cavalryman Jackson had ever known. Twice, he had ridden around the Union army. In last week's battle, Stuart had discovered the Union's right flank in the air. This intelligence was responsible for the South's triumph in the Wilderness.

"Yes, it brings out the rose," Jackson said.

Stuart grinned and sniffed the red flower sticking out of the buttonhole above the stiletto.

"Is General Rodes away?" Jackson asked. He headed toward the back of the house.

"He left for Orange Court House on time."

"Good, good." After the staff meeting, the rest of his corps and two brigades of Stuart's cavalry would join Rodes' division on the long journey to Pittsburgh.

Jackson's adjutant, Major Sandie Pendleton, met the two generals as they came into the backyard. He handed them cups of what passed for coffee in the Confederacy these days. Any other young man, not yet 23, might find it daunting to be the assistant adjutant general of the Second Corps and be responsible for, among other things, organizing the corps' march from the Rappahannock to Pennsylvania, but the blue-eyed, lantern-jawed Pendleton thrived in the position.

"Everyone's here," Pendleton reported, "but General Ewell brought his wife."

Jackson frowned at the irregularity. He glanced at the bald headed Ewell seated next to a pretty, blonde widow at the mess table. Ewell was returning to duty after losing his leg last summer at the Battle of Groveton. Jackson was pleased to have him back. Ewell was an aggressive fighter, unafraid to commit his troops to battle. Unfortunately, Ewell's aggressiveness could only be activated if he was told *precisely* what to do. For Old Baldy was a man who was good at following orders but never initiating them. Which explained his contentment at obeying the dictates of his new wife, even down to the amount of milk he poured into his coffee.

General Jubal Early greeted Jackson as he took his seat at the head of the table. Early was a small man, gray with age, bent to pieces with arthritis, and prone to the occasional profane outburst. Jackson overlooked the profanity when Early forgot who he was talking to. A raised eyebrow from Jackson was usually enough to remind him.

"General Ewell, I'm glad you're back," Jackson said. "This corps has missed you. We're not the same with you gone."

Ewell flushed at the kind words. "It's good to be back. If it would please the General, I'd like to introduce my wife. General Jackson, this is the Widow, Mrs. Brown." His face lit up with the happiness of a newlywed. "My dear, this is General Jackson."

Mrs. Brown rose and curtsied. Her black crepe veil fluttered in the breeze.

Jackson didn't know how to respond to the odd arrangement. He sipped his coffee and waited for inspiration to strike. Next to him, Stuart sat ramrod straight like a setter on a pheasant. His blue eyes flashed with curiosity, and he quivered at the promise of a secret to ferret out. Jackson took another sip of coffee and decided to leave the matter with the cavalry leader. Stuart would breathlessly report all the reasons Ewell was calling his wife by her dead husband's name before the army marched five miles down the road.

Jackson set down his mug. "General, congratulations on your marriage. I'm happy for you. Now, having said that, a staff meeting is no place for your wife." He smiled at the Widow Brown. "I suggest you go into the house and have breakfast with my wife and daughter."

"I'm not going anywhere," the bride insisted. "I'm here at my husband's request. He needs me." She fixed Ewell with a piercing stare. When the stare failed to gain a reaction, she poked him hard in the ribs.

Thus roused, Ewell came to his wife's defense. "I've come to rely on Mrs. Brown since our marriage. She's proven to be an immeasurable help."

"What possible help could she give you at a staff meeting?"

"I counsel him in all types of matters," Mrs. Brown answered for her husband. "Therefore, I'll remain." She planted herself in her seat, opened her fan, and began to cool herself.

"No, you will not!" Jackson raised a warning eyebrow at Ewell. "Don't force me to make it an order."

Ewell snapped to attention at the bark of command in Jackson's voice. He gave his wife a pleading smile. "I'll be fine, dear. Go, and have a nice visit with Mrs. Jackson."

The Widow Brown shot Jackson a withering glare. She appealed to Ewell. "I'll go, if that's what *you* wish, dear."

He nodded. The fan closed with a crack. She jerked to her feet and stalked across the yard.

"In the future, I'll make sure she doesn't attend any more staff meetings," Ewell eagerly assured Jackson.

"What do you mean in the future? Surely, you don't intend to bring her along?"

"She'll remain safe behind the lines."

"She'll remain in Virginia!"

The back door slammed shut. Ewell flinched. "How do I tell her?" He whispered.

"I suggest you tell her gently."

Early choked on his coffee. Jackson stared at him. "Is there something you find amusing this morning, General?"

Early's shoulders shook in laughter. "No, sir."

Jackson looked around the table and saw that most of the men were having a hard time containing their laughter. Except for A.P. Hill, who looked ghostly. "Are you feeling any better?" Hill was suffering another bout of the mysterious illness he had contracted during his West Point days.

"I'm ready to go," Hill said.

"Good to hear. Now, if there are no further distractions, let's get down to business."

Pendleton handed Jackson a file.

Chapter Three

Abraham Lincoln, sixteenth President of the United States, at least of those northern and western states that had stayed the course upon his election, stared out the White House window. At the moment, he was ignoring the table full of generals just returned from Virginia. They were a thoroughly whipped contingent and listening to them chilled him more than the cold, damp room or the dispiriting scene unfolding in the streets beneath his window.

The ruins of the Army of the Potomac, whose sole purpose was to restore all the states to the Union, marched through the muddy, empty streets and a soaking spring rain: heads down, shoulders slumped, and guns dragging in the mud. No cheering throng welcomed them. The few citizens dashing through the rain didn't even acknowledge the army's passing. The weary mules struggled to draw the heavy cannon through the mud. The mules were not the only ones who were exhausted. The soldiers, the Cabinet, the Congress, and the nation were exhausted, too. And so was Lincoln.

The last telegram he had received from Virginia forewarned of disaster. The Eleventh and Twelfth Corps had surrendered, the Third and Fifth Corps had been severely damaged, and Commanding General Joseph Hooker had been captured.

Lincoln sighed to the very depths of his tortured soul. "What will the country say?" He said to no one in particular. "How will I be able to explain this defeat?" He tugged at his tie as if the black strip of material was strangling him. "How will I be able to convince the nation that we must carry on?"

He returned to the table, sat down, and studied each general: Reynolds, Couch, Sickles, Meade, and Sedgwick, in turn. "For we must carry on, gentlemen. We can't allow the lives lost to be sacrificed in vain. No, that I *cannot* ask from the nation. Now, tell me, what are we to do about the Army of Northern Virginia?"

"Permission to speak freely?" General John Reynolds asked.

Lincoln was relieved to hear the fire in Reynolds' voice. Maybe some spark of battle remained within his generals. He waved his hand in permission.

"Sir, you need to get out the way and let us do our jobs."

"I don't believe I'm in the way." Lincoln observed his generals' careful, neutral expressions and realized he was the only one in the room with that opinion.

"I'm sure General McDowell wouldn't agree," Reynolds said. "Or General McClellan..."

Lincoln interrupted angrily. "If I hadn't interfered with General McClellan, he'd still be sitting on the Virginia peninsula bombarding me with telegrams demanding more men and supplies."

"That's because you forced him to take the field before he felt the army was ready. And you denied him the reinforcements that were a necessary part of his strategy."

"I had to protect Washington."

"No, you had to answer Congress' demands that you do something about Jackson running loose in the Shenandoah Valley."

Defeated, Lincoln sighed.

"Exactly." Reynolds smiled sympathetically. "Your political realities dictate to you, and you, in turn, dictate them to your commanders. And when they fail, the newspapers scream, Congress turns up the heat, and you summarily dismiss them. It's public; it's messy; and it's humiliating."

"What do you suggest?"

"That you trust your generals to get the job done. We want to win this war as much as you do."

Lincoln sat back in his chair and stretched out his long legs. The War Department's file on Reynolds did not differentiate him from any of the other generals in the army. He was a West Point graduate who served in the Mexican War and had been brevetted twice for bravery. He did most of his active duty out west. When the war began, he was the Commandant of Cadets at West Point. As for his conduct, the file described him as a soldier's soldier: smart, fearless, and beloved by his men. But the defiance in the dark, flashing eyes was not in the file. While the rest of the generals sat staring at the table, Reynolds dared to challenge his commander-in-chief on the very way he was running the war. "Take command, and I'll give you all the leeway you require."

Reynolds shook his head. "We both know you can't do that. You're up for reelection next year, so you must have victories. General Grant's triumphs out west are too far away to matter. You must win in Virginia, so the newspapers can trumpet your success in bold headlines. You need the nation to know this war will successfully end."

"You are very astute, General. If you'll not come to my rescue, to whom shall I turn?" He gazed at his generals again.

"Your new commanding general is sitting in his room at Willard's Hotel," Reynolds told him. "Send for General Hancock. He'll give you the victories you need."

"I don't know much about him."

"Find out. You won't be disappointed."

Winfield Scott Hancock sat outside the president's office fidgeting with his hat. Two hours ago, a runner had appeared at his hotel room with orders to report to the White House; the president needed to speak to him. Hancock arrived promptly at three o'clock, only to have the White House usher inform him that Lincoln was running late. The usher gestured to a bench against the wall and asked Hancock to wait. That had been 30 anxious minutes ago.

Hancock crossed to the window. He straightened his tie in his reflection, smoothed his mustache, and raked at his goatee. All his grooming couldn't stop his heart from thudding in his chest or his stomach from churning. Satisfied that he looked calm and collected, at least on the outside, he looked past his reflection and down into the street below. The sun had come out from behind the clouds and was attempting to dry the large mud puddles in the middle of the road. The sidewalks teemed with people hurrying about their business with such sublime casualness, Hancock wondered if they even cared that a battle had been fought and lost no more than a week ago.

The office door opened, and a young man stepped out. "General Hancock?" Hancock turned from the window. "I'm John Hay, the president's secretary. He'll see you now." Hay led the way into the office. Lincoln sat behind his desk, reading what appeared to be a dispatch. "Have a seat," Hay whispered, pointing to one of two chairs in front of the desk.

The President signed his name and handed the document to Hay. The secretary left them alone. "I apologize for the delay, General." Lincoln took off his spectacles. "Too many papers to sign. An occupational hazard."

"No apology's necessary."

"I'm glad you've agreed to see me." Lincoln walked around the desk and collapsed into the chair next to Hancock. "I hear you're called Superb. I have many nicknames and none of them superb." He smiled ruefully.

"Don't let the newspapers get you down, Mr. President," Hancock said. Lincoln sat slumped in his chair; his eyes dull with fatigue. He was thin, as if the weight of the war was whittling him down to nothing. "Strong leaders are easy targets."

"Would you mind being a target?"

"Sir?"

"General Hancock, I'll be honest with you. I'm desperate for this war to end." He rubbed his brow with a weary hand. "I need a man who'll fight. I thought that man was General Reynolds, but he turned me down. Instead, he suggested I give the army to you. I've looked at your record. It's very impressive. Will you help me? Will you take command?"

Hancock's heart stopped pounding and his palms stopped sweating. In one unexpected moment, he was being offered the army; the culmination of a 20-year career, spent mostly occupying insignificant positions in out-of-the-way posts because his superiors considered his talent to count mules and bullets an irreplaceable skill. Now, at last, he was being given a chance to prove what he long believed about himself; that his genius was for war and not bookkeeping. He wouldn't waste the opportunity. "It will be my pleasure to serve."

"What needs to happen for the army to return to the field?" Lincoln asked. Then he grinned. "Even though I don't want to interfere with your command, I can't have the army sitting in Washington forever."

"I'll meet with my corps commanders tonight and have a comprehensive plan on your desk within the week." Hancock stood. "With your permission, Mr. President, I'll get to work."

"Permission granted."

Chapter Four

Near Johnstown, Pennsylvania
June 1863

Jackson rode out of camp in a bright mood that was perfectly matched by the beautiful summer day. Last night's rain had broken the oppressive humidity, and the cool breeze whispering through the birch and tulip trees was received as a blessing from Heaven. Joyfully, he threw up his hand and offered a prayer of thanksgiving to God.

The capture of the Allegheny Arsenal had gone off without a hitch. The commandant had surrendered the large armory and all its supplies upon demand. The Second Corps had marched in and stripped the fortress of weapons, horses, and other needed provisions. The corps' wagon trains now stretched for tens of miles and grew daily thanks to the raids Stuart's cavalry conducted throughout the countryside.

As Jackson rode along, Henry Heth's brigade of Virginians raised a cheer for ole Stonewall, the nickname he had earned during the war's first battle. *"There stands Jackson like a stonewall..."* South Carolinian General Bernard Bee had cried to rally his shattered troops. Overnight, Thomas Jonathan Jackson, a professor of Natural and Experimental Philosophy at the Virginia Military Institute, had ceased to exist, and, in his place, stood the indomitable Stonewall Jackson, hero of Manassas, the Valley, and Chancellorsville.

Jackson reined up and watched the sweaty, dusty soldiers pry loose the iron rails from the ground. It wasn't even noon, and the brigade had destroyed over 15 miles of track. An enormous bonfire crackled and popped in a near-by field. The rails were dragged over and thrown on top of the flames. When the iron softened, the rails were corkscrewed into uselessness.

Jackson smiled in satisfaction. Believing that the South couldn't win a war of attrition against its more populous and industrialized neighbor, he had sat down two winters ago to outline an invasion plan guaranteed to bring the war to a quick end. To accomplish this goal, he had to discover a way to halt the production of supplies that allowed the Army of the Potomac to recover rapidly from its many defeats. Jackson had analyzed the problem from every angle until he had arrived at a solution. The northern economy was fueled by coal. Therefore, if the coal's flow could be disrupted: the munitions factories would close, the naval blockade of southern ports would fall, jobs would be lost, and, perhaps, the war-weary citizens would rise up and demand that the Lincoln administration let the South go in peace. The Union loss at Chancellorsville provided Jackson several uninterrupted weeks in the western coalfields to do all the damage he could.

Jackson headed north to where the remainder of the Light Division was engaged in the destruction of the Pennsylvania Canal. He saw a fly-tent pitched under a copse of elm trees. He was leading Little Sorrel toward the tent when a shout warned him to stop. He pulled up just in time. Four soldiers, carrying a large boulder in their arms, crabbed by him on their way to the canal.

A.P. Hill met him in front of the tent. The change of scenery and diet had vastly improved his health. His sickly pallor had been replaced by a tan. His green eyes sparkled with vitality. He had also gained weight, not filling out, but certainly filling in his uniform.

"The men have warmed to their work," Hill said, pointing at the soldiers heaving the boulder into the canal.

"I've seen your handiwork for miles, General," Jackson said. "I'm very proud of your boys. By time you're finished, it'll take the Yankees a year to make repairs."

A shout caught their attention. Four riders raced toward them. Jackson recognized his brother-in-law and his adjutant, but not the other two riders.

"Couriers from General Lee!" Pendleton exclaimed, his face bright with excitement.

One of the couriers retrieved a dispatch from his wallet and handed it to Jackson. He broke the seal and scanned the contents.

"The Yankees left Washington ten days ago. General Lee has ordered us east with all possible speed," Jackson told the assembled group. He reached into his saddlebag, drew out paper and pencil, and wrote:

June 21, 1863
3:15 pm
Near Johnstown

General Lee,
The Second Corps will be on the road tomorrow at dawn.
Look for us on the turnpike.

T. J. Jackson
Lt. Gen.

He folded the paper and handed it to the courier. "How soon will you be able to return to General Lee?"

The courier secured the message in his wallet. "Immediately."

"Good, good. Mr. Pendleton, make sure they get something to eat before they leave." He turned to Hill. "General, your division will remain behind. Complete the destruction of the railroads and canal as quickly as you can. We'll be in a fight soon, and I'll need you."

"Yes, sir," Hill replied.

Jackson read Lee's note again. He was not surprised by the news. The Second Corps' presence in western Pennsylvania had forced the Army of the Potomac to march before it could recover from its loss in the Virginia wilderness. Now, all the Confederates needed to do was find good ground and destroy the enemy. Jackson bowed his head and began to pray.

"Sir, General Johnston has arrived."

Lee looked up from his cavalry's latest report on the position of the Union army and saw his adjutant, Major Walter Taylor, framed in the tent's doorway. A sudden, sharp pain stabbed behind his left eye. "Tell him I'll be right there."

Taylor disappeared with a nod. Lee strained to hear, if not the words spoken between his adjutant and Johnston, at least the tone of the conversation. He heard what he expected to hear. Taylor was deferential, as usual. Johnston was polite, but his cordial words scarcely hid his anger.

Lee picked up the source of that anger: a copy of a telegram Jefferson Davis had sent to Johnston in Mississippi at the beginning of May. The telegram contained two lines: *Relieved of command. Report to General Lee for reassignment.* By having Johnston report directly to Lee, the president had neatly sidestepped any confrontation with the furious Johnston. Unfortunately, Davis' fancy footwork had landed the mess squarely in Lee's lap. He breathed a prayer for wisdom, pulled on his jacket, and stepped out in the early morning cool.

Fog blanketed the small valley where Lee's headquarters were billeted. Through its wispy clouds, the diminutive Johnston looked spectral. "Joe, I hope you had a pleasant trip." Lee struck a friendly note.

"It would have been more pleasant if I knew why I've spent the last week chasing you through the Valley and into Maryland," Johnston snapped. He slapped his quirt against his boot; each smack louder than the one before.

"Let's have a seat." Lee motioned toward some chairs under a clump of trees. Johnston stalked off. "Would you like some coffee?" Lee asked when he caught up.

"What I want is an answer!" He was balanced on the edge of his chair, reminding Lee of a tiny bird ready to take flight at the first sign of danger. The quirt was silent, but color was rising in his face and veins were popping out on his bald forehead.

Lee settled back in his seat. "I was just as surprised as you when I found out that General Longstreet had been assigned command of the armies out west."

"Do you honestly expect me to believe that you had no say in whether your First Corps' commander was reassigned?" He twirled the quirt in his hand.

The back of Lee's neck grew hot. He took a deep breath. Now answer. Calmly, he counseled himself. "It's the truth, Joe, whether you choose to believe it or not."

The quirt came to rest on Johnston's lap. "Why?" For a brief moment, his blue eyes revealed his anguish at being dismissed so abruptly from command, but it was only a glimpse. His eyes hardened in anger.

"Politicians." Lee gestured to let Johnston know that he didn't agree with the decision. "The news from Vicksburg was growing more desperate with each passing hour. Longstreet guaranteed them victory. In my opinion, the Cabinet made a rash choice."

"I could have saved Vicksburg if Davis would have just given me the time I needed," he said defensively. The quirt slashed the air for emphasis.

"No one knows that better than me."

Johnston softened at Lee's reassurance. "Why was I ordered to report to you?"

"With Longstreet gone, I was hoping you'd take the First Corps," Lee said conversationally. He knew he couldn't remove the insult from his request. Until he was relieved, Johnston commanded the Department of Mississippi and all the armies between the Appalachians and the Mississippi River.

Johnston flew back in his chair. Furious, he pointed the quirt at Lee. "What makes you think I'd be satisfied with Longstreet's scraps? Or any of the scraps Richmond insists on feeding me?"

Lee tugged on his jacket sleeve and steeled himself for what was coming next.

"This army belongs to me," Johnston said, his voice like a whip. "When I recovered from my wounds, I should have resumed command. You stole it from me."

Swiftly, Lee cut him off. "President Davis made that decision. Not me. I won't be vilified for obeying orders."

Johnston glared at Lee but said nothing. Suddenly, he jumped to his feet. "The First Corps!" He paced between the chairs; the quirt returned to action. "You must get some perverse pleasure in humiliating me, Robert!"

"You've known me since West Point, Joe." Lee struggled to keep his voice even. "Have you ever known me to take a perverse pleasure in humiliating anyone, let alone my oldest friend?"

The quirt ceased its assault on his boot. Johnston slumped in his chair. Lee looked him in the eye, but Johnston hunched forward and began a careful examination of a wagon rut in front of him.

"You can return to Richmond and wait for another command. You'll probably get one in South Carolina or Florida. But, Joe, what a waste of your prodigious talent." When Johnston didn't answer, Lee changed tack. "I need your help. I'm not well."

At the news, Johnston jerked his head up, a worried look on his face. He reached out a hand and rested it lightly on Lee's arm before awkwardly withdrawing it. Lee was relieved at the gesture, no matter how clumsy. It proved that some remnant of their friendship had survived the dispute over command of the army.

"It's my heart," Lee continued. "I've suffered some attacks this winter. They've weakened me."

"I'm sorry, I didn't know."

"Not too many people do. I'm able to do my duty, but if I should become incapacitated, I must have someone able to take command."

To the right, the corpsmen were loading trunks into a wagon. Johnston watched them intently. The moments dragged. "I can't," he choked out. "You ask too much."

Lee opened his hands in supplication. "I know the sacrifice I'm asking you to make, but there's no one else I trust with the army."

When Johnston turned back, there was a coldness in his stare that chilled Lee.

"And if you become incapacitated, the army would be mine?" He asked.

Lee nodded.

"On that condition alone, I'll do it." He jerked to his feet. "I'll have my baggage sent from Richmond. When can I meet with my division commanders?" He was all business.

"I'll have them assembled within the next hour. In the meantime, can I interest you in that cup of coffee?"

"No." He stomped away.

Lee watched him go until the mist swallowed him up; the quirt once more beating a staccato rhythm on his boot.

The army rendezvoused in a grassy field in Huntingdon County. Jeb Stuart came through the woods, joyously waving his plumed hat. Lee stopped Traveller, his grey gelding, and waited for his young major general.

Lee smiled at Stuart. "You're a sight for sore eyes."

"Oh, General! You should see the stores we captured at the arsenal. And the food! I haven't eaten so well since before the war."

Lee observed Stuart's new finery. "And clothing!" A cloud fell over Stuart's face. "Did I say something wrong?"

"No." Stuart sagged in disappointment. "I managed to buy a new cloak, hat, and plume."

"Then what's the matter?"

"I couldn't find a pair of thigh high boots, and I wanted them most of all."

It was all Lee could do not to laugh at Stuart's crestfallen face. "I'm sorry for the boots, but could I persuade you to take me to General Jackson anyway."

"Yes, sir." A huge smile broke out on Stuart's face. "And don't worry on my account. Pennsylvania's a big state. I'm sure to find a pair of boots somewhere. Perhaps in Harrisburg!"

Stuart spurred his horse and rode off. Lee urged Traveller forward. He could no longer contain his laughter. The mission had gone very well indeed if the only complaint was that Jeb Stuart had not been able to find a new pair of boots.

Chapter Five

The Susquehanna River
Near Duncannon, Pennsylvania
June 1863

Major General John Buford, recently promoted to head the Army of the Potomac's cavalry corps, tipped his canteen and took a long drink of water. He poured the rest of the canteen's contents over his head in an attempt to cool off. The temperature had to be close to 100 degrees, and the stifling humidity made it feel 20 degrees hotter. Behind him, his men were cooling off in the Susquehanna. Jackets, vests, shirts, and boots littered the riverbank. Horses waded into the shallows to drink, unmindful of the boisterous soldiers splashing about them.

Buford secured his canteen and retrieved his portfolio from his saddlebag. He squinted into the late afternoon sun. Last night, his scouts had reported that Lee was on the New Bloomfield Road, a three-day hard march from the Susquehanna. So this morning, Buford had his men up and on the road before dawn, scouting the countryside for good ground to prevent the Rebs from crossing the river and capturing Harrisburg. The day long search had produced no substantial results until his scouting party had burst from the tree lined road into this large clearing.

Buford mopped his forehead with his sleeve then quickly sketched the area. Satisfied with his effort, he closed the leather folder and called for his horse. He wanted to get the information back to Hancock as quickly as possible.

Ten miles south of the Susquehanna, at a spot where the woods swallowed up the road in a canopy of green leaves, a sharp report of musketry punctured the quiet. Up ahead, Buford saw white puffs of smoke and the silver flash of muzzle barrels. His troopers wasted little time. They jumped off their horses, pulled their rifles from their saddle boots, and dove behind the remains of a crumbling cobblestone fence.

Buford slid behind the fence. He raised his field glasses and peered into the lengthening shadows. A blue flag emblazoned with a white palmetto tree unfurled for a brief moment. He cursed in irritation. Up ahead wasn't some Reb scouting party but Wade Hampton's cavalry brigade.

Captain Norris dropped down next to him. "General."

Buford raised his hand to silence his aide. The rapidity of the Rebs' gunfire had caught his attention. He listened intently then slammed an angry fist into his palm. Hampton had repeaters!

At the opening of the spring campaign, Buford had noticed a weakening in the South's cavalry. A weakness that didn't come from a lack of skill, but rather from a lack of supplies: fodder for the animals and replacement horses for the men. With new technology, like the repeater, the Union cavalry had finally begun to gain the upper hand on their formidable opponent. But now, equally armed, thanks to Jackson's successful raid on the Allegheny Arsenal, and riding the best horseflesh in Pennsylvania, the South's strength had been resurrected.

Colonel Devin collapsed beside him.

"How are the boys?" Buford asked.

"It's not the Rebs that's doing the damage, but this infernal heat," Devin complained.

Buford peered over the wall. Neither side had gained an advantage in the hour long skirmish. "Okay, enough! Mount up and return to the ford. We'll cross the river and make our way back to the army."

Devin hurried to obey. Buford looked through his glasses at Hampton's line. He shook his head in frustration. Every last Reb was armed with a repeater.

By time Stuart reached the field, the sun was low on the horizon. Hampton's men stood in small groups, whispering back and forth, death in their faces. Despite the oppressive heat, Stuart shivered. He waited for someone to greet him, but the men ignored him.

Hampton's adjutant walked over. His eyes shone with unshed tears. He tried to speak but couldn't find his voice. Stuart shivered again. "General Stuart." The adjutant's voice broke, increasing Stuart's fears. "General Hampton has been wounded. Sir, it's a mortal blow."

For a moment, Stuart stood rooted in place. He heard the words but was unable to grasp what the man had said. Hampton dying? "Where is he?" Stuart questioned, his own voice no more than a murmur.

"A mile back. Doc's with him now."

Stuart followed the adjutant to a bend in the road. A circle of men, gray silhouettes against the dusk sky, worked feverishly over a stretcher. Stuart stumbled forward. He peered into the dim light and saw Wade Hampton lying on the stretcher. Blood drenched his shirt front, and his sweat-streaked face was deathly pale behind the fierce dark beard. His eyes were closed.

Stuart knelt down. "General Hampton," he whispered, afraid that he was too late and Hampton was dead.

To his relief, Hampton opened his eyes and smiled. "I'm glad you're here with me at the last." Stuart bent low to hear the fading voice. "I prayed you'd come. There have been times I haven't treated you with the respect your abilities and talents deserve."

"That's not true," Stuart protested, even though he knew it was. Hampton believed Stuart not serious enough for the responsibility of command.

"It is, and you must forgive me."

"You've served the Cause with honor, fought with valor, and now die with glory. I'll have Sweeney write songs extolling your virtues. We'll teach them to our children, so your memory may live and never fade away."

"Will you look after my men?" He asked, his breath labored.

"Of course, I will. They'll forever be known as Hampton's Brigade."

That seemed to satisfy him. He stopped his struggles and lay still for a long moment. "Tell my men…" The doctor stooped over him, but Hampton waved him away. "Tell them…I loved them like they were my own sons." He closed his eyes. One long breath eased from him.

Stuart backed away from the stretcher. He gulped once, but couldn't prevent his tears from falling. He took out his handkerchief, wiped his eyes, and blew his nose. "Major McClellan," he called to his adjutant. "I want you to ride to General Hampton's headquarters and take temporary command. If the men need anything, let me know immediately. I need to report to General Lee."

But Stuart didn't go to Lee. Once he passed the army's pickets, he dismissed his aides and rode to East Waterford where the Second Corps was bivouacked. He barged into Jackson's tent. "Wade Hampton's dead," he announced. Then he began to weep.

Dawn was more than four hours away when Jackson rode into Lee's darkened headquarters. He roused the sentry and sent him to wake the general. Underneath the ash and half-burnt logs, embers in the campfire still glowed orange with heat. An owl hooted at him from the branches of a tall sycamore tree. Lee hurried into the light, tying the belt of his black silk robe around his waist.

"Is there trouble?" Lee asked.

"I've come about the Union cavalry Hampton ran into this afternoon."

Lee sighed. "Hampton!" He shook his head in regret. "His death's a blow." He picked up a stick and stoked the fire until it blazed to life. "Have you seen General Stuart?"

"I left him asleep in my tent. He took Hampton's death hard."

"So I've heard. I'm surprised it would affect him so deeply, considering the state of their relationship."

Jackson stared into the fire. "I believe we live our lives as empty vessels, designed to collect all the joy and sorrow destined to come to a man throughout his life. Unfortunately, it seems that life hands out more grief than joy. No man is immune to loss. When my first wife and child died, I thought I would shatter into pieces. Only the mercy of Almighty God kept me in those black months.

"If the war hadn't come, perhaps our cup would have never known the devastating fullness of death and grief. But war fills the cup rapidly. Who knows what death will be the drop the overflows it, or when it'll happen. The death of his darling daughter did much to fill General Stuart's cup. So did the death of Major Pelham. Hampton's death was only the drop that overflowed it."

Jackson stepped aside so a corpsman could set a coffee pot on the fire. When the corpsman departed, he continued.

"When Turner Ashby died, his death was that drop for me. I wept for him, for my young students dead on Henry House Hill, even for my mother who died when I was seven. It's an anguish we can't deny, no more than we can hold back the sun from rising. So strong men weep like children because we're not as strong as we think we are. Then grace comes to us, and we can go on because we know our Lord is a man of sorrows and acquainted with grief.

"The Lord will keep General Stuart in His strength, and he will once more be consumed with finding thigh high boots and riding happily into battle. That's how we'll bear this war. Knowing that weeping endures for the night, but joy comes in the morning."

Jackson drained his cup of the last vestiges of the rich coffee and turned to the pressing matter that had brought him to Lee. "I believe General Hancock means to seize the Duncannon fords. Sir, we can't give away the ground just because the Yankees are closer to the river. We must get there first."

Lee, now dressed, took a piece of toast from a basket. "It is a race we can't win. And in this heat and humidity – Jackson saw him frown – you'll end up with miles of stragglers."

Jackson would not be put off. "Sir, I wouldn't ask if I wasn't sure that I could arrive at the fords with my men intact."

Lee scraped creamy Pennsylvania butter across his toast "How many men will you need?" He took a bite.

"Early is at the head of my column. And I believe Hood is at the head of the First Corps' column." Lee nodded in confirmation. "I'll take them and the Stonewall Brigade. Plus two brigades of cavalry."

Lee wiped his hands on a napkin. "Go on!"

Chapter Six

Jackson stood on a rise that overlooked the river town of Duncannon on the western shore of the Susquehanna River. With a critical eye, he appraised the sun-burnt landscape. Not only did he have to defend the fords of the Juniata and Susquehanna Rivers, he also had to hold the New Bloomfield Road until Lee arrived with the rest of the army. Jackson stared west down the very road in question while the weary soldiers of Early's division tramped past him.

Behind him, to the north, were the town and the fords. To the south, the rise faded into Sherman Creek. A large mountain jutted up south of the creek and dominated the terrain. Jackson pulled his field glasses from their case and peered south. The road that ran parallel to the river was empty except for a farmer driving a wagon laden with produce to one of the nearby villages.

In front of the rise was a large clearing of parched grass framed by thick woods. The New Bloomfield Road cut the woods and field in two. Two hundred yards from where Jackson stood, the road dipped down, hiding the rear of Early's division as it swarmed toward the river.

"The Stonewall Brigade's about three miles back," General Fitzhugh Lee, known as Fitz, informed Jackson. The portly Fitz commanded one of Stuart's cavalry brigades.

"Any news from General Hood?" Jackson asked. He peered across the gray river to see if he could place his artillery on the eastern shore. Fitz indicated there was not. "Please find out."

Jackson returned to his deliberations only to be interrupted by the arrival of another Lee. This time it was General William Henry Fitzhugh Lee, General Lee's second and favorite son and Fitz's cousin. Everyone but his father called him by his childhood nickname of Rooney. Lee called him Fitzhugh.

"General Stuart sends his compliments," Rooney said. Like his cousin, he led another of Stuart's brigades.

"How is General Stuart this morning?"

"Better," Rooney smiled, his mouth barely visible in a face full of whiskers. "He sends word that the Yankees are getting underway."

"How far out?"

"Ten miles. They should be here sometime this afternoon. They're moving rather leisurely in the heat. If you'll excuse me, General Stuart gave me orders to burn the bridge over the creek."

Jackson dismissed him. He sighed in relief. He had won the race and arrived with his columns intact.

Reynolds rode into Hancock's headquarters and strode over to the fire where Hancock, Buford, and General David M. Gregg, one of Buford's division commanders, were involved in an intense discussion. He hoped the coffee pot had not been packed away and was delighted to see the blue and white speckled pot still nestled in the fire. The mugs however had been packed. He asked Win for his.

A courier rode up and handed Hancock a note. He scanned it; then angrily folded it.

"I plan to cut cross country and get on Lee's right flank," Gregg said, finishing the conversation interrupted by Reynolds' arrival.

"I want constant updates, General. No surprises," Hancock said.

"No surprises," Gregg agreed. He saluted and hurried to his horse. Buford excused himself as well.

"Well, let's have it," Reynolds said, pointing at the paper.

Hancock handed him the message. Reynolds read it. Sedgwick's Sixth Corps had failed to make its 15 miles yesterday, but Uncle John was confident he could still make Duncannon by nightfall. Reynolds returned the note and poured another cup of coffee. "Delays are inevitable, Win, you know that."

"I know," Hancock replied, still angry.

"Relax! You've won the race. Lee's still 20 miles away. So, have a cup of coffee." Reynolds held up the cup. Hancock declined. "Well, I'll see to my men. Now, stop worrying. What could possibly go wrong?"

At noon, Reynolds received an urgent message from Buford. He had run into Confederate cavalry two miles south of Sherman Creek. He needed infantry help with all due haste.

Stuart, dust covered but exhilarated, rode up to Jackson. "The First Corps has holed up in the woods over there." He waved his hand toward the southwest. "The Second Corps is an hour down the road. That makes 40,000 Yankees converging on this position."

Jackson stroked his beard and absorbed Stuart's news.

"You're thinking we're going to need more men, right? Because, that's what I'm thinking."

Jackson glared at him. "Since you understand our situation so well, I want you to ride to General Lee and ask him for some help."

Without another word, Stuart pivoted his mare and galloped down the New Bloomfield Road.

"Major Pendleton!" Jackson said, choking on the dust Stuart's departure had kicked up. "Please inform General Hood he's about to have company. Lieutenant Morrison, tell General Early the same."

John Bell Hood's division, reinforced by Gordon's brigade from Early's division, managed to hold off Reynolds' latest assault. But the tall Kentuckian, with the flashing eyes and the long blonde beard, had grave doubts whether his weary men could do so again. Ten minutes ago, Rooney Lee's troopers had mounted up and rode off, leaving a gaping hole in the line. To fill the breach, Hood ordered his men to the right, but the result was less than desirable. His line was so tautly drawn that all the Yankees had to do was push and it would snap in pieces. His request for more men had been denied by Jackson. So, somehow, he had to find a way to hold his overextended and exhausted division together.

Pendleton rode up.

"Major," Hood said before Pendleton could speak. "I need cannon fire poured down on the Yankees the moment they come out of the woods. They're overpowering me. I need everything General Jackson can spare."

"I'll tell him, sir."

Shouts along the line announced the Yankees' approach.

"Now, Major," Hood barked in dismissal.

Pendleton plunged into the woods and wound his way through the dense trees. Union artillery exploded overhead. Without warning, his mare collapsed from underneath him. He pitched head over heels and slammed onto the hard ground. The wind was knocked from him and his right leg felt on fire.

Petrified, Pendleton tried to breathe, but his lungs refused to fill with air. He forced himself to relax. As suddenly as his breath left, it returned. He took a gulp of air. Then another. He wanted nothing more than to lie in the shade and breathe in and out, but the white hot pain in his leg demanded his immediate attention. He tried to stand, but every time he moved his leg, waves of agony raced through his body. Just ahead, he saw a tree. He dragged himself over to it, careful to keep his leg still. He rolled over and sat up. He saw his mare lying dead; a large wound in her side.

His trembling fingers moved down his thigh. Blood gushed from a hole and ran down his leg into his boot. He knew if he didn't stop the flow, he would bleed to death. He fumbled at his jacket but could not grasp the buttons. He clenched his hands in tight fists. When his shaking ceased, he tore at the buttons. The jacket opened. He jerked out his shirttail and tried to rip it, but the coarse material refused to give way. He sobbed and gnawed at the hem until he chewed a hole wide enough for his fingers to fit through. He counted to ten and ripped with all his might.

In weary victory, he stared at the wide strip of cloth in his hands. He steeled himself and raised his leg. It exploded in pain. A constellation of white and red stars burst before his eyes. He ignored the searing agony and passed the cloth beneath his leg. It was too much. He turned his head and vomited into the leaves. The world spun drunkenly about him. He closed his eyes. He was so tired. How easy it would be just to go to sleep and slip away.

He forced his eyes open and shook his head to clear it. He dug through the moist, decaying leaves for a stick, but his search came up empty. Tears coursed down his cheeks.

"I am in the woods! There has to be a stick nearby. There has to be!" He sobbed. Finally, his clawing fingers stumbled upon a stick half-buried in the dirt. He jerked it out and rested it on his thigh. He brought the opposite ends of the cloth together and tied a knot around the stick. He twisted the stick until it wouldn't twist anymore. Had the bleeding stopped? He couldn't tell.

He lay down on a soft bed of pine needles. Everything around him faded into darkness. The last thing he remembered was the flash of blue-gray eyes.

"What are you doing?" Hood demanded. "I asked for artillery during the last attack. Where was it?"

Jackson held up his hand to blunt Hood's verbal assault. "I didn't receive your request, sir." There was a strong warning in Jackson's voice for Hood to tread lighter.

Hood doused his anger. "I sent your adjutant…what's his name…oh, yes, Pendleton, to tell you that I needed cannon fire down on that field."

"Captain Smith, have you seen Major Pendleton?" Jackson's voice rose in alarm. Like Joe Morrison, the pale and slight James Power Smith served on Jackson's staff as an aide-de-camp.

"No, sir, I haven't."

"Please tell Colonel Crutchfield that I want the Yankees broken up before they reach our position. Is that understood?"

"Yes, sir." Smith spurred his mare and galloped away.

"General Hood, please show Lieutenant Morrison where you last saw Major Pendleton." Jackson turned toward his brother-in-law. "Joe, I want you to ride back to this position with great care. Sandie may be hurt and unable to call for help."

Morrison followed Hood back down the rise. Jackson bowed his head and began to pray.

Lieutenant Colonel Ira Grover hurried his malingers into formation. During the last assault, the Rebs had bent like a green twig. They hadn't snap, but the splinters and fractures were clearly visible. The Confederates needed to be hit again before they could bring up reinforcements. Grover heard Reynolds shouting at the men to hurry. He smiled. Reynolds could sense victory, too.

The drums began their roll, and the command was given. Grover led the 7th Indiana out of the shelter of the trees and across the hard, sun-baked ground. From across the river, the Confederate guns unleashed a tremendous bombardment. Shot, solid and grape, came hurtling toward them.

"Steady, men!" Grover said. Huge holes were blown into the line ahead of him. He stepped over a private who no longer had legs. This was the worst part of battle: to stay in formation; to move forward while shells burst all around, ripping, maiming, and killing; and to ignore the anguished cries for help even when those cries came from lifelong friends, or worse, your brothers or relatives.

A shell drove through the line to his left, mowing down his men. The young flag bearer crumpled and died. A grizzled old veteran caught the flag. He hoisted it high, but the flag hung limply from its staff. There was no breeze. The regiment had been fighting in the humid, heavy air all afternoon. His men ignored the chaos and continued to cross the field just as he had trained them to do.

When the Hoosiers were 50 feet away, the Rebs unleashed a terrific volley.

"Return fire!" Grover ordered.

His men lowered their guns and fired. The Reb line disintegrated. Those who weren't wounded or dead fled. "Charge bayonet!" Grover shouted. Eagerly, his men sprang forward.

They hadn't gone more than ten feet when Grover heard an insidious Rebel yell. It was so loud and close that the hairs on the back of his neck stood on end. He pivoted. The New Bloomfield Road was packed with gray uniformed soldiers forming an attacking line of their own.

"About face!" Grover yelled. His men wheeled left 180 degrees. The newly arrived Rebs fired. The Hoosiers went to pieces.

"Has Lee arrived?" Reynolds yelled at Hancock the moment he rode up.

"No, according to Gregg, Lee's still miles away."

"Then who is that?" Reynolds pointed in the direction of the New Bloomfield Road.

Hancock raised his field glasses. "I don't know," he confessed.

Reynolds seethed in impotent rage. "Damnation, Win! What's Gregg doing? What else don't I know? Is the entire Reb army descending upon my left flank?"

"Are you finished?" Hancock barked. Reynolds nodded meekly. "Good. I'll bring up the lapse in intelligence with Buford tonight. But right now, we've enough time to make one more assault before dark. We're going to demonstrate against both flanks and strike the center. If we hit them in the center, they'll give way."

The soldiers of the Stonewall Brigade and the recently arrived soldiers of Kershaw's, Wofford's, and Barksdale's brigades faced west, not seeing the setting sun or the salvation of approaching darkness. All they saw were two corps of the Army of the Potomac rolling toward them like a mighty tidal wave. Closer and closer the deluge came, growing in size and menace. The wave crashed against the rise and washed the gray troops from its path. Urgent shouts and anguished cries intermingled with the smell of gunpowder and blood. The Confederates slashed at the Yankees with bayonets, fists, or whatever else they could lay their hands on, but the Yankees were too strong. Jackson's men were driven backward step-by-begrudged-step toward the river.

Jackson watched his center collapse. Movement on his left revealed Hays' Louisiana Tigers running to his assistance. From his right, there was no movement. The Yankees' demonstration had frozen Hood in place. "Mr. Smith, please see what help General Hood can send."

Jackson turned to give another order. Stunned, he gasped, "Mr. Hotchkiss! What are you doing here?"

The Second Corps' cartographer smiled. "I brought you a gift." He pointed behind him. Jackson saw General Robert Rodes riding up the rise followed by his division.

A funereal pallor, black as night, hung over Hancock's headquarters. All unnecessary noise had been stifled, and the corpsmen carried out their duties in hushed and whispered voices. Hancock sat at the head of his mess table with Reynolds and Second Corps Commander, Darius Couch, on his left and right. None of them spoke. They just stared at their plates in stunned silence, their minds replaying the bitter moment when the army had been pushed off the rise by Rodes' arrival. Now, adding insult to injury, the strains of *Dixie* could be heard from the New Bloomfield Road. Lee was arriving. What little appetite Hancock possessed, evaporated. He pushed his plate away.

Reynolds pushed away his plate as well. "I've been thinking."

"That's encouraging," Couch replied. He doggedly picked at his beef.

Hancock grinned. "What about?"

"Maybe God does fight on Jackson's side. Maybe he really is a general in the Army of the Lord, and that's why he keeps whipping us."

Couch dropped his fork. "Surely, you don't believe that."

"Do you have another explanation for the arrival of not one," Reynolds held up one finger, "but two," he added another finger, "divisions at the precise moment to turn the battle? One, I would chalk up to coincidence or just dumb luck, but two? I think that falls under Divine intervention."

"You're not suggesting that prayer is the key to winning battles, are you?" Couch asked incredulously.

"Scoff all you want, Darius, but that ole Presbyterian is doing something very right. I believe I'll pray especially hard tonight. What could it hurt?"

"Not a thing," Hancock chuckled, his humor and appetite restored. He pulled his plate to him and attacked his food.

There was a flurry of activity just outside the reach of the fire's light. Buford strode over to the table. He threw himself into a chair and stripped off his gauntlets.

"Well?" Hancock asked.

"General Gregg sent two couriers to warn us that three brigades had been dispatched from Lee's column. I just checked. They didn't make it back."

Hancock loudly exhaled. In all likelihood, Gregg's scouts had either been captured or killed. "And the second time?"

Buford poured a cup of coffee. "There's no way Gregg could have known. He was confined to Lee's right. Rodes came from the left."

"All right," Hancock said, satisfied with Buford's explanations.

Meade rode up.

"Coffee, George?" Reynolds asked.

Meade waved no. He looked tired and older than his 48 years. He collapsed next to Couch, raising a small dust cloud. "We did the last three miles in the dark."

The generals were treated to a rousing rendition of *Bonnie Blue Flag*.

"What's the plan for tomorrow, Win?" Meade asked over hurrahs for Southern rights.

"Besides John's plan to spend the night on his knees in prayer, I don't have one, yet." Hancock laughed at Meade's quizzical expression. "John, why don't you explain your theory on Jackson's success."

Reynolds refilled his coffee cup and did so.

Pendleton felt a cool rag on his head. He opened his eyes and found himself staring into blue-gray eyes.

"Welcome back," Jackson said.

He became aware of his surroundings. He was in a hospital bed, his hot wool uniform replaced by a linen night shirt. A stained and mended sheet, recently washed (he could smell the strong lye soap) covered him. Jackson sat on the edge of the bed, smiling down at him.

His leg! It didn't hurt any more. Terrified, his mind jumped to the worse possible conclusion. He began to weep. "Is it…Do I…" He could say no more.

"You're fine. You still have your leg. The tourniquet you made saved your life. That, and the unrelenting efforts of Lieutenant Morrison."

Tears of fear turned into tears of joy. “Remind me to thank Joe when I see him,” Pendleton replied. He was very sleepy, but there was something else pressing down on him, worrying him. *What was it?* He remembered. “The battle…”

“Is won for the day.”

His eyes defied him and closed of their own volition. “Sir…”

“It’s okay, Sandie. Go to sleep.”

He obeyed.

Chapter Seven

Once more Jackson stood on the rise and looked west at the woods framing the large clearing and the New Bloomfield Road. The sun was directly overhead. Yesterday afternoon, as he stood in the heat and dust, he didn't think it could get any hotter. Compared to today, yesterday was a fair spring day. It was only noon, but the thick, humid air was suffocating. Sweat poured down his face. Behind him, Gordon's Georgians rolled four large wooden barrels to their position left of the rise. A young private, laden down with dripping canteens, hurried after them, and a bucket brigade noisily formed from the river to the barrels' new home. Jackson wiped sweat from the field glasses' eye pieces on his lapel. He raised the glasses and refocused on the woods in front of Ewell's position. "There's movement in those woods. Captain Smith, please inform General Johnston that the Yankees are moving to his right."

"Yes, sir," Smith said.

When Smith returned from his errand, Jackson's attention was concentrated on the woods in front of the Light Division. He could see a long column of men snaking through the woods from the Yankee's position across Sherman Creek. He lowered his glasses and turned to Smith. "Well?"

"Sir, I don't think he believed me."

Jackson scowled in irritation. Little Sorrel was brought forward, and Jackson rode off toward the right flank.

"Good day, General Jackson," Johnston said.

Jackson ignored the annoyance in Johnston's voice. Last night, during a brief meeting, Johnston had made it perfectly clear that he expected Jackson to stay on his side of the field and not meddle in First Corps' affairs. "The Yankees have been winding their way through the woods for the last hour," Jackson said, meddling anyway.

Johnston's face burned scarlet at Jackson's impatient tone. He raised his field glasses and looked in the direction Jackson indicated. A long moment passed. "No sir, I don't see any movement."

Jackson re-examined the area and saw the faint outline of men picking their way through the trees. "I don't know what to tell you, General, but they're out there and headed toward your flank."

"I'll keep a sharp eye." Was all Johnston said before riding away.

Jackson watched him depart for a shocked minute, then spun Little Sorrel around and went to find Lee.

"What's the matter?" Lee asked as he rode up.

"The Yankees are moving into position on our right." Jackson pointed toward the field and woods.

Lee's face revealed his alarm. "Are you sure?"

Jackson nodded. He walked with Lee to the Light Division's position in the center of the line. "Look into the woods right in front of you. Find a spot a hundred yards in where the sun shines through the trees. Keep focused there and watch."

Lee peered into the woods. He gave a start before gazing up into the cloudless sky. "Could it be a natural occurrence?" He asked, his field glasses focused back on the woods.

"I don't believe so. It started in front of General Ewell's position and has been moving right ever since."

"We would see those people when they came out of the woods onto the road." Lee indicated the road he marched down last night.

"You probably didn't notice it in the dark, but the road dips down. That's why the Yankees didn't see Wofford's brigade until they were on the field."

Lee examined the spot again. "Do you know how many?" Jackson shook his head. "Okay, I'll make the necessary adjustments."

Relieved, Jackson rode back toward Sherman Creek.

Lee and Jackson were standing with General Early at the creek bank when Union artillery unleashed a deafening barrage. Generals and aides dove to the ground, hands over their heads. There was no respite. Every cannon in the Union Army was honed in on the defenses along the creek.

"A *feu d'enfer*," Lee said to Jackson during a lull in the shelling.

Early took advantage of the stillness and hurried his men to safer regions nearer the river.

Lee brushed dust from his uniform. "An old Napoleon tactic. General Hancock is attempting to break up my left flank with his artillery. Once he does, he'll throw his strength against it and overwhelm it."

Jackson wasn't convinced. "General, I watched the woods for the better part of two hours. The Yankees have moved a considerable force through them."

"Do you know how many?" Lee questioned.

"No, I don't."

"I've instructed General Johnston to keep a close eye on the woods. In the meantime, I must prepare for the attack on my left. I'm afraid you may not have enough men."

"My lines are secure," Jackson assured him.

"Even so, I'll ask General Johnston to send us what he can spare. I believe we should err on the side of caution."

"Yes, sir." Jackson could say nothing more. Shells screamed overhead and drowned out all conversation.

The artillery barrage ceased, and a silence descended upon the battlefield. It didn't last. A symphony of sounds erupted: the roll of drums, the shouts of officers, the rattle of muskets, and the sure steady stamp of thousands of boots smacking the ground. The Union's Second Corps tramped out of the woods toward Early's division. Kershaw's and Barksdale's brigades, dispatched by General Johnston from his extreme right, filled in the line and reinforced the creek's defenses. Lee nodded in approval. His army was more than able to receive those people's attack.

Unexpected cannon fire from the right! Lee whirled Traveller around in time to observe a Federal corps march from the woods in front of his denuded right flank. He shuddered in horror when another Federal corps marched out of the woods straight at his center.

From across the river Confederate artillery thundered, but it only delayed the onslaught. Those people reformed after every explosion and continued their advance. The first line reached the bottom of the rise. Semmes' Georgians stood and delivered a scorching volley. The Yankees fell back in confusion. A second wave of blue-coated soldiers pushed past their wounded comrades and thronged the fortifications.

Lee dispatched an aide across the river with orders for Hood's division, held in reserve after yesterday's fight, to secure his damaged right. But how long would it take Hood to form up his men? He needed immediate help. If his flank was turned, he would lose the battle. Lee sent Major Taylor on the gallop to Jackson. When Taylor returned, Jackson was with him.

"General Lee, the Yankees are only demonstrating against my flank. If I strip men away, they will attack in earnest," Jackson protested strenuously.

"McLaws cannot hold those people back by himself!" Lee exclaimed, angry not only at Jackson's argumentative ways but at himself for being so brilliantly fooled.

"I have Dole's and Iverson's brigades in reserve. You can have them." Lee nodded his consent. "Lieutenant Morrison…"

"I heard, General!"

Stuart rode up to see if his cavalry could offer assistance.

"General Lee, we need to sweep the field with the bayonet. If we don't seize the offensive, we'll be defeated," Jackson declared. All three generals turned when the Light Division guns began to bark.

Lee only paused a moment before giving his consent. Jackson galloped away. He had no sooner gone when a sweating Johnston rode up. "We're losing the right flank," he reported, unable to keep the panic out of his voice. "My men can't hold any longer."

"I'll drive them back," Stuart said. He hurried off before Lee could stop him.

"I don't think General Stuart's cavalry will make any difference," Johnston stated.

"I'm afraid you're right," Lee said. "That's why we're going to sweep the field, starting with the left flank."

Johnston balked like a stubborn mule. "Sir, my men are in no condition to do that. They're fighting for their lives."

Lee was grim. "We have no other choice."

Hancock rode back and forth between two poplar trees at the edge of the field. He was wearing a groove in the hard earth, waiting for Lee to strip his left flank in order to save his battered right. Through his field glasses, he saw Reynolds' men turn the cannon around on the Confederates. But for some inexplicable reason that defied logic, Jackson's men sat tight behind their fortifications. The end of Couch's line was already engaged at the creek. The rest of the Second Corps trudged across the rutted field and linked up with the Sixth Corps.

The Rebel yell detonated over the field. *What on earth?* Hancock watched with a mixture of awe and dread as Jackson's defenses emptied, and 30,000 screaming Johnny Rebs ran straight at Couch's advancing lines. Couch's men slowed, unsure how to handle the new development. In the hesitation, one man turned and pushed his way through the tight formation. Two men joined him. Then a platoon here and there. The trickle quickly turned into a torrent. Hancock could hear Couch bellowing at his men to keep moving. His orders made no impact. More than half his corps was running in the direction of the woods.

Hancock rode into the stampede. "No, boys, you can whip them! Turn and fight!"

The gray troops slammed into the remainder of Couch's men and pushed them off their feet. More soldiers bolted toward the rear.

"Rally to me!" Hancock shouted at the men flowing past him. "Rally to…" He couldn't breathe. He glanced down at his spotless white shirt. A small black hole and a spattering of blood stained it. At first, he didn't realize the blood was his because he didn't feel any pain. In fact, he felt nothing at all. Not his hands on the reins, the hot sun burning his cheeks, or the nerves of battle that had gripped him the moment Reynolds marched out of the woods. He tumbled from his horse and didn't even feel the hard ground when he landed.

Someone grabbed his hand and called his name. Hancock opened his eyes and saw Couch kneeling above him. *Poor Darius! He looked so scared.* "Put Meade in." His attempts to stand failed. He couldn't feel his legs. How odd.

Couch pushed him back to the ground. "No, no. Lie still, Win!

"Darius, tell John…the….army belongs…"

Couch held the limp hand a moment before tenderly placing it on Hancock's chest. He stood. "Lieutenant Burt, tell General Meade that he must put his men in now! Lieutenant Potter, find General Reynolds. Tell him that General Hancock is dead and command has passed to him."

Couch willed himself not to look at Hancock. He needed to stay focused on the battle. He gathered up his reins. A shell blasted nearby and knocked him to the ground. His horse spooked; the reins whipped free from his gauntleted hand. He scrambled to his feet and saw Rebs no more than ten feet away.

"Surrender! Surrender!"

There were five of them shouting and looking for an excuse to shoot. Slowly, Couch raised his hands. He felt a bayonet prod his back. His captors herded him in the direction of the Confederate line.

"How far do you think we should let the men chase those people?" Lee asked Jackson as the Second Corps receded from view.

"Until the Yankees either surrender or are dead."

Lee smothered a laugh. "That far, eh!"

A group of dirty soldiers approached with Jackson's former West Point classmate at the end of their bayonets. "We caught ourselves a Yankee general," they bragged to Jackson. "General Hill said we was to bring him to you."

"Thank you, gentlemen," Jackson said. "I'll take charge of the prisoner."

"Does that mean we can go back and chase us some more Yankees?" They asked, their heads swiveling between Jackson and Lee.

Lee laughed and pointed toward the field. "Sure, chase them all you want."

Their faces lit up in excited smiles. "Come on, let's go." They hustled back down the rise.

"Do you need anything, Darius?" Jackson asked Couch. "Some water or medical attention?"

"No, Tom," Couch replied with a shake of his head.

"Major Taylor," Lee called, "please escort our prisoner to the provost guards. Make sure he receives anything he needs."

Jackson suddenly chuckled. "Imagine the boys wanting to get back to the field so they could chase more Yankees. Probably hoping to capture another general."

He was still laughing when Major McClellan rode up. "General Stuart is down," he announced through his tears.

Chapter Eight

A mob hid Stuart from view. Every soldier had an idea on what should be done for the cavalry leader and expressed those opinions at the top of their lungs. They quieted when Lee and Jackson approached. Jackson pushed his way through and stared down at the injured man. Stuart lay in the dust. His face was pale, and his eyes were closed. Rivers of sweat had left traces of their descent on his dirty face. His hands clutched his right side. Blood ran through his fingers.

"Fetch Doctor McGuire," Jackson said to Smith, referring to the Second Corps' chief medical officer. He knelt down in the dust, but Stuart didn't acknowledge his presence. "Jeb," he whispered.

"Now, I know I'm dying," Stuart groaned. "You've never called me that before."

Jackson half-laughed, half-sobbed in response. He swung around and propped Stuart's head gently on his knee.

"It's nothing," Stuart insisted. His lips were so constricted with pain that Jackson could see the impression of his teeth in them. Stuart opened his eyes. "I didn't mean to worry you, sir," he apologized to Lee.

Lee's face went pale. He knelt down next to Stuart, who removed one hand from his wounded side and clutched desperately at Lee's hand. Lee caught and held it. "I'm not going anywhere," Lee promised. Stuart closed his eyes and sighed.

Jackson carefully opened Stuart's fighting jacket. The red checked shirt beneath was blood soaked. He began to probe the wound.

"No, no," Stuart whimpered pitifully. He pushed Jackson's hand away. Tears tracked more rivers through the dust on his face.

"Okay," Jackson relented, "We'll wait for Doctor McGuire." He looked at Lee and shook his head. *How could Stuart survive such a severe wound?*

"Flora," Stuart whispered, "she'll take it hard."

"You're not going to die, Jeb," Jackson said.

"Stop calling me that! It's not natural." He writhed in pain.

An ambulance pulled up, and Doctor McGuire jumped down from the back. Lee tried to stand to make room for the doctor, but Stuart refused to let go of his hand.

McGuire took a large stride over Stuart's legs and knelt down on the other side. "General Stuart, how are you?"

"I'm afraid it's bad," Stuart confessed.

For a wild moment, Jackson thought he was going to lose control of his emotions. Waves of fear beset him. *How could he endure this war without this young man's teasing ways?* He became aware of McGuire calling his name. "I'm sorry, what?"

"Help me remove his coat."

Lee let go of Stuart's hand, but Stuart opened and closed his hand until Lee grasped it again. Stuart's grateful smile was overtaken by a grimace of pain. McClellan plucked up the discarded jacket and folded it gently over his arm.

Jackson whispered to Stuart. A constant stream of chatter that made little sense but distracted the cavalry leader from McGuire's examination. Finished, the doctor stood and motioned for the corpsmen. They carried a blood-stained stretcher over to Stuart.

"Doctor?" Jackson asked.

McGuire's bleak face said more than Jackson wanted to know.

The corpsmen tried to lift Stuart onto the stretcher, but he refused to let go of Lee's hand. Lee murmured to him, but still, Stuart refused. Lee pried Stuart's fingers from his own. The corpsmen laid Lee's young major general on the stretcher.

"General Jackson," Stuart called as the stretcher was raised into the air. He waved a feeble hand.

"I'm right here." Jackson grasped Stuart's hand.

"I want to know if you'll look after Flora and the children for me. Please."

Jackson wished Stuart would stop talking about dying. He needed to fight death, not surrender to it. "Of course."

"There are papers in my baggage. A will, bank records, a life insurance policy."

Jackson looked helplessly at Lee.

"Son, you don't have to worry about anything," Lee said.

Stuart burst into tears. "I wish I could have seen the baby."

Jackson squeezed Stuart's hand. "You'll see your baby. I promise. Now, General, I order you to fight. Fight and get well."

"Aye, aye, sir," Stuart said obediently.

The stretcher was loaded into the ambulance. McGuire climbed in next to Stuart. The driver flapped the reins, and the ambulance drove off.

"If he dies," Lee's voice cracked and tears welled in his brown eyes, "I shall never stop weeping." He turned away.

Jackson sank to his knees and began to pray.

***

The tent flap opened. From his hiding place in the shadows of the pine trees next to the operating tent, Jackson saw a drawn and weary McGuire step out into the night air.

"Well?" Jackson asked, his heart in his throat. He came into the light to better gauge McGuire's reaction.

McGuire rubbed his eyes. "He's alive."

Jackson offered up a prayer of thanksgiving. McGuire took off his bloodstained apron, folded it, and set it on a small pile of linens near his feet. He put his hands on the back of his hips and arched backwards. "I got the bleeding stopped and repaired the damage." He straightened up. "If peritonitis doesn't set in, he'll live. He's drifting in and out of consciousness, but you can see him if you like."

Jackson walked into the tent and smelled the lingering aroma of chloroform. A small lantern burned overhead. Stuart lay sleeping on the wooden operating table. Bandages swathed his right side. In the pale gold light of the lantern, he appeared frail and vulnerable. A wave of protectiveness washed over Jackson.

"My dear Stuart, when we get to Harrisburg," he whispered, "I'm going to make it my duty to get you a pair of thigh high boots, even if I have to commission some Yankee cobbler to make them."

Stuart smiled in his sleep. All of Jackson's pent-up anxiety gave way, and he began to weep.

Lee slipped inside the private tent where Stuart now lay recuperating. A candle burned low on the corner table, casting shadows on the tent wall and across the bed. An empty chair sat next to the bed. Lee sank down on it and listened to Stuart's shallow but healthy breaths. He reached over and picked up Stuart's hand. There was no fear or pain in it now. He brushed a lock of hair from Stuart's forehead. "I've never told you this, but I need your laughter, Jeb. You've always been a constant source of a joy to me. Since the first day I met you at West Point." He leaned over and kissed Stuart on the forehead.

Stuart slowly opened his eyes. "Am I going to live?" His asked hoarsely.

"You'll hold your baby."

"Good," Stuart fell back to sleep.

Lee held Stuart's hand for a few minutes longer, then laid it back on the bed. He stood and took another long look at his young major general. Good, Stuart had whispered. What a blessed understatement. It just wasn't good; it was more than wonderful. When Lee returned to his headquarters, he was smiling.

Abraham Lincoln collapsed into a chair; John Reynolds' telegram clutched in his trembling hand. His heart beat so wildly that, for a hopeful, happy moment, he believed he was having an attack. If God was merciful, his overburdened heart would shatter, and he would die and finally be free of this war. How could he weather this latest storm? For this defeat was worse than Chancellorsville or even Second Bull Run. What would the country say now!

Lincoln put his face in both his hands and allowed one mournful sob to escape. Where could he turn for help? His mind went to the only place possible. Out west was his salvation. Out west was the one general who fought and won. He grabbed his coat and rammed his long arms into the sleeves as he ran past Mr. Hay. He ignored the chief usher at the front door and beat a path through the crowded streets. Death must be in his face, for the people melted out of his way with horrified expressions on their faces. Yes, that was fitting, for he was the Angel of Death. Because of his stubborn insistence to see this war through to victory, thousands of men had died on a hot, dusty field in Pennsylvania, just as they had done in the Virginia wilderness. But out west was his avenger. All he had to do was summon him, and all would be righted.

Lincoln's hand shook as he wrote the telegram. He handed it to the young clerk with the same indescribable relief a sinner must experience when God forgives him of his sins. The click-clack of the telegraph key sent his message to Tennessee. General Ulysses S. Grant was ordered east to take command of the army.

Chapter Nine

Harrisburg, Pennsylvania
July 4, 1863

A light drizzle fell as Lee rode into Harrisburg. To his utter amazement, the streets were lined with enthusiastic residents waving handkerchiefs and shouting his name. Last night, Stuart's scouts had informed him that the roads to Philadelphia teemed with refugees, and the empty houses he had passed on the outskirts of the city had confirmed the report. So, this raucous crowd, behaving as if his long column was a Fourth of July parade and not an occupying army, came as an unexpected surprise. Lee tipped his hat in acknowledgement, not really knowing what to make of the spectacle. To his right, Johnston, looking equally perplexed, acknowledged the shouts. Not so, the men from Pickett's division marching behind. Unlike their commanding general, they knew exactly what to do: flirt with the pretty girls, accept the bouquets of wilted summer flowers showered upon them, and exchange catcalls with the men not in uniform.

"Where's Jeb Stuart?" Someone shouted. The demand ricocheted through the crowd. "Where's his plumed hat?"

"It seems the fame of General Stuart's hat is known everywhere," Lee quipped to Johnston's amusement.

"I suppose they won't be satisfied unless General Stuart dashes down the street and asks all the pretty girls to dance," Johnston replied.

There would be no dancing, for Stuart was still Doctor McGuire's reluctant patient. Ordered to lie quiet and rest, Stuart had cooperated with the doctors and orderlies for an hour before making a series of cantankerous demands that taxed McGuire's bedside manner.

"Why can't you just behave?" The doctor asked after Stuart rejected a pillow because it was too hard. "Major Pendleton is right across the yard and does everything I say."

"Oh, he would." Stuart wrinkled his nose at McGuire's praise of the obedient adjutant. "I'm bored. No one has visited me today."

"General Jackson and General Lee are sitting with Sandie." McGuire held up his finger to quiet the request on the tip of Stuart's tongue. "General Jackson says they'll come and visit you next."

"Why didn't they come and see me first," he demanded anyway.

McGuire sighed in exasperation. “Sandie is getting out of bed today, and the generals wanted to be there.”

Stuart lapsed into silence. McGuire restrained his laughter until he was outside the tent. *Poor Stuart, he wanted out of bed, too.*

The exhausted adjutant was safely tucked back into bed. Under Jackson’s supervision, Pendleton had walked from one side of the tent to the other. It wasn’t an easy trip. Leaning heavily on a crutch, Pendleton traversed the five feet of ground, stopping every foot to rest. Sweat poured down his face. The arm clutching the crutch trembled with fatigue. He fell once, but Jackson was there to catch him. A smile of encouragement sent the young man on his way. After a 20-minute rest period, Sandie navigated his way back to bed and gratefully sought its covers. He was asleep before Lee and Jackson could say goodbye. They stole out of the tent and were met by Stuart’s baritone.

“...Went around McClellan,

“We’re the boys who went around McClellan...”

McGuire hailed them from across the yard.

“Bully boys, hey! Bully boys, ho!”

“Well, he sounds like he’s getting better,” Lee remarked to McGuire when the doctor joined them.

“If you want to have a good time, jine the cavalry!

“Jine the cavalry! Jine the cavalry!”

“Yes, he’s better. I wish he’d choose a different song, though. He’s been singing that one non-stop for the past hour.” McGuire shook his head in mock disgust.

“If you want to catch the Devil,

“If you want to have fun...”

“What’s his prognosis, Doctor?” Jackson asked.

“If you want to smell Hell,

“Jine the cavalry!”

“He’s going to be fine. He’s weak, though you wouldn’t know it by listening to him. He’s going to need plenty of bed rest. And bed rest doesn’t mean sitting in a saddle. It means lying flat on his back in bed. I don’t want those wounds reopening.”

“We’re the boys who crossed the Potomicum,

“Crossed the Potomicum...”

“He does have a fine singing voice,” the tone-deaf Jackson observed.

"Crossed the Potomicum,

"We're the boys who crossed the Potomicum..."

"Can we see him?" Lee asked.

"Please do, then perhaps he'll hush," McGuire laughed.

"Bully boys hey! Bully boys ho!

*"If you want to have...*I'm so very glad to see you!" Stuart exclaimed when he saw them in the tent door. "You've saved me from my boredom. Doctor McGuire has ordered me to lie still, but I don't know if I can. I don't think it's in my nature."

"Well, you gave us quite a fright, so I insist that you listen to Doctor McGuire and do everything he says. Even if it's against your nature," Lee gently rebuked him. He sat on the chair next to the bed.

"But no one comes to see me!" Stuart wailed.

"That's not true," McGuire said, coming into the tent. He bore a small tray containing a vial of medicine and a glass of water. "Why just last night, Sweeney entertained us to all hours of the evening. You had yourself quite a little hootenanny. General Pickett's sat with you and so have General Early and General Hays." He mixed some powder into the glass. "General Hill has sent three runners asking about your condition. So take your medicine and stop your complaining." He handed the glass to Stuart.

"More medicine," Stuart grumbled, but he drank it. He grimaced with wild exaggeration at its taste. He held the glass out.

McGuire took it and set it on the tray. "Now, be a good patient and no more singing!" He implored before leaving the tent.

"So, what do we have planned for today?" Stuart asked, looking first at Jackson standing at the end of his bed and then to Lee.

"We," Lee stressed the word, "are going to visit the good folks of Harrisburg."

Stuart's pale face was instantly alert. "Are you expecting any trouble?"

"I don't believe they'll greet us with open arms, but Fitzhugh will make sure nothing happens to us," Lee replied.

"I think Rooney'll do a fine job, but I'd feel better if you took Fitz with you, too. I don't think you can be too cautious in this instance. Oh, I wish I was going!" He pounded the bed in frustration.

"I wish that, too," Lee said. "But you need to concentrate on getting well." He glanced at his watch. "Now, we must be going."

"So soon!" Stuart protested, trying to sit up. "You just got here!" He collapsed back on the bed.

"You need your rest," Lee ordered.

"Fine!" He crossed his arms in disappointment.

"Stuart, how about I spend the entire evening with you," Jackson said, earning a grateful smile from the patient.

They waved goodbye and had gone no more than a few feet from the tent when Stuart rejoined his interrupted song.

"Then we went into Pennsylvania,

"Went to Pennsylvania..."

"My name is Robert E. Lee," he announced to the crowd jammed into the town's square. "My army will be requisitioning the houses and property of Harrisburg 24 hours from now."

Lee's words threw a bucket of cold water on the carnival atmosphere. A chorus of angry murmurings started up.

"I want to assure you that my army will not behave in the manner yours do. We'll not burn your homes or steal your valuables and send them south to be prized by our women and children," Lee continued, ignoring the crowd's anger. "When we leave your city, your homes and businesses will still be standing. You have my word."

There were no cheers for the Confederates when they rode out of the city. Rooney and Fitz, along with Pickett's division remained behind to keep order.

The house Jackson selected for his headquarters was a three-story mansion, which sat at the end of a wide, tree covered avenue. The mansion hosted steep steps climbing up to a wrap-around porch. Black shutters provided a handsome contrast to the whitewashed walls. Large windows faced west and promised warmth on cold winter evenings. Chestnut trees in the yard, taller than the house, provided cool shade for the summer. The upstairs contained enough bedrooms to house Jackson's staff. The downstairs hosted a large kitchen, a dining room for entertaining, a parlor with a view of the avenue, and a formal living room. While his brother-in-law was impressed with the mansion's size and grandeur, even comparing it to Cottage Home, the Morrison plantation in Lincoln County, North Carolina, it was the library that had won Jackson over. From floor to ceiling, the shelves were crammed full of theological books. Jackson stared at the extensive array of titles and could think of no finer room in which to pass the winter.

This morning, he had emptied the shelves of commentaries on Psalms, Proverbs, and Ecclesiastes. By lunchtime, he was surrounded by books, comparing what each author had to say about his favorite scriptures. A knock on the door roused him from his studies. "Come in!"

The door opened halfway. "The ambulance has arrived," Jim Lewis announced. Jim was a middle-age black man without a hint of gray in his jet black hair. Hired a year ago to be Jackson's cook, he had proven to be fiercely devoted to the general. Devotion Jackson quickly rewarded with more responsibility. Jim's kingdom expanded from the kitchen to engulf the entire headquarters. He was a benevolent monarch, though, ruling over Jackson and his staff with an iron-fist gloved in loving velvet.

Jackson stepped out onto the porch and shielded his eyes against the glare of the noonday sun. Pendleton limped up the walk. Jackson hastened down to help. "Sandie, welcome home." He took the young man's arm, and, together, they started the slow climb up the steep staircase. When Pendleton stopped for the third time to catch his breath, Jackson found his weakness frightening; a sobering reminder of just how close his adjutant had come to death.

Pendleton collapsed on the top step. "I need to rest for a moment," he gasped.

A sharp gesture from Jackson brought Jim instantly to Pendleton's side. "The general done fixed you a real nice room in the front parlor," Jim said, helping Sandie to his feet. "You'll be sharin' it with General Stuart." He practically carried the young man out of the hot sun and in to the house.

The corpsmen unloaded a stretcher. Stuart lay on it.

McGuire hopped down from the wagon. "I hope you know what you're getting yourself into," he said with a laugh.

Jackson did. In the course of Stuart's confinement, the usually happy-go-lucky cavalier had disappeared. In his place was a prickly, petulant patient: all sharp barbs and surly behavior.

"Good afternoon, Stuart," Jackson said.

"General Jackson," Stuart growled in response.

Jackson ignored Stuart's bad temper. He supervised the stretcher as it was borne up the stairs and into the parlor. Pendleton was already situated in the bed next to the wall. His wounded leg was resting on two pillows.

"Where's Jim?" Jackson asked, pulling back the sheets on the bed next to the window.

"He decided I looked thirsty, so he went to make me a pitcher of lemonade," Pendleton reported.

The corpsmen maneuvered the stretcher into the room and laid it on the floor. They picked up the frail cavalry leader and placed him gently in the bed. Jackson tried to arrange the covers around Stuart's shoulders, but Stuart slapped his hands away and snapped the sheet and thin blanket into place.

"He can sit up for two hours at a time," McGuire instructed Jackson from the door. "He's only allowed broth for meals. He still needs rest, so you might want to restrict the flow of visitors that come and go all hours of the day and night."

"I can't help it if I'm popular," Stuart retorted. With a groan of pain, he sat up and stared out the window. "Doctor, can I sit outside on the porch?"

"I think that will be all right, as long as you don't attempt to walk to the porch on your own or sneak off to your headquarters when General Jackson's not looking. But not in the early morning or late at night. I don't want you getting sick because of the damp."

"How much longer am I going to be your prisoner?" Stuart cried, vexed. "It's been weeks of lying in bed or sitting in a chair."

"One more week should do it. Then I'll allow you to move around a bit."

"I think I will sit on the porch, if that is okay *with you*." He made a sullen face.

McGuire called for the corpsmen. Stuart was carried out of the room. Pillows and blankets were brought and hastily arranged in a comfortable chair. A pitcher of Jim's lemonade was set on a table next to the chair. An hour later, Jackson laid aside a commentary on Psalms and went to check on his charges. Pendleton was asleep, but Stuart was happily holding court with a porch full of soldiers.

Chapter Ten

"Mr. President, General Grant has arrived," John Hay announced to Lincoln and a grieving John Reynolds, lately returned from Pennsylvania where Winfield Scott Hancock had been laid to rest with full military honors.

Lincoln jumped to his feet and, in the anticipatory moment, felt relief wash over him like a gentle rain. Here was the one general who could win against the Rebels! "Show him in."

Grant burst through the door, his vitality a sharp contrast to Reynolds' sad weariness. He was of average height, ginger hair and beard, round-shouldered, and dressed in a seedy and rumpled uniform.

Lincoln rushed forward and pumped his hand. "Welcome to Washington, General." He motioned for Reynolds to come forward. "Do you know General Reynolds?"

Grant shook Reynolds' hand. "We were at West Point together."

"Nice to see you again, Sam," Reynolds said.

"We've much to discuss, so let's get right to it." Lincoln settled back in his chair. "I'm sorry to summon you to Washington under such trying circumstances, but General…" He raised his hands in defeat. Suddenly, his fears spilled out in a torrent of anguished words. "I don't know what to do. If there is a place worse than Hell; I am in it. The Army of the Potomac has been decimated and needs over 15,000 troops to return it to full strength, but the governors inform me they have met their enlistment quotas and have no more men to send."

Lincoln sighed and ran his fingers through his hair in agitation. "The Rebels have torn up the railroads in the Pennsylvania coal fields. Once the current stockpiles are exhausted, there'll be no more coal to continue the blockade or manufacture cannon and rifles. The people are growing impatient. The Secretary of the Treasury has no money and has informed me he can raise no more. The bottom is out of the tub. What shall I do?"

Grant pulled a cigar from a silver case. "Do you mind, sir?" He held up the cigar. Lincoln didn't. Grant lit it, sat back, and puffed out cloud after cloud of smoke. He erupted. "Do, sir?" He threw the cigar in a brass spittoon next to his chair. "Do? Why get after them, of course."

Lincoln smiled; his first real smile in a very long time. Grant had not disappointed him. He leaned forward in his chair and placed his elbows on his knees. "How do we do that? Get after them?"

Grant removed another cigar from the case. "We set ourselves to the relentless pursuit of Lee. Where he goes, we go. We harass him. We fight him every chance we get. We don't let up. We set out from Washington, and we don't return until victory is assured."

Lincoln wanted to leap to his feet and shout hallelujah! How many times had he implored his generals to do this very thing only to be lectured by them that he didn't understand strategy and tactics? "General Grant, I am ready to confer on you the rank of lieutenant general and promote you to general-in-chief of the army. Will you accept?"

Grant puffed on his cigar. "If you will allow me to appoint General Sherman to command the armies in the western theater…"

"Done!" Lincoln rubbed his hands together. "When will you get after Lee?"

"General Reynolds, how soon do you think the army will be ready to march?" Grant asked.

"I don't believe we'll be ready until spring. We've lost too many good men and a large portion of our leadership. The men are demoralized."

"Victories are the key to restoring morale. Let the army savor a few of those, and the men will run to battle," Grant said to Lincoln's immense relief.

"What do we do in the meantime, General Reynolds?" Lincoln hoped Reynolds was just being overly cautious, and the army would be able to combat the Confederates before the autumn rains made the roads impassable.

"Introduce General Grant to the troops and let him repeat the things he said to us. It will be like a strong tonic."

John Hay stuck his head into the office. "I'm sorry to interrupt, but Secretary Seward needs to see you in the Cabinet Room. He says it's urgent."

Lincoln stood. "Please excuse me, but duty calls."

"I understand." Grant threw his cigar stub into the spittoon.

"It's been a real pleasure meeting you, General Grant. Let's plan on meeting again tomorrow afternoon."

Lincoln shook Reynolds' hand. "General Reynolds, I've sent a letter to Almira Hancock expressing my condolences for her loss. This army will miss General Hancock's immeasurable contribution."

"I know she'll appreciate the gesture," Reynolds said.

Hay escorted the generals from the office. Lincoln returned to his desk and gathered up some papers. He started to laugh. "Get after them, General Grant. Get after them."

Jackson walked down the tree covered avenue on his way to Lee's headquarters. Soldiers, lounging about in the late summer sun, saw him coming. They emptied both houses and porches, filled yards and sidewalks, and bombarded him with questions about the army's future plans or the latest rumor spreading through the ranks. The men also sought updates on Pendleton and Stuart. For Pendleton was popular and Stuart more so.

Jackson dutifully answered each question before he peppered the men with questions of his own. Were they getting enough to eat? Were they keeping up with their morning drills? The soldiers pulled on their tightening waistbands as proof positive that the commissary was doing a fine job supplying them with flour, milk, and meat; and they good-naturedly groaned at the strictness of early morning drills.

"Good, good," Jackson said with a wave goodbye.

He turned a corner and ran into a small platoon of soldiers; their faces were streaked with sweat and soot, and their clothes reeked of gunpowder.

"How goes it, gentlemen?" He asked.

"Demolishin' bridges is a dirty business, sir," A filthy corporal answered. He scrubbed at his face with a handkerchief. "Some of them trestles are iron. Cain't be burnin' 'em. So, General Ewell had us call up Colonel Crutchfield. The Colonel, he was a marvel, sir, real genius. He walked all around them trestles, then called for a cannon. He blasted away at it for…what do you think, Joe…yeah, me too…about an hour, sir, and the whole thang, why it tipped over just like my granddaddy on Court Day. We plan to blast the other trestle tomorrow morning."

"Thank you for that inspiring report," Jackson chuckled. He started past them.

The corporal blocked the sidewalk. "Sir, if it ain't being too pushy, when do you think we might be headin' east to Philadelphia or New York?"

"That decision belongs to General Lee."

He shrugged. "Oh, I like it here and all." The men around him agreed. "We've plenty to eat and a roof over our head to keep out the rain, but I'm hankerin' for home." A look of longing crossed his smudged face. "General, I got me a little spread in the Valley with a mountain for a backyard. It's a beautiful sight. Especially in the fall. These mountains are pretty, too…but it ain't home, if'n you know what I mean."

"I do indeed," Jackson agreed.

The corporal's face brightened with an idea. "Hey, General, after the war, you would sure be welcome to come over for supper. My wife's a good cook. And my farm ain't too far from Lexington."

"I'd like that very much, Corporal."

The men buzzed with excitement. The corporal grinned at them. "Is there anything the General likes? I could send my wife a list to help her plan a menu."

"Nothing special. But no pepper. Pepper doesn't agree with me." In fact, Jackson believed just the whiff of pepper caused his right leg to go numb.

"I'll tell her, sir," the corporal promised with a salute. "No pepper."

"If you gentlemen will excuse me, General Lee's waiting."

"Tell the general hey from the 4th Virginia." The corporal stepped aside and let him by.

As Jackson neared the small clapboard house that served as Lee's headquarters, he saw Lee standing on the walk with Rooney. Rooney's gelding waited patiently for his master, his black tail swishing at bottle flies buzzing about.

"General Jackson." Lee waved him over. "You're a most welcome sight. Perhaps, you can help solve a disagreement my son and I are having. He has turned down my supper invitation. He claims he has to see to some pressing matter."

Rooney groaned. "What Father's failed to tell you is that I've had dinner with him every night for the past two weeks. You'd think he'd be tired of having me underfoot."

"If I had my way, I'd install you in the bedroom next to mine, so you would be underfoot until spring." He patted Rooney on the shoulder. Jackson smiled. Lee never looked happier than when he had his children near.

Rooney held up his hands in surrender. "All right, you win. I'll come for supper tonight."

His surrender earned him another pat, this time on the cheek. "Bring Rob, too." Rob Lee, the youngest of Lee's sons, served on Rooney's staff. "And see if you can round up your cousin."

Rooney assured his father he would do as he was told. He gathered up his reins and made his goodbyes. Lee opened the gate and gestured for

Jackson to enter first. The cobblestone walk was shaded by a large wooden trellis covered with red roses.

"How's General Stuart?" Lee asked.

"Easier to live with now that he can have solid foods. He gave me strict instructions to admonish you for your lack of visits."

"You can tell my young major general that I'll stop by tomorrow morning."

On the porch, Jackson saw Johnston sitting on a high-back chair, reading a newspaper. The First Corps Commander looked up and greeted Jackson as he came up the steps. Ever the gracious host, Lee ushered Jackson into another high-back chair.

Lee pointed to a small table. "I have lemonade and fresh-baked cookies."

On the table sat a pitcher of lemonade and a half dozen tall glasses. Next to the pitcher was a plate of cookies. Lee sat down on the porch swing. When the swing settled to a stop, he picked up the plate of cookies and held it out to Jackson.

Jackson took one. It was still warm to the touch. "I met up with some of the boys of the 4th Virginia on my way here. They wanted me to tell you 'hey.'"

"That's kind of them," Lee said. From next to him on the swing, Lee picked up two newspapers and handed them to Jackson. Jackson popped the rest of the cookie in his mouth, brushed the crumbs from his hands on his pant leg, and accepted the papers. "Fitzhugh just brought me these. It seems General Grant's been promoted to general-in-chief of the army. I sure wish General Longstreet was here to advise us on his friend."

Jackson skimmed the headlines. An article describing Grant's recent campaign in Tennessee caught his eye. At great length, the reporter detailed Grant's blast furnace approach to war. His army had rampaged through the countryside, stripping the land of crops and livestock, stealing personal property, burning down homes, and impoverishing women and children. He became aware that Lee was speaking to him. "I'm sorry, sir," he apologized.

"You seem deep in thought," Lee said.

"I was just thinking of a story my Uncle Cummins told me when I was a boy. He was at a tavern when a fight broke out between two long time rivals. They battered one another until one of them fell to the floor and gave up. But the man's relatives hauled him to his feet, gave him a hunting knife, and shoved him toward the other man. It was at that point, Uncle Cummins said, that the man understood what kind of fight he was involved in. It was a fight to the death. By bringing Grant east, Mr. Lincoln has handed the Army of the Potomac the knife and shoved it back in the fight."

He passed Lee the newspaper and pointed to the article. "This war will not end until one of us is unable to fight. So, we must kill every last one of them. Then, and only then, will they let us go in peace."

Stuart sat on the mansion's front porch listlessly reading a novel and making bored sighs with every turn of the page. Jackson fell into the chair next to him. "What are you reading, Stuart?"

"I don't know." Stuart slammed the book shut and set it down on the table next to a pitcher of iced tea. "How was the meeting?"

"Do you remember General Longstreet talking about his friend, Sam Grant?" Jackson poured a glass of tea. Stuart nodded. "Seems he's been promoted to general-in-chief of the army."

Stuart made a face, but Jackson couldn't tell if he was interested or bored. A group of soldiers strolled by the gate and hollered up at them. Stuart waved and hollered back.

"When I left, General Lee gave me this to read to you." Jackson plucked a folded paper from his pocket. "He thought it might cheer you up." He cleared his throat, sat up straight, and read in his most official voice. "Major General James Ewell Brown Stuart, the Congress, in accordance with the War Department, has bestowed upon you the rank of lieutenant general. Signed, Jefferson Davis, President."

Stuart was dumbstruck. He took the letter from Jackson and read it twice. A shadow passed over his face. "I didn't receive this promotion because I was wounded, did I?"

"Why would it matter?" Jackson asked. He drained his glass and smacked his lips.

"I guess it doesn't." Stuart read the letter again. "I just wanted to earn my promotion by my efforts in the field. I'd hate to think I received it because people felt sorry for me."

Jackson gave him a curious look. "I don't know anyone who feels sorry for you."

"Well, you did when you held me at Duncannon and called me Jeb."

Stung by the comment, Jackson flushed red. "Is that what you think? That I felt sorry for you," he barked.

Stuart flinched like he had been slapped. "I'm sorry."

Ashamed of his waspish tone, Jackson reached over and gave Stuart's arm an affectionate squeeze. "It's my fault. I shouldn't have snapped. You earned that promotion when you found Hooker's flank at Chancellorsville."

Stuart shrugged, but Jackson knew by the hunch of Stuart's shoulders that his apology and assurances had failed to mollify the younger man. Stuart picked up the book and began to read. "Okay," he said. He angrily turned a page.

But, it wasn't. A frigid breeze had descended upon the porch. Stuart continued to flip the book's pages. Jackson poured another glass of tea and debated whether he should confess to Stuart the feelings that assailed him while he waited to hear whether the cavalry leader would live or die.

"Stuart…"

"Why do you call me that?" Stuart interrupted testily. He slammed the book shut. "Before I was wounded, you called me General Stuart. Now, you just call me Stuart."

"Does it bother you?" Jackson asked.

"No, I was just wondering." He re-opened the book.

Jackson had a choice to make. The safer choice was to retreat to his office and wait for the storm to blow over. The second, more difficult choice was to make a clean breast of his feelings. Well, his favorite maxim instructed him never to take counsel of his fears. He took a deep breath and began.

"I didn't call you Jeb because I felt sorry for you," he said softly. He tightened and loosened his grip on the tea glass. "I was too busy being scared that you would die."

Stuart closed the book. "Oh." He stared at Jackson with shocked eyes.

Jackson took a deep breath. "I was only seven when my mother became too ill to take care of me and my brother and sister. My older brother, Warren, was sent to live with my mother's relatives. My sister and I went to live at Jackson's Mill. When Uncle Cummins came to fetch us, I hid in the woods. I sat beneath the branches of a pine tree and begged God to let me stay with my mother." He took a sip from the glass. "I experienced the very same feelings outside the operating tent. I prayed God to spare your life because I didn't want to lose another…brother."

Stuart's face didn't change. He opened the book, closed it, and opened it again. "I don't know what to say," he finally said.

"I don't think words are necessary, unless you want to disown me." Jackson was half-terrified Stuart would do just that.

Tears pooled in Stuart's blue eyes. "Do you mean it?"

Overcome by emotion, Jackson could only nod.

"No, then that's the last thing I'd do," Stuart assured him with a pleased smile. "Brother! I like it," he laughed merrily.

Jackson suddenly felt five years old and as happy as the afternoon he had chased Warren into the general store. Between them, they had a penny to spend. In those days, laughter had come as easy as breathing. When he said goodbye to his mother, the laughter had died away. It had been reborn in Stuart, whose teasing ways made him feel as young and carefree as he had been in that store, laughing with Warren.

The gate clicked open. Doctor McGuire strode up the sidewalk. "General Stuart, I have a surprise for you."

"Another surprise!" Stuart's face lit up. "Where is it?"

"There!" McGuire pointed down the wide avenue.

Stuart rose. Major McClellan was leading Virginia, Stuart's favorite mare. Stuart's aides rode along with big smiles on their faces. Curious soldiers trailed behind, creating a spontaneous parade. Stuart made his way down to the gate. Virginia saw him and strained to be released. McClellan let her go; she trotted over to Stuart. He stroked her neck, buried his face in her mane, and inhaled.

"This doesn't mean you're free to tear about the town or countryside," McGuire lectured, "but you can walk, and that does not include trot, cantor, or gallop, today and tomorrow. Then we'll see."

Stuart put his foot in the stirrup and pulled himself into the saddle. A stab of pain ripped his abdomen, but he ignored it.

"How does it feel?" McGuire gestured toward Stuart's wounded side.

"Like home." Stuart patted Virginia on the neck. He waved to Jackson, who was watching from the porch, then nudged the mare and went down the street at a slow walk. He returned in time for supper, sore, but happy.

Chapter Eleven

PRESIDENT ANNOUNCES COAL SHORTAGES THIS WINTER

> Due to the sabotage of the railroads in western and eastern Pennsylvania by the Rebel army, the President announced that the country may experience a coal shortage this winter. He did not discount coal rationing to alleviate the scarcity but said that factories providing munitions and other supplies for the war effort will continue to have uninterrupted coal supplies. When asked about the naval blockade of southern ports, Secretary of War Edwin Stanton said that the blockade would continue.

A fervent wave of patriotism met Lincoln's announcement. The women proclaimed how they welcomed the chance to show the enemy the sterner stuff from which they were made. Within a week of the announcement, store shelves emptied of wool and flannel. Knitting circles sprang up like dandelions on a spring lawn. Over the clackety-clack of their knitting needles, they spurned the privations facing them and produced mountains of knitwear. When the bottom fell out of the thermometer and the wind turned to ice, the women lined their skirts and coats with newspapers and rags and boasted how resolute they were in their suffering. Devotion to the Union was enough to keep them warm.

COLD SNAP PRODUCES SHARP RISE IN COAL PRICES

> Ten days of sub-zero temperatures have produced a 22% increase in the cost to heat a home for a week. Factory owners predict this increase will force lay-offs or shut-downs. The War Department was quick to reiterate that factories producing war supplies would continue to receive coal at a discounted price.

Coal was rationed on a first-come, first-served basis. Every day, the men of the house, whether age eight or eighty, rose well before dawn to stand in long lines. They stomped their feet and blew on their hands to keep warm and prayed that the day's allotment would last until it was their turn. One day, the men trudged through a half foot of freshly fallen snow to find the warehouses closed. A sign on the gate announced there would be no more coal for the foreseeable future.

NUMBER OF UNEMPLOYED RISES
PRICE OF KINDLING TRIPLES IN THREE WEEKS

> Cincinnati city officials announced that one-half of the city's factories have closed. Approximately 10,000 men have been thrown out of work. When asked about the recent price jump in kindling, Mayor Leonard Harris issued a statement that his office was currently investigating allegations of price gouging.

Unable to get their hands on the tiniest lump of coal or afford a stick of kindling, the freezing citizens cannibalized their homes and yards. They cut down the majestic oaks, maples, and elms that had served for decades as sentinels against the hot summer sun. When the trees had been reduced to ash, they chopped down banisters, sliced up dressers and bureaus, before burning china cabinets, dining room tables, and elegant sideboards. Still the wind blew, the snow fell, and the cold gripped them. Only when there was nothing left to burn, did the freezing capitulate and pay five times what it cost them last year for a cord of wood.

FOOD PRICES RISE DRAMATICALLY

> Yesterday, this reporter witnessed the greed of speculators as they swarmed a train upon its arrival at the station. With fistfuls of greenbacks, the profiteers bought up the cargo and whisked it away to warehouses to wait for the inevitable price increase. "The price of flour has risen ten dollars in the last week," Herbert Chase, proprietor of Chase's Mercantile said. "My business is in trouble. Many of my accounts are over three months in arrears, but in this current economic crisis, my customers can't pay. Without cash, I can't compete with the speculators."

One frigid afternoon, anger at the speculators and profiteers boiled over. An armed mob looted the warehouses surrounding the rail yards. The police waded into the angry throng and found themselves under attack.

Their response was quick and brutal. When the rioters were finally dispersed, nine people lay dead in the snow. The riots raged until a snowstorm raced up the coast and forced everyone indoors. The wicked weather only suppressed the fury. It seethed under the surface and waited for an opportunity to reassert itself.

LINCOLN ORDERS HALT TO NAVAL BLOCKADE
COAL ASSIGNED FOR NAVY TO BE DISTRIBUTED TO CITIES

> In an attempt to alleviate the coal crisis, President Lincoln ordered a halt to the naval blockade of southern ports. Coal reserved for the Navy will be shipped to the cities within a week.

It was good public relations but did very little to ease the shortage. New York City ran out of its allotment in four hours.

REBEL CAVALRY DESCENDS ON COUNTRYSIDE
PHILADELPHIA AND TRENTON RAIDED
PITTSBURGH CITIZENS REPORT JEB STUART IN CITY

> Fort Pitt Foundry reported that Reb cavalry raided their factory yesterday and carried away over fifty cannon destined for the Army of the Potomac. C. Sharpe & Company claimed that over 3,000 breech-loading rifles were stolen in another raid. The Rebs have raided Wilkes-Barre's industries and hauled away ammunition, uniforms, and other supplies meant for the army. During one twelve hour period, raiders stopped three trains headed for New York City and carried off over 150 wagon loads of dry goods. What they could not carry away, they burned.

Stuart approached Jackson about raiding New York City. "Why have you come to me and not General Lee?" Jackson asked from behind the big desk in the library.

"Because you'll say yes."

"I do say yes. But the decision isn't mine. When you talk to General Lee, you can tell him I endorse your plan."

Lee approved, and Stuart and Rooney's brigade set off. At this latest assault upon their property and security, the politicians demanded Grant do something about the thieving Reb cavalry.

A SURPRISE ANNOUNCEMENT FROM THE WAR DEPARTMENT
MAJOR GENERAL PHILIP SHERIDAN TO LEAD CAVALRY

> The Army of the Potomac suffered a painful blow when Major General John Buford died of typhoid in December. His position was filled yesterday by General Philip Henry Sheridan, a West Point graduate and former division commander in the Army of the Cumberland's XX Corps.

"I don't know why you told the President I can stop the raids," Sheridan complained to Grant.

Sheridan was a man all out of physical proportions. He possessed a chunky body and a short neck and legs. His long arms caused Lincoln to quip that Sheridan could scratch his ankles without having to bend his knees.

"The President was adamant that Stuart be stopped." Grant blew on his hands. His breath was frosty white in his unheated office. "Just do what you can, will you?"

Sheridan shrugged. "Sure, why not. I've got a hankering to look at Stuart anyway. I've never seen a peacock before. Well, except in a zoo."

"Be careful! This peacock will shoot at you."

Sheridan stormed up the banks of the Susquehanna with 8,000 men. When he threw his troopers across the river, he found the Confederates well entrenched. Twenty-two bloody minutes later, he pulled back. In the quiet after the battle, he paced the banks of the gray river and contemplated the best way to dislodge the Rebs. He heard a rustling in the trees across the river. To his surprise, Stuart rode out to the river's edge and tipped his plumed hat in his direction. Sheridan glowered. Stuart smiled and burst into song. He disappeared back in the trees, and the song faded away. An intense hatred ripped through Sheridan's heart. How dare that strutting peacock, all decked out with plumes, cloak, and shiny thigh high boots (Jackson had kept his promise and given Stuart the boots for Christmas) mock him. "I'll see you dead!" He shouted across the river.

Laughter floated back to him.

SHERIDAN DEFEATED ON THE BANKS OF THE SUSQUEHANNA

> General Sheridan was handed three quick defeats along the shores of the Susquehanna. Total casualties were 50 dead and 146 wounded. Sheridan retreated to Washington with his tail tucked firmly between his legs. A heavy snowstorm in central Pennsylvania has put a halt to the Rebel raids.

The bored soldiers in Harrisburg greeted the snowstorm with three cheers. Word spread. Starting tomorrow morning, the Army of Northern Virginia's Second Annual Snowball Fight would commence, pitting the First Corps against the Second.

Unaware of the tradition, Johnston was on his way to see Jackson when he became one of the battle's first casualties. He raged up the mansion's steps. To his immense irritation, he saw Pendleton throwing a snowball up in the air and guarding the side yard. Smith was guarding the opposite side.

"My position is clear," Morrison called from the backyard.

"Colonel Pendleton!" Johnston barked, perturbed that Jackson would allow his aides to be so frivolous with their time.

Pendleton made one more sweep of the yard and abandoned his post. "Yes, sir."

Johnston dug snow from his collar. "I want you to go down there," he pointed to the street, "and find which insolent soldier threw that snowball at me. I want him brought up on charges."

"General, meaning no disrespect, but…"

"But what?" Johnston snapped.

"General Lee approved it, sir."

Johnston recoiled, the thought anathema to him. "General Lee? He knows the men are running around like children, throwing snowballs at their superior officers."

The front door opened; Jackson came out on the porch. Three snowballs sailed in from the front yard. Johnston ducked behind the porch railing.

"Come inside, General," Jackson said, dusting the remains of a snowball off his jacket. "You're likely to draw much fire standing out in the open like that."

Johnston scurried into the foyer.

Pendleton followed the generals into the house. "Will you be needing me, General?" He asked Jackson.

"No, you're free to return to your post."
Pendleton ran out of house.

CONGRESS PASSES CONSCRIPTION ACT
35,000 MEN TO BE DRAFTED INTO ARMY
$500 WILL BUY SUBSTITUTE

> To rebuild the Army of the Potomac and augment the armies in the west, Congress passed a new conscription act calling for 35,000 new recruits. Social reformers and immigrant leaders objected to the substitution policy, stating that it took unfair advantage of the poor. When asked about the policy, a member of the draft board said that he only cared about meeting the quota.

The cities erupted. From Augusta to Chicago, people marched through the streets, held rallies, blockaded entrances to factories still churning out war supplies, and set government buildings ablaze. Just when Lincoln thought the Union would dissolve into anarchy, the former Commanding General of the Army of the Potomac, George McClellan, strode onto the national stage.

McClellan authored a series of editorials begging for calm. He attended rallies in Philadelphia, Trenton, and New York City. Speaking to over 10,000 people on the steps of Independence Hall, McClellan declared, "We are all victims of the arrogance of this administration and its petty crusade against the South. But it's our gallant men in uniform who suffer the most from Lincoln's war of vindictiveness."

His gray eyes filled with tears. The crowd hushed at his obvious distress. He allowed one tear to drop from his eye. Just one. Any more would have ruined the effect.

"When President Lincoln dismissed me after my victory at Antietam, I vowed that I would never come to his aid again. Alas, I must break that vow. Not for Lincoln's sake. No! But it's for my beloved soldiers that I now implore you to report to the draft boards…"

He almost lost the crowd. They began to boo. A snowball hit the door behind him. He didn't flinch. His eyes swept over the sea of angry people. Then he smiled, just like a loving father smiles at his quarrelsome children, perfect white teeth under a perfect brown mustache. The crowd immediately repented of their boorish behavior, came to attention, and waited for him to command them.

"If we abandon our men this winter, they'll return to us in flag-draped coffins this summer," he continued. "Do not forsake our soldiers in their dark hour of despair. Let's do what's in our power to do, so all our men come marching home!"

McCLELLAN SAVES THE UNION AGAIN!
McCLELLAN OFFERS TO LEAD ARMY OF POTOMAC

> Major General George B. McClellan spoke to an enthusiastic crowd at Independence Hall on Thursday. In a short but emotional speech, McClellan urged the crowd not to abandon the soldiers in the field to the "vindictive policies" of the Lincoln administration. A magnanimous offer by McClellan to put aside his differences with the president and lead the Army of the Potomac was the catalyst that ended the riots. Since reproducing the text of his speech in this newspaper, over 3,500 men have reported to the draft boards.

Lincoln tossed the newspaper on his desk. "It's the again I mind the most," he quipped to Stanton. "I know I should be grateful. After all, our Young Napoleon managed to quiet the cities and save my war of vindictiveness, but I can't be." He put his feet up on the desk and leaned far back in his chair. "I'll give Little Mac this. He's proving to be a better politician than general." Lincoln laughed bitterly. "He's maneuvered against his enemy," he pointed at himself, "with a hasty bravery he didn't show on the peninsula or in Maryland."

"General Grant wanted me to remind you about his suggestion to postpone the fall elections," Stanton said. "He is adamant that if you did, Lee would have no reason to stay in Pennsylvania."

"I understand General Grant's point of view, but I don't think it'd be wise." Lincoln stretched his arms over his head. "The people must have their say on the war."

"If your mind is made up…" Stanton fluffed his iron gray goatee with his fat hands. "Is it?"

“No.” Lincoln’s feet found the ground again. “I told General Grant that I’d keep the option open.” He picked up the paper. “Again! Tell me, when did he save it the first time!”

Chapter Twelve

Harrisburg, Pennsylvania
Early April 1864

The rattle of musketry pierced the air. The screams of the wounded rose over the exploding artillery shells. A man stumbled past. His arm was missing from his shoulder down and half his face had been blown off. Pendleton felt sick.

Smith galloped up. “The General needs you,” he yelled over the shrieking shells.

Pendleton nodded and rode to where Jackson was shouting orders at Joe.

“Mr. Pendleton, tell Hill to advance immediately!” Jackson’s eyes flashed fire. Blood dripped from a wound in his hand. The blood formed a small pool on the ground. The pool spread throughout the battlefield. Pendleton shuddered. The Light Division was situated on a high ridge. The only way to relay the order would be to ride through the hottest part of the field. He would be killed for sure. His leg throbbed in pain; a warning not to tempt death twice.

“Mr. Pendleton, are you listening to me?” A ghoulish sneer contorted Jackson’s face. Pendleton stared at Jackson and wondered why he had never noticed how pitiless those blue-gray eyes were. “Are you refusing a direct order?” Jackson’s wounded finger poked Pendleton’s chest, staining his shirt with blood.

Tears flowed down Sandie’s cheeks. He didn’t know Jackson was capable of this type of cruelty. Before he could explain that his leg was on fire, his throat closed shut.

“Smith!” Jackson turned his back on his adjutant and repeated the order. Smith galloped off. “Mr. Pendleton,” Jackson growled contemptuously, “what are you still doing here? Cowards belong in the back with the shirkers.” Again, Pendleton wanted to explain about his leg, but Jackson wouldn’t let him. “Now!” Jackson pointed toward the rear.

In slow motion, a shell whistled overhead. Pendleton followed its trajectory. It was headed for Smith, but Smith didn’t see it. “Jimmie!” He screamed with all his might. “Jimmie!” But Smith couldn’t hear him because the shell was exploding; killing him. “Jimmie!” He screamed again.

Pendleton woke with a start. Frantically, he glanced around. He was in his room in the mansion. He sat up. His heart slowly eased its wild thumping. Had his cries wakened Smith? No, Smith's soft snores continued uninterrupted. His roommate had been known to sleep through artillery barrages, so it would take more than a cry of terror to rouse him.

There were footsteps in the hall. The bedroom door slowly opened. Pendleton lay back down and pretended to be asleep. Jackson entered the room and paused. Then he walked over to the foot of the bed. "Sandie," he called softly. He waited a long moment before fading into the shadows. The closing door signaled his departure.

Pendleton waited until the master bedroom door shut. He sat back up and wrapped his blanket around his shoulders. Five days ago, Stuart's spy in the War Department had sent word that the Army of the Potomac was preparing to leave Washington. Ever since, his sleep had been plagued by this reoccurring nightmare. It ate at him as he went about his duties. What if his subconscious was sending him a message? What if he was a coward? It happened, sometimes, to soldiers after they were wounded. Had it happened to him? The scar on his leg tingled; he rubbed at it.

He half-believed it had. It certainly was cowardly to pretend to be asleep when the general came into the room. And so was lying yesterday at breakfast when Jackson asked if anything was worrying him. The lie still bothered him.

"I should have just told the truth," Sandie whispered to himself. "The general would have understood."

But, then again, what if Jackson didn't? What if Jackson decided he couldn't risk his adjutant failing to deliver a crucial order in battle and replaced him? Sandie bit his thumb in worry. No, he couldn't risk Jackson or anyone else knowing what feared him. Exhausted, he flopped back down on his pillow. What should he do? He was no closer to an answer when he fell back into a restless sleep.

On a quiet Monday afternoon, news reached Harrisburg that the Yankees had crossed into Pennsylvania. As the news rippled down the army grapevine, Grant's legions swelled in size and strength. By suppertime, the army descending upon the Confederates had grown to 250,000 troops and 2,000 cannon.

"General Johnston, is it true?" Members of the 88th Virginia asked the petit general as he strolled past their headquarters.

"Is what true?" Johnston asked.

"That the Yankees have over 250,000 troops?"

“Stuff and nonsense,” Johnston answered with a sharp slash of his hand. “General Stuart is out gathering information on the strength of the enemy now. I doubt Grant has more than 150,000 men.”

Still, if Johnston was correct, it meant the Yankees doubled their own strength. “What do we care?” A sergeant shrugged after Johnston departed. “We’ve always been on the short end of the stick when it came to numbers. I say let them come. One hundred thousand or one million. We’ve licked them every time we faced them. It’s time to end this thing. I’ve been gone from home long enough.”

Two days later, the order went out. Each man was to cook three days rations. The army would be crossing the Duncannon fords tomorrow at dawn, heading south.

Chapter Thirteen

Thirty miles from Harrisburg, the Susquehanna made a wide meander east before sweeping south again. The city of Marietta guarded the entrance of the meander, while a quickening deep current, a few miles north of Columbia, guarded the exit. On the eastern shore, there was a thick parcel of marsh land, a quagmire, filled with trees – some alive, but most of them dead and decaying. Two creeks moseyed through the five-mile-wide bog, in no particular hurry to empty into the river. Ten days ago, these creeks, teeming with spring rain, had overflowed their banks. Now, they gurgled along with no more than a few inches of water covering their rocky bottoms. The road to Marietta circumnavigated the marsh before heading north to the next crossing.

Jedidiah Hotchkiss led Lee and his lieutenant generals north along the western shore of the river. They came to a rickety bridge that spanned the Susquehanna and ended at a wide path leading into the marsh. The generals sidestepped rotting planks and jumped over holes as they picked their way across the structure. The bridge groaned under their weight, but it held, much to Jackson's prayerful relief. They followed the path until it met another trail, which ran north to south through the marsh. They turned south and twisted and turned through the bog, which stank of decaying plant life. The path came to a dead-end at a drop-off to one of the creeks. On the other side of the creek was a tangle of hickory trees covered with thick green leaves and small yellow catkins. The creek ran east a few hundred yards before it disappeared into the marsh.

Jackson climbed down the bank and splashed through the water. Without waiting to be asked, Stuart followed. They scrambled up the other side and instantly sank in mud that threatened to separate them from their boots. They slipped and slid forward. The ground finally hardened at the edge of the hickory grove. They threaded their way through the trees and wound up on the top of a large clearing. Below, green fields dotted with white clover and yellow dandelions spread before them. In the far distance, Columbia's church steeples were visible. Both men looked back the way they came. The hickory grove hid the creek and the path.

"The Yankees could find the path," Stuart warned.

"They could."

"But you don't think so."

“We just waded through 20 feet of mud.” Jackson glanced at his boots. “At least four inches deep. What would you do if you popped through those trees and found yourself sinking in that muck?”

“I’d post pickets.”

“Why?” Jackson snapped, supposing Stuart was being difficult on purpose.

“I’d never leave my flank unprotected if you were in the neighborhood.”

“The battle is that way.” Jackson pointed toward the river. The Confederate defenses were visible from the small hilltop.

“Yes, but my flank’s vulnerable this way.” Stuart jerked his thumb back toward the grove of trees.

Jackson made a slow survey of the terrain. He smiled. “But what if I wasn’t on the left flank, but the right.”

Stuart thought about it for a moment. “Then I’d be more inclined to relax and think I wasn’t in immediate danger.”

Without a word, Jackson headed back to the path.

“Well?” Lee asked as Jackson climbed up the creek bank.

“We can hurt them,” Jackson said, giving Stuart a hand up. “First, we’ll need to disguise the path so it can’t be seen from across the creek. Any ideas, Mr. Hotchkiss?”

“I can think of a few,” the cartographer replied. He sized up the underbrush for use as possible camouflage.

When the generals arrived at the trails’ intersection, Lee asked Hotchkiss where the path north ended.

“At the road to Marietta.”

“Is it visible from the road?”

Hotchkiss nodded.

“Hide its entrance, also,” Lee said.

“Now all we have to do is convince the Yankees that General Jackson isn’t where he is,” Stuart said cryptically. He sat down on a log and began to scrape the mud off his boots.

“Let me explain,” Jackson said. They recrossed the bridge, leaving Stuart to catch up.

The next morning, Sheridan led a scouting party up to the river bank. He whipped out his field glasses and made a careful survey of the gray troops as they constructed their defenses. The ramparts covered the approaches from the river. Artillery rested on higher ground behind the fortifications. Satisfied that the Second Corps occupied the right flank and the First Corps held the left, Sheridan ordered his men north up the small hill.

At the hickory grove, Sheridan dismounted and wove his way through the trees. He stepped into a sea of mud and almost fell. He grabbed a tree branch and pulled himself free. He stalked along the edge of the grove and jabbed a stick into the mud every 50 feet or so. The ground never changed. Just muck as far as he could see.

"So, are we going through there?" Sheridan's adjutant asked when Sheridan emerged from the hickory trees.

"No, and I don't think the Rebs are either. Place is nothing but mud."

Sheridan remounted and skirted the bog until he came to the Marietta Road. He sent a platoon toward the city to picket the next crossing. Satisfied with his reconnaissance, he headed back to the army. At noon, he met up with Grant and Reynolds.

"What do you have?" Grant asked between puffs on his cigar.

Sheridan gave a detailed description of the area. "Our left flank's protected by the current. It's miles to the next crossing. Even if the Rebs wanted to flank us, we could easily spot such a maneuver."

"The right flank?"

"Protected by miles of marsh. I posted pickets at the next crossing."

"Where was the Second Corps positioned?" Reynolds asked.

"On the Rebs' right flank."

"Are you sure?"

Sheridan flared with impatience. He didn't like having his information questioned. "Yes, I'm sure," he snapped so rudely that Grant shot him a warning glance.

"I just…"

"Oh, for crying out loud. Jackson isn't the boogie man. When are you going to quit being afraid of him?"

Reynolds flushed bright red. "General, it would behoove you to remember who you're addressing. If you ever speak to me like that again, I'll have you cashiered."

Sheridan appealed to Grant.

"I'd sign that order." Grant flicked an ash.

"My apologies." Sheridan hated to apologize almost as much as he hated having his information questioned.

Grant ground out the cigar with the toe of his boot. "General Reynolds, I understand your concerns."

Sheridan smirked at the condescension in Grant's voice.

"I'll put the Sixth and Ninth Corps on our flanks. That should protect them well enough." Grant turned to Sheridan. His demeanor dismissed Sheridan's actions even if his words didn't. "General Reynolds knows these particular Rebs better than we do. If he has a concern, we should listen. Understood?"

"Yes, sir. Will there be anything else?" When Grant dismissed him, he rode away at a gallop.

Lee watched those people march to the river. Swagger would be more precise, he thought. They didn't seem to be the least bit concerned that his army was just across the water. A small city of white tents sprang up in range of Confederate artillery.

"Colonel Alexander," Lee called to the First Corps' artillery chief, "I think we should remind those people that we're here."

Alexander wiped his muddy hands on a towel. "What do you have in mind, sir?"

"Why don't we test some of the guns General Stuart liberated this winter?"

A smile erupted on Alexander's weary face. With a chuckle, he directed his best gunners to load the ten big cannon in the center. "We're ready, General."

"Then do your duty."

The guns rang out in the gathering twilight.

Meade ducked as 20 pound canisters crashed into his camp. All around him, men scrambled for shelter. He fumed in fury. He couldn't retaliate. His cannon were still two miles back. "Corporal, quit hiding and move those horses to the rear. Colonel, tell the men to move back out of the reach of those guns before they break us to pieces. No one runs. If I see anyone running, I'll shoot him myself."

General Daniel Sickles, now commanding Couch's Second Corps, charged over to Meade. "Why aren't we pouring fire on the Rebs?"

"My cannon haven't come up yet."

The barrage ended, reminding Meade of a small spring shower. No one would have known it had rained if it weren't for the puddles left behind. No one was hurt, but tents smoldered, wagons were overturned, broken barrels of flour dusted the ground like a late spring snow, and two stands of rifles had been obliterated. Grant and Reynolds dashed up.

"It seems my good friend Robert Lee wanted to remind us he was across the river," Meade said with a half-hearted chuckle.

"I say bring up the cannon and let him have it," Sickles declared.

"I already told you, Dan, my cannon haven't come up yet."

Sickles glared across the river. "The impudence!"

Grant laughed. "Pull the men back out of range of their guns. Tomorrow will be soon enough to fight."

Chapter Fourteen

After Stuart's scouts relayed word that the Yankees had left the shores of the Susquehanna, Jackson went to work and concealed Early's, Rodes', and McLaws' divisions, along with Rooney's and Hampton's brigades. He sequestered them in a secluded clearing north of the bridge. Jackson laid down the law. No campfires, no talking, no unnecessary noise of any kind. Violators would be bayoneted. The men spent the chilly night not moving or breathing lest the provost guard drag them before Old Jack. Those who could sleep, did. Those who could not, whispered softly to each other and waited for the sun to rise.

At midnight, Jackson sent Pendleton, Morrison, and Smith over the bridge. Morrison and Smith were tasked with watching the Yankees encamped on the hill next to the marsh. The two aides were to signal Jackson when the Yankees broke camp to join this morning's battle. Pendleton was given the far more difficult assignment of spying out where the Yankee picket line was posted on the Marietta Road.

Before Stuart returned to the fortifications, he had warned Jackson that if the pickets were too close to where the path exited, the Yankees would spy Rooney's brigade entering the road and all would be ruined.

"What if the cavalry just waited on this side of the river until I launched the attack?" Jackson asked.

"There's no way both brigades could ride to your support in time. Now, if the pickets were closer to their campfires, Rooney could go almost to the bend without being discovered."

"Mr. Pendleton," Jackson called.

The young men stepped off the bridge and were instantly swallowed up by an impenetrable darkness and an overwhelming stench. They groped their way down the path and paused at the intersection to gather their bearings.

"You be careful," Pendleton said. He turned north toward the road. He hurried a few feet down the path and listened. Morrison's and Smith's footsteps faded away. In the smothering darkness, he suddenly felt abandoned and alone. Trees blocked out the night sky. He raised his hand in front of his face. It only came into view when he pressed it against his nose.

His scar began to tingle. He lectured himself not to give in to silly imaginations, but the scar ignored the lecture and continued to tingle, then burn. By time he reached the end of the path, it was throbbing, and he was limping.

His heart pounded wildly as he peered at the twisted branches and leaves that disguised the path's exit. In his mounting terror, Colonel Hotchkiss' benign camouflage transformed into a mass of wriggling copperheads. He tried to move, but his legs had put down roots. The scar screamed in protest.

"Okay, just start by doing something small," he whispered to himself. "Push a few branches aside. After all, they can't hurt me."

His fingers came in contact with leafy softness. The snakes returned to what they were: harmless twigs and branches. Carefully, Sandie made an opening. The road to Marietta lay before him. It might not be his dream filled with shells and blood, but it was still the stuff of terror.

"Please God, help me be brave," he prayed.

He put one leg through, then a shoulder, his head, and then the other leg. He was through! He gulped in air as if he had just run ten miles. He returned the brush to its original position. His legs were wobbly, but at least the scar no longer throbbed.

Sandie greeted the stars like long-lost friends. The night was still black as ink, but it was not the suffocating darkness he had just endured. He could see about three feet in front of him, but felt like he could see forever. He eased down the road, straining to hear any sound, and freezing whenever he did. In his ears, his footsteps sounded like artillery blasts. Any attempt to soften them failed. The Yankees would hear him coming, and he would be caught for sure. He silenced the fears that caused his heart to accelerate and the scar to prickle and walked on.

He heard voices! No more than ten yards in front of him. He made a mad dash toward the marsh. CRACK!! He glanced down. His foot rested on the broken halves of a large stick. He dove under a log, positive his hammering heart would lead the Yankees straight to him.

"Did you hear that, Charlie?" The voice was young.

"Hear what?" Charlie sounded bored.

"Sounded like something in the marsh, right over here."

Footsteps approached. Two Yankees stood over him framed in starlight. Sandie held his breath.

"Probably another deer." Now, Charlie was perturbed.

"Could be Rebels!"

"Could be ole Stonewall himself come single-handedly to flank us. Don't be stupid, Dan. Now let's get back." Charlie stalked away.

"It could have been Rebels," Dan said, disappointed.

"Willie!" Charlie shouted down the road. "Come and get this fool brother of yours. He thinks Stonewall Jackson's after him."

"I don't either!" Dan declared and ran after Charlie.

Sandie waited until the footsteps died away. He crawled from beneath the sheltering log, careful not to make a sound. He crept along the edge of the marsh. The road started to make a wide sweep to the right. He had gone no more than a few feet when he heard the pickets. He dropped to the ground and tiptoed into a thicket of trees; his eyes peeled for any stick or other noise maker.

The hours dragged by. Pendleton dozed off, woke, dozed again. His head snapped forward. He was alert. It was dawn. The road stretched out before him. He could make out the trees framing the other side. To his right, the guards were restless. Footsteps approached.

"About time you got here." Charlie was still perturbed.

"Stop your grousin'. We ain't late. We got orders to pull back closer to camp."

"Cain't see nothing from back there."

"I don't make the orders; I just follow 'em. Now, you want to be relieved or not?"

Charlie admitted he did. He and his men retired up the road.

Pendleton inched his way out of the marsh; his legs numb and uncooperative. When the feeling returned to them, he shadowed the soldiers. When he observed where the new picket line was posted, he smiled. The general would be pleased.

Morrison spent the night leaning against a hickory tree. His head pounded from the marsh's stench, and his stomach turned flip-flops. Beside him, Smith snored. Morrison was too anxious to sleep, but it didn't prevent him from envying Smith's ability to do so. He made himself comfortable, tried in vain to ignore the odor, and kept a sharp eye on the Yankees.

Joe sat up, drawn by movement among the sea of tents. The Yankees were stirring. Fires were stoked to life, and the aroma of coffee and bacon wafted into the grove to compete with the stench. He poked Smith, who woke with a jerk.

Smith rubbed his eyes. "How long have I been asleep?"

"For a while."

He rooted through his haversack. "Want some cornbread?"

Morrison shook his head. He was too nervous to eat.

An hour after sunrise, the Yankees assembled and marched down the hill. When the last soldier disappeared from view, Morrison waded through the mud and slid down the creek bank. He climbed up on the other side and ran full speed down the path and over the bridge. Jackson was waiting for him. At his appearance, the men, already formed up in columns of two, marched soundlessly to the bridge, now reinforced to hold both infantry and cavalry. At the edge of the clearing, the cavalry saddled their horses. Jackson's last minute instructions were to be quick and quiet. Twice, he pressed the need for Morrison and Smith to get the men in position as swiftly as practicable.

Morrison ran to the head of the column. He led Dole's Georgians on the double-quick into the marsh, down the path, and to the creek. To avoid the pioneers assembling a makeshift bridge over the creek, he jumped into the shallow stream and scrambled up the other side.

Colonel Hotchkiss was there, testing the planking he had laid over the mud to speed the men on their way. The planking rocked back and forth unsteadily; the far end disappeared into the muck. Hotchkiss stepped off, slipped in the mud, and almost fell. He grabbed onto his aide and righted himself. He gave the order for the planking to be re-laid. When it was in place, he walked the bridge's length. It didn't budge. Satisfied, the cartographer gave the all clear.

Morrison sent the first pairs of soldiers across with an admonishment to hurry. Under their combined weight, the planks and their supports sank into the mire. Mud oozed over the sides, flowed to the center, and created a small lake of sludge. As the Georgians hurried across, the planks sank lower and lower. Two soldiers stepped forward, but their shoes remained in the sludge.

"I was afraid of this," Hotchkiss whispered to Morrison as he watched the soldiers wrestle their shoes from the mud.

"Can you fix it?" Morrison asked.

"If I had more time. Right now, the best we can do is relay the bridge when it becomes too..." He gestured at the planking to indicate what he meant.

Morrison groaned. How long would it take if the planking had to be re-laid every half hour? Only 100 soldiers had crossed safely, and the boards were barely visible. Hotchkiss' men re-positioned the bridge. Soldiers pounded across. The planking disappeared into the depths of the mire.

"Joe," Smith called. He held up his watch. The first assault had just commenced. "We're never going to make it at this rate." He shoved the watch back into his pocket. A private wrenched his shoes from the mud and struggled toward the aide. Smith grabbed him by the elbow and hauled him to dry ground.

"Take off your shoes and socks," Morrison ordered the surprised soldiers waiting their turn to cross. They sat down, took off their shoes, and stripped off their socks. It worked – a little. The speed increased, but the line still moved too slowly. Iverson's brigade combated the mud and crossed. Ramseur's North Carolinians took their place.

The second assault began with an awesome cannonade. Morrison fought back his rising panic. He urged the men to hurry, practically pushing them onto the makeshift bridge.

"How goes it, Mr. Morrison?" It was General Early. General Gordon stood next to him.

The planking made a whooshing sound as it was lifted from the mud.

"It's not."

When Hotchkiss gave the all clear, Early stepped onto the bridge. It dropped a few inches. Mud poured in from all sides. The lake reformed in the center. "I see your problem," he laughed. Morrison gave him a hand as he slid back toward the creek bank.

"Suggestions?" Smith yanked another soldier clear of the mud.

"Send the men down the creek."

Morrison was aghast. "They don't have any shoes on."

"What's the matter, Mr. Morrison? You never waded in a creek when you were a boy?" Early pulled 15 soldiers from the column. "You men, wade down that creek until you come to your place in line. Tell those on the bank to help you out."

The men jumped down. Morrison flinched at the noise.

"Quietly!" Early snapped.

"General, there are rocks down here," one of the men complained.

"Of course there is, Private. It's a creek. Now stop your bellyaching and move out." The men were a little too forceful with their splashing. "Quiet!" He repeated.

The third assault on the Confederate line brought a courier from Jackson with a message: Faster!

So Morrison went faster. The creek was jammed with soldiers. Pairs of soldiers crossing the planking became triplets. He waited longer to reset the planking. When Hotchkiss re-laid the bridge, he prowled the creek bank and demanded speed over efficiency. Soldiers were admonished to press on!

Barksdale's brigade turned into Kershaw's, which turned into Wofford's brigade. Only Semmes' brigade remained. Then the cavalry.

Keep pushing men! Keep pushing! We're almost there! Morrison snuck a peek at his watch. A little more than four hours had passed since Dole's Georgians had slogged through the mud.

Down by the river, all was quiet. The battle was over. In the silence, Morrison heard the thunder of horse hooves. The cavalry was crossing the bridge across the Susquehanna. He wiped his forehead and sighed in relief.

Smith flung up his hand. Without another word, he disappeared into the hickory grove. Semmes' men struggled into position.

Smith reappeared. "The Yankees are returning." Panic filled his voice. "How much longer?"

"The cavalry's crossing now."

The last of the men were hauled from the creek.

"Mr. Morrison!" Jackson stood before him.

"We barely made it," Morrison said, expecting a rebuke from Jackson.

"God has blessed our efforts, Captain," Jackson smiled. "He would not have us go down to defeat today."

Jackson waded through the mud. Smith gave him a hand onto dry ground. Careful to stay hidden in the hickory grove, Jackson raised his field glasses. Morrison saw him nod in satisfaction.

Grant was very pleased by the discipline and courage the men displayed during the battle. That didn't mean there wasn't room for improvement. Logistics were sloppy, and the corps took too long to reform after each assault. He was with Reynolds, Meade, and Sickles going over a list of concerns when the hill to their right exploded in havoc. The Rebel yell rolled down the rise, followed by the sharp report of musketry.

"What the…?" Grant drew his field glasses from their case and saw the Ninth Corps stampeding down the hill as if they were being chased by the very demons of Hell.

"If I had to guess, I'd say that's Jackson flanking us," Reynolds replied, his tone filled with an unspoken "I told you so."

"Well, that's just bloody brilliant." Grant was admiring. "Why are you two just standing there?" He asked Meade and Sickles. "Go see what help you can give General Burnside."

Meade and Sickles threw themselves in their saddles and galloped away.

"How do you stop them?" Grant asked Reynolds. He pointed at the river of soldiers now headed toward the rear with thousands of screaming Confederates chasing after them.

"They usually stop on their own when they get to Washington."

Grant glanced at Reynolds to see if he was joking; he wasn't. What if the Ninth Corps did run all the way back to Washington? The men were making no attempt to turn and fight.

From across the river, another Rebel cry resounded. The rest of the Army of Northern Virginia poured over the Union pontoon bridges.

Chapter Fifteen

Jackson sat outside his tent cleaning the mud off his boots. As he vigorously applied brush to boot, he brooded over the failure of this morning's battle. The breakdown had occurred with Johnston. The First Corp Commander had panicked when the Yankees began to skirmish with Anderson's division, which was guarding the pontoon bridges in case Jackson was forced to retreat. Johnston sent a series of messages that had escalated from concern to terror. Finally, he informed Jackson that unless Jackson broke off the attack immediately, he would have no choice but to recall Anderson, cross the river, and abandon Jackson to his fate. Frustrated by Johnston's lack of aggression, Jackson had halted his advance and hurried his men across the very bridges Johnston claimed he could no longer protect. Once his troops were safe on the Confederate side of the Susquehanna, Jackson ordered the bridges cut loose. As he watched them float down the river, he complained to Stuart about the lost opportunity to destroy the Yankees.

Pendleton approached. "General, if you're not busy, could I speak to you for a moment."

"Have a seat, Mr. Pendleton." With the brush, Jackson gestured to an empty campstool. "How are the men?"

Pendleton sat down, picked up the other boot, and cleaned it with a rag. "Exhausted but exhilarated."

"Good, good."

Pendleton didn't say anything but put all his energy into cleaning the boot.

"What did you want to talk to me about?" Jackson handed Pendleton the brush.

"Before we moved out, you asked if something was bothering me."

"I did."

"I was having nightmares." The brush scraped heavily across the boot, sending mud in all directions. "They started the night General Stuart told us about his spy in the War Department."

Jackson held up his hands to shield himself from the flying dirt clods. "Yes, that would be about right."

"I should have told you." He breathed heavily from his exertion with the brush. "Especially after you asked."

Jackson took the boot from the young man. "I believe you want to tell me now, but for some reason, you're afraid."

"In the dream, you give me an order, but I freeze. So, you're forced to send Jimmie in my place. He's killed." Pendleton's voice was low.

"But that's not all, is it? For you could have told me that easily enough."

"I didn't want you to replace me."

Jackson faced him. "Do you believe me so stern that I would do something like that?"

An averted head caused Jackson to be filled with remorse. The young man *was* frightened of him. "Oh, Sandie! I can't imagine what it was like to lay under that tree and almost bleed to death. But this morning, you proved your courage."

"I was scared," he confessed, tears sparkling in his eyes. He picked up the boot and buffed it with the rag.

"We're all afraid."

The rag stopped in mid-air. "Not you! You don't even flinch when shells rain down on your head."

"Even me. We just have different things we're afraid of. I'm not afraid of dying. The Lord has set the time of my death. I can't alter it, so I don't concern myself with it. If every man believed the same, they'd be equally brave." Jackson took the boot away again. "I'm sorry you felt that you couldn't come to me with this, and I'm sorrier still if I've somehow made you afraid of me."

Pendleton dropped his head. "I just don't ever want to disappoint you."

"Sandie, look at me." Jackson waited patiently until his adjutant raised his head. "I'm very proud of you. That's what you need to remember." The fear faded from the young man's eyes, and he smiled joyfully. "There'll be many opportunities for you to be afraid on the battlefield, just never take counsel of your fears, and you'll be fine."

"I won't," Pendleton assured him. He picked up the boot and applied rag to leather.

Jackson laughed. "I think you've got that boot clean enough. I need to pay my respect to General Barksdale's brigade. His death is like a hard blow to the stomach."

"Would you like some company?"

"Certainly! Let's round up Stuart. He always knows the right things to say in these types of situations." He slipped on his boots. "Good as new!"

***

Jackson leaned against the fortifications; the wood rough against his elbows. Behind him, soldiers of Ewell's division gathered in the gray, gloomy dawn. Rain clouds, low enough to touch, crowded out all hint of sunlight.

Across the gray Susquehanna, he heard the sounds of an army hastily preparing for battle. Grant was rushing to unleash his assault before the rains fell. Mist rose from the river and shrouded the pioneers pounding the pontoon bridges into place.

Tree branches rustled above him. Jackson looked up and saw a sniper braced in the fork of an oak. A puff of wind blew the mist clear and exposed the work team. The sharp bang of gunfire was followed by a splash. The sniper smiled at Jackson in triumph. He reloaded and waited for the breeze to blow. The tree rustled. Another shot; another splash.

Union artillery pounded. Shells burst through the white mist. Jackson ducked as a shot sheared branches, twigs, leaves, and the sniper from the tree. The soldier staggered to his feet. He shook his head a couple times then threw Jackson a woozy smile. Besides some abrasions on his face, he appeared unharmed. He hitched up his pants and climbed another tree further back. The wind blew, the mist parted, and the sharpshooter took aim. Jackson smiled when a body hit the river. Mississippians didn't make it a habit to miss from such distances.

Despite the sniper's marksmanship, the bridges moved closer. In this morning's staff meeting, Lee had advised his corps commanders that he wouldn't contest the river.

The pounding stopped. The bridges were in place. A rider sent by Stuart warned of the impending attack.

The Yankees poured out of the fog like water from a well spigot. The bugles sounded. The wind whipped battle flags – red, blue, green – the only color in a colorless landscape. The Yankees formed up in front of the Confederate defenses.

From his vantage point, Jackson heard the order given to fire. His men unleashed a withering volley. The Yankees in front of the fortifications simply vanished. Load! Fire! Load! Fire! The blue lines receded. Load! Fire! Load! Fire! More soldiers backed away from the fence. Another volley; they fled. A bolt of lightning slithered to the ground. The storm clouds emptied.

***

Grant stood in the doorway of his tent somberly smoking a cigar. Reynolds splashed up. “John, what brings you out in this weather?” Grant asked.

Thunder rumbled and a flash of lightning lit up the miserable camp, which was in the process of transforming into a huge mud puddle. It might be only late morning, but it was as dark as dusk.

Reynolds ran under the canopy. “I came to tell you the river is up.” He looked around for a coffee pot but didn’t see one.

“We’ll disengage, of course.” Grant puffed on his cigar. “Do you have casualty figures yet?”

“Not yet. Preliminary figures put the dead, wounded, and missing for the last two days at approximately 5,000. I think they’re high.”

Grant bowed his head; his face hidden in shadow. He didn’t say anything but continued to smoke his cigar in silence. When he finished, he motioned Reynolds inside. A map, weighed down by various paperweights, lay on the table. Reynolds’ eyes lit up. A coffee pot! He poured himself a cup and gulped it down.

Grant’s hand swept over the map. “I propose we head to the mountain passes south of Chambersburg and cut Lee’s communications and supplies. He’ll be forced to follow us.”

“He’s well supplied thanks to Stuart.”

“He’ll follow us.”

Grant was positive, so Reynolds dropped the matter. “This rain won’t make crossing the river easy.”

Grant lit another cigar. “We have pontoons.”

Reynolds poured another cup of coffee. “Maybe we can trick the Rebs into thinking we’ve retreated to Washington.”

“No tricks,” Grant said swiftly. “I want them to pursue us. If I thought it necessary, I’d leave a trail of bread crumbs.”

Reynolds examined the map. “Lee only needs to follow your bread crumbs a short distance before he realizes where you’re headed. He could reach the passes before us.”

“That’s why we must be gone by this evening.”

“Okay. I’ll order General Sheridan to find a good place to cross.” Thunder shook the tent. “The rain’s turned the roads to mud, though.”

“What’s a little mud?” Grant tapped an ash.

Reynolds laughed. "You wouldn't say that if you'd been here to participate in the Mud March."

Grant shook his head in amusement. "This army certainly has had its share of travails."

"Most of them self-inflicted. I'll have the wounded removed to Lancaster. We should be ready to move out sometime after supper."

"That'll be fine." Grant folded the map.

Reynolds ran back out into the rain. It was really coming down.

Chapter Sixteen

Near Schwenksville, Pennsylvania
Middle of May 1864

My young lieutenant general certainly has an eye for good ground, Lee thought, examining the lush series of swells that descended into a deeply banked creek. What made the landscape more appealing was its location; a mere two-day march from Philadelphia. According to the newspapers Stuart had brought back from a new round of raids, the entire city was up in arms at the thought of Rebels at their doorstep. Headline after headline excoriated Grant for being caught with his pants down, or, more specifically, marching in the wrong direction. The Great Gallop Across Pennsylvania, as the editors had penned the Army of the Potomac's mad dash from Chambersburg, was on the front page of every daily newspaper in the Union. The army might be averaging 20 miles a day in the heat, humidity, and rain, but it wasn't fast enough to satisfy the nervous citizens of Philadelphia, New York, or Washington City.

The Great Gallop was the entire point of Lee's move east. The memory of Jackson's analogy of the knife fight had stayed with him during the winter. Jackson was correct. This was a fight to the death. It was all win or all lose, and Lee didn't plan to lose. Grant understood the stakes. That was why he had moved south; to force Lee on the offensive. Lee had moved east to stay on the defensive, to make those people look foolish, and to terrorize a shaky North ready to rebel against the Lincoln administration.

Jackson had approved the daring strategy. "Always mystify, mislead, and surprise the enemy whenever possible," he had said with a pleased smile.

Now, if Lee could only make Johnston understand his reasoning, he would be a happy man. From the Susquehanna to the Schuylkill, he had been forced to listen to Johnston first lecture, then hector, then bemoan this "disastrous decision." Endless conversations about supply lines, communications, and the horrors of trying to escape from eastern Pennsylvania if the worst befell the army, and it lost along the banks of Shippack Creek.

"You're needlessly risking the army," Johnston had argued.

"Not needlessly." And with those words, Lee had ended the conversation.

Yes, it was a risk, but it was the only move he could make. And from the headlines and editorials screaming that Lincoln do something about Grant's incompetence, the risk was reaping great dividends. Grant would arrive, breathless and weary, and throw his great army at Lee's fortified position, not caring if his men lived or died. The casualty lists would mount, the anarchy in the cities would re-ignite, and, with his great hope beaten again on Northern soil, Lincoln would be forced to let the South go.

A tree crashed to the ground. Members of Pickett's division denuded it of branches with amazing skill. The once noble tree would soon be a part of the large ramparts being erected at the top of the hill. The rain-swollen creek and its banks were being stripped of boulders and large rocks. Under Johnston's exacting eye, a steady stream of wagons lugged the rocks to the top of the rise to be incorporated into the newest section of the wall. To Lee's left, Hood's division fortified the left flank at Keyser's Mill. From the mill pond, the fortifications climbed the hill, made a sharp left, and rode the ridge. The Second Corps was hard at work securing the right flank at the point where the waterway elbowed its way from south to east.

Jackson rode up. "General Lee, this line does us no good," he said before Lee could say good morning. "Armies are not called out to dig trenches and throw up breastworks." He waved at the men flailing away with shovels. "No, their purpose is to find the enemy and strike him. All we will be able to do here is hold them off. We won't even be able to pursue them once we beat them back. Their cannon on the opposite hill will make that impossible."

"Have you seen the latest newspapers?"

Flummoxed by the question, Jackson stared at him.

"The editors are very upset with General Grant and Mr. Lincoln. Incompetent was the adjective they used over and over again. You really should read them. I'll have them sent right over."

"But the line!" Jackson insisted, but with less fury. As Lee intended, all the protest in his Second Corps Commander had been doused.

"Is exactly as I designed. It allows us to inflict great casualties with minimal damage to ourselves."

"Well, if you will excuse me," Jackson said, still discomfited, "I'll see to my men."

"Certainly." Lee watched him ride off. He had to wonder how Jackson ever acquired the *nom de guerre* of Stonewall. For he more resembled an eagle soaring over the battlefield than an immovable, stationary object. It was a mystery. Lee was still musing on it when Taylor arrived with a question that forced his thoughts elsewhere.

Carnot Posey's brigade of Mississippians held the angle. Half the brigade sloped down the hill to link up with Cadmus Wilcox's brigade of Alabamians. The other half stood on the high ground next to Pickett's Virginians. Posey focused his field glasses and saw Union artillery already in place. The Yankees must have brought up the guns immediately upon their arrival late last night. "I believe the Yankees plan to attack us this morning, boys."

"Are you sure, General?"

The answer came from Union artillery. The large guns opened fire. Shells blasted the ground in front of the Mississippians. The men ducked behind the wall as dirt, rock, and shrapnel hurled toward them. The guns rang out again. With a sigh, the Mississippians settled back against the stout wall to wait out the barrage.

"General, can we git something to eat? It's been three hours worth of shellin', and they ain't come yet," some men complained.

"They're coming now," Posey replied.

The soldiers scrambled to their feet and looked down the hill. The long blue lines were jumping into the creek, lower now than when the Confederates first arrived. The Yankees waded across with ease. Tomorrow may be a different story if the rain clouds moving through the area since dawn decided to stick around.

The Yankees climbed out of the creek and reformed at the bottom of the hill. The Confederate artillery barked. Hundreds of shells whistled through the air and crashed into the line. The Yankees scattered.

"They ain't that tired," a private laughed to Posey. "Did you see them skedaddle back into the crick?"

The Yankees popped their heads up and crawled out. Another round of shot resent half the troops scrambling for refuge beneath the creek's bank. Their commanders unleashed a severe tongue lashing designed to separate the most cowardly man from his hiding place. It did the trick. The creek emptied. Huge holes were blasted throughout the entire line, but not one soldier ran. The advance was sounded. The Yankees marched up the hill.

The Confederate line crackled with musket fire. The Yankees lowered their heads and pressed on. Halfway up the hill, the lines swung to the right.

Posey stared in disbelief. The bulk of the Union army was headed right at him!

He ordered one concentrated volley before ordering his men to fire at will. Tired or not, the Yankees showed resolute bravery. They withstood the murderous fire spewing from behind the wall. The field filled with the dead and dying, and still ramrods were shoved into barrels and return fire tore into the Mississippians.

Posey checked his left. Wilcox's brigade was sustaining heavy losses. A gap had opened between the two brigades. He spurred his horse down the hill. "Cad!" He shouted over the gunfire. A bullet ripped through his open jacket. "What's happening on your right? Your men keep pulling back!"

"I'll take care of it," Wilcox assured him.

Satisfied, Posey returned to the angle. The gunfire abated. The Yankees retreated down the hill. They jumped into the creek and climbed out the other side. They went no further. There would be another assault.

On the Confederate side of the wall, the wounded were helped into ambulances or carried to the back toward the field hospitals. The dead were dragged away.

Johnston rode up. "Let's go talk with General Wilcox."

Johnston and Posey joined division commander Richard Anderson and Wilcox in mid-conversation. "Do you need reinforcements?" Anderson asked Wilcox.

"My men took a beating, but we should be able to hold," Wilcox replied.

"General Posey?" Johnston asked, giving Posey every opportunity to contradict Wilcox's assessment.

"Are you sure, Cad?"

The usual nervous and fussy Wilcox nodded calmly. It was enough to convince Posey.

"If you need reinforcements, send a runner. I have Laws Brigade in reserve." Johnston said before galloping up the hill.

"Don't waste any time," Anderson ordered his brigade commanders. "If you need help, send word to General Laws."

Posey had no sooner returned to his position when the Yankees began their slow ascent up the hill. He held his breath. Would they turn? His heart lurched. There it was! Another right oblique. The Yankees were trying to break him.

His men defended their portion of the Pennsylvania countryside like it had been in their family for generations. The gunfire became a roar;

individual shots merging into one continuous sound, broken only by the rapid boom of artillery. Through the hazy gunsmoke, Posey observed Wilcox's brigade fall back down the hill. Yankees clambered over the wall and into the gap between the two brigades.

"Mr. Hancock!" Posey screamed at his aide. "Tell General Laws to hurry."

Hancock had only gone three feet when he pulled up. He shouted and gestured. Posey couldn't hear the aide but raised his glasses in the direction of the frantic gestures. He saw two of Laws' brigades sprinting up the hill. Guns lowered, Laws' men fired into the Yankees on the Confederate side of the wall then enthusiastically applied the bayonet. Not wishing to test the deadly steel, the Yankees reversed course and scampered back over the wall to safety. Slowly, the Federals were driven back down the hill. Posey watched them. This time the Yankees did not stop. They waded the creek and marched up the hill to their camps. It was over for the day.

The rain beating against his canvas tent was like a mother's lullaby to Reynolds. He did his best sleeping under such conditions, so it took his adjutant, Colonel Rosengarten, several tries at waking him before he sat up with a start. "What's the matter?"

"General Grant requests your presence down at the creek."

Reynolds acknowledged the request with a groan and threw back the light blanket. He yawned, stretched wide his arms, and pulled on his boots. Another yawn and stretch, and he was ready to go.

As he rode down the hill, he could see that the creek was out of its banks and slowly creeping up the sides of the hill. Grant prowled along the water's edge while John Sedgwick threw pebbles into the water. Both turned at his approach. Grant's look was thunderous; Sedgwick's sublime. Reynolds hailed them both and gestured toward the stream. "I guess last night's rain was too much for the creek."

"The creek's flowing backwards," Grant informed him.

Reynolds studied the current for a moment. It was true. The water was moving in the wrong direction.

"The Rebs have dammed it," Grant said. "They're also digging a trench in front of their right flank. It seems they've been at it for a couple of hours now."

"If I didn't know any better, I'd think Lee has a spy in our midst," Reynolds chuckled. For the Rebs were protecting the very spot Grant had planned to attack this morning.

"The answer's not that complicated," Sedgwick said. He twisted the ends of his mustache in irritation. "Early this morning, General Custer was involved in a little altercation with Reb cavalry. I think it alerted Jeb Stuart to the increased activity on our left flank." He left his mustache alone and directed his next comment to Grant. "General, I know Sheridan refuses to believe that Stuart is a worthy opponent; but I served with Stuart in Kansas. This country's not foaled a better cavalryman. It's time Sheridan regarded him with more than scorn."

Reynolds took a step back from the rising creek. "I agree with General Sedgwick."

Grant threw his cigar on the ground. "Let's concentrate our energies on this morning's battle, shall we?" He barked.

Reynolds rolled his eyes at Sedgwick. As long as Grant protected Sheridan, there would be no reason for the cavalry leader to change his thinking or ways.

Reynolds asked Sedgwick for his field glasses. He focused on the Confederate's right flank. The Rebs had made remarkable progress on the trench. Plus, they were moving artillery to the other side of the creek. The only feasible place to attack was at the angle. "If we can break through there again," he told Grant, "we can trap Jackson between the flooded creek and the trench."

Grant agreed. "Sound the assembly."

Stuart smiled like a proud father as the Yankees concentrated their formidable strength on the Confederate center and the reinforced angle. His brainchild to dam the creek, dig a trench, and flood it with creek water to protect Jackson's right flank had done the trick.

"General Stuart!" Fitz called him away from admiring his handiwork. "We have company."

Stuart turned his field glasses in the direction of Fitz's point and saw Yankee cavalry crossing the creek on a makeshift bridge. "Where's Rooney?" He asked, stowing his glasses in their case.

"Setting up a defensive position about 100 yards from here."

"Major McClellan." Stuart wrote out a note. "Please take this to General Jackson with my compliments." He turned to Fitz. "Let's go and give Rooney some help."

Stuart joined Rooney at a small tributary. At the mouth of the rivulet, the water formed a small pool. Rooney anchored his left to the pool and his right on the tributary itself. Major Beckham had placed his horse artillery on the high ground to the right, which gave the cannons command of the field. Fitz ordered his brigade to Rooney's right.

Stuart urged Virginia across the small stream. She carefully picked her way across but stumbled on the spongy ground. Stuart patted her neck in encouragement. Ten yards from the edge of the tributary, the ground re-hardened. He returned to his side of the stream. "It's a good line, Rooney. We can hold them until help arrives from General Jackson. Here comes Major McClellan now."

"General Jackson is sending you both the Stonewall Brigade and Nicholls' brigade. They were forming up when I left," the adjutant dutifully reported.

"Remind me to thank General Jackson after we whip these Yankees," Stuart laughed.

"Here they come," Rooney remarked calmly.

"Major McClellan, instruct Major Beckham to fire at will."

From across the stream, Stuart heard the bugles sound the retreat. He peered through his glasses. Horses were rushed from the rear, and the blue line in front of Rooney's troopers fell back. "Ah, they're running away," he said to Rooney in disappointment.

It was the arrival of the Stonewall Brigade that had turned the tide of the battle. Intermittent gunfire still crackled up and down the line, but the majority of the Yankees were already mounted and headed back across the creek. Stuart glanced up the hill at the long column of infantry hurrying toward them. "General Nicholls is going to be upset that he missed all the excitement."

He turned back around. Rooney was sitting very still, his eyes wide with surprise. "Oh, Jeb," he whispered. He collapsed.

Stuart caught him and held him close. "Rooney? Rooney? NO! NO! NO!"

Chapter Seventeen

Fitz heard Stuart's shouts. He glanced over. Stuart was clinging to Rooney's slumped body while trying to dismount. He has half-in and out of the saddle. Virginia danced under his indecision. Fitz spurred his mare and raced over. He threw himself from the saddle. Stuart was tugging on Rooney, but to no avail.

"What can I do?" Fitz asked.

"I think his leg is caught," Stuart gasped, breathless from his struggles.

Fitz saw Rooney's left foot pinned in the stirrup. He freed it and ran around to where Stuart still struggled to keep Rooney upright. Fitz took his cousin in his arms and sagged under Rooney's weight. Stuart dismounted and slapped Virginia's flank. She trotted out of the way. Together, they dragged Rooney from his saddle and laid him on the ground.

Fitz dropped down next to the wounded man. There was a blackened bullet hole in Rooney's jacket right above the heart, but very little blood. He quickly unbuttoned Rooney's jacket. Without warning, Stuart seized his arm and jerked it away. Furious, he raised his head to bark rude words at Stuart, but Stuart's tear-stained face, drawn tight in sorrow, stole the words from his throat.

"No!" Fitz waited for Stuart to contradict him. "No!" He begged in a choked whisper. Stuart reached out to him. He fell against Stuart's shoulder, his sobs muffled in Stuart's fighting jacket. "This will break his father's heart," he said when he could speak again.

At the thought of telling Uncle Robert that his favorite son was dead, a shiver of dread raced down Fitz's spine. And no matter how much he dreaded the task, Lee needed to be told before news reached him via the army grapevine, or by some soldier who reveled in being the bearer of bad tidings. He said so to Stuart. "Do you want me to do it?" He asked, wiping his eyes.

The blood drained from Stuart's face. "No, I'm…was…his commanding officer. It's my responsibility."

Fitz closed Rooney's brown eyes. His tears splashed Rooney's cheek.

"Fitz." Stuart stood over him. "When the ambulance comes, take Rooney to his tent. I'll bring General Lee there."

***

"General Stuart," Lee called with affection. He was seated beneath a leafy tree, eating a small lunch. "Come, have a glass of buttermilk." He held up his glass.

At Lee's invitation, a wave of tears threatened to engulf Stuart. It would take more than Lee's favorite cure-all to fix this. He fiddled with his saddle, breathing in and out until his eyes stopped stinging. Only a few more minutes, he rallied himself, then he could fall to pieces. He walked over and knelt down next to Lee. "Rooney set a strong line." He placed a gentle hand on Lee's arm.

Lee's eyes widened in apprehension. "Is he hurt?"

One tear slipped down Stuart's cheek. Beneath his hand, Lee's arm stiffened. "I'm so sorry, sir, but Rooney is dead."

"Are you sure?" The words were breathless.

"He died in my arms."

Lee's brown eyes filled with tears; his noble face became a sorrowful mask. "Where is he?" He choked out. He gripped Stuart's hand and crushed it against his arm.

"Fitz took him back to his tent so you can say goodbye." Before his eyes, Lee aged 20 years. Impulsively, Stuart leaned over and kissed his cheek. "I'll fetch Traveller."

When he stepped away, Lee caught his hand. The once strong grip was vulnerable and helpless.

"Jeb, I'm glad you're here with me," he whispered. "Your presence makes it bearable."

"I won't leave you," Stuart promised.

When Lee and Stuart rode into Rooney's headquarters, the small crowd of aides milling in front of Rooney's tent rushed towards Traveller.

"You men, find something else to do!" Stuart said harshly. They hesitated. "Now!" At Stuart's raised voice, they scattered.

Fitz came out of the tent; his cheeks wet with tears. "I'm so sorry, Uncle Robert."

Lee patted him on the shoulder. "Is he in there?" Lee gestured toward the tent.

Fitz pulled back the flap. Like a sleepwalker, Lee walked inside. Stuart and Fitz followed. Stuart swallowed hard when he saw Rooney lying on his bed, dressed in his finest uniform; the gray wool not stained by the road or frayed by the years of campaigning. His yellow sash fell gracefully at his side. Fitz had even strapped Rooney's handsome sword around his waist.

Lee bent down and arranged his son's hair. It took a few moments before he was satisfied. Then he kissed Rooney's forehead and stroked his cheek. He fell into the chair next to the bed. He picked up his son's lifeless hand. "He's so cold. Jeb, fetch me his blanket."

Stuart pulled a blanket from the trunk at the end of the bed and covered the still form. Like he had done with the hair, Lee fussed with the blanket until he was satisfied with its arrangement. He picked up Rooney's hand again.

"We'll be out front if you need anything," Stuart said.

"You won't be far, will you, Jeb?" Lee's eyes were full of worry.

"No, I'll be right outside."

Outside the tent, the sun was shining, and the birds were singing in the birches, unmindful that this day had been visited by death and sorrow. Stuart shivered at the contradiction. He and Fitz dragged chairs in front of the tent to protect Lee from the steady stream of mourners arriving to pay their respects.

Fitz jumped to his feet. "Rob! In all the commotion, I forgot about Rob. Will you be okay alone?"

"Go!"

Stuart poured a cup of coffee. He stared out into space too numb and exhausted to do anything more. Maybe tomorrow he could make sense of all the emotions and memories assailing his heart. Right now, he was just thankful that his exhaustion kept his tears at bay.

Lee began to weep: torrents of sobs that burst over Stuart until he believed he was going to drown in Lee's sorrow.

Stuart stood and faced the tent. He tugged on his beard in indecision. He knew he should go in and comfort the grieving father, but he shrank back. For once in his life, he was at a loss for words. If only his beautiful Flora was here. She would know what to do. If only…Jackson! Why hadn't he thought of Jackson sooner? Calm, cool Stonewall was the perfect antidote to this overwhelming tragic hour. Yes, his good and gallant Jackson would know all the proper words to comfort Lee.

From behind him, there came a rustling. Stuart whirled around and faced four troopers with their hats in their hands. Tears streaked down their cheeks. "We've come to pay our respects," they told the cavalry leader.

"Do you want to help?" Stuart questioned sharply. They nodded eagerly. "Then you stay out here and chase away anyone who comes near except for Fitz, Rob, or myself. Do you understand? Oh, yes, General Johnston can stay, too. But that's it. Can I trust you to do that and not go in there," he pointed to the tent, "and make a spectacle of yourselves?"

"Yes, sir," they assured him, glad to be of service.

"If General Lee calls for me, tell him I'll be gone only for a moment." Stuart ran to Virginia.

"Good afternoon, General Stuart," Pendleton called. "Would you like some lunch?" Smith and Morrison helloed him also.

Stuart ignored them. He stalked across the yard and burst into Jackson's tent. "Rooney Lee is dead. I want you to come with me."

Jackson set down his pen. "Come with you where?"

Stuart picked up Jackson's jacket from off the bed and held it out. "To Rooney's tent. General Lee's sitting with the body. I want you to go and comfort him."

Jackson balked. "Oh, Stuart, I'm not very good at that kind of thing. Besides, I didn't know Rooney all that well. Why not ask General Johnston? Or Reverend Lacy? Surely, they can be more of a comfort than me."

Stuart felt the ground dissolve beneath his feet. He hadn't counted on Jackson refusing. He threw the jacket across the tent. It bounced against the canvas wall and slid to the ground. "I can't stand it!" He sobbed.

The next thing he knew, he was in Jackson's arms.

"Please," he begged, "he's all alone."

"It's all right. I'll go with you," Jackson whispered.

At the gentleness in Jackson's voice, Stuart began to weep.

"Who's there?" Lee's voice was rough with anger.

Jackson stood behind Lee and waited for his eyes to adjust to the dimly lit tent. "It's General Jackson. I didn't mean to startle you. I've come to sit with you and Fitzhugh. If that is acceptable to you."

Lee's nod was so small that Jackson almost missed it. Since Lee occupied the only chair in the tent, Jackson sat down on Rooney's trunk.

Lee was sprawled in the chair, his frame shrunk and shriveled in agony. He held Rooney's hand, but his eyes stared straight ahead, seeing nothing. Tears streamed down his pale face and soaked the front of his shirt.

Jackson remembered the joy he had beheld on Lee's face last summer as he scolded Rooney for not coming to dinner. To see Lee in such obvious pain…his heart filled with compassion for the suffering man.

Now that he was here, Jackson felt a compulsion to say something. But the speeches he had rehearsed on the way over had vanished from his mind. So had all Scripture. The only thing he could think to say was I'm sorry, but somehow that phrase seemed to be more about his pain than Lee's.

Jackson shifted uncomfortably. The trunk squealed in protest. He came to attention and glanced at Lee in embarrassment. Thankfully, Lee hadn't heard. Besides being incredibly hard, the trunk placed him at Rooney's feet. Jackson felt like a ghoul staring at the young man. He averted his eyes and stared at a large stain on the tent wall above Rooney's head instead.

The canvas tent was hot in the noon sun. Jackson's collar pinched and a bead of sweat traced its way down the side of his face while another raced down his spine. He was wiggling his handkerchief from his pocket when another screech filled the tent. He froze. Lee glanced at him, but with unseeing eyes. Then he turned his head and gazed at his son. A small sob escaped him, and his tears flowed anew.

Since he was doing nothing for Lee, Jackson decided to leave and fetch Reverend Lacy. He would just tell Stuart that it was for the best. "General Lee." He kept his voice soft so not to impose on Lee's grief.

"I use to tease him, this big son of mine," Lee interrupted. His smile held the ghosts of memory. "I told him he was too big to be a man but too small to be a horse. See, how he's missing his fingertips." He indicated the hand he was holding. The tips of Rooney's fore and middle fingers were missing. Jackson had never noticed the deformity before. "Fitzhugh was eight when he sliced them off with straw cutters." Lee smiled again. He let go of Rooney's hand and placed it tenderly on the bed. He fussed with the blanket for a few moments. "I worried about him constantly. Never knowing what scrapes he would get into next."

The tent flap opened, and Rob walked in. Jackson was surprised to see him. He knew from Stuart that Rob had been confined to the hospital for the past week with a severe case of dysentery. Rob's ashen face grew paler when he caught sight of his brother lying on the bed. He gulped. Lee rose and swallowed him up in a hug. "Bertus, how will we tell your mother?"

At the mention of his mother, Rob wept. Lee gathered his youngest son even closer. Tears coursed down Lee's cheeks, wetting Rob's hair.

Jackson rose from the trunk. Once more, it protested with a loud screech. He was almost to the door when Lee caught his jacket. "You're not leaving, are you?"

"I thought I'd go fetch Reverend Lacy," Jackson murmured.

"I want you to stay."

Jackson was torn, but Lee's eyes pleaded with him to stay. He relented and returned to the trunk. Before he sat down, he took out his handkerchief and wiped his forehead.

Lee let go of Rob and collapsed back into the chair. Rob sat at his father's feet. He wept soundlessly, his body trembling from fever and grief.

Lee wiped his eyes. "General Jackson, I've been sitting here trying to remember the words of Molly's favorite hymn. All I can remember is *'Jesus, I my cross have taken…'* Do you know the words?"

"Jesus, I my cross have taken, all to leave and follow Thee,
"Destitute, despised, forsaken, Thou from hence my all shalt be,
"Perish every fond ambition, all I've sought, and hoped and known,
"Yet how rich is my condition, God and heav'n are still my own."

"That's it!" Lee exclaimed. "Perhaps Jeb can sing it for us. Jeb!"

Fitz stuck his head in the tent. "He stepped away for a moment."

"Tell him I need him." Fitz nodded and retreated. Lee stroked Rooney's cheek. "I don't want him buried in Pennsylvania. His mother will want him close."

"Don't worry, sir, I'll see that he gets home."

Jackson felt Lee's eyes on him.

"Thomas Jackson, you've done me and my sons a great kindness today." Then he smiled. Jackson saw that his tears had stopped and his pale face was composed. He placed a loving hand on Rob's shoulder. "We won't forget it. I still remember the talk we had after Hampton's death. I never imagined that one death could fill the cup and overflow it. Thank you for allowing me a father's grief."

There was a knock on the canvas flap. "It's General Stuart. Fitz said you needed to see me."

"Come in, Jeb," Lee said.

Stuart crept into the tent. He raised a questioning eyebrow at Jackson, who nodded. Stuart sighed in relief.

"Jeb." Lee caught his hand. "I want you to tell me stories about Fitzhugh. Fitz, please come here!"

Fitz came in, and Lee repeated his request. Stuart sat down on the cold ground next to Lee. Jackson made room for Fitz on the trunk.

"I want you boys to tell me all the things I don't know about my son."

Jackson, Stuart, and Fitz stepped out into the pale moonlight. Inside, Lee and Rob were saying their final goodbyes to Rooney. A pinewood coffin sat in the clearing.

Jackson pointed at the coffin. "Stuart, I don't want General Lee to see that."

Fitz and Stuart dragged the pine box into the deeper shadows.

"General Jackson! General Jackson!" Jackson heard terror in Rob Lee's voice. He ran into the tent and saw Rob cradling his father in his arms. Lee was unconscious. "He just collapsed!" Rob cried.

Stuart and Fitz burst into the tent.

"Go fetch Doctor McGuire!" Jackson ordered Stuart.

Stuart pushed Fitz out of the way and vanished into the night.

"Whose tent is nearer?" Jackson asked Fitz. "Yours or Stuart's?"

"Mine."

"Let's take him there."

Chapter Eighteen

Phil Sheridan sat by the fire and stared moodily at the dancing flames. Grant sank into the chair next to him. "What did you want to see me about?" Sheridan asked. His boots sought the warmth of the fire.

Grant took a cigar from his pocket. "I want to know why General Custer was skirmishing with the Rebs this morning." He picked up a twig and stuck it into the flame. It blazed to life. He blew it out and used the smoldering ember to light the cigar.

"I sent Custer to determine the Rebs' strength in preparation for today's attack. When the enemy blundered into his party, he had to defend himself."

"He should have exercised more caution."

Sheridan shrugged. "Perhaps."

It was an epiphany. He had been wrong about Phil and Reynolds right. "Well, Custer is directly responsible for today's defeat."

Sheridan stiffened. "How so?"

"His blundering alerted Jeb Stuart to the fact we were concentrating on Lee's right flank." Grant took one last puff from his cigar and threw it in the fire.

Sheridan laughed in derision. "Jeb Stuart doesn't have the wherewithal to determine such things."

"Really?" Grant said roughly. "It seems to me he had enough wherewithal to bring up infantry support in this morning's battle." Grant could tell his words hit their mark. "Now, you can hold Stuart in contempt for his plumes and all the other affectations that have gotten under your skin, but you must," Grant thrust an admonitory finger into Sheridan's face, "must change your attitude about his ability to fight. I'll give you the necessary time to adjust your thinking. If you can't, then I'll replace you with someone who respects Stuart's capability. Do I make myself clear?" He took out a new cigar.

"Yes," Sheridan said sullenly.

"Good." He searched for another twig. "Now, that army over there is giving both of us fits. What do you suggest I do?"

"To tell you the truth, sir, we need to move off from here and make Lee chase us."

"Oh, no," Grant laughed, "I can't afford to make that mistake twice. I'm all for moving off this ground. So, tomorrow, go out and find me a piece of land that gives Lee no choice but to attack me." He finally found a stick and stuck it into the fire.

"My men will be ready to go at first light."

"Splendid." Grant lit his cigar.

The smell of coffee reached Lee in the blackness. He knew he wasn't in familiar surroundings. This wasn't his bedroom at Arlington or his tent. No, the smells and feel were all wrong.

There were voices: anxious and worried. Lee wanted to wake and relieve the anxiety, but he knew something terrible waited for him in the light. Here, sheltered by the darkness, he couldn't remember what it was.

He wasn't alone. Someone was seated next to him. Someone familiar and safe. The person left his side. When the person returned, the aroma of coffee was strong. Lee wanted a cup, but the warnings were sounding: Don't wake up! Don't remember!

The darkness called to him to return to a place where his memories were happy and carefree. He could be at Stratford Hall one moment or riding the trails of Arlington with Mary the next. Now, he was returning from the Mexican War. His children were pouring out the door…Warning bells began to ring: Don't remember your children! Not your children!

Next to him, the person put a hand on his forehead. The hand next touched his arm. A hand on his arm! A tear tracing its way down a familiar face! A face as beloved as any son! Fitzhugh! He opened his eyes. "Fitzhugh is dead."

"I'm sorry, sir."

Lee turned his head. He saw Doctor McGuire seated beside him. "Where am I?"

"You're in your nephew's tent. General Jackson brought you here after you collapsed."

It all came back to him. The hand and the tear belonged to Jeb Stuart, who had brought him the news of the death of his son.

"How long have you been having heart trouble, General?" McGuire fixed a powder.

"It started while we wintered on the Rappahannock."

"You have medicine?"

"Yes."

"Good. You had a minor heart seizure, which I believed was brought on by grief. I want you to take this." McGuire handed him the powder, now swirling in a glass of water. "I'm also going to order one week's bed rest."

Lee sat up and drank the medicine. "How can I rest with those people not even a mile from our position?"

"General Johnston and General Jackson can handle the army for a week, I should think." He took Lee's pulse.

"I can't remain in bed…"

McGuire cut him off. "Sir, I understand, but you're ill. If you push yourself here, you may do permanent damage to your heart."

Lee closed his eyes and surrendered. "Doctor, where's General Stuart? I need to see him."

"He and General Jackson are preparing Rooney for his trip home."

Lee tried to push the thought of his son sealed up in a pine box from his mind, but the image stubbornly refused to leave. Tears coursed down his face. He didn't bother to wipe them away.

McGuire handed him a handkerchief. "Would you be more comfortable back at your headquarters? I can arrange for an ambulance to take you."

"Thank you, Doctor, for everything," Lee said, indicating the handkerchief. "Is Rob still here?"

"No, I sent him back to the hospital. General Johnston's outside. He's been waiting all night. I wouldn't oppose a short visit if you feel up to it."

"Please."

"I'll order the ambulance." McGuire exited the tent.

"Robert." Johnston slipped into McGuire's vacated chair. "I'm so sorry."

Lee began to weep. "I can't believe he's gone." He waved the handkerchief in front of his face. "I've cried so many tears since I've heard the news, I'm surprised I haven't run out."

Johnston reached over, grabbed Lee's hand, and gave it a small squeeze. "I'm afraid it's an endless reservoir. It's been almost 20 years since Preston died in Mexico, but something will suddenly remind me of him, and the tears will start flowing of their own volition. They say time heals all wounds. It doesn't."

Lee's shoulders sagged. He couldn't imagine living the rest of his life with this gaping wound in his heart. Johnston squeezed his hand again.

"I didn't mean to sound so hopeless. It won't always hurt as much as it does at this moment." Johnston gave a consoling smile. "Your faith will sustain you and so will the comfort of your friends. Even now, the hours after I received the news that my darling Pres was dead are still a blur. But I do remember your sudden appearance in the breastworks at Padierna. You held my hand and wept with me."

"I wish I could have done more."

"You did enough." Johnston handed Lee his handkerchief. "Here, this one's dry. What I'm trying to say, and not very well, is that Pres hasn't left me. And Fitzhugh won't leave you either. Death doesn't have the power to steal them away from us." Johnston rose and embraced him.

"Thank you," Lee whispered. Johnston stepped back, his eyes shiny with tears.

McGuire entered the tent. "If you're ready, General."

Johnston stiffened and his face grew hard. "Give us a moment."

"Not too long," McGuire admonished before retreating.

"About the army, Robert. When will I have the order giving me command?" Johnston demanded coldly.

"I'll have Colonel Taylor send it to you within the hour," Lee mumbled, too stunned by Johnston's abrupt change in demeanor to say anything else.

Johnston nodded once then left the tent. Lee burst into tears again. This time he didn't know if his tears were for Fitzhugh or for himself. Until this moment, he hadn't realized just how much he missed Joe's friendship. But the unresolved quarrel over rank and position had stolen him away, just when Lee needed him the most.

Chapter Nineteen

Under the guise of doing paperwork, Walter Taylor sat at the common table guarding Lee's tent. Since command had been transferred to Johnston, there was no reason for Lee to be disturbed. Taylor was ready to risk life and limb to protect Lee's privacy. The sounds of jangling spurs and slap of scabbard against leather boot warned him of an intruder. A squinting look into the sun revealed an angry Stuart bearing down on Lee's tent. Taylor sprang up so quickly that papers and reports scattered in every direction. He flung himself in Stuart's path. For a moment, he thought Stuart was going to roll right over him, but the cavalry leader pulled up. "What can I do for you, General?"

"I need to see General Lee."

Taylor stood his ground. "General Lee is asleep." Stuart tried to circumvent him. Once more, Taylor placed himself between Stuart and Lee's tent. "Perhaps you should take your problem to General Johnston. He has temporary command."

"I know that," Stuart snapped. "I've just came from a staff meeting." He tried to side-step the adjutant. Taylor mirrored his movement.

"Sir, I'm sorry. I have my orders." Taylor kept his voice firm. Stuart side-stepped in the other direction, but Taylor anticipated his move and once more blocked his path.

"Walter, is that General Stuart?" Lee called from the tent.

Taylor glared at Stuart. "Yes, sir. He was just leaving." He tried to shoo Stuart away before Lee emerged from his tent, but the cavalry leader was having none of it.

"Tell him I'd like to see him," Lee said.

"Sir, Doctor McGuire said you were to rest."

Lee appeared in the doorway. His hair was mussed and his eyes were sleepy. "I'm sure I can rest and talk to General Stuart at the same time. Doctor McGuire didn't ban visitors, did he? Do you think we could have some buttermilk? Would you like that, Jeb?"

"Yes, sir." Stuart slipped inside the tent.

"That will be all, Walter." Lee closed the flap. He sized up his fuming young lieutenant general. "What's wrong?" He sat down on his bed and swung his feet up.

Stuart paced back and forth, from desk to bed, a short space that had him turning every three steps, making Lee dizzy just to watch. "General

Johnston has been in command of this army for less than three hours, and he already called General Jackson and me into a staff meeting."

"General Johnston is an efficient administrator, and those people are across the creek," Lee reminded Stuart.

Stuart stopped pacing. "Well, he informed us that this army will be retreating to South Mountain." He waited for a reaction. When he did not receive one, he detonated. "Maryland!"

"I see." Lee couldn't believe Johnston would do something so contrary to his stated wishes. "Did he give a reason?"

"He had a list of reasons." Stuart threw his hands up in the air. "He said you refused to hear his concerns about communications and then insinuated I wasn't supplying this army properly. So, he needed to correct our course. I told him he was abusing his position by attempting a *coup d'état*." Stuart flung himself into Lee's desk chair.

Lee smothered a smile at Stuart's fierce temper. "How did General Johnston respond?"

"I don't remember. General Jackson gripped my arm so hard, he bruised it." Stuart rubbed at the spot.

A corpsman entered with two glasses of buttermilk. He handed a glass to Lee then placed the other one on the desk in front of Stuart.

Lee sipped his buttermilk and stared at Stuart until Stuart started to squirm. "Did you really accuse him of attempting a *coup d'état*?" Stuart nodded like a chastened schoolboy. "What am I going to do with you, Jeb," Lee said affectionately.

"I don't know, sir."

"Drink your buttermilk."

Stuart took a big gulp.

Doctor McGuire entered. "Good morning, General Lee. How are you feeling?"

"General Stuart has brightened my morning by telling me about the staff meeting." He winked at Stuart, who smiled. It's such a sunny smile, Lee thought.

"Has he now?" McGuire didn't bother to hide his disapproval.

Lee came to Stuart's rescue. "Oh, don't be angry with my young lieutenant general. He was right to come to me."

Stuart jumped to his feet. "If you don't need me for anything else, I'll be on my way."

Lee knew Stuart wanted to make good his escape before McGuire spoke harshly to him. "Go on, Jeb. But you'll come back and visit me?"

Stuart nodded before running out of the tent.

"General Lee." McGuire pulled the desk chair next to the bed. He gestured for Lee's hand. Lee surrendered it with a contrite smile. "You're an educated man. I shouldn't have to explain to you the concept of bed rest." McGuire took Lee's pulse.

"You don't," Lee assured him, "but General Johnston will be around to see me within the next half hour or so. After that, I'll rest. I promise."

McGuire shook his head, mixed a powder, and handed it to Lee, who drank it down like a good patient.

"Sir," Lee heard Taylor call, "General Johnston's here to see you."

He put down his Bible and glanced at his watch. Twenty-five minutes had elapsed since Stuart's departure. Right on time, he chuckled. "Walter, tell him to come in."

Johnston stepped into the tent. At once, Lee could tell he had suffered a severe blow. His coloring was high. He was also rigid with anger, which gave him an odd, angular look, almost as if an invisible string was jerking him along. "I hope you're feeling better." Even his voice was rigid.

"I am," Lee said, a touch of frost in his voice.

"I have just concluded a staff meeting. General Jackson and I conferred on a new strategy." Johnston jerked a portfolio from underneath his arm and slammed it down on the desk. Then, with a whoosh, he opened it and unfolded a map so forcefully, Lee was afraid he was going to rip it. Lee walked over to the desk. "We're going to withdraw tonight to Springville, a small city on the Schuylkill." With a stabbing finger, Johnston pointed to the city. "General Jackson informs me that the city is laid out much like Fredericksburg, with heights behind the city similar to Marye's Heights."

Lee didn't know if he should just thank Johnston and hope the First Corps Commander wouldn't bring up the confrontation with Stuart, or open Pandora's Box and get the argument out of the way before the army marched. He chose the latter. "Is there anything else?" Lee sat on the foot of the bed and waited while Johnston bent himself in all the appropriate places so he could sit in the chair.

"Yes, I'm going to bring charges of insubordination against General Stuart and General Jackson."

"What did General Jackson do!"

Johnston's eyes narrowed. He stiffened even more. "Since you didn't ask me about General Stuart, I'm going to assume the moment he bolted from the meeting, without permission I might add, he came straight to you and tattled."

"Is it true that you proposed to retire this army to South Mountain?" The back of Lee's neck began to heat up in anger.

"Yes, I did," Johnston responded brusquely.

"I didn't give you the army so you could ignore its primary objective. If you pull a stunt like that again," Lee made a warning gesture, "I'll rescind my order and put General Jackson in command."

Johnston catapulted from the chair. He folded his map, closed the portfolio with another whoosh, and slammed it back under his arm. "You've disapproved of the way I fought this war since I abandoned Yorktown two years ago."

Suddenly, Lee was exhausted. It was the same old argument, and he was tired of having it. "No, I disagreed, that's all," he said wearily. He rubbed his forehead with the heels of his hands. Since the army wasn't retiring to South Mountain, he chose to move on. "Since you plan to bring General Jackson up on charges, I'm going to assume that he agreed with General Stuart's remarks."

Johnston slammed the portfolio on the desk and sat back down. "I gave General Jackson every opportunity to disavow General Stuart's comments, and he would not. He even threatened me."

Lee recoiled. He couldn't imagine Jackson doing such a thing.

"He told me if I was going to charge General Stuart with insubordination, I'd have to do same to him. So I am." Johnston stared daggers at Lee. "You're far too lenient with General Stuart," he lectured. "His conduct falls well short of the mark of a lieutenant general."

"General Stuart's behavior is my concern and no one else's!" Lee yelled.

Maroon with anger, Johnston launched himself to his feet. "I'll forward the charges to you."

"Fine!"

"Now, if you'll excuse me, I need to make preparations for tonight." The invisible string jerked him out of the tent.

Spitefully, Lee waited until Johnston had ridden away before he stepped out of his tent. "Walter, except for Rob and General Jackson, I don't want to see anyone. Oh, and I'll see General Stuart anytime he comes by. I'm going to follow Doctor McGuire's prescription and get some much needed rest."

***

Stuart pulled his desk from his tent and dragged it across the common area to the welcoming shade of a large oak tree growing at the edge of a field. The morning sun was warm. Spring was turning to summer, and the field was awash with wildflowers. He reached down, plucked a flower, and smelled it. Marvelous!

A yawn surprised him. Stuart stretched his arms and allowed the yawn to consume him. He was tired enough to sleep for the rest of the day and night but was too anxious to do so. He feared every horse hoof was bringing orders for the army's retreat to South Mountain. He was not the least bit sorry for the angry words he had spoken to Johnston. They needed to be said. They could have been said differently, more tactfully, he admitted to himself. Well, he would have to stand by them, for he was certain Johnston would haul him up on charges. But the threat of court martial was a mere annoyance at the moment. His real worry had to do with General Lee.

Lee had looked so tired this morning. Not that he expected Lee to recover from such a devastating loss overnight. But Lee had aged when he learned about Rooney. At the time, Stuart thought it had to do with the sudden shock of death. But it had not dissipated in the last 24 hours. Lee still looked like an old man. When he came out of the tent, he had even moved like one. Stuart realized Lee was close to 60, but Lee had always acted like a man 15 years younger. What if he never recovered his vitality? Stuart had seen it happen before. The loss of a loved one leading to the deterioration and death of the one left behind. He wanted to help; he just didn't know how.

Then there was the fact that Lee was treating him differently. He was calling him Jeb and speaking in a tone that didn't have the ring of command to it. It was softer, friendlier, and more familiar. Dare he think it? He dared. It was fatherly.

He smiled at the thought; embraced the idea. Then he shook his head to clear his mind of such a silly notion. He grabbed a report and attacked it with vigor. But was it foolish to think this way? He asked himself. He leaned back in his chair and replayed this morning's conversation in his mind. No, he wasn't imagining it. Lee spoke to him the same way he spoke to Rob and Rooney and, to a lesser degree, Fitz. The formality of command had vanished. And he liked it. Oh, how he liked it when Lee called him Jeb.

Something brushed up against his leg. Startled, Stuart glanced down and saw the young gray and white cat that had taken to hanging around his tent the day the cavalry had arrived from the Susquehanna. The cat had been hungry, so he had fed it. With that simple act, he had found himself the owner of a cat. He was not so sure he liked this new responsibility. Especially after finding cat hair this morning on the buffalo robe that covered his bed. The cat serenely gazed up at him. Then it stretched itself, curled up next to his desk, and went to sleep.

Jackson approached, carrying a chair from the dining table. The moment Jackson plunked the chair down in front of the desk, Stuart launched a pre-emptive strike. "I'm not going to apologize."

"That's one sorry looking cat." Jackson gazed at the young cat. It was sleeping on its back; its belly toward the sun.

"Well, that's not its fault," Stuart said sympathetically. "It's a Yankee cat."

"You're going to have to tell it goodbye because we're heading out at dusk."

"Not to South Mountain!" Maybe Johnston had been able to convince Jackson of the necessity of such a retreat.

"No, General Johnston and I had a very productive meeting after your rude departure. He's agreed to stay in Pennsylvania for the time being."

Stuart wasn't upset at Jackson's choice of adjective. He had been rude. "So, where are we going?"

"Springville on the Schuylkill River." The cat rose and sat at Jackson's feet. "General Early will be leaving around sunset. I need a tight screen on him. I want no surprises."

The only one surprised was Jackson, for the cat suddenly sprang into his lap.

"Well, what do you know," Stuart said with obvious envy. "I've fed the silly thing for days now, and it won't even let me pet it. It knows you less than five minutes and treats you like long lost family."

Jackson smiled at Stuart. "Obviously, it's a very intelligent cat." The cat curled up in Jackson's lap and went to sleep.

"I thought so until a minute ago."

Jackson laughed. He reached into his haversack, pulled out a map, and handed it to Stuart. "Early and Ewell will cross the bridge north of the city; Rodes and the Light Division at Perkiomen Junction to the south. Your men will need to take possession well before they arrive."

Stuart studied the map. He wrote a few notations along the edges. Jackson cleared his throat. "Now, let's talk about this morning."

Stuart pointed his pencil at Jackson. "I already told you, I'm not going to apologize."

"Don't be stubborn," Jackson counseled. "You were wrong to speak in such a disrespectful tone to a superior officer. And, you were wrong to storm out of the meeting. But I don't think you were wrong in your sentiments."

"For bolting the meeting, I have no excuse. I lost my temper."

"I did tell General Johnston that if he brought you up on charges, he'd have to charge me, too." Jackson scratched the cat between its ears.

Stuart smiled in gratitude. "That's right loyal of you."

Jackson returned the smile. "Loyal or foolish, I haven't thought it through yet."

"We do need to discuss this bruise on my arm from where you pinched me." Stuart rolled his sleeve up and revealed an angry welt turning various shades of black and blue.

"I was trying to prevent the disagreement from being resolved at 20 paces." Jackson picked up the cat and set it on the ground. "Think about the apology. And get some sleep. You have a busy night ahead of you." With that, he left Stuart sitting under the tree.

The cat made its way over to Stuart and looked expectantly at his lap.

"Well, if you're coming, come on."

The cat jumped up. It turned three times, plopped down, and slept while Stuart wrote up orders to his brigade commanders.

From Stuart's headquarters, Jackson made his way to Lee's. "Good morning, Colonel," Jackson called to Taylor from atop Little Sorrel. "Or is it afternoon?"

"It's still morning. Barely," Taylor replied with a small chuckle. "Sir, the general left word that he wanted to see you, but I'm afraid he's resting."

Jackson held up his hand. "Don't wake him on my account. I just came to find out how he's doing." Lee made a sudden appearance. "I hope I didn't wake you, sir," he apologized.

"No, unbeknownst to Walter, I've been up for the past hour writing Mrs. Lee. Will you come and keep me company?"

Jackson handed Little Sorrel's reins to Taylor and followed Lee into the tent.

"How are you feeling, sir?" Jackson swung the chair away from the desk and sat it at the foot of the bed.

"Better than when you last saw me. I'll always be grateful for what you did for me and Fitzhugh." Lee could feel another wave of tears building up. To forestall it, he changed the subject. "General Johnston came to see me. He told me about the meeting. It must have been quite contentious, for he is going to bring both you and General Stuart up on charges…What's wrong?"

Jackson dropped his head in his hands. "I told him if he brought Stuart up on charges, I would resign my commission and return home. I regret the words, but I can't disavow them."

At Jackson's announcement, all the air rushed from Lee's lungs. "I couldn't bear to lose you over this matter," he said in a strangled voice.

"I feel terrible adding to your troubles, but it's a matter of honor."

"Jeb will follow you."

"That's for Stuart to decide. But don't underestimate his devotion to you."

Lee felt like a drowning man caught in the midst of a raging sea. Fitzhugh dead! Jackson resigning! Jeb following! Everyone was leaving him to bear the load alone; a burden that was slowly killing him. "You're my right arm. I can't lead this army without you."

Jackson smiled sadly but didn't take back his words.

"Thomas Jackson, I want you to listen to me," Lee exploded in wrathful frustration. He wouldn't take another blow without fighting back. "If you resign your commission, I'll resign mine also. Jeb will follow us. Where will that leave the country?"

Jackson stared at him. "Sir, that's coercion."

"Is it?" Lee raised his eyebrows in surprise. "And there was no coercion in your words to General Johnston?"

"No, I was too angry to be that clever. That's why I spoke hastily."

"Well, let me know what I'm to do? Should I start packing?" Lee rose, reached under his bed, and pulled out a canvas valise.

Jackson laughed, a worn and tired laugh. "Of course I'll stay."

"Thank you." Tears of relief flooded his eyes.

Jackson's face turned red. "No, don't thank me. If I had controlled my temper, you wouldn't be needlessly fretting." He laughed again. "You'd think that three grown men could learn not to behave like belles squabbling over beaux. Please, accept my apology."

Lee smiled. "I think we're all exhausted and far from home."

Jackson nodded. A yawn caught him off guard.

"When's the last time you've slept?" Lee asked.

"About 36 hours ago. When I'm done here, I'm going to seek the comfort of my bed."

"Don't let me keep you." Lee escorted Jackson to the door. "Promise me – it was a command – that you'll come to me if any concerns arise during the march."

"I promise. Please feel better soon. We miss you when you're not in command."

Chapter Twenty

GRANT DEFEATED AGAIN
2,500 DEAD AT SHIPPACK CREEK
GIVE US MCCLELLAN!

The last headline brought McClellan a great deal of satisfaction. But no longer would he settle for mere command of the army. Now, he wanted the White House. The White House and retribution for the public humiliation he had suffered at the hands of Lincoln, who dared to think, in his arrogance, that a backwoods politician knew more about combat than a West Point graduate! Oh, how rewarding it would be when he was the master, and Lincoln the one contemptuously dismissed from his presence.

McClellan folded the paper and set it next to his breakfast plate. While salting his eggs, he did some hasty calculations. The honeymoon Grant had enjoyed with the public was over. He had murdered it with the Great Gallop and the licking the army had received once it had caught up with Lee. That meant the people were once more searching for a savior to guide them from the quagmire of this war. McClellan had no hesitation in accepting the role. Since the first shots were fired along Bull Run Creek, he had known it was his destiny to save the Union.

His butler entered and held out a white calling card. McClellan wiped his hands and examined it. *Mr. Henry Bicknell. Democratic Society of Trenton.* How propitious! "Show him into the study, James."

McClellan took a bite of toast and swallow of coffee. In the hall mirror, he straightened his tie and brushed crumbs from his mustache. A moment later, he burst into the study, oozing presidential gravitas. "Mr. Bicknell." He shook the man's hand.

"General McClellan." Henry Bicknell was a small man with a big potbelly, a large walrus mustache, and not much hair on his head. McClellan towered over him. "Have you seen the morning papers?"

"I've only glanced at the headlines," McClellan replied noncommittally. He sat down behind his desk. "Please, have a seat. Would you care for some coffee? I could have some brought."

"No, thank you." Bicknell plopped down on the red leather chair in front of the desk. "I have come on behalf of the Society to invite you to speak at tonight's gathering." McClellan didn't reply. "I can promise you a large crowd," Bicknell added enticingly.

McClellan leaned back in his chair and put his fingertips together. "I do have a few ideas I'd like to share."

"General, you'll not find a friendlier venue."

McClellan choked back his eagerness and remained silent.

"I know it was presumptuous of me, but I've notified the newspapers that you would be speaking," Bicknell volunteered. "Plus, the leadership committee gave me strict orders not to take no for an answer. If you decline, I'll just be back here within the hour with reinforcements."

Perfect! Newspapers meant a wide circulation of his speech. McClellan smiled. "Well, I wouldn't want you to get in trouble with the leadership committee."

"Does that mean yes?"

"That means yes."

Bicknell stood and jerked his too small coat down over his too round stomach. "Tonight then. At seven. You know where the Society is housed? Good."

By dinnertime, the large brick structure was swamped with people desperate to find a seat. When every chair in the salon was occupied, and the silk-covered walls were lined with spectators, people piled into the small anterooms on the first and second floors. Both halls were filled and so was every step on the grand staircase. Latecomers jostled each other in the street. They pushed and shoved to get a coveted spot near the open windows, trampling Mrs. Bicknell's jonquils into the mud.

Inside the salon, men debated the correct course to end the war. Heated words bounced about the room. The women listened to the arguments: eyes dancing and fans fluttering with excitement. Who could have known that politics could be so stimulating and dangerous? Why, the night might just end in a duel or two. The ladies found it thrilling to be eyewitnesses to the possibility of bloodshed. Usually, they only heard about such goings-on second or third hand. They put their heads together and clucked like hens.

Precisely at seven, Henry Bicknell stepped onto the small platform to a smattering of applause. "Ladies and gentlemen, like you, I'm anxious to hear what General McClellan has to say. So without further ado, I present Major General George McClellan."

McClellan bounded on stage. He wore his full dress uniform. A blood-red sash was tied around his waist. The sash's fringe swished above his polished boots. His scabbard had received an extra coat of polish, and it also glistened in the gaslight. The moment he appeared, the crowd rose in a thunderous ovation. Stay humble! He counseled himself. Look down! Be demur! But he failed. The acclamation poured over him like an intoxicating spirit. He drank of its heady water until the applause started to fade. To appear in control of the room, he raised his hands and asked for quiet. Obediently, the crowd took their seats. McClellan stood perfectly still until all eyes were focused on him.

"As the war enters its fourth year, the time has come to ask the one question those in Washington are afraid to ask. Can this war be won?"

The room broke out into a lengthy debate on the merit or folly of continuing the war. McClellan tried to find a moment to reassert himself, but the audience had forgotten he was there. He started to speak over them, when, from the front row, his wife raised a subtle eyebrow, a reminder to be patient. After all, he was supposed to be a reticent candidate called reluctantly from exile to save the Union from destruction. McClellan willed himself to relax and wait until the argument ran its course.

"Mr. Lincoln has much to show for four years of bloodshed," he resumed when he was once again the center of attention. "The Union has captured the Mississippi River and the Port of New Orleans. We hold Missouri and Kentucky. Virginia has been split in two. Yet, Mr. Lincoln has made some disastrous decisions. None worse than refusing to send me the reinforcements I asked for on the Virginia peninsula. Had he done that, this war would have ended two years ago. If I decide to run for president…"

He closed his eyes and waited. Would the crowd approve or disapprove of the notion? As one, they stood to their feet and poured out their greatest ovation of the night. He could even hear them cheering his name in the streets. He held up his hands. "I haven't decided. Yet," he scolded with a winsome smile.

The crowd moaned. From the back, someone began to chant his name. *McClellan! McClellan!* The chant grew louder and louder. For a brief, exhilarating moment, McClellan thought the men were going to whisk him from the podium, place him on their shoulders, and march him around the salon. He was somewhat disappointed when they didn't. They were content to shout themselves hoarse.

"Tonight, I want to tell you where I stand," McClellan said when all was quiet again. His hand fell on the gold hilt of his sword. "That's what you've come to hear, isn't it?" The audience assured him they had. "I'm on the side of the fighting man! Praying every night for Generals Grant and Sherman. Desiring to see the Union restored and slavery forever abolished off this great continent." He lowered his voice. "But I'll not abandon my men, and they'll always be my men, to that petty Illinois tyrant, who tramples our rights underfoot while he feeds our men into the meat grinder of his personal vendetta against the South! No, I'll not abandon the men who fought for me at Gaines Mill, Malvern Hill, and Antietam to the likes of Lincoln.

"He must be removed from office. That's where I stand. He's the enemy of the fighting man. If it becomes my duty to oppose him in the presidential election, then I will." His voice began to crescendo. "Your duty will be to vote for responsible leadership in November. So, let us each do our duty, just as our men in the field, under tremendous fire, do theirs!"

His final words released a hurricane of emotions: tears from the ladies and huzzahs from the men. McClellan sprang down off the platform, embraced his wife, and shook hands with Mr. Bicknell.

Hundreds of hands were thrust at him. He shook them all and spoke to countless faces, thanking them for coming, for their support. Tonight was the first step in raising an army whose sole purpose would be to sweep him into the White House. He smiled in triumph. President George Brinton McClellan!

The morning sun streamed through the windows, painting the coffee pot on Stanton's desk in a pallet of reds and pinks, but the Secretary of War didn't notice nature's handiwork. His mind was occupied with more important things. Well, actually, one thing: George McClellan. Scattered across his desk were various newspapers filled with rapturous accounts of McClellan's speech at the Trenton Democratic Society. Editorials speculated on whether McClellan would seek the Democratic nomination. This speculation particularly irked Stanton. He didn't understand why the editors chose to play coy. McClellan might have couched his speech in "ifs" and "mays," but any fool knew that the Young Napoleon was running for president. And a McClellan candidacy represented a very real threat toward Lincoln and, more importantly, the radical cause: emancipation of the slaves and vengeance toward the South. To safeguard the cause, McClellan had to be cut off at the knees before his candidacy gained popular support. Once it did, Lincoln would have no choice but to oppose Little Mac in the upcoming elections. With Sherman stalled at Chattanooga and Lee having his way in Pennsylvania, Lincoln was not guaranteed victory in November.

Late yesterday afternoon, Stanton dismissed his aides, took out paper and pencil, and formulated a plan of attack. One that would neutralize

McClellan, shore up Lincoln's shaky support, and keep the war raging until the South was crushed under heel.

His secretary entered and announced that Senator Charles Sumner and Congressman Thaddeus Stevens were in the anteroom. "They're not in a pleasant mood," he said, stifling a yawn. "They've let it be known that they don't like being summoned to secret meetings at the crack of dawn."

Stanton didn't care whether they were happy or not. It was enough they had come. "Show them in."

The handsome, clean-shaven Sumner, newspaper clutched in his fist, charged into the office ahead of the stern and bewigged Stevens.

"Good morning, Senator. Mr. Stevens," Stanton said.

"Have you seen this!" Sumner stormed. He waved the offending newspaper to emphasize his point and almost clubbed Stevens in the head with it. "What's happening to us?"

"We're losing," Stanton stated bluntly.

"When does the president propose to stop losing and start winning?" Sumner asked. He sat down and refused an offer of coffee.

Stevens poured himself a cup. He took a small sip then replenished it. He added a little cream.

"He believes he has the right generals in place," Stanton answered, pleased by Sumner's rage. Stevens' feelings were safely concealed behind his puritanical face. Only the speed in which his spoon stirred the cream revealed his thoughts.

"Little good they're doing us," Sumner sighed.

"The president believes, given enough time, Grant and Sherman will win the war."

Sumner laughed in disbelief. "Time? The conventions are just around the corner."

"The president has a calendar."

"What have you heard from Sherman?" Stevens interjected.

"Actually, the news is quite good. Chattanooga's about to fall."

"You don't have any telegrams from Grant, do you?" Stevens asked.

Stanton shook his head. "I didn't call you here to discuss the latest war news. I need your help in convincing the president to suspend the election until after the war is won." The faces before him went blank. "Grant believes Lee is staying in Pennsylvania in hopes of influencing the election…"

"Well, it's working!" Sumner waved his newspaper.

"The Constitution guarantees elections," Stevens said. The spoon created small waves in the cup.

"Since when has constitutional guarantees stopped us?" Stanton replied.

An uncomfortable silence filled the room.

"So, you're suggesting we do away with the election," Stevens said.

"No, postpone," Stanton clarified. "If Grant is correct, and I happen to believe he is, then postponing the election gives the Rebs no incentive to remain. They return to Virginia. That means, in the headlines at least, we're winning. It can only help us." He rose and came to their side of the desk. "Grant's strategy will win the war. But not by November. And that's what we want, correct? To win the war and free the slaves. Plus, Grant's strategy guarantees the South pays for its rebellion with a price it can't bear."

The spoon stopped its circuitous route around the china cup. "Victory and vengeance." Stevens smile was malevolent. He returned to the coffee pot and poured a fresh cup. He added a splash of cream. "What do you want from us?

"A Congressional proclamation requesting an executive order postponing the fall elections."

"What's our justification?" Stevens asked.

"Why not tell people the truth," Sumner offered.

"Unless Grant's wrong and Lee doesn't retreat," Stevens told him. The spoon started spinning again. "If Lincoln receives such a proclamation, will he ignore it?" He asked Stanton

"It'll be my job to make sure he doesn't."

The two men became solitary islands of political computation, each calculating whether he had enough votes to get such an unorthodox proclamation passed, and, if not, what type of coercion would be necessary to force the reluctant on board.

"Can we tell our colleagues about Grant's theory?" Sumner asked.

"You can share with them anything I've said here. But I must have the proclamation before the armies meet again. If Grant is victorious, the president won't postpone the election, no matter how many proclamations you send him."

Sumner was confused. "But if Lee retreats, we won't need to postpone the election."

"What if Grant gets bogged down in Virginia?" Stanton asked.

Sumner sighed in concession. "McClellan wins the election. He's always been lenient toward the South."

"So is the president," Stevens remarked. The spoon tapped the edge of the cup. He sipped his coffee.

"That's true," Stanton agreed. "He'll want to restore the South to the Union without retribution. At the moment, I don't have an answer for that problem."

"The House will issue the proclamation. How about the Senate?" Stevens looked at Sumner.

"I'll see it done in the Senate. I do expect your support, Mr. Secretary."

"You have my support and Secretary Chase's as well."

Stevens stood. Sumner followed suit. "We'll have the proclamation to the president by this evening," Stevens said, handing Stanton his coffee cup.

"Secretary Stanton's here," John Hay informed the President.

"Show him in." Lincoln placed two documents on the center of his desk. Stanton burst into the office. "Sit down, Mr. Secretary." Lincoln waited until Stanton was comfortable. "You should know that I've had quite a busy morning. Being manipulated is exhausting work." Stanton refused to be ashamed, and Lincoln admired him for it. "I have here a Congressional proclamation in support of an executive order postponing the election. It seems Congress is afraid that if," Lincoln put on his glasses and read from the document, "the election was held before the successful conclusion of the war, voters in the South who do not support the rebellion will be disenfranchised and unable to exercise their constitutional rights." Lincoln put the document down and stared over the rim of his glasses at Stanton. "I must give Mr. Stevens and Senator Sumner credit for coming up with such an original and compelling reason for me not to submit my name and policies to the good people of this country."

Lincoln picked up the next document. "Then this morning, I received a telegram from General Grant asking me if I had reconsidered my stand on postponing the election. I didn't think it a coincidence that both these documents arrived on my desk within hours of each other. I telegraphed the general and asked if he knew of the proclamation." Stanton shifted in his seat. "He was prompt in getting back to me. No, he didn't know about the proclamation. He had telegraphed me at your request."

Stanton took off his glasses and cleaned them with his handkerchief. He held them up to the morning light, wasn't satisfied with what he saw, and began the cleansing process all over again.

Lincoln removed his spectacles and tossed them on the desk. "I'm waiting for an explanation."

"I wanted you to know that there is support in Congress for postponing the election."

"Let me set you straight on this issue," Lincoln said heatedly. "If I decide that postponing the election is sound military strategy, then I will. So, you can stop scheming with the Radicals. Their political agenda doesn't have a say in this." His anger cooled slightly. "But, I don't think we need to resort to such an extreme measure. The news from Tennessee is good."

"Chattanooga's not Atlanta. That's harsh, but that's how the people will view it." Stanton put on his glasses.

Lincoln frowned. "You're not particularly cheerful this morning, Mr. Stanton."

"No, I'm not. I'm not trying to force your hand or manipulate you, but you're running out of time. If you delay, and the Democrats anoint McClellan, any decision about the election will not be viewed from a strategic standpoint, only a political one. You'll be accused, rightly or wrongly, of playing politics with the election."

Lincoln glowered at Stanton. He picked up the proclamation with distaste. "Here's my solution. I'm going to put this away." He opened his desk drawer, slid the document in, and slammed the drawer shut. "But I'll keep General Grant's telegram on my desk. If he loses again, God forbid, I'll postpone the election. Then the Congress, who can only stand in the direction the wind is blowing, can impeach me. For such an act will surely cause the wrath of the nation to fall upon me. At least General Grant can redeem the time it takes me to be impeached to win the war."

"I don't think it'll come to that." Stanton smiled slyly. "That's why I had Congress issue the proclamation. Yes, they'll huff and puff and make headlines. But how can Congress impeach you if you only did what they implored you to do."

"Have you studied at the feet of Machiavelli, Mr. Stanton?" Lincoln laughed, his good humor restored. He leaned back in his chair and put his feet up on the desk.

"Machiavelli was just misunderstood," Stanton quipped.

Lincoln turned somber. "I'm afraid we're all going to be misunderstood if we're forced to do such a thing. No, history will not regard us kindly."

Chapter Twenty One

From the heights behind the small city of Springville, Jackson watched the Yankees lay their pontoon bridges across the muddy, calm waters of the Schuylkill River. Four, no five, were in various stages of completion. He could see the engineers feverishly working, while sharpshooters nervously prowled the length of the bridges. They needn't be so anxious. Like Lee at the Susquehanna, Johnston had decided not to contest the river. He was more than content to wait for the Yankees behind the fortifications Jackson had constructed. Jackson thought it was a mistake to let the Yankees come unopposed, but Johnston, still smarting over Jackson's refusal to renounce Stuart's remarks, rebuffed his arguments.

The bridges were completed to the relief of the engineers. They hastened back to the Union side of the Schuylkill. Once they were safe, the soldiers merged into a dark river of Federal blue. They poured over the bridges and separated into tributaries that flowed through the streets. At the edge of town, the tributaries rushed together and pooled at the bottom of the hill. From across the river Union artillery roared. Shells hurtled toward the Confederate defenses.

Jackson ordered his artillery to respond. Solid shot and grape rained down on the Yankees at the foot of the hill. They scattered, but the dispersal was only temporary. The order was given, and the Yankees began the long climb up the hill.

Jackson was awed by the parade ground precision displayed by the Yankees. Battle flags snapped in the breeze. Pipes and drums played martial tunes. The blue-clad soldiers marched with guns resting on their shoulders, bayonets shining in the sun. Jackson's spine tingled at the handsome display. How right was Lee when he said, "*It is well that war is so terrible, lest we should grow too fond of it.*"

So immense was the army ascending upon the Confederates that the Union line of battle extended well past Jackson's right flank – defended by the Light Division. The Yankees stopped and the soldiers leveled their rifles. A sheet of flame flashed through a cloud of blue smoke. The first line of Jackson's defenders appeared to have been assailed by the very fires of Hell. His men had simply been blown away. Just like that, war became a terrible thing. The cries and shrieks of his wounded rose above the gunfire.

Hill refused Heth's brigade at a 90 degree angle, but the act was as useless as sticking a finger in a dyke to hold back the sea. Jackson sent Morrison to the rear for Nicholls' and Jones' brigades held in reserve.

His men withstood the second blow, returning like for like. The same held true for the third and fourth volleys, but the fifth and sixth staggered the gray troops backwards.

Jackson focused his field glasses on his weakened flank. The acrid smoke from rifles, muskets, and cannon concealed the desperate fight.

Colonel Morgan, Hill's adjutant, galloped up; his horse lathered in sweat. "The Yankees have broken through!" Morgan swung his mount around without waiting for a reply.

Pandemonium greeted Jackson's arrival at Hill's field-quarters. Heth's men were surrounded. Lane's brigade was trapped between the surging Yankees on their immediate right and the Yankees in their front.

"I have reinforcements coming. Can you hold until they arrive?" Jackson shouted over the musket fire.

"No, sir," Hill declared. "My line is about to give way."

The sudden, sharp bark of artillery caused Jackson and Hill to start in surprise. Under the cover of dust and smoke, Major Beckham had brought up his battery of horse artillery. Like angry wasps, the shower of grape drove the Yankees back. Beckham advanced his cannons and unleashed another swarm. The blue column reeled back like a rope violently shaken at the end.

From the front of the ramparts, the bugles trilled retreat. The Yankees fired one last volley and backed down the hill. But it was not the retreat of an army in defeat. At the bottom of the hill, the Yankees re-pooled. They would return.

"General Johnston is down." A dust covered General Mackall informed Jackson. "He was thrown from his horse. He's unconscious at the moment and has been taken to the rear."

Jackson nodded. "Mr. Pendleton, please inform General Lee that I've assumed command. Ask him if he'd like to join us. If not, tell him I'll do my best." Jackson turned his attention to Johnston's chief-of-staff. "Now, what's the situation on the left flank?"

"We're in desperate straits," Mackall lamented. "General Johnston believes we're outnumbered two to one."

Jackson swung up on Little Sorrel and headed toward the First Corps. Mackall trailed behind, talking non-stop gloom and doom the entire way. Jackson paused when he saw Hood, harried and overwhelmed, barking orders to his aides. “General Hood, surely Texas will not allow this line to be breeched!”

“No, sir!” Hood thundered. “My men will not surrender one inch of ground to the Yankees.”

“Excellent, sir! Don’t be afraid to use the bayonet!”

“I’ll throw stones if I have to. My portion of the line won’t yield.”

“I didn’t think it would,” Jackson said with a triumphant smile. He hurried to view the rest of the line he had inherited.

Against overwhelming odds and with some rough bullying on Jackson’s part, his men had held. On shaky legs, the Second Corps watched the Yankees descend the hill. Prayerfully, they waited to see if they would reform for another assault. God heard their prayers. The Yankees began the slow march toward the river. As one, Jackson’s men collapsed to the ground in exhaustion.

“General Rodes, get the men up,” Jackson barked. “The battle’s not over.”

Soldiers within the sound of his voice groaned, but Jackson angrily stared at them with an expression they both understood and feared. They hurried back to the line.

Jackson kept an impatient eye on the receding columns, waiting for that moment when the Yankees, believing they were no longer in any danger, relaxed.

“Come on,” he muttered. “Come on.” There it was! “Colonel Crutchfield, fire every gun you have down on that town.” Beside him, the men gathered up their guns.

The concussion from the cannon shook the ground like an earthquake. The Yankees disappeared behind a lead curtain of shot and grape. The curtain parted and revealed the blue river crashing through the streets.

Jackson yanked his sword from its scabbard and swung it over his head. “Sons of the South! Let’s give those Yankees something to run from!” He pointed the sword down the hill. The Army of Northern Virginia raced over its breastworks, the Rebel yell on its lips.

Goosebumps raced up Jackson’s spine. The thrill of parade ground precision could never compete with the wonderful spectacle of his men in pursuit of a routed enemy.

“Come on, you brave men!” Jackson shouted. “Give them the bayonet!”

From his right he heard the bugle's cry. Stuart galloped down the hill, hollering and waving his hat as if he was chasing a fox across the English countryside. Four thousand horsemen, in columns of four, thundered behind him.

Jackson rushed toward the left flank. Morrison and Smith freed their pistols from their holsters. He was preparing to put spurs to Little Sorrel when he heard Morrison shouting.

"Sir, it's Colonel Taylor!" Morrison pointed back at the center of the defenses.

Annoyed to be halted, even by Lee's adjutant, Jackson swung Little Sorrel around and waited for Taylor.

"General Lee requests you join him."

Jackson shook his head.

"It is an order, sir," Taylor said apologetically.

"General Lee!" Jackson protested this unexpected yank on his leash. Gunfire erupted in the city. The battle was engaged. He should be down there!

"I'd prefer it if you stayed with me." Was all Lee said.

Jackson chaffed under the words. "But someone has to direct the men." To add weight to his words, he rocked forward in his saddle and pointed down the hill for extra emphasis.

Lee was inflexible. "General Stuart is there. He'll manage the situation just fine."

"But…"

"No."

Like a bitter pill, Jackson choked down the order. He jerked his field glasses out of their case and scanned the new battlefield as it developed between the buildings and along the bank. He could see Stuart, cape whirling about him, barking out unheard orders. The men formed up and poured volleys into the Yankees, who hastily returned fire.

Lee watched medics, ambulances, and corpsmen stream out of the city and up the hill, now carpeted blue with the Union dead and wounded. "I'm tired of General Grant taking advantage of my good nature and assuming I'll allow him full access to the field he just lost," Lee said heatedly to Jackson. "Not today! We've beaten him three times. It's high time he acknowledges that fact. Have General Stuart clear the field."

***

Accompanied by Colonel Rosengarten and two of Sheridan troopers, Reynolds rode through the maze of ambulances parked at the edge of town. Corpsmen and medics milled around, waiting for someone to sort out the situation. The Reb cavalry didn't prevent the wounded from reaching help. Once the injured were clear of the patrolling gray troopers, medics rushed out to help them. As Reynolds passed the triage area, doctors shouted questions at him. Reynolds ignored the questions. He was afraid he would take his still simmering anger out on the good doctors.

And he was angry. At Grant, Sheridan, and the ruthless manner in which they prosecuted this war. When Lee forbade the medics the field, he had suggested to Grant that they both go under a white flag and seek Lee's permission. Grant had bluntly refused. Enraged by the refusal, he had stormed off.

Reynolds exhaled; a sharp sound of frustration. When the war started, he had tried to work up the same hatred for the "enemy" that fueled Sheridan's twin thirsts of conquest and vengeance. But he couldn't. He had served with some of those men up on the hill, had fought with them, and, during his stint at West Point, had even educated them. That didn't mean he didn't want the Union restored or Pennsylvania liberated from the horrors of war. But to hate as cold blooded as Sheridan. No, he didn't have it in him.

Halfway up the hill, he was met by a vibrantly dressed officer riding a beautiful red mare. He introduced himself with a gracious smile and smothered a laugh when he discovered the officer was none other than Sheridan's nemesis: his peacock in the flesh! "You're known to me by your splendid reputation, General Stuart. I'm General Reynolds. I've come to ask General Lee's permission to collect my wounded and bury my dead."

"Major McClellan," Stuart called. "Please convey General Reynolds' request to General Lee."

Reynolds took in all of Stuart's many splendid accessories. He picked his favorite and complimented it. "That's a nice hat."

"Why, thank you." Stuart beamed with pleasure. "I like it."

They sat in silence until Reynolds couldn't stand the uncomfortable hush any longer. He rushed to fill it with his voice. "Where are you from, General?"

"Patrick County, Virginia. About a stone's throw away from the North Carolina border."

A small group of riders came down the hill.

"Oh! It's General Jackson." Reynolds heard Stuart announce. In spite of himself, Reynolds felt a sudden thrill at the prospect of meeting *the* Stonewall Jackson.

He couldn't have been more disappointed. If Stuart was all color and flash, Jackson was all gray and drab. His uniform was covered with an inch of dust, and his jacket was missing two buttons. His weather-stained kepi's bill was broken, and the material was so faded, Reynolds couldn't tell what color it actually was. And Jackson's horse! It was a sorry sorrel, no larger than a pony.

Stuart made the introductions.

"I'm pleased to meet you, General Reynolds." Jackson touched a finger to the broken bill. "General Lee grants a 24 hour cease fire. He also extends any aid you may need."

Reynolds turned and waved his arm. The ambulances lumbered from the city.

Jackson cleared his throat. "The next time you request a cease fire, General Lee expects General Grant to make it in person."

Reynolds nodded tiredly and made his goodbyes. A little ways down the hill, he whirled about. "General Jackson, about Chancellorsville. That was the finest piece of soldiering I have ever witnessed." Suddenly embarrassed by his forwardness, he put spurs to his mare and galloped down the hill.

Chapter Twenty Two

Lincoln's office door opened cautiously, almost regretfully. John Hay slipped in, but Lincoln ignored him. He knew what his secretary was going to say, and he didn't want to hear it. Hay cleared his throat and said it anyway. "Sir, Secretary Stanton is here to see you."

Lincoln scowled. The vultures were already circling to pick clean his political bones. Stanton didn't even have the good manners to wait until the body grew cold. The news from Springville was only an hour old. The horrendous impact of over 4,000 men dead, wounded, or missing hadn't even sunk in. After the catastrophes of Fredericksburg, Chancellorsville, and Duncannon, Lincoln had truly believed that the situation couldn't get any worse. What a naïve fool he had been. If last summer he had been in a place worse than Hell, then where had he descended to now? For this new place, with its torment and agony, was ten times more excruciating. How could he escape? If juniper trees grew in Washington, he would seek one out and sit under it.

"Well?" Hay asked.

"Show him in." Lincoln pivoted his chair and stared out the window at the Virginia hills.

Stanton crept into the office. "I've received more news from the Schuylkill. General Sedgwick is dead. General Burnside has been captured," he reported dutifully.

"No more news." Lincoln swung back around. He held up his hands in an effort to ward off any more calamities. "I can't bear to hear it." He blew out his breath. "Why can't we win? I'm so desperate to win."

"We were all mistaken to believe this war would be over in three months."

Lincoln glowered at his Secretary of War. "Let's get to the real reason you're here."

"You did say you'd postpone the election if Grant lost again."

Lincoln put his head in his hands. "I don't want to make this decision." He raised his head and stared at Stanton, hoping his Secretary of War's sharp legal mind could fashion an escape. Stanton stared back, his eyes and face neutral. An old courtroom trick. One, Lincoln had successfully employed a time or two…or seven. Stanton wasn't giving away what he was thinking. Lincoln stood and resumed his study of the Virginia landscape. "Let it be decided on the battlefield or at the ballot box, but not by me. Not this way."

"If you want it to be decided at the ballot box, all you have to do is nothing."

"Yes, I know," Lincoln snapped, annoyed at being reminded. He returned to his desk and oozed into the chair as if all his bones had suddenly disappeared. "To so flagrantly violate the Constitution makes my critics right about me." If it were possible, he oozed lower.

"I think you're over analyzing it, Mr. President, to your credit," Stanton said with the first hint of sympathy Lincoln had heard in his voice since his arrival. "History will show that your executive order forced Lee from Pennsylvania."

"Have you the gift of sight, Mr. Stanton?" Lincoln chuckled. His spine materialized and he sat up. "What if we lose the war?

"I don't know what you want me to say." There was impatience in Stanton's tone. "General Grant has presented a strong argument on why you should postpone the election. I agree with him. You have Congress' backing. But in the end, you must decide whether it's something you can do in good conscience. The only thing I would add is that time is running out."

Lincoln plucked a paper from his desk and held it up. "This is an executive order postponing the election on the grounds of the Congressional proclamation." He handed it to Stanton. "What I want, the moment the war ends, is a constitutional amendment denying any president the right to do this again." He waved a deprecatory hand. "Yes, it reveals me as a hypocrite, but I've endured worse name calling than that. So, if you can promise me the amendment, I'll sign the order and have it released in time for the evening papers."

"If you win the war, you can have whatever you ask except lenient terms for the South."

"I may even get that," Lincoln said with a faint smile. "Hand me the order." Stanton did. Before he could change his mind, Lincoln signed his name and returned the order to Stanton.

Stanton blew the ink dry. "It's the right thing to do."

"It's a dangerous thing to do. If it brings us victory, it will be worth it." Lincoln spun back around in his chair and resumed his examination of the Virginia countryside.

***

LINCOLN SIGNS ORDER TO POSTPONE ELECTION
ELECTION WILL OCCUR AFTER WAR ENDS
UNION VICTORY WILL ENSURE RIGHTS OF ALL CITIZENS

"He can't do that!" McClellan exclaimed. He threw the newspaper he had been reading across the study.

Henry Bicknell watched the pages scatter and blanket the other side of the room. "I'm afraid he has."

"We'll fight it in court!"

"You'll lose. Even if the case goes before the Supreme Court, it'll just be a showdown between the Judicial and Executive branches over executive power. The Supreme Court may issue a ruling, but Lincoln will simply refuse to obey. And since he has that Congressional proclamation asking him to postpone the election, it's unlikely Congress will impeach him for doing so."

McClellan picked up his letter opener and twirled it in his hand. "You can also remove a president by assassination."

Bicknell flinched at the picture McClellan presented. "You don't mean that."

"No, I'm just frustrated." McClellan's reply was a little too quick for Bicknell to believe him. "During my command, he opposed me every step of the way. Now, he's doing so again!" McClellan slammed the letter opener down on the desk. "He just declared himself Caesar with the full support of Congress."

There was a knock on the study door. "What is it, James?"

At McClellan's query, the butler entered. "General, a crowd has gathered outside. They're asking for you."

Bicknell waited until James departed. "What are you going to say?" He asked, concerned that McClellan might repeat the assassination line.

"I don't know. But don't worry, Mr. Bicknell, I'll be inspiring."

That's what Bicknell was afraid of. He took one more anxious look at the brooding McClellan then went to inform the crowd that the general would be right out.

Four days later, McClellan was back in his study; his brow drawn in concentration. Before him sat a half-completed speech for the Philadelphia Democratic Society. The Trenton newspapers had printed his impromptu porch speech, and it had been well received. Henry Bicknell sat on the brocade couch sorting through a huge stack of invitations sent by democratic societies all along the East Coast.

Newly appointed as McClellan's personal secretary, Bicknell's apprehension about McClellan's veiled assassination threats had evaporated. After all, in the 15 minutes McClellan had addressed the captivated crowd outside his house, he didn't *exactly* call for the death of the president, although he nearly crossed the line three times. But as Mrs. Bicknell had put it so succinctly at breakfast, "This is no time to be principled, Henry. McClellan is going to be president. It's a mere jump from personal secretary to say, campaign manager, to, well, who knows."

Who knew indeed? He could very well end up in the cabinet or ambassador to the Court of Saint James. *Ambassador Bicknell!* He quickly hitched his star to McClellan's wagon.

The door crashed open. James stood in the doorway: his face white and his eyes double their normal size. "What's happened?" McClellan asked in alarm.

Before James could say anything, four soldiers barged into the room. "General McClellan?" A tall sergeant with a limp asked.

"I'm General McClellan."

"I have a telegram for you." The sergeant handed it to McClellan, who scanned it. McClellan's face turned green.

Bicknell rushed over. "What does it say, General?" McClellan wordlessly gave the paper to Bicknell. It was an arrest warrant issued by General Grant. McClellan was being court martialled for speaking contemptuous words against Lincoln. "He can't do that!" Bicknell's cry was tragic. For he if could, there would be no Court of Saint James.

"This is just one of Lincoln's dirty tricks," McClellan said calmly.

"No, sir, this order came direct from Pennsylvania," the sergeant said. "Corporal, place the general under arrest."

The corporal stepped forward, a pair of manacles in his hands.

"Are those necessary?" Bicknell stared in horror at the chains.

"General Grant's orders."

McClellan put his hands in front of him. Two small metallic clicks echoed in the study. "Don't worry, Mr. Bicknell, I'll be vindicated."

"If you're ready, General." The guard marched McClellan out of the room.

By time Bicknell ran out to the porch, the small procession had disappeared down the street and around the corner.

***

Stuart's head pounded and his stomach turned somersaults. He screwed his eyes shut, opened them, and read the headlines again. No, the papers still proclaimed the news. Lincoln had postponed the election. Stuart gathered up a wide assortment to take back to Lee.

"Hey!" The clerk yelled as Stuart walked down the aisle toward the door. "That'll be 25 cents."

"Pay the man, Fitz," Stuart ordered. He slammed the store door behind him.

Lee read the first headline, looked up at Stuart in shocked misery, and had Taylor order Johnston and Jackson to report to him immediately. Johnston arrived first. He had fully recovered from the mild concussion he had suffered during the battle. He read the headline and dropped into the nearest chair.

"Gentlemen, what seems to be the problem?" Jackson asked the doleful men upon his arrival.

"This!" Stuart said theatrically. He held up a newspaper so Jackson could see the headline.

LINCOLN SIGNS ORDER TO POSTPONE ELECTION

Jackson grabbed the newspaper. He sat down next to Stuart and thumbed through the small stack of papers on the table. Every headline proclaimed the same news. "I'm beyond words." He looked at Lee and Johnston. "Of course, we go home."

"Home!" Stuart exclaimed, astounded that the combative Jackson would suggest such a thing. "We're winning here!"

"We are," Jackson agreed.

"Then why all this defeatist talk. Let's march on Philadelphia." Stuart slammed his hand on the table to show his commitment to his plan.

"What will we do with Philadelphia once we get it?" Lee asked.

Stuart was getting ready to make a tart reply when the words died in his throat. The sun had come out from behind a cloud and illuminated Lee. In its harsh light, Lee appeared fragile, as if he would shatter under the slightest pressure. It broke Stuart's heart. Well, he would not add to Lee's burden by arguing the point "If you think it's best we return; then we return. Is there enough time for my men to avail ourselves of Pennsylvania's storehouses one last time?" Stuart gathered the papers from off the table and tossed them on the ground.

"Do you wish to go raiding, Stuart?" Jackson teased.

"I just don't think we should leave empty-handed."

"I agree," Lee said. "I want Pennsylvania stripped bare from the Schuylkill to the Susquehanna. Take only what the army can use. Pay for all you take. Understood?"

"Yes, sir," Stuart nodded eagerly.

"General Jackson, I'm going to approve your request that General Harvey Hill and his Richmond troops march north to reinforce us. I think it prudent just in case General Grant decides to impede our retreat." He stood. "If there's nothing else, gentlemen."

Stuart waited until Jackson and Johnston had left the table. "General Lee..."

"Yes."

"I was hoping you'd come to my headquarters for lunch," Stuart said, determined not to take no for an answer. Lee needed cheering up and cheered up he would be.

"Not today, I'm tired."

"I can promise a good piece of beef and seven days worth of gossip I've been saving up." He gave Lee his most winning smile.

Charmed, Lee's face lit up. Stuart was encouraged. He almost looked like the old Lee.

"You go have Traveller saddled," Lee relented, "while I fetch my hat and gloves."

Stuart almost ran to do so.

"Telegram for you, sir," John Hay announced. Lincoln stood at the window watching the traffic stream by, his mind hundreds of miles away in Pennsylvania. Fourteen days had passed since he signed the executive order, and, for 14 days, Hay had walked into his office with a telegram from Grant informing him that Lee was still on the heights behind Springville.

Lincoln held out his hand, opened the envelope, and removed the slip of paper. He whooped in glee and read the telegram aloud: "*Lee retreating. We are in full pursuit. U.S. Grant.*"

Chapter Twenty Three

Near Ephrata, Pennsylvania
End of June 1864

"What do you have?" Stuart asked his scouts. The two men were squeezed into the bell tower of a Lutheran church. Stuart was breathless from the climb and losing a battle in ridding himself of the spider webs clinging to him. He pressed in next to them. "These things aren't going to go off, are they?" He pointed to the bells.

"They haven't so far. And we've been up here close to three hours," Sergeant Owens replied.

Stuart gave one more dubious look at the bells and turned his attention to the Pennsylvania valley spread out before him. He held out his hand. Owens gave him a pair of field glasses. Stuart raised them and focused. The entire valley was no more than a foot away. He lowered the glasses and stared at Owens in disbelief. The valley was filled with Yankees. "Who are they?"

"Second Corps," Major Williams said. "Fifth Corps' baggage passed through about an hour ago."

"So fast." Stuart's mind whirled with possible scenarios. "They're not even a day behind us."

"Sir, they're turning south," Williams reported.

"South?" Once more Stuart was aghast. "Do you know where?"

"That road leads through Lancaster to Columbia," Williams reported. "So do the other roads the Yankees are traveling down." He fanned himself with his hat and blew up a great deal of dust.

Stuart raised the glasses, and, between coughs, stared at the Yankees tramping down the main road. "They'll make Lancaster by sundown."

"Yes, sir, and if Columbia is their goal, they'll cross the river by tomorrow evening or the next morning at the latest."

"They're almost in front of us." Stuart returned the glasses to Owens. "Okay, I've to get out of this oven." He descended the staircase two steps at a time. Once outside, he breathed deeply. "If I ride all night, I should reach the army by dawn." He took a drink from his canteen and gazed at his two exhausted scouts. "I know you men are tired, but I need you to track these Yankees. If it looks like they'll cross the Susquehanna sooner than we discussed upstairs, I need to know."

"Yes, sir."

Stuart swung up on Virginia and headed back to Lee.

There was movement besides his camp-bed. Jackson rolled over and saw Stuart strip off his gauntlets and cape. Next came the sword and the other falderals he wore. Stuart lay down on the ground and wrapped himself in his cape. Jackson sat up, pulled his shawl from the end of the bed, and covered the cavalry leader.

"Stuart," he said.

Stuart grunted.

"Is it bad?"

"Yes."

"How far back?"

"Half a day. A full day at the most."

Jackson flopped on his back and threw his arm over his face. Half a day! That meant a race through the mountains to the Potomac. He groaned and sat up. He stepped over the snoring Stuart, sat down at his desk, and lit a candle. It was nearly four in the morning, but sleep had fled. He pulled out a series of maps. If it looked like they were going to be caught from behind, he needed to find a place where the army could turn, dig in, and fight.

Grant rode down the Hanover Road along side Reynolds and Meade. The setting sun cast its lingering glow against the stone walls bordering the dirt road. The clouds of dust kicked up by the horses danced and swirled in the rapidly dimming light. The army had crossed the Susquehanna two days ago. Early reports trickling back from Sheridan put the Rebs close to the mountain passes. Grant was still hopeful that he could catch the Confederates before they made it through the mountains. If not, he would settle for trapping Lee against the Potomac. A rider approached. Grant pulled up, hoping it was Sheridan. He was not disappointed.

"The Rebs are at Gettysburg," Sheridan reported. "They've turned and are digging in."

"Less than a day's march away." Grant smiled at the opportunity to do more damage to Lee.

"There's more," Sheridan yawned. He rubbed his eyes with his fists. "We met some refugees who told us that a division of Rebs arrived three days ago from Chambersburg. It seems Lee has called up reinforcements from Virginia."

"How many?" Grant asked.

"Twenty-five hundred, give or take." He yawned again and stretched, coming dangerously close to striking Meade in the face. With a glare, Meade pushed his hand away.

"We must have hurt them worse than I thought at Springville." Grant took out a cigar and lit it. "Were you able to ascertain where they're digging in?" He nudged Kangaroo, his gelding, forward.

"Yes and no. Their cavalry denied us entry into town, but the refugees told us the Rebs were digging in along McPherson Ridge and Oak Hill."

"There are good hills east of town," Reynolds informed Grant.

"Yes, but we're going to have to get at them where they are. I doubt they'll come to us." Grant tapped an ash.

"We'll whip them this time," Sheridan declared, his dirty face fierce with determination.

"I'll settle for mortally wounding them," Grant said, curls of smoke wafting before his face. "I don't want Lee in Virginia at his present strength." He rubbed his hands together. "Gentlemen, we may very well be in battle tomorrow, depending on whether the Rebs fight us for the town."

"It'd be nice to have a victory under our belt before we return to Virginia," Meade said.

Grant impatiently smoked his cigar. "I must define victory very differently than you seem to. For I see nothing but a long string of victories from the start of this campaign to now." The others laughed. "I sense doubt in you. Well, let me educate you on the victories this army has won."

"I look forward to it." Meade nudged Reynolds in the ribs.

"At the Susquehanna, it may have appeared that we were licked, except I learned the lesson I had been reluctant to learn. Lee and Jackson are formidable opponents, who should never be underestimated. No matter how impossible a situation appears; expect them to do it. There have been no more ambushes since the Susquehanna. So, even though we technically lost, I believe we scored a great victory."

"Better watch it!" Reynolds teased with a boyish grin. "If you stretch the definition of victory any further, it'll break."

"No danger of that." Grant puffed away on his cigar.

The breeze blew the smoke into Sheridan's face. He coughed loudly.

"I always look at two things in a battle," Grant continued. "What I did right and what I did wrong. If I don't correct what I did wrong in the next fight, then I would count the previous one a failure. I corrected that particular weakness."

"Shippack Creek?" Reynolds asked.

"That wasn't my lesson to learn. It was Phil's."

"Why was it mine?" Sheridan asked indignantly.

"Because you refused to consider Stuart a worthy opponent just because he likes feathers in his hat."

Sheridan snorted in disgust; Grant laughed. "But I believe that has been corrected. Am I not right, Phil?" Grant's eyes twinkled in amusement.

Sheridan grunted and rode away, scattering dust and rocks in his wake.

"I'll take that as a yes!" Grant called after his departing cavalry leader. "Leadership now has the right frame of mind to continue our assault on Lee." Grant flourished the cigar at Meade and Reynolds.

"So, you count it a victory even if you don't hold the field at the end of the day?" Meade shook his head in disbelief at Reynolds.

Grant sighed in mock exasperation at Meade's bewilderment. "General Meade, war is more than who holds the field at the end of a battle. That type of thinking is why Lee has run roughshod over your generals in the past."

"I think Lee's abilities might have something to do with it," Meade growled.

"From this point forward, I'll stipulate to Lee's military acumen, if you promise not to remind me of it every chance you get," he barked at them.

Rebuked, Reynolds and Meade nodded contritely.

"Last winter, I read all the reports of this army's encounters with the inestimable Robert E. Lee. What I discovered was each commanding general tried to win the war with one spectacular victory in order to fuel their political ambitions."

Meade and Reynolds acknowledged the truth of Grant's assertion.

"My strategy is quite different. I don't have any political ambitions, so I don't need the spectacular victory." He smiled mischievously. "Are you following?"

"Every word," Reynolds laughed.

"And gentlemen, my strategy is working." His cigar went out much to his consternation.

"I don't see how you can believe that," Meade argued. "We've lost a lot of men."

"Well, General Meade, I should be appalled that you don't recognize the brilliant strategy you're a part of." Grant relit the cigar and puffed out a small cloud of smoke. "Since the end of April, we've managed to deny Lee the very thing he wanted. He is now in full retreat to Virginia, wounded more severely than I could have hoped. How is that not victory?"

"The papers…"

"Ah, the omnipotent editors," Grant said facetiously. "Tell me, General Meade, can some editor, holed up in New York City, with no knowledge of military affairs, know more than we about who is winning and who is losing."

"I would say no, but…"

Grant held up his hand to stop Meade. "No buts."

Meade stubbornly stuck to his argument. "What they write determines what the people believe about the war."

"And what will those editors write when Lee slips over the Potomac and is once more confined within the borders of Virginia?" Meade chuckled in appreciation. "What will the editors write and the people believe when the names of battles keep bringing us closer and closer to Richmond?"

Reynolds waved cigar smoke from his face. "That we're winning."

"That we're winning," Grant repeated in triumph. "So, on the outside it may look like Lee has cleaned my clock in the last three engagements, but who has retreated over 120 miles. Not me. I'm in full pursuit, and, when I catch him, I'm confident that I'll deliver another hammer blow and severely injure him. I would say smash, but I wouldn't have you believe that I'm trying to win the war in one battle." His eyes danced in merriment. "But if that should happen, I'll accept the results, of course."

"Of course," Reynolds teased.

"If it doesn't, then I'm prepared to continue my pursuit until Lee can no longer place an army on the field. That is why I continue to keep our troop levels at such high numbers and throw everything I have at him. I can afford to lose ten men to his one. I'll continue to bleed him until he can no longer stand. And then he will come to me and surrender his army." With that, Grant urged Kangaroo forward into the approaching night.

Chapter Twenty Four

It was dark when Stuart led a limping Virginia to the corral at the rear of Camp On-the-Way-Back. She had gone down hard after stumbling in a hole. Stuart had somersaulted over her head onto the ground. Once he stopped seeing stars, he scrambled to his feet and grabbed her reins before she did herself more harm. He ran a hand down her shivering matchstick leg. His careful examination revealed a skinned knee, already swelling, but thankfully, no broken bones. She was in agony, though. Slowly, he walked her back to headquarters, resting her whenever she needed: cajoling, praising, and begging her to keep walking. Then came that horrible moment when she balked and refused to take one more step. He emptied his pockets of sugar lumps and bribed her to continue.

"Jack!" He called to his groom.

The small, wizened old man seemed to materialize out of thin air; but then he always did. This unusual habit of sneaking up on him used to startle Stuart, causing his heart to thump every time Jack appeared. Now, he just took it for granted and didn't even bat an eyelash when Jack performed his magic.

"What do we have here?" Jack said in his ever-changing accent. Tonight, Jack was Irish. Yesterday, he had been French Creole. But he was a genius with horses, so Stuart overlooked his eccentricities.

"She went down hard." Stuart stroked Virginia's nose.

Jack felt the leg. Virginia nickered in pain. Stuart tightened his grip on the cheekpiece to prevent her from pulling away from Jack's probing hands.

"Know more in the morning." Jack stood and crossed to his trunks. Stuart peered over his shoulder while the groom plucked out an odd assortment of roots, jellies, and salves. "You want Maryland saddled?"

Stuart's eyes glinted with excitement. "That won't be necessary."

"So, you'll go claim the stallion now," Jack laughed, his elfin body shaking all over.

The stallion was a sixteen hand, midnight-black thoroughbred Colonel Baker had brought back from a raid north of Shippack Creek. He was a grand fellow; the desire of all the troopers. While the army waited for the Yankees to gallop across Pennsylvania, Stuart could be found down at the makeshift corral watching the thoroughbred gallop across the yard.

Stuart strolled up to the corral's gate. He watched the stallion watch him for awhile. There was intelligence in the thoroughbred's eyes. The stallion threw his head and raced around the large pen. Stuart smiled in anticipation. There was also speed in the legs. He undid the latch and walked into the corral. When he did, the stallion streaked away. The animal came to a halt and tossed his head in such a high-spirited manner that Stuart laughed with delight. He had a bridle in his hands and enough sugar lumps in his pockets to stay hours. He made hushing sounds and approached slowly so not to spook the horse. But the thoroughbred, for all its spirit, had become lonely for human companionship. He allowed Stuart to pet him, then stood submissively while Stuart slipped the crownpiece over his ears. He meekly followed Stuart out of the corral and back to Stuart's headquarters.

As Stuart neared his tent, McClellan loomed up before him.

"So you got him!" McClellan exclaimed, admiring the stallion up close.

"You knew I would sooner or later," Stuart chuckled.

"My money was on sooner. By the way, General Lee wants to see you."

"Okay," Stuart replied wearily. His bumps and bruises throbbed in protest. "Could you send someone to saddle this big brute? My tack's at the corral. Jack knows where."

Stuart changed his shirt and splashed water on his face. Ten minutes later, he galloped along, admiring the smooth gait of the stallion. He pulled up outside Lee's tent and noticed the animal wasn't even breathing heavily.

"Jeb, that's a fabulous stallion," Lee said, coming out of his tent. He circled the animal; patting him here and poking him there. "Every bit as tall as Traveller." Stuart joined Lee in his inspection. "What happened to Virginia?"

"She wrenched her leg in a gopher hole. She went down hard and so did I. No broken bones on either of us, but she's plenty sore. So, I went and confiscated this beast."

"Are you alright?" Lee looked Stuart over in the firelight.

"I'm fine. It's not the first time I've been thrown from a horse," he laughed merrily.

"You must be more careful. I couldn't bear it if you were hurt."

Stuart nodded at Lee's paternal admonishment.

"What's his name?" Lee lifted a hind leg and inspected the hoof for damage. "He's going to need new shoes."

"I haven't named him yet."

"Why, you must. Tonight."

"Well," Stuart said eagerly, "I was thinking of something Roman, like Caesar." He really liked the name Caesar. Thought it fit the stallion's breeding and the imperial way he carried himself.

"No, not Caesar." Lee disagreed so vehemently that Stuart struck the name from his list. "This is a war horse. He needs to know who he is."

They circled the stallion again.

"Do you want to stay with the Roman theme? Okay." Lee thought for a moment. "How about Centurion?"

Stuart tried it out. "Centurion. Do you like that, boy?"

The horse snorted and pawed the ground. Both men laughed at the timing.

"It's settled then." Lee patted Centurion. "You and General Stuart will do great exploits together."

They made one more circuit around the stallion.

"What did you need to see me about?" Stuart asked.

"Nothing in particular. I was looking for supper company and thought of you. I hope you don't mind."

"Not at all," Stuart replied, happy that Lee had invited him.

"The rest of my staff will be joining us. Ah, here comes Colonel Long now. I had fried chicken prepared because Fitzhugh once told me it was your favorite."

Stuart followed Lee to the table.

Jackson was sitting at his desk, issuing a very long list of orders to Pendleton when Major McClellan stuck his head into the tent. "General Stuart says good morning and hopes the day finds you well. He's on the outskirts of town between the Hanover Road and the York Pike. He would like to meet with you there on a pressing matter."

"Tell Stuart that the morning finds me well. Mr. Pendleton and I'll be along within the hour."

"Yes, sir." A few moments later Stuart's adjutant stuck his head back in. "I should warn you, he has a surprise for you."

"Thank you, Major," Jackson laughed, wondering what Stuart was up to.

"Do you think he has a new toy?" Pendleton asked.

Jackson shrugged. With Stuart, it was hard to know.

***

Jackson almost didn't recognize him astride the black stallion. Stuart saw him and waved. He gathered up the animal and raced across the field; the thoroughbred devoured the distance with ease. Stuart galloped around Jackson and Pendleton then drew up with a flourish. With a large roguish smile, he patted the animal.

Jackson ignored the display. "You wanted to see me?"

"Is that all you have to say?" Stuart sulked in disappointment.

"Don't waste my time, General. I'm a busy man," Jackson barked irritably.

"He's just jealous of my exceptional new mount," Stuart said to Pendleton, unimpressed by Jackson's anger. Pendleton smothered a smile.

"Yes, yes," Jackson laughed, "he's a monster."

"He's not a monster; he's magnificent," Stuart protested.

"Does the beast have a name?" Jackson took in the sleek animal. Stuart always did have an eye for quality horseflesh. And this stallion seemed to be a rare find, all muscle, and, from the display Stuart put on, lightning speed.

"Centurion. General Lee named him."

"It suits him," Pendleton said.

"It does, doesn't it? Why General Lee…"

"You didn't bring me all the way out here just to show off your new mount, did you?" Jackson interrupted. Once Stuart got on the subject of horses, it was hard to get him off of it.

"No, sir." Stuart turned all business. "My scouts have Yankee cavalry encamped on the Hanover Road about eight miles away. Behind them is the Ninth Corps. The Second Corps is on the York Pike and the First Corps behind them. My scouts were unable to probe any further. The Yankees should be here sometime this afternoon. If you want me to hold this position, then I'll need considerable help."

Jackson frowned. "Where do you suggest we pull back to?"

"There's not a piece of ground from here to McPherson's Ridge worth fighting for."

"I hate just to give them the town."

"Me, too. But they're coming from the east 100,000 strong. I'd need the entire army to hold the town."

"Why Stuart, I thought you could hold off the Yankees all by yourself. Isn't that what I read in the papers?"

"Now, he's jealous of my popularity," Stuart said to Pendleton, who laughed.

"Pea green!" Jackson retorted. He stared down the dusty road. Unfortunately, Stuart was correct. The town would have to be sacrificed. "Mr. Pendleton, please inform General Lee that I agree with General Stuart's assessment of the situation. If that's acceptable to him, I'll see it done. I'll wait here for his answer."

"Do you want to ride him?" Stuart asked, once Pendleton had left.

"I didn't think you'd ever ask."

Stuart handed the reins to Jackson.

Jackson swung himself up. "He's beautiful." He tapped Centurion and raced down the road.

Grant and Reynolds sat under a tree, a map of the local area spread out in front of them and the remains of their half-eaten lunch shunted off to one side. Sheridan dashed up. Without waiting for an invitation, he threw himself out of the hot July sun and under the welcoming shade of the tree.

"The Rebs have evacuated Gettysburg, sir," Sheridan announced, a little disappointed that he didn't have to fight his way into the town. "We ran off some pickets where the roads join up by the cemetery. There's a brigade of cavalry milling around the seminary. They're using the cupola to spy out our movements. Do you want me to drive them out of there?" He asked this last part eagerly.

"There's no hurry. Once the Ninth Corps is up, you can go ahead and take the seminary," Grant said. He made two marks on the map and folded it. "When it's in your control, please notify General Hunt to move artillery to the base of the hill. Tell Hunt not to be stingy. There'll be no more screaming Rebs coming over their breastworks to sweep the field. Our men are too conditioned to drop their guns and run the instant they hear that damnable yell. I'm putting an end to that behavior right here. If the Rebs even attempt to come onto my side of the field, I'll blast away at them until they're the ones running for cover."

"Yes, sir." Sheridan stood. "Will there be anything else?"

"No, that'll be all." Grant took out a cigar and lit it. "John, I'm going to make a confession. Ever since your encounter with Stonewall Jackson, I've been envious."

"I thought you were at West Point with him." Reynolds lay down in the grass and fanned himself with his hat.

"I was a first-year man. He was a plebe. Would you have noticed him?"

"Probably not," he said with a yawn.

"If I'd known 20 years later that I'd be tangling with him in Pennsylvania, I'd have invited him to dinner every night. That way, I could have gained some insight into his theories on warfare."

"Oh, his beliefs are easy enough to understand," Reynolds said sleepily.

Grant nudged Reynolds' boot. "Please enlighten me."

Reynolds protested having to forego his nap and sat up. "Simply put, Jackson believes he's leading the Army of the Lord. He fights for God's glory."

"I heard he had religious tendencies," Grant said with just a hint of distaste.

"I wouldn't call them tendencies." Reynolds scratched his back against the rough bark of the tree. "That means he's only religious when it suits him. That's not the Thomas Jackson I've learned about."

"Is he a fanatic?"

Reynolds made a face. "I don't know if I like that word. It makes Jackson sound like he suffers from a mental defect."

"So, he thinks God is directing his steps." Grant puffed on his cigar. "Interesting."

"I think so. Even though I've said it in jest, I wonder if it isn't true that God fights for him."

"For slavery? Absolutely not," Grant said harshly.

"Not all the Rebs are fighting for slavery," Reynolds countered. From the remains of the lunch, he picked up an apple. "If we could ride up and ask Jackson point blank why he's fighting, I'll wager this apple," he held it up and showed Grant its attributes, "that slavery isn't among his reasons."

"You seem to know pretty much about him." Grant snatched the apple from Reynolds' hand and took a huge bite.

Reynolds shook his head. "It's all second hand knowledge gathered from newspapers or prisoners. The only time I met him was at Springville. I did tell him that his flank march at Chancellorsville was a brilliant piece of soldiering."

Grant's eyes widened in surprise. "You didn't tell me that! What did he say?"

"I didn't wait for a reply. Maybe I should have."

Grant took another bite of the apple. They heard the drums of the Ninth Corps. "Duty calls," Reynolds complained. He stood and brushed dirt and grass from his uniform.

Grant continued to chew on the apple. "General Reynolds, if you should gain any more insight into Jackson's philosophy, please tell me."

Reynolds nodded then hurried down the road to greet the Ninth Corps.

From the seminary's copula, Stuart watched the Ninth Corps march up the Hanover Road. He figured they'd be on the outskirts of town in less than 30 minutes. He also noticed Yankee cavalry skulking about the eastern side of town.

"Major Williams, I'm going to start the evacuation. Keep a sharp eye on that cavalry brigade. This is prime real estate. I'm surprised the Yankees have let us sit here this long unopposed. Once the infantry comes up, they'll have no need for such largesse. If you need me, holler down. Any questions?"

They had none, so Stuart disappeared down the ladder. Major Williams peered at the Yankees. Yes, they were still coming. He yawned in boredom. From below, he could hear Stuart dismiss the brigade. Williams followed the horses as they trotted up the Chambersburg Pike. Listlessly, he turned his field glasses back on the Yankees. Still on the road; still marching closer. Another yawn seized him.

"Have you heard the latest about General Stuart?" Sergeant Owens asked.

Williams settled back for a good laugh.

Stuart was breathing heavily by time he reached the third floor. One more look at the Yankees to make sure they had no designs to attack today then back to the line.

McClellan was waiting for him at the top of the steps. "I was just coming to see if you needed anything. I saw the brigade leave."

"We're next. I'm going to have one more look…"

Stuart was interrupted by someone racing up the stairs and screaming his name. When the trooper burst onto the third floor, all he was able to gasp out was "Yankees."

McClellan ran into one of the classrooms and stuck his head out of the window. "They're on top of us!"

Stuart hurried upstairs, climbed the ladder, and heaved himself into the copula. His sudden appearance surprised his scouts. Stuart stared down into the street and realized the horrible truth. The Yankees *were* on top of him. "Downstairs now!" He ordered his scouts.

Stuart dashed out the backdoor. A squad of Yankees came around the side of the building. Stuart grabbed Centurion's reins. A shot rang out. A bullet whizzed past Stuart's ear. He ducked, and, from the protection of the stallion's massive body, saw a smoking pistol in Sheridan's hand. Stuart swung up and spurred the thoroughbred in the opposite direction; right into another squad of troopers. Blocked from jumping the side fence and making his escape up the Chambersburg Pike, Stuart drew up and raced toward the back fence. An entire Federal brigade chased after him.

"Go on, Major!" Stuart yelled at McClellan. "Get out of here! I'll hold them off!" He wheeled Centurion around and pulled out his LeMat. The Yankees zigged and zagged to avoid his marksmanship. Two didn't zig or zag fast enough and went down. Stuart kept shooting until he emptied the revolver.

"One hundred dollars in gold to the man who kills Stuart!" Sheridan yelled at the top of his lungs.

Stuart spun Centurion around to follow his aides but saw the back fence blocked by a sea of blue uniforms. He took a quick survey of the yard. He was almost hemmed in. Almost! There was still one route open. It was risky and depended entirely on his ability to judge the quality of horseflesh beneath him.

Stuart gave Centurion the signal. He raced diagonally from the center of the yard to the back corner. Bullets whizzed over his head. On the other side of the fence, a dozen Yankees scurried to cut him off. Stuart gathered up the thoroughbred and set him on the fence. As Centurion launched himself upward, Stuart feared the stallion's effort might not be enough.

A gunshot echoed. Jackson pulled out his field glasses and observed Stuart swinging up on Centurion. A dozen Yankees were closing in on him.

"We have trouble," Jackson said to General Daniel Harvey Hill, his brother-in-law. The dark haired, solemn Hill was married to Anna Jackson's older sister, Isabella. Jackson looked around to see what help he could send, but the men in his immediate area were armed with shovels and not rifles. The cavalry brigade up from the seminary was well on its way to the rear.

Several more shots were fired. Jackson raised his glasses again. Stuart stood alone in the center of the yard, shooting at the Yankees, while his staff sailed over the back fence and galloped up the hill. Jackson kept his glasses trained on Stuart. The Yankees had him surrounded. They would capture him, or worse, kill him, because Stuart wouldn't surrender. Then Centurion was racing toward the back corner of the yard with Stuart stretched out over his neck. More gunshots, this time from the Yankees. Centurion launched himself over the fence.

Jackson put down his glasses and stared at his saddle. He couldn't watch his dear Stuart murdered before his eyes. "Did he make it?" He asked Harvey Hill, his voice so constricted with fear that it was no more than a whisper. "Did he make it?"

"He cleared the fence. That's all I know," Harvey Hill replied.

Unable to stand the suspense any longer, Jackson raised his glasses. He didn't see Stuart until Centurion burst from a small grove of trees. A few moments later, the Yankees poured through, but Stuart was pulling away. His staff rushed to his aid. They pulled their rifles from their saddle boots and opened fire on the Yankees. Rather than test Southern marksmanship, the Yankees eased off and headed back to the seminary.

When Jackson joined the excited troopers, they were listening to Stuart describe his great escape. "General Stuart, are you hurt?"

"Yes, I am!" Stuart was indignant. "Those fool Yankees have impugned my honor. Do you know that tiny little man offered 100 dollars to any Yankee who could kill me? One hundred dollars! Here, I was thinking that my scalp was worth at least 500, maybe even a 1,000," he laughed. His cheeks were bright red with excitement.

"That's nothing to joke about!"

Stuart had never heard Jackson use this tone with him before. With others, yes, but never with him. All laughter was quenched.

"What I want to know is how you let the Yankees get that close to you?" Jackson demanded.

"That's a very good question." Stuart directed an angry glare at his scouts, who, at least, had the decency to be remorseful that their lapse in duty almost ended in his death.

"You had pickets posted, didn't you?"

"Until I saw the Yankees were almost in town. I was getting ready to evacuate the seminary when they burst in on us."

"You posted no one in the copula to guard against such a thing?"

Now it was Stuart's turn to bristle. "I most certainly did!"

"I want their names. By tonight, General!"

Even though Jackson had every right to demand such a thing, Stuart thought it a horrible breach of etiquette to do so in front of his staff. He addressed his aides. "The rest of you are dismissed. I'll be along directly." He waited until they were gone before he pitched into Jackson. "They're my men. I'm well able to punish them in the manner I see fit."

"Not this time." There was steel in Jackson's voice. "I want their names. Their blatant disobedience almost cost me the loss of a fine officer."

"You don't trust me to discipline my own men!"

"No, you won't be as harsh as you need to be."

"You must not trust me at all!" He glared at Jackson and waited for an answer.

Jackson walked Little Sorrel a few feet then collapsed on the ground. Stuart watched with interest. He hadn't expected Jackson to give up so quickly.

Stuart sat down next to him. "Look at us! Aren't we quite the pair?" He pushed Jackson on the shoulder. "Fighting each other instead of the Yankees! Don't worry. Major Williams and Sergeant Owens will be punished for disobeying my express order to keep a watch on the Yankees."

Jackson shook his head. "It's not that."

"What is it then?" Stuart asked, bewildered. He thought names were what Jackson wanted.

"You've no idea what it was like; watching. I thought they had killed you."

"Well, I was a little worried myself." Stuart held his thumb and index finger about an inch apart. Jackson laughed. "Were you able to watch long enough to see Centurion take that fence? He cleared it by ten feet easy." He proceeded to give Jackson a total recount of his harrowing escape. The more he spoke, the more daring and brave he became. The Yankees multiplied by the hundreds.

Colonel Rawlins burst into the den of the small brick house Grant had commandeered for his headquarters. He hurried past Reynolds, who was slouched in a chair. He halted at the desk and quickly explained that two Rebs had appeared out of the darkness with a white flag and a note. He held out the note. Grant dismissed his adjutant and unfolded the slip of paper.

"Who's it from?" Reynolds asked.

"Stonewall Jackson!"

Reynolds bolted up, consumed with curiosity.

"He requests a meeting and has sent his adjutant to bring me to the rendezvous point. He assures my safety on his word of honor. You know him." Grant passed the slip of paper over the desk. "Do we trust him?"

"By we, I'm hoping you'll allow me to go with you, and yes, I believe we can trust him." Reynolds read the note.

"Do you have any idea what he wants?"

Reynolds refolded the paper. "Perhaps he has come to ask for our surrender."

Grant chuckled. "Who could have imagined that we'd be meeting him so soon after our conversation? Maybe we can ask him about his theories on war." Grant grabbed his hat, gauntlets, and a couple of cigars for the ride.

"You don't expect him to answer, do you?" Reynolds followed Grant from the office.

"You never know. He may be in an expansive mood."

Grant and Reynolds followed Pendleton and Morrison up the Mummasburg Road. In the starlight, trees threw their shadows across the road like slats in a window. The Union generals rode into the darkness then back into the light. Grant heard horses approaching before he saw two shadowy figures emerge from underneath a large tree on his left. He examined the soldiers. Which one was the vaunted Stonewall Jackson? One of the men sat ramrod straight on the back of a tall charger. The other figure was slumped over a horse no larger than a pony. Convinced that the ramrod straight soldier was Jackson, he was taken aback when the other spoke.

"General Grant? I'm General Jackson."

While Jackson and Reynolds renewed their acquaintance, Grant used the shadows to perform a frank examination of his opponent. He felt let down by the slouching man, even though he was dressed in an ornate jacket with plenty of gold braid. Why, Jackson was – he sought for a word and hated the one he came up with – common. Where was the ten-foot tall hero chiseled from granite the Yankee papers wrote about daily?

"Your cavalry came very close to capturing our General Stuart," Jackson said.

Grant was flabbergasted. Surely, Jackson had not come to complain about that!

"During his escape, General Stuart reported that your cavalry leader, General Sheridan, I believe…"

Reynolds indicated it was.

"Promised a hundred dollar bounty to any soldier who managed to kill General Stuart. Is it your policy to place bounties on the lives of our generals?"

Grant was glad his face was semi-hidden in the shadows, so Jackson couldn't witness the flush of anger rising in his cheek. "No, sir, it's not!"

"Then I should assume General Sheridan acted without your knowledge or permission."

Grant's face grew hotter. "I give you my word."

"Can I expect the bounty to be lifted?"

"Immediately!"

"Good, I had hoped that would be the case." Jackson's sternness slackened. "Thank you for meeting me. I'll have Mr. Pendleton escort you back to your lines."

"That won't be necessary," Reynolds interjected. "Your word that we'll be unmolested will suffice."

"You have it."

Grant felt a poke on his arm. He glanced over and, in the moonlight, saw the challenge in Reynolds' eyes along with an accompanying gesture. Did he really dare ask Jackson about his theories on warfare? Well, why not?

"While we're all together," Grant said swiftly before common sense stopped him. "Perhaps you can help resolve a difference General Reynolds and I have concerning your theories on combat."

"You're asking me about my war doctrine?"

"Well, yes," Grant admitted with a rueful smile.

A long silence passed.

"No, I think I shall keep my secrets," Jackson replied, a hint of amusement in his voice.

"Then perhaps after the war?" Reynolds asked.

"If God is merciful to us, and we come through this war unscathed; come, visit me in Lexington. Though, I think we'll be well tired of the subject by then."

Nods took the place of spoken goodbyes. Grant and Reynolds swung back toward their lines.

"General Grant!" Jackson called. "Could you please let General Sheridan know that General Stuart was rather insulted over the cheapness of the bounty. He thought he should have been worth five times the amount."

Grant didn't respond. He pivoted in the saddle and watched until darkness swallowed up the generals and aides. "So that was Stonewall Jackson!"

"What do you think?" Reynolds asked.

On that, he was not ready to make his thoughts known. "I think I'm going to lay into Sheridan something fierce when we get back. There's no excuse for that type of behavior!"

They rode along in silence. Suddenly, Grant burst into laughter. "Can you believe General Stuart! Insulted over the cheapness of Sheridan's bounty."

"Well?" Lee asked Jackson when he came into the tent.

"It's taken care of."

"Thank you for your help in this matter," Lee said. "There's no need for General Stuart to find out about this."

"He won't learn of it from me or my aides. Will there be anything else?"

"No."

Jackson saluted and left. Lee returned to his paperwork.

Chapter Twenty Five

The Union artillery began its assault on the Confederate defenses. White puffs of smoke floated on the breeze like low lying clouds before cascading down the hill and covering the assembling army in wispy smoke. The smooth green turf dotted with yellow dandelions became pockmarked as the artillery slowly found its range.

Lieutenant Colonel James Gwyn of the 118th Pennsylvania stood on the Chambersburg Pike and assembled his men for the assault on the Rebs' Second Corps. "Does everyone have a full canteen?" He asked the men gathered around. They all nodded, grunted, or gave some indication that they did. "How many rounds do you have?" The answer was anywhere from 30 to 60. "I told everyone last night they were to have 60 rounds," he barked. "Why do some of you have less than that?" The answer was that the quartermaster had run out. "I don't think this army has run out of bullets," Gwyn rebuked. "Not with the all trains coming from Washington."

Gwyn glanced around and saw one of Meade's aides. "Major, where might I find ammunition?" The major directed him to the trains on the right. Gwyn sent those who failed to draw 60 rounds to the trains on the double-quick.

"Do you have any idea who we're going to attack?" A young, nervous private from Philadelphia asked. He was one of the new enlistees that had caught up with the army after the battle at Springville.

Gwyn glanced through his field glasses. "Looks like it's the Light Division," he said when he saw a battle flag he recognized.

The private paled. "They're pretty good, ain't they?"

"Yes, but we're better."

"Yeah, we are."

"What's your name?

"Danny Breslaw."

"Don't worry about the enemy, Danny," Gwyn counseled. "Just do your duty. You have 60 rounds?" Danny confirmed that he did. "Full canteen?" He nodded. "Said your prayers and wrote your mama?" He nodded again. "Then it's in God's hands."

That satisfied the lad, and he went to sit down under one of the shade trees. He didn't have long to wait. The drums began to roll the assembly.

"Form up, men," Gwyn called. The last few stragglers from the trains ran up and slipped into place.

The order to advance was given. Gwyn's regiment began the long climb. His men had only taken three steps before the Reb artillery unleashed its fury. The drums changed their cadence. "On the double-quick, boys!" Gwyn yelled.

The artillery intensified. The long line ran at full speed. From behind their defenses, the Rebels opened fire. Soldiers collapsed on Gwyn's right and left. He ignored the cries for help and fixed his attention on the breastworks before him. Calmly, he fired, reloaded, and fired again. He put his hands in his cartridge box only to discover that the box was almost empty. Gwyn peered through the smoke at the Confederate line. Were the Rebs damaged? No, they were still there; deadly as ever.

At his feet, Gwyn heard a cry for help. It was the young private from Philadelphia. Without thinking, Gwyn reached a hand down. A minié ball exploded in the middle of his chest. Gwyn crumpled onto the Pennsylvania soil he loved so dearly. The world faded from view. He was ushered into the presence of God.

Under a white flag, a mortified Sheridan trotted up the hill toward the Rebel defenses. In his pocket, a message from Grant to Lee requesting a ceasefire. Sheridan didn't know why he had to be the one to deliver it. The army was full of captains. Why not give one of them the note. He cursed. Here came the peacock to witness his shame. Sheridan jerked his gelding to a stop.

He thrust the note into Stuart's face. "With General Grant's compliments."

Stuart waved the note away. "I believe General Lee said that General Grant was to come in person."

Sheridan scowled. "Why don't you be a good little lackey and send the note to General Lee. I doubt he has given you the authority to speak for him," he snapped furiously and held the paper out again.

Stuart shrugged. "If you insist." He took the paper and handed it to McClellan.

Sheridan glowered at Stuart. Stuart, up to the challenge, glowered back. McClellan returned with a huge smile on his face. "General Sheridan, I'm to inform you that General Stuart has authority to speak for General Lee on this or any other matter."

Sheridan cursed again and galloped down the hill.

When he returned, Grant and Reynolds were with him. Once more, Stuart intercepted the Union generals halfway up the hill.

"Good morning, General Stuart," Reynolds said with a smile. "We meet again. May I introduce General Grant. I think you already know General Sheridan."

"Good morning, General Reynolds," Stuart said brightly. "General Grant, how can I be of assistance?"

"I would like to meet with General Lee about the disposition of my wounded and dead," Grant said.

"Major McClellan, please convey General Grant's wishes to General Lee, with my compliments," Stuart called to the aides milling about. One of them, McClellan, Grant gathered, cantered up the hill.

While Grant waited for Lee's answer, he made use of the opportunity to admire Centurion. Behind him, Sheridan huffed in impatience. Stuart bubbled over with excitement about Centurion's fine qualities.

And there certainly are many of them, Grant chuckled to himself, liking Stuart immensely.

Riders cantered down the hill. Stuart's excitement now bubbled over in his announcement that it was Lee.

Lee didn't wait for introductions. He glared at Sheridan then brusquely asked what Grant needed.

"I'm requesting permission to collect my dead and wounded," Grant replied.

"Will you need any assistance from us?" The brusqueness remained.

Grant shook his head. "But it's kind of you to ask."

"In the future, General Grant, I would appreciate it if your cavalry leader would show the proper respect due General Stuart," Lee said, anger clipping his words. "General Stuart may not have been insulted by the term lackey, but I am. If General Sheridan is unable to do so," another glare at Sheridan, "please don't send him to ask anything from me again. I would be disinclined to grant his request."

Grant took umbrage at Lee's correction of his man. "Well, passions do get inflamed." He wondered how much of Lee's anger had to do with the bounty.

"Passion I understand. Disrespect and rudeness, I will not tolerate." Lee wheeled about and cantered up the hill. Stuart followed, trailed by a parade of aides.

Grant whirled about and visited his own angry glare at Sheridan.

Sheridan held up his hand. "I only called Stuart a lackey…" he began defensively.

Grant cut him off. "I don't want to hear it."

"You can explain it to me though," Reynolds said. "Let's say in an hour, my quarters."

"Sir, General Sheridan is here," Rosengarten announced.

Reynolds put down the report he was reading and went to the tent's door. He peeked out and saw Sheridan standing beneath a shade tree: hands on his hips and a scowl on his face. Reynolds steeled himself and stepped out of the tent. Sheridan refused to acknowledge his approach.

"General Sheridan, let's have a seat out of the sun." Reynolds led Sheridan to a collection of chairs scattered beneath a canvas canopy. A sporadic breeze blew, but it was not enough to cool the day. "I've been thinking about General Lee's comments…"

"I'd like to say my peace, if you don't mind," Sheridan interrupted coldly.

"By all means."

"You don't like me." Sheridan pointed his finger at Reynolds. "You've made it obvious that you resent me leading your cavalry." Another thrust of the finger. "Well, I resent the little morality plays you stage at my expense every time you have an audience. This morning was the last straw. You didn't need to come to Gregg's headquarters and deliver that smug, holier-than-thou speech to my men about the evils of bounties. I had already removed the prize on the peacock as General Grant ordered. You only showed up to humiliate me." The finger came close to jabbing Reynolds.

"Even though I've given you permission to speak freely, I'd tread a little lighter if I were you." Whereas Reynolds was willing to allow Sheridan the freedom to vent his frustration, he was not about to let himself be poked in the chest.

Heedless, Sheridan plowed on. "Ever since I've arrived from the west, you've made it a point to hound me." The finger went back into action. "I'm sick and tired of you constantly belittling and correcting me just because I want to kill Rebs and end this war. If you have a problem with my aggressiveness, then I suggest you find a way to come to terms with it."

"Finished?" Reynolds asked the red-faced man. Exhausted, Sheridan nodded. "Then let me disabuse you of the more egregious errors in your tirade." Sheridan turned a disdainful face toward him. It took all of

Reynolds' self-control to keep his voice calm. "First of all, I do respect your abilities, your fearlessness, your commitment to your men, and your loyalty to this nation. If you feel you're disrespected, I'd say welcome to the club. Since you've joined this army, you've disrespected my opinions and orders. Now, I don't lose sleep because you don't like me, but you'll respect my rank. I'm not your equal," this time it was Reynolds' finger thrust angrily into Sheridan's face, "I'm your superior."

A vicious glare replaced the disdain on Sheridan's face.

Reynolds ignored it. "Furthermore, I'm concerned about your anger. After listening to your diatribe, I think I'm justified. You're spinning out of control, General." Sheridan was about to respond, but Reynolds cut him off with a sharp gesture. "A bounty and an insult can be remedied. The bounty was wrong, and I can tell by the way you're stiffening your spine, you don't agree with me. But I do believe that you've heard General Grant on the subject and there will be no more bounties issued. One of these days, your anger is going to get the better of you and cause the deaths of good men. I'll not allow that to happen."

"Sir, how does it help my relationship with the men if you're quick to reprimand me every chance you get," Sheridan spat out.

"Obey my orders as readily as you obey General Grant's, and you won't be reprimanded."

Sheridan shrugged. "I'm a hard driving cavalry leader. That's what General Grant likes about me."

"But I must like you as well. Whereas I don't mind the hard driving part, I do mind the churlish, angry, hateful parts a great deal."

"Sir, I'm sorry if I showed you any disrespect," Sheridan said tightly. "It won't happen again."

Reynolds searched the bland face to see if Sheridan meant what he said. Unable to determine, he decided to proceed on the basis that the cavalry leader meant it. "Apology accepted."

"Thank you, sir." Sheridan jerked himself up. "If there's nothing else, I'll be on my way."

"No, you can go," Reynolds said in dismissal.

Chapter Twenty Six

Jackson entered the small hospital tent. A blast of heavy, hot air slapped him in the face. He began to pour sweat. He reopened the flap to allow the breeze in, but it did little good. He stripped off his jacket and loosened his collar. In a shaft of sunlight, he saw Isaac Trimble lying under a faded blanket, his face contorted in pain. "General Trimble," he whispered.

"Who's there?" The old man wheezed in distress.

"It's General Jackson."

Trimble held out a pale hand. "How are my men? They were hurt badly this morning."

"General Pender took fine care of them." Jackson placed his jacket on the back of the chair before sitting down. He took Trimble's hand. There was no strength in it. Trimble's usual florid face was drained of all color. Even the thick black mustache had lost its vibrancy.

"He rallied them with shouts of 'remember Trimble,'" Jackson told the dying man. "They fought with such fierceness, I'm sure the Yankees are still licking their wounds."

"They're good men," Trimble said with a hint of pride in his voice.

A bowl of tepid water sat abandoned on a small bedside table. A bloodstained rag floated in the water. Jackson wrung the rag out and placed it on Trimble's burning forehead.

"I wanted to thank you for giving this old man an opportunity to prove his worth to his country," Trimble said.

"And you did."

"Thank you for the rank." Trimble closed his feverish eyes. "I know you fought those politicians in Richmond for it."

"You earned it with your zeal to whip the enemy. I just wish I had a whole division of men with your fighting spirit. And now, you're leaving us just when we need you the most."

"I go to a better place," Trimble opened his eyes and smiled at the canvas ceiling. Jackson wondered if he saw angels coming to escort him to Heaven.

"Is there anything I can do for you?" Jackson plunged the rag back into the water.

"No, sir," he wheezed.

He replaced the rag on Trimble's burning forehead. "I will miss you, Isaac Trimble."

"We'll meet again in Heaven, General Jackson." Trimble closed his eyes and died; the smile still on his lips.

Jackson stepped out of tent and into the afternoon sun's blazing rays. All around him, the wounded from this morning's battle lay shoulder-to-shoulder on the ground: their eyes closed against the piercing sun. A pile of amputated arms and legs were heaped high by a large outbuilding. The bloody stumps were covered with black flies. He could hear a young soldier call for his mama over and over again. Doctors and orderlies rushed by him.

It was a good thing the army was leaving for Virginia this evening. For the last three days, the Army of Northern Virginia had held off its stronger foe. But this morning, Harvey Hill's raw recruits had thrown down their guns, abandoned Johnston's right flank, and attempted to run back to Richmond. It took all of Lee's persuasiveness to corral the frightened men back to the line. Johnston had shored up his flank, but at great cost. General Perry's Floridians had suffered near ruin fighting off Meade's Fifth Corps until the 6th and 12th Virginia could enter the fray and turn the tide. The First Corps had held, but only by the skin of their teeth.

On Jackson's side of the line, Ewell had received the brunt of the attack. Twice Ewell's men had broken, but Rodes had quickly fed his reserve brigades into the breach. Even though Jackson knew his corps had been damaged, he was still stunned when Pendleton had brought him the preliminary casualty list. If the numbers were correct, his corps had suffered more wounded in today's battle than it had in all the battles combined since leaving Harrisburg.

"General Jackson!" A soldier ran over to him. "My name's Joe. I'm a member of the 4th Virginia. Last summer, our corporal invited you to dinner. He owned a farm, not too far from Lexington."

Jackson vaguely remembered the conversation. "Private, I don't have time…"

Joe drew back at Jackson's tone. He held up his hand in apology. "Beggin' your pardon, General. I just wanted to let you know that Bob was kilt this morning."

Jackson was regretful about his impatient tone. "I'm sorry to hear that."

Joe smiled through his tears. "He had his wife rid the house of pepper and everythin'." He sighed, a mournful sound. "I guess I'll be havin' to write her and tell her the bad news. I ain't lookin' forward to it." He took out a red bandana and blew his nose.

"Please send her my condolences."

"Will do. Well, I best be gettin' back." Joe saluted and disappeared behind a large tent.

Jackson's legs went numb. He staggered over to a campstool and sat down heavily. A deep sense of loss assaulted him. His chest heaved in sobs. He closed his eyes to dam up the tears threatening to flow. How strange that it was this Bob's death and not Trimble's death that overflowed his cup. Jackson didn't know Bob or even where Bob's farm was located. Yet, he could still recall the look of pleasure on Bob's dirty face when he had agreed to come to supper.

"General Jackson?"

Marshalling his strength, Jackson swallowed back his tears. He opened his eyes and stared up at Doctor McGuire. Jackson waved at the wounded lying around him. "Will you be ready to march within the next few hours?" His voice grew stronger with every word.

A bucket of water sat on a table not far from Jackson. McGuire plunged a cup into its depth. "We will." He handed the cup to Jackson.

"How many men will you leave behind?" These were the wounded, too critical to move. Jackson drained the cup. Strength returned to his legs. He stood, strode to the table, and plunged the cup into the bucket.

"Approximately a 1,000. There are an additional 250 men who won't live to see the sunrise."

Pained by the loss of good men, Jackson released his grip on the cup and left it at the bottom of the bucket.

"Doctor McGuire! Doctor McGuire!" The urgent summons came from one of the operating tents. McGuire exhaled in exhaustion. He waved goodbye to Jackson and disappeared into the tent.

General Ewell was standing with his aides when Jackson rode up.

"How are the men?" Jackson asked. He watched the end of Ewell's column slip down the sun-hardened road.

"Tired, beat-up, but eager to get home."

"Good. Maybe that eagerness will keep them pushed up and making good time."

Ewell heard the inflexibility in Jackson's voice. "General, I'll keep the men moving," he said, regretful in having to be so tough on them. "But sir, my boys were roughly handled this morning."

Jackson's face was impassive. "I know."

"Aren't we asking too much from them in this heat and humidity?" He waited for a reply but received none. "A forced march of 35 miles to be completed in 16 hours no less."

"When the men get to Funkstown, they'll have a proper rest," Jackson replied. "In the meantime, you stick to the schedule. I'll be with the Light Division."

"Yes, sir."

"See you in Virginia." Jackson tapped Little Sorrel and departed. Ewell followed his men down the darkening road.

Chapter Twenty Seven

Funkstown, Maryland
July 1864

Jackson heard a blanket go down beside him. He opened one eye and saw Stuart standing between him and a sleeping Lee. "Are you hungry?"

"No, just tired. How was your trip?" Stuart stretched out on the blanket.

"Quiet without you."

There was laughter from Stuart, but it quickly faded into the even breath of sleep. Jackson rolled over and went back to sleep.

Daylight disappeared while the Light Division slept. So did Ewell's division, which rose on schedule to begin the final leg of the trip: a five-hour march from Funkstown to Falling Waters. Jackson woke to the aroma of stew and coffee. As soon as he sat up, Pendleton gave him a pile of accumulated messages. Except for Harvey Hill's men delayed at the river waiting for Rodes men to cross, everything was progressing according to schedule. Lee handed Jackson his own pile of messages. All from Johnston, meticulously detailing the First Corps' crossing at Williamsport. Jackson read quickly. McLaws had been delayed for an hour when three of Hood's wagons broke down in the river. Since McLaws had fallen behind schedule, Johnston was giving Pickett and Anderson two hours of extra rest. He had every confidence both divisions would clear the river well before dawn. Besides these small hitches, Johnston was pleased to report that all was proceeding smoothly.

"Someone want to wake Stuart?" Jackson asked. Stuart was still asleep, snoring noisily.

Morrison volunteered. A nudge on Stuart's shoulder produced the desired results. The cavalry leader sat up and sniffed the air. "I smell stew!"

Jackson laughed. Never in his 40 years had he met anyone who went to sleep faster or woke up quicker than Stuart. And when he did wake, he was always alert and cheerful.

Stuart took a bowl from Jim and sat down next to Lee.

"General, we expected to see you yesterday," Lee admonished.

"It couldn't be helped." He swallowed a large bite of stew. "I've been keeping a close eye on the Yankee cavalry chasing after us on the Emmitsburg Road. If we're delayed, we'll have a fight on our hands."

"The best way to avoid that is to get on the other side of river," Lee said. He called for Traveller.

"Do you want me to check the progress at Williamsport?" Stuart asked.

"No, General Johnston has the situation well in hand," Lee said. "Ride with me a while."

Jackson maneuvered his watch and searched for a glimmer of light in which to read the time. No matter how he moved the watch, it remained hidden in the dark. He glanced up at the sky. The stars and moon had disappeared behind thick clouds. *When had they rolled in?* The wind was whipping up, too. It was no longer the gentle, cooling breeze he had welcomed an hour ago. He tapped Stuart on the arm.

"I know," Stuart said ominously. "I've been smelling it for the past thirty minutes."

"Smell what?" Lee asked.

"Rain. Moving in from the south."

Lee brought Traveller up short. "Are you sure?"

"I wish I wasn't, but this nose," he tapped it, "was thoroughly trained on the Kansas prairie."

A bolt of lightning slithered and snaked its way to the horizon. A moment later thunder rumbled low and insistently. Without warning, the windows of heaven opened and rain poured down.

General Early was hurrying his troops across the river when thunder shook the ground.

"Harry," he called to General Hays. "How much longer?"

Large raindrops splattered the dusty ground and plinked in the river. A low flash of lightning was followed by another roll of thunder.

"Sir, shouldn't we recross?" Hays asked. "If the Potomac floods, General Jackson will need our strength."

"Orders!" Early shouted. "Tell the men to recross on the double-quick. Find General Jackson," Early barked to another aide. "Tell him we've remained on this side of the river."

Jackson was soaked to the skin. His raincoat provided very little protection from the driving rain. The gale force winds stole words from his mouth. In the inky blackness, he couldn't see Lee next to him. The moment the rain fell, Stuart had ridden off to make sure the Yankees didn't use the storm to ambush the struggling column as it stumbled forward in the ankle-deep mud.

Hill pulled up in front of Jackson. "The men are exhausted, General."

"I realize that, but we must get to the river," Jackson shouted over the wind. "If there's a remote chance we can cross, we have to take it."

"They have to rest. A half hour?" Hill pleaded.

Jackson relented. The men pulled their bedrolls over their head and slept where they dropped. Pendleton led Morrison and Smith under one of the wagons. After a brief consultation with Hill, Jackson and Lee followed. The wagon kept them from the rain, but the wind swirled about, freezing them to the bone. When the rain slackened, Jackson ordered the march to continue.

"These are the worst conditions I've ever marched in," Morrison said through chattering teeth.

"That's because you weren't with the army during the Romney Expedition," Pendleton replied, water dripping off his nose. "When the march began, the weather was balmy, almost spring like. Most of the men threw their coats and blankets in the baggage wagons. I thought it was a good idea, so I discarded my coat and blanket also. That night the weather turned wicked. Snow, icy roads, and temperatures close to zero. The wagons had fallen behind, so no one could retrieve their items. I spent two long nights sleeping in the extreme cold." He shivered at the recollection. "No, I'd rather be wet than an icicle."

"I was so cold during the Fredericksburg campaign," Smith volunteered, "that it took me to May to thaw out. So, I agree with Sandie. This isn't so bad."

"These youngsters," Lee laughed to Jackson. "I wonder if they'd have been able to withstand the conditions we endured in Mexico."

"Intense heat, flea-infested sands, lack of food, valleys choked with thick chaparral, and impregnable fortresses," Jackson listed with great drama.

"We're familiar with the lack of food part," Pendleton remarked. Smith and Morrison added their hearty endorsements.

"This storm reminds me of the time I crossed the pedregal to deliver plans to General Scott's headquarters," Lee said.

A crack of thunder caused everyone to cringe. So did the following lightning flash.

"What's a pedregal?" Smith asked when everything turned black again.

"It's a large lava bed about 15 miles wide. Let's see, how shall I describe it? It looked like a sea frozen in the midst of a terrible hurricane, but instead of waves, there were razor-sharp rocks and fissures. When the lightning flashed, I would fix my bearings on Zacatepec, a large rocky formation where General Scott's headquarters were located. When the light went out, I felt my way through the rocks with only my memory and sense of direction to guide me. I made it, though. Soaked and exhausted, I made it." Lee smiled at the memory.

"I'll say this on my aides' behalf," Jackson said, wiping rain from his eyes. "If I had ordered them to storm Chapultepec by themselves, they'd have carried it. I reviewed Mr. Pendleton's plan to deploy the Stonewall Brigade during the great snowball fight. He shows real talent."

"I'll have to remember that in case I need another division commander," Lee teased.

A clap of thunder drowned out Pendleton's retort.

The sky was a dismal gray by time the Light Division reached the river. The men from Ewell's and Early's divisions were scattered around. Blankets were tossed over tree limbs in a futile attempt to keep the rain off those sprawled underneath. Jackson and Lee rode up to the Potomac. It flowed past them with great speed.

"The good news is the Yankees will remain a full day's march behind us." Jackson said.

"We'll know more when the rain stops. In the meantime, we wait," Lee said grimly.

There was no sun, but had it appeared, it would have been noon when Stuart made his way back to camp. Jim had spread canvas tents beneath the baggage wagons to keep the exhausted men off the water-logged ground. The small space was jammed with bodies. Stuart crawled under the lead wagon and over Pendleton and Smith. He squeezed in between Jackson and Lee.

"You're wet," Jackson complained, when Stuart lay down next to him.

"And cold. Do you have an extra blanket? Mine's wet."

"No."

"Can I have yours?"

"No."

"Will you share?"

"No."

"Not even share! Why not?"

"Because you're a notorious blanket thief."

Half a blanket was thrown over his damp jacket. Stuart turned and faced Lee.

"Thank you, General! Unlike some people, you're a true Christian."

"You'll regret it," Jackson warned. "He'll wrestle that blanket away from you within the hour. He's very persistent."

Lee smiled. "We can't have General Stuart come down with the ague, can we?"

"No, we can't!" Stuart pulled on the blanket. It didn't budge. Another tug. Nothing.

"You get half and no more." Lee wagged a playful finger at Stuart.

"Okay." Stuart closed his eyes and went to sleep.

The cold and damp woke Lee. He sought his blanket, but saw it firmly in the grasp of his young lieutenant general.

"I warned you, sir," Jackson laughed. "He just can't help himself."

In the murky light, Lee saw Jackson sitting up, his blanket thrown over his shoulders.

"I want to take a look at the river while the rain's stopped. Care to join me?" Jackson asked. Off went the blanket and on went his black raincoat.

"I suppose I need to face it, so I can plan what to do next." Lee found his rain poncho folded at his feet. He slipped it over his head.

A few minutes later, the generals stood at the edge of the Potomac. The usually benign waterway was an unrecognizable monster. The brown river rolled like water boiling in a pot. Logs, bloated animals, and tree stumps swept by them. Jackson threw a stick into the water. The current carried it from sight within seconds. The river would be out of its banks within the next few hours.

Lee pointed to the rain swollen clouds. "It appears it'll rain all night. Perhaps the morning will favor us with blue skies."

They returned to the sodden camp and found Stuart awake and drinking a cup of coffee. My Maryland, his chestnut gelding, was saddled and waiting.

"Leaving us again?" Jackson asked.

"Unfortunately." Stuart swung into the saddle. "Save me some food. I'll be hungry when I return."

"In that case, I better find you your own blanket," Lee said severely, though his brown eyes danced in amusement.

Stuart laughed merrily. "Can you make it two? I get very cold at night." He saluted and rode into the twilight.

A drop of rain hit Lee's cheek. He sighed and headed for coverage under the wagon.

Chapter Twenty Eight

Major Smith's rain gauge indicated that four inches of rain had fallen before the Army of Northern Virginia woke to pleasant blue skies, mild temperatures, and a rising river voraciously gobbling up the low lying areas. Since yesterday, the trains had been moved twice, and Dr. McGuire was making arrangements to move the wounded another mile inland.

Lee stood at the water's edge contemplating how best to protect the five divisions trapped in Maryland. Traveller strained at the end of his reins, his bit slipped so he could munch the green grass. Last night, Stuart had reported that three Union corps were strung out between Emmitsburg and Smithsburg, a little more than half a day's march away. Union cavalry had occupied Funkstown and Hagerstown. The only good news was that two Federal corps remained stuck in Pennsylvania where the roads were still impassable.

Lee whipped a hickory switch through the tall, wet grass. One thought crowded out all others: his decision to do battle at Gettysburg. Grant's large army had marched faster than Lee could believe possible. At Carlisle, Johnston had argued that the army couldn't safely cross the Potomac before the Yankees caught up with them. He had pressed Lee to turn at Gettysburg where there was good ground along the heights west of the city.

Lee's inner voice warned him to keep going; that his lead over Grant was sufficient. He had always obeyed that voice – over every argument, no matter how sound or reasonable. But Johnston kept insisting. Since Joe was always hesitant to fight, Lee had given added weight to the argument. He had silenced his inner voice and relented. But what had that decision wrought? Half his army was trapped against a raging river while Grant's massive army bore down on them.

Lee sighed, a despairing sigh. He was so tired of wrestling with his grief and doubts. Now, guilt over his decision to turn kept him up at night accusing him of…He took a deep breath. Recriminations did little good. Except…He stopped the thought dead in its tracks. Another deep breath to focus and to push his doubts away.

Right now, he had another decision to make. If he consolidated his meager forces at one ford or the other, the army would stand a better chance of fending off Grant's legions until the Potomac fell. The trade-off was that the men, wounded, and trains wouldn't be able to cross the river in one night. Lee didn't want to sacrifice one wagon. The army would need all its spoils once it returned to war-ravaged Virginia.

If Lee kept Jackson across from Falling Waters and Johnston at Williamsport, the army could slip over the river in one night. The most obvious drawback to the idea was the long miles separating his forces. If those people attacked a ford, they could overrun its defenses before help could arrive from the other ford. Grant would then march on the remaining corps and crush it.

With his mind far from made up, Lee rode into the Second Corps' soggy headquarters. Jackson met him at the tent door and invited him to take a hike up the Downsville Road. They passed Early's and Ewell's divisions hard at work erecting fortifications. The men shouted and waved. Lee waved back. Without warning, Jackson left the road and tramped through the knee high grass toward the woods. Lee caught up to him at the entrance of a path. Jackson pointed to his right. Lee saw another path's opening.

"Let's take a walk in the woods," Jackson said with a small smile. Forty minutes later, the paths merged into one. Jackson explained that in another mile, the path turned west toward Williamsport and exited into a large field two miles east of Johnston's defenses. "I call it a rabbit trail. I'll use it to disappear from behind my defenses and re-emerge on the flanks of a divided army."

As the two men headed back to Jackson's headquarters, Lee made his decision. Both fords would be defended. Before heading to Williamsport, Lee requested Ewell's division be assigned to the First Corps. With Anderson's division severely hurt at Gettysburg, Johnston would need the extra manpower. Jackson dispatched Ewell within the hour.

The only fly in the ointment was the cavalry. Part of Stuart's men was already across the river, and the wagon train needed extra guards to protect it from the marauding Yankee cavalry. There was just too much territory for the overextended division to cover. A worried Stuart informed Lee that his men could be in the wrong place at the wrong time and unable to provide any support at all. Lee told him to do his best.

Stuart was afraid his best wasn't going to be good enough. He posted Hampton's brigade to guard the approaches to Williamsport. To reduce the area the brigade had to cover, Colonel Baker was pulled back almost on top of Johnston's lines. Videttes were posted further north, but Stuart was nervous about their isolation. The pickets could be gobbled up before warnings were sent to Williamsport. Grumble Jones' Laurel Brigade protected Johnston's left flank and the wagon train assembled along the water's edge. Fitz's men ranged between Falling Waters and Williamsport. Chambliss' troopers guarded the road leading from Downsville to Falling Waters. Chambliss was Jackson's first line of defense. Stuart hoped that he had successfully covered all the approaches. When he saw Chambliss riding across the water-logged field, waving his hat and shouting, he knew he was wrong. Putting spurs to Centurion, Stuart hurried to intercept the colonel.

"Yankees!" Chambliss pointed back in the direction he came. "They're coming cross country."

Stuart raised his field glasses and saw the landscape carpeted with blue troopers. Could he outrun the Yankees to Jackson's defenses? He glanced at Chambliss' lathered gelding and decided against it. "Major McClellan, notify General Jackson that I need support on the double-quick." McClellan galloped off. "Colonel Chambliss, there's a drainage ditch about 600 yards south. Let's set the line there."

Stuart dismounted and drew his repeater from its boot. He handed Centurions' reins to an aide and took his place on the line next to the men of Rooney's old brigade. Major Beckham unlimbered his cannon on the left. Knowing artillery would alert Jackson faster than McClellan, Stuart ordered Beckham to fire and keep firing. The dismounted blue troopers sprang forward; a solid blue wall. "Fire at will!" Stuart shouted. He leveled his rifle and emptied its contents into the advancing Yankees.

The ditch turned into a trap. The Yankees' superior numbers allowed them to overlap the Confederate line. Stuart was outflanked and in danger of having his retreat cut off. He ordered Beckham to take half his horse artillery to the right and drive the Yankees back. The extra firepower made little impact. The flanking maneuver continued.

"Sir, we're almost out of ammunition!" A private shouted at Stuart. He held up his cartridge box just in case the cavalry commander didn't believe him.

Stuart nodded. It was time to go. Centurion was brought up. "Colonel Chambliss, I'm going to alert General Jackson that we're on our way. Don't stop until you're behind the infantry. Tell Beckham to abandon his cannons. I don't want him captured. I can always get more guns. I can't get another Beckham." He spurred Centurion toward Jackson.

***

"I can't tell you the satisfaction it brought me to see the peacock running away," Sheridan crowed to Grant. "He got behind his infantry before I could catch him, but make no mistake, he was scared, and he was running."

"How are the roads?" Grant asked his mud-splattered cavalry leader.

"Terrible. I don't think the sun dried them one bit," Sheridan sulked, resentful of the sun's inability to perform such a simple task.

"Can I pass infantry down them?" Grant was equally resentful.

"Yes, but it will be a tough row to hoe. And artillery. Forget it!" He threw up his hands in frustration. "The cannons will sink to their hubs."

"The river?"

Sheridan brightened a little. "Still rising."

"Can you get after the Rebs tomorrow?"

"That's why I've come." He smiled gleefully.

"Colonel Rawlins, ask General Reynolds to join us." Grant sat back and lit a cigar. "Phil, when's the last time you had something to eat?" He pointed to the leftovers on the table. "Help yourself."

Sheridan wrinkled his nose. "I'm not hungry."

Grant fixed him a plate anyway. He scooted it over. "How many men did you lose?"

"Thirty-five dead, 67 wounded. My rough estimate is that I did five or six times the damage to them." Sheridan stabbed a potato. He thrust it in his mouth and chewed noisily.

Reynolds arrived and sat next to Grant. He reached for the coffee pot. "How are things in Maryland?" He asked Sheridan.

Sheridan gave him a rundown of his fight with Stuart, punctuated by flourishes of his fork and knife. "And I can hurt them again tomorrow if you'll give me the First Corps."

Reynolds poured another cup of coffee. "What about the roads?"

Sheridan bristled. After their recent encounter, he feared Reynolds would say no just for spite. "They're a mess. Even more so, the further north you travel. But Doubleday is west of Smithsburg, less than ten miles away. If he leaves his baggage and artillery behind, he can join me in Hagerstown by noon."

Reynolds sipped his coffee. "What's your plan?"

"I want to hit the Reb defenses at Williamsport. Develop their strength."

"Are you sure one corps is going to be enough?"

"It should. Only Johnston is at Williamsport. Jackson remains across from Falling Waters."

Grant's eyebrows shot up in surprise. "Lee hasn't consolidated his forces?"

Sheridan added another helping of potatoes to his plate. "No, Jackson sent Ewell to Williamsport. That's all the information I've been able to gather. To find out more, I need infantry."

Grant leaned back in his chair. "Take them! I'm tired of just sitting here waiting for the roads to dry."

Reynolds wrote up the orders. Sheridan pushed his plate away, the potatoes half eaten. "If you'll excuse me, I need to get a fresh horse."

Chapter Twenty Nine

Lee's field office was nothing more than a captured Federal ambulance, which had been easily converted into an workplace with the addition of a table, chair, and a never ending supply of despised paperwork. On beautiful mornings like this one, Lee was glad to abandon his musty tent, tie up the ambulance's canvas sides, and take advantage of the sunshine and breeze.

He had just recently returned from an unpleasant confrontation with Johnston over the construction, or rather, the lack of construction of the Williamsport defenses. Yesterday had been wasted. The fortifications were not even half-built, and no artillery had been moved into place. Johnston hemmed and hawed, excused and justified, but Lee pressed the point. The bulwarks must be finished. Tonight! Johnston's agreement was sullen, but at least the First Corps Commander had agreed. Upon his return, Lee had found word waiting for him from Stuart. The Union's First Corps was in Hagerstown, only an hour's march from Johnston's unfinished defenses.

Stuart rode up, singing at the top of his lungs. "Hallo! General!" He sang out.

"Come in, Jeb! You're in fine voice this afternoon."

"Perhaps I should have made my living on the stage." Stuart struck a theatrical pose then burst into laughter.

How he loved that laugh! "You can't ride horses on stage," Lee said. "And from the moment your father threw you up on your first pony, you were hooked." There was more laughter from Stuart. "No, you're fulfilling God's destiny in the army." Lee pointed to a small stool in the corner of the ambulance. "Have a seat."

Stuart did as he was told. Most of him disappeared behind the table. Only his hat was visible to Lee.

Lee picked up Stuart's morning dispatch. "Have you heard anything more?"

"No, but I did increase my pickets, so we won't be surprised like we were yesterday."

"How did that happen?" He questioned his junior officer.

Stuart didn't evade the question. "The Yankees avoided my pickets by cutting cross country."

"Losses?"

Musket fire from the west! Stuart jerked himself up and jumped down from the ambulance. The small wagon rocked back and forth. Lee caught a file before it fell to the floor. He shaded his eyes with the file and watched Stuart galloped off. Yes, his young lieutenant general was a natural cavalryman!

When Stuart arrived on the field, he found Hampton's men engaged in a pitch battle. The brigade was spread out along a dilapidated wood fence, half rotted and fallen. The Yankees were pressing hard, but the South Carolinians were holding. Further west, Stuart heard more gunfire. The Yankees must be attacking the wagon train, which explained where the Laurel Brigade had disappeared to. Stuart sent a courier to find out if Jones needed assistance.

From his temporary headquarters under a large willow, Colonel Baker, his left leg bleeding from a large gash, barked orders to his aides. "I'm sorry, sir," he said when Stuart rode up. "But the Yankees caught us by surprise. They avoided the roads and came cross country."

Gunfire banged along the fence.

"They did the same to Colonel Chambliss yesterday," Stuart said.

"I estimate the Yankees' strength at nearly 5,000 men. Right now, their biggest problem is trying to cram all that strength into such a narrow front. My men are stretched too thin. I have over 100 dead. Sir, the First Corps is about a mile back on the turnpike. I don't know what, if anything, is behind them."

"Were you able to send word?" Stuart asked.

"Yes, sir. To both General Johnston and General Jackson."

"How long ago to General Jackson?"

Baker pulled at his whiskers. "No more than 30 minutes."

Stuart's heart sunk. The courier wouldn't even be halfway there. Ten troopers ran past them. "You men!" Stuart shouted. "Where are you going?"

"Our lines are breached!" An agitated corporal explained between wheezes. "Colonel Black ordered us to set up a new line about a hundred yards east of here. The rest of the men will follow as soon as practicable."

"Major McClellan! Tell Fitz I need him here on the gallop." Stuart wrote in his notebook, ripped out the page, and handed it to another aide. "Take this to Colonel Chambliss."

"I can't wait for Fitz," Baker pleaded. "I'll be massacred."

"I'll go and speak with General Johnston." Stuart gathered Centurion's reins. He swung up in the saddle and pointed to the Yankees surging over the fence. "In the meantime, keep them back!"

"Yes, sir," Baker said. He mounted up and followed his men.

Lee rode down his chaotic line. Five soldiers labored by carrying a large log. They threw it onto a pile of brush; a desperate breastwork that wouldn't hold back the Yankees. Lee glared at the half-finished defenses. If the First Corps survived this afternoon, the fortifications would be erected tonight, even if he had to build them himself.

Lee came upon Johnston and division commander Richard Anderson. "How does it look?" Lee asked, interrupting the men's conversation.

"General Stuart's men have pulled back and are anchoring our flank along the river," Johnston reported. His unruffled demeanor did much to calm Lee's anxiety. "General Wilcox is deploying now. General Perry is ten minutes away. But we shouldn't expect any help from General Jackson. Word hasn't reached him yet."

"Can we hold?" Lee questioned.

Johnston motioned for Anderson to answer.

"Yes, sir," Anderson spluttered. Johnston gave him a hard stare, which put steel in the division commander's backbone. "My men will drive them back." This time, Lee believed him.

"Sir." It was General Pickett, all curls and cologne. "We have company down the turnpike." He pointed north.

Lee raised his field glasses. The road was blue with soldiers. "How long do we have before those people attack?" He asked Johnston.

"An hour; maybe less." Johnston put down his field glasses. "No artillery that I can see. Roads still must be bad."

"General Johnston." This time it was General Nicholls. "General Ewell sends his compliments. His men are securing the right flank. Chambliss' brigade is beginning to arrive."

"General, if you'll excuse us, General Anderson and I will see to the line," Johnston said. Pickett made his excuses and returned to his Virginians.

"General Nicholls, inform General Ewell that I need a brigade sent to the left flank," Lee said. After this morning's confrontation, Johnston had moved a handful of cannon into place. Lee sent word for Colonel Alexander to pour fire down on those people.

Lee hurried to check the right flank. As he passed Pickett's Virginians, they cheered his heart by vehemently promising him the Yankees would not get past them. Ewell's men shared the same sentiments. Cannon thundered from behind him.

"Here they come!" Someone shouted.

Lee watched the blue lines sweep forward. His men were in place. He breathed a sigh of relief and offered up a prayer of thanksgiving. His men had done it. Under the wire, but they had done it. The line would hold. For today, at least. Tomorrow would have to take care of itself.

Chapter Thirty

Surrounded by soldiers, Lee stood and listened while Johnston held forth at great lengths about his completed fortifications. Right behind Lee, three privates from Kemper's brigade added a humorous commentary to Johnston's pompous remarks. Lee's shoulders shook with suppressed laughter.

"Now, we will have a demonstration of the artillery train," Johnston intoned. He gestured imperiously at Colonel Alexander.

Deliverance came in the form of Jeb Stuart. Lee's relief quickly turned to dread. Stuart's tense, weary face warned of bad news. Lee steeled himself.

"Good morning, sir," Stuart said. "My spies – determined not to be surprised again, Stuart had sent spies into Funkstown and Hagerstown to keep an eye on the Yankees – report the First and Fifth Corps are preparing to leave for Williamsport. General Jackson sends his compliments. He is coming with all haste. I also want to report that the river has crested."

Johnston addressed the group of men crowding around Lee. "Okay, men, you heard General Stuart. Those shovels aren't going to hold the Yankees back." The men groaned in mock protest, but broke up and headed to their camps to gather up their weapons and eat a quick bite of cornbread.

"I don't want to add to your burden," Stuart stifled a yawn, "but I'm sure the rest of the Yankees will be headed this way soon. The Fifth Corps has artillery with them. It means the roads have hardened."

Jackson joined them. "General Lee, Early and Hill should be here within the hour." Jackson turned his attentive stare upon the exhausted cavalryman. "Stuart, I want you to assume command at Falling Waters."

"I don't want to," Stuart said, annoyed by the order.

Jackson's brows came together in anger. "I don't care."

Stuart appealed to Lee. His plea produced a surge of protectiveness in Lee, but he fought it. Jackson must have a good reason to be so brusque with Stuart. "I'm sorry, Jeb. You have your orders."

"It's not fair!" He cried. Again to Lee. "I want to dance at the ball."

"Stuart," Jackson warned.

"Fine!" With that, Stuart tapped Centurion and galloped away.

"Was it necessary to send him away like that?" Lee reproved.

"I did it for his own good." Jackson rubbed his chin. "According to Major McClellan, Stuart has had four hours of sleep in the last 72 and a mouthful of cornbread in the last 24, unless you've fed him." Lee had not.

"With the Yankees descending upon us in the next day or two, we're going to need him fresh. Jim is making him his favorite breakfast, and Major McClellan promised me he'd convince Stuart to sleep. I'm hoping he'll pass the afternoon dreaming of Flora. But if Falling Waters is attacked, it'll most likely be by cavalry. He's the best man for the job."

"I'm glad to know you have his best interest at heart," Lee chuckled. "I suppose he'll forgive us."

"Eventually." Jackson dismounted and gestured toward the fortifications. "So what's our strategy?"

"To beat them back."

Sheridan chafed in irritation. Today's attack was being led by Meade, which meant the assault would be as conservative and cautious as the old grandpa riding besides him. Meade would be content to play it safe and wait for Grant and the rest of the army to arrive.

"General Meade," Sheridan said politely. He knew Meade didn't care for his hard hitting ways, so he was careful not to give Meade reason to act on his antipathy. "We hurt the Rebs yesterday and the day before that."

"So General Doubleday informs me," Meade said roughly.

Sheridan waited to see if Meade would say more, but Meade had gone silent. He prodded again. "I think we should press them."

"I'm not marching through the mud to host a tea party, General."

"Can I ask what you have planned?" Sheridan was a study of nonchalance.

"Your cavalry will protect my flanks."

Sheridan seethed; he didn't want to baby-sit flanks. "Sir, if I see an opportunity, will I have the freedom to act?"

Meade chewed on his request. "We'll have to see what the day holds, but right now, I'd have to say no. There's no reason to risk two corps when the army is a day behind us, and the river is up."

Sheridan choked on his anger. "Sir, the Rebs are also dug in across from Falling Waters."

"Fully aware of that, General."

"Perhaps, I could send a brigade or two to see if we could capture the ford. If we could, it would hamper Lee's ability to escape," he volunteered.

"I don't know if I can spare the manpower."

Sheridan pretended he hadn't heard Meade's reply. "How about I send Custer's Wolverines. Just to scout it out. After yesterday's beating, I suspect

Jackson has left Falling Waters to reinforce Lee. The ford could be there for the taking."

"Think Jackson just left it gift-wrapped for us like an early Christmas present?"

It took a moment before Sheridan felt he could answer in a normal tone. "No, sir, I don't. But if there's a chance we can capture the ford, I think we should take it."

"Custer is young," Meade challenged.

"Sir, he's one good cavalry man. He'll ascertain the situation and act accordingly."

Meade didn't answer. Sheridan was getting ready to ask again when Meade spoke. "Excellent thinking, General. Permission granted."

Stuart felt a hand on his shoulder. He opened his eyes and saw McClellan squatting down next to him. The expression on his adjutant's face said it all. "How many?" Stuart threw off the blanket and took out his watch. He had been asleep all of 45 minutes.

"One brigade." McClellan gave him a hand up.

Stuart stretched his arms over his head and leaned back until all his vertebras snapped and cracked. He jumped down into the trenches and stood next to Generals Archer and Lane, whose brigades had been left behind by Jackson to guard the ford. He stroked his beard then burst into laughter.

He climbed out of the channel and addressed the soldiers crowding around. "The brigade coming down that road is very small and no match for us. What I propose we do is let the Yankees believe these defenses are empty."

"How are we going to do that?" A Tarheel called out.

Stuart smiled mischievously. "We're going to hide in these here trenches and pretend no one is home. The Yankees will come down the road, see the breastworks, but no soldiers. They will let down their guard, and, when they do, we'll slip loose the dogs of war." A murmur of acceptance rumbled through the men. "Now listen up! Spring this trap too early, and the quarry escapes with little damage. Spring it too late, and they may turn and rend us. So, what we need is someone who knows how to spring the trap perfectly."

"Do you know someone like that, sir?" Another soldier shouted.

Stuart smiled again. "I'll be over there," he pointed to a stand of spruces to the left of the fortifications," waiting just like the spider does when the fly comes to investigate the harmless little web." Gleefully, he rubbed his hands in anticipation. "Now, I know these next few moments will be anxious ones. Some of you will want to peek, or worse, to fire." All frivolity left him. "You must not give into the temptation. If you do, our quarry escapes. So you must trust me."

"We do, General!" They called in unison.

"When I fire, stand up and deliver such a scorching volley that the Yankees will fear the names of Lane and Archer forever!"

They let out a cheer, but Stuart stifled it. "From now on not a sound." The men scrunched down in the mud. Stuart climbed the sturdiest of the pines and hid among the green needles. Feeling like a human pincushion, he broke off the more aggressive branches sticking him through his pants and jacket. Once situated, he stood still. The branches stopped moving. He was hidden.

Custer saw breastworks stretched across the Downsville Pike, blocking access to the river. They were immense, constructed mostly from dirt. The surrounding woods were unruly, and the trees so thick that the sunlight penetrated only the first few feet. The fortifications bristled with cannon, yet for all its menace, the defenses appeared abandoned. He didn't believe that to be the case. He held up his hand and looked about, trying to catch a hint of life, a whiff of ambush.

"What do you think, General?" Captain Osborne whispered.

"I don't know, Captain." Custer strained to hear a sound that would alert him to the presence of troops. He heard nothing but silence. "I don't know."

He gave the signal and his troopers followed. He paused every few feet to scan the landscape and listen. He ordered his scouts to scour the woods for a path or a trace; any break that would allow his men to be flanked. They uncovered nothing.

Everything he saw and heard told him that all the Rebs must be at Williamsport, but his gut told him that a soldier of Jackson's caliber would never leave these defenses undefended. "Dismount!"

Still not a sound. Custer relaxed. The breastworks were indeed abandoned.

Custer walked to the front of the fortifications. "Let's occupy these defenses. Major," he called to his aide, "go back and tell General Sheridan that we are in possession of the ford."

It took some effort, but Custer managed to scale the large mound of dirt. He turned and found himself staring down into the eyes of 1600 Rebels. There was a shot from the stand of spruces to the left. Custer tumbled backwards off the breastworks.

The campfire's flame shot up into the night sky. Grant smoked his cigar in silence. Reynolds sat next to him, drinking cup after cup of black coffee. The roads had proven to be a formidable adversary. Since sunup, the men had slogged their way down the Chambersburg Pike. The artillery and wagon trains had churned the roads into channels of slush, which made the navigation of them all but impossible. When the sun had disappeared behind the horizon, Grant had called a halt, still a five-hour hard march from Hagerstown.

"Well, the men gave it a valiant try," Grant said. "Any word from General Warren?"

"Nothing encouraging." Reynolds poured out the rest of his coffee in distaste. "He's about 20 miles behind us."

"In the meantime, the river keeps falling." Grant threw his cigar into the fire. At the rate the Sixth Corps was traveling, it would be two or three days before Warren crossed the border. He said so.

"You didn't expect him to travel any quicker with the Second Corps tearing up the roads before him, did you?"

It wasn't the answer he wanted.

Sheridan arrived and dragged a chair to the fire. He brought a plate of biscuits with him. He devoured the first biscuit, swallowing it almost whole.

"How'd it go?" Grant asked, ready for some good news.

"It could have gone better," Sheridan scowled and tore a second biscuit in two.

"How's that?" Reynolds questioned.

"By injecting General Meade with some aggressiveness. He showed little stomach for the fight."

"I'm sure General Meade assessed the situation and responded appropriately," Reynolds said coldly.

"I was there, and, no, he didn't," Sheridan snapped. "His old womanish ways cost me 300 men and a good general." He popped half the biscuit in his mouth.

"Explain yourself!" Reynolds barked.

Sheridan swallowed. "I received permission to send Custer to Jackson's defenses across from Falling Waters. He was ambushed by a couple of brigades Jackson left behind to guard the ford." Sheridan poured himself a cup of coffee. "Besides those brigades, Lee had his entire force assembled at Williamsport. And General," he gulped the coffee and gasped when it scalded him, "we should have finished the Rebs today. But Meade stepped aside and let them up."

Grant interrupted the argument before it escalated. "Sheridan, I expect a full report on what happened to Custer, but right now, I want you to fill me in on what's happening at Falling Waters." He pulled another cigar from his pocket.

"All I can tell you is that Jackson is dug in."

"It's not a sham?" Grant questioned sharply. *What was Lee up to?*

"No, his breastworks were quite extensive and bristled with cannon. I can ask Custer's aides if they remember anything else."

"What are you thinking, General?" Reynolds asked Grant.

"I'm thinking I don't care much for the idea of Jackson on my flank. I want to know what he's doing there."

"Then that should be our priority." Reynolds fixed his gaze on Sheridan. "Tomorrow, your sole aim is to break through Stuart's screen and find out what Jackson is hiding. We need to know if there are any small roads, wagon traces, or riding paths that Jackson can exploit during the battle."

"You'll have it." Sheridan finished off the plate of biscuits.

"And General, if you can hurt the Rebs, don't hesitate to do so," Reynolds said.

Sheridan smiled in delight "I won't."

Chapter Thirty One

Stuart stumbled from Pendleton's tent. The common area was deserted. The only sign of life was a rabbit hopping into the woods. "Hello!" He called. A mockingbird screeched in response. He took out his watch. It was 8:00. It had been 12 hours since Jackson had sent him into Pendleton's tent with orders to sleep.

Jim came from behind the tents. "Mornin', General."

"Morning, Jim." Stuart stretched his back. "Where is every one?"

"They're hidin' the exit to the rabbit trail."

Stuart vaguely remembered Jackson talking with Colonel Hotchkiss last night at supper about camouflaging the path's exit. "Well, I guess I should join them. Could you have Centurion brought around?"

"No, sir, not until you eat somethin'. General Jackson's orders."

Stuart put his hands on his hips in anger.

"I'm just doin' what I'se been told, so you can spare me the fierce look. Once you eats, then you can have your horse."

"You do realize I'm a lieutenant general in this army," Stuart puffed in exasperation.

"I don't answer to you, but to the general," Jim informed him. "Now, sit down and eat!"

Stuart sat down. He grabbed a mug and the coffee pot. He splashed the brown liquid in and loudly grumbled about Jackson's dictatorial ways.

"General Stuart, how comes you speak so dis'pectfully about the general?" Jim stood before him, a small plate in his hand. "He lovin' you and worryin' about you likes he does. He nursed you back to health after your woundin' and everythin'. I never thought you could be so ungrateful. Here!" Jim slammed the plate down on the table. "You gots two biscuits 'cause the general gave you his." He stalked away.

Stuart stuck his tongue out at the retreating figure and heard laughter from behind.

"What's the matter, Jeb?" Lee asked. He tied Traveller's reins to a small post.

"No one was supposed to see that," Stuart replied, annoyed that Lee of all people had.

Lee grabbed one of the mugs from the center of the table. He lifted it up. "I'll take a cup of coffee, if you don't mind." His brown eyes danced in delight. Stuart poured him a cup.

"Now, I hopes you'll forgive this Virginny man for speakin' so sharply with you," Jim lectured upon his return. "But I cain't allow you to talk that way 'bout the general." He saw Lee. "General Lee, mornin', sir. Can I get you something to eat?"

"No, it seems you have your hands full keeping General Stuart in line."

"It's a full time job," Jim complained with a weary sigh. He set a plate down in front of Stuart. "Two eggs, just likes you like them, and four strips of bacon. Once you cleans your plate, I'll release your horse." Jim retreated to his kitchen.

Lee's laughter rang out.

"Did you ride all this way just to laugh at me?" Stuart barked.

Lee stopped laughing. "What's wrong, Jeb? I've never known you to be deliberately rude."

Stuart was ashamed of his outburst. "I'm sorry."

"It's okay." Lee helped himself to a strip of bacon. "I take it General Jackson's not around."

"He's camouflaging the rabbit trail. Didn't you see him when you rode in?" Stuart asked, his face puckered in concern. Coming from his headquarters near Williamsport, Lee should have ridden right by Jackson and his work party.

Lee shook his head. "I rode along the river."

Stuart scowled and crashed his knife down on the table. "Please don't do so again. It's too dangerous. I don't have pickets along the river. Any Yankee scoundrel could be lying in wait to kill you."

Lee's eyes widened at Stuart's lecturing tone. "I was in no danger. I rode through General Ewell's pickets and General Early's pickets also. I even had breakfast with General Hill."

"All the same." Stuart angrily wiped up egg yolk with a biscuit.

"I'll stay away from the river trails." Lee crossed his heart. "Promise."

Stuart nodded in satisfaction. "I'm heading to the rabbit trail myself, so you can ride with me, if you like." He pushed away his plate. "Jim!" He hollered. "I ate every bit of my eggs and bacon. General Lee will vouch for me. Can I have my horse now?" He looked at Lee. "Honestly, have you ever had to beg for your horse before?" He flushed in embarrassment.

"I don't remember an instance."

"Hey, I have an idea," Stuart said, turning from grumpy rain cloud into sunshine. "Why don't you ride Centurion down the rabbit trail and learn firsthand all his fine qualities."

"If you want me to."

A corpsman brought around the liberated Centurion. Stuart looked the stallion over and adjusted the tack. He gave the thoroughbred two lumps of sugar. "This is General Lee," he whispered in Centurion's ear. "He's the finest horseman I know. Show him your stuff, my man-of-war." Stuart patted the stallion and handed the reins to Lee, who swung up on Centurion's back and waited while Stuart made friends with Traveller. When Stuart was situated in the saddle, Lee headed out of camp. "I remember you saying this horse was fast."

"Want to race?" Stuart asked with a wicked laugh.

Lee tapped the stallion and sped down the road. Stuart caught up with him at the entrance to the first path.

"Jeb, he's magnificent!"

"I told you so." Stuart was excited by Lee's choice of adjective. He thought Centurion magnificent, too. "And I'm right. He runs because he enjoys it."

"Yes, he does. I've never ridden a horse with his speed."

"General Stuart! General Stuart!"

Stuart swung around and saw a courier galloping toward them.

"Do you want me to wait?" Lee asked. Stuart shook his head. Lee turned Centurion and raced down the path.

The rabbit trail lay abandoned, the tools hidden away, and all traces of activity nullified. The courier had brought word that a large force of Union cavalry was headed toward Falling Waters. Stuart was in the woods where Jackson had posted him with orders to protect the path's existence at all cost. Through the pines and scrub, Stuart caught glimpse of a Yankee flanking party weaving its way through the woods. He signaled Colonel Beale to take a handful of men and swing around behind the Yankees. When the blue-clad soldiers were ten yards away, Stuart opened fire. Terrified, they retreated into Beale's waiting arms and surrendered.

"The way's clear behind us, General," Beale reported.

"And it seems General Jackson has routed the enemy," Stuart said, as the skirmish in the clearing came to a sudden end. "I leave you in command, Colonel. I'll be with General Jackson."

Stuart picked his ways through the trees. He heard urgent shouts but couldn't make out what the shouts were about. The calls grew more urgent. Something bad had happened! Stuart burst from the dark woods and squinted against the blinding sun. Slowly, his eyes adjusted to the light.

When things came into focus, he observed soldiers formed in a tight circle, not far from a small stream.

Someone was down! But who? Joe Morrison darted from the crowd; a canteen in his hand. Fear froze Stuart's veins. He scanned the area, trying to find all the faces he loved. At the stream, 20, maybe 30 feet from the anxious crowd, was Little Sorrel, riderless. Not his good and gallant Jackson! And before Stuart knew it, he was running across the wide field.

Chapter Thirty Two

Stuart squeezed through the press of men and saw Jackson lying on the ground; his head resting on Pendleton's lap. His jacket was off and a scarlet stain was spreading across his shirt. His eyes were closed, and he didn't respond to the activity around him. He's dead! Stuart thought wildly.

He knelt beside Jackson. He refused to look at Pendleton, for he didn't want his worse fears confirmed. His eyes fell on Lee, but Lee's face was a tight mask void of all emotion.

"We've sent for Doctor McGuire." He heard someone say.

"General Jackson?" His voice shook in terror.

"The rabbit trail?" Jackson murmured.

Relieved to hear Jackson's voice, Stuart laughed merrily. "Just some Yankees hoping to flank us and catch us by surprise. I surprised them instead. Perhaps I should have been here, protecting you," he teased.

"It's a scratch. Bullet grazed my side." The words came out in gasps of pain.

"Then why are you the center of all this concerned attention? You've drawn a larger crowd than I had at Duncannon, and I was bad hurt," he challenged, feigned outrage in his voice.

Jackson opened his eyes and smiled. "Jealous?"

Morrison pressed in next to Stuart. "Sir, I brought water." He held up the dripping canteen. Jackson shook his head.

Stuart reached into his pocket and pulled out a handful of sugar lumps. "Joe, do me a favor. Go catch Little Sorrel before he wanders away." He held out the sugar; Morrison refused.

"Go on, Captain," Lee said. "Little Sorrel will come to you."

Morrison handed Stuart the canteen. With one more desperate look at his brother-in-law, he took the sugar and went to round up the Morgan. Lee knelt down and took the canteen from Stuart.

Carefully, Stuart lifted Jackson's shirt. "Who has a knife?" Thirty knives were thrust at him. He selected one, cut a slit in Jackson's undershirt, and carefully ripped the material. He was not careful enough; Jackson flinched in pain.

"General, would you like some water?" Lee asked. This time Jackson agreed. Lee poured a small amount into Jackson's lips. "More?" Jackson turned his head away.

Stuart gestured for the canteen. He dumped its contents down Jackson's rib cage. The water turned red.

"Stuart, what are you doing?" Jackson gasped, writhing in pain.

"General Stuart, perhaps you should stop!" Pendleton's plea was almost a command. Stuart ignored the adjutant and inspected the wound. The bullet had produced a nasty gash and a broken rib or two, but thankfully, it was no worse.

"I can tell by my young lieutenant general's face that you're going to be fine," Lee informed Jackson.

Stuart placed his hand upon Jackson's cheek. "You old faker."

"I told you it was a scratch. It's just painful to breathe."

A loud clatter from behind announced the arrival of the ambulance. Doctor McGuire jumped down from the back. The crowd parted for him like the Red Sea before Moses. Stuart hovered over McGuire while the good doctor examined Jackson's wound.

"It doesn't appear to be serious," McGuire said, wiping his hands on a towel. "I want you to come to the hospital, so I can make sure those broken ribs haven't damaged the lung. Other than that, I think you're going to be fine."

"That's what Doctor Stuart said," Jackson replied, his words still gasps of pain.

"Then Doctor Stuart can ride along to the hospital. That way he can lend me more of his medical expertise. Now, if someone will fetch me the stretcher."

Jackson woke, chilled from the night air. *Where was his blanket?* His hand only groped an inch before it struck an unexpected barrier. It all made sense "Stuart!"

"Ssshhh! I'm asleep." Stuart had squeezed himself on the small camp-bed and was lying pressed against the tent wall.

Jackson retrieved the blanket. "Get out of my bed."

Stuart sat up. "Is that any way to treat your nurse? Confine him to sleep on the damp ground without a blanket. Talk about ungrateful."

"Don't make me laugh, it hurts."

"Doctor McGuire left you some powders. Do you want me to fix you one?" Without waiting for an answer, Stuart crawled toward the end of the bed, shaking the cot until Jackson thought he was going to be shaken right out of it.

"No, I don't want to take any more powders."

"Okay. Hey! While I'm down here, do you have another blanket in your trunk?"

Jackson gasped in exasperation. "Just my winter one."

Stuart opened the lid and plunged his hand in. A few minutes later, he fished out the blanket. He crawled back up the bed. Jackson endured another shaking. Stuart lay back down and, with great ceremony, spread the blanket over him. "Ah, much better."

"No, it's not better," Jackson said, his words edged with laughter. "You're jiggling me to death."

"Good night." Stuart's pretend snores filled the tent.

"My dear Stuart, why are you here?"

"I told you; I'm your nurse."

"Stuart!" Jackson's tone demanded an explanation.

Stuart rolled over and raised himself up on his elbow. "If it had been me that had been wounded this afternoon, where would you be?"

"Not crammed in next to you on a camp-bed designed for one person that's for sure."

"I think it's rather cozy." Stuart yawned and plopped back down on the bed.

Jackson turned his head and saw the white of Stuart's shirted back. He surrendered. "Well, scoot over, then. You're hogging the bed. I feel like I'm sleeping on the edge of a cliff." Stuart complied. "And I don't want to wake up tomorrow and find my blanket has disappeared in the night!"

"I have my own blanket." Stuart shook the winter one for effect.

"Then I'll see you in the morning."

"If you need anything before then, anything at all, just let me know, and I'll fetch it for you."

"Good night, my dear Stuart."

"Good night, General Jackson," Stuart replied happily. Then he was asleep.

Chapter Thirty Three

General Daniel E. Sickles marched his Second Corps six miles down the Downsville Pike before calling a halt. When the men fell out for a brief 15 minute rest, he asked General Gregg and Captain Osborne to join him. "What am I facing, Captain? What's down that road?"

"Pretty much what you see here. Woods to your left and open field to your right until the woods from the west enclose the road," Osborne answered.

"How many miles from the road to the Reb flank?"

"About four miles." It was Gregg who answered.

"Did you see any place where they could flank me?" Sickles asked Osborne.

"The only thing I saw was the Rebs protecting their escape route across the river."

"Is that so?" Sickles made a deliberate survey of the area. Both Grant and Reynolds had warned him repeatedly to be on the alert for a Jackson flanking maneuver. "Did Custer have scouts check out those woods on the right?"

"Yes, sir. Our scouts found no trailhead or pathway the entire trip in," Osborne reiterated. "Jackson is planted behind his defenses because he has nowhere to go until the river falls."

Sickles stroked his mustache while he thought. "General Gregg, I want the edge of the woods scrutinized as we march in. If you find a path, let me know immediately. General Reynolds is real nervous about Jackson being so far away from Lee. Thinks we have the making of another Chancellorsville. He has given me the task of stopping it. Is that clear?"

Gregg saluted and rode off. "Let's get the men up!" Sickles called. "I want to get there before noon."

The Second Corps marched down the road and into the waiting guns of Colonel Crutchfield. His lead elements put their heads down and hurried into position. Sickles had a few choice words for Grant and Reynolds, who had assured him that the Rebs were clinging to their defenses by their fingernails. His first contact with the enemy didn't reveal weakness, but the same tenacity he always faced when lined up against Jackson's Corps. The dead and wounded began to mount.

***

It was two in the morning when Jackson left Doctor McGuire at the temporary hospital down by the river bank. Today's casualties had been lighter than Jackson had expected. With the thick woods and his heaviest cannons securing his flanks, the Yankees had little choice but to converge on his center where a heavy concentration of artillery and infantry kept them off his fortifications. Jackson prayed the damage he inflicted would be remembered by the Yankees when they attacked again later this morning.

After sunset, a grim-faced Stuart had returned from Williamsport. He had thrown himself down before the fire and recounted the harrowing battle at the other ford. Anderson's division had almost been obliterated. General Posey had been killed in the opening moments of the battle; General Perry, an hour later. Wilcox's and Wright's brigades had sustained heavy losses. Only two things had saved the First Corps: the Ninth Corps' late arrival on the field, which delayed Grant's attack, and darkness. Another assault and Stuart was positive that Anderson would have given way.

He did have some good news though. During the battle, the wounded and most of the trains had crossed the river. That freed up the Laurel Brigade to ride to Falling Waters once Jackson unleashed his assault on the Yankee's left flank. Not only that, but as he was leaving Williamsport, Anderson's division was wading through the waist high water. As soon as Anderson was safe in Virginia, Ewell's division would follow. Pickett was scheduled to cross during tomorrow's battle. Chambliss would cover his retreat and then provide any support the Second Corps needed.

At Falling Waters, the river was still too deep for Jackson to slip away. The raging river had washed away the pontoon bridge that Rodes and Harvey Hill had used to cross. So, Major Harmon, the Second Corps' Quartermaster, had cobbled together a makeshift bridge from dismantled barns and confiscated boats. At dawn, he would lay his bridge, and General Rodes would march his division over to take command of the fortifications.

Jackson returned to his field-quarters. It was deserted except for Smith, who was pacing back and forth in front of the fire. Smith saw him and ran over.

"Mr. Smith, please tell General Early it's time to go. And Smith, Early's men straggle badly. Not this time. If there was ever a time to keep his columns pushed up, it's today. I reminded him of that last night. If you see his men falling behind, remind him again."

Jackson swung up on Little Sorrel and headed down the path. At the exit, he found Stuart sitting tall on Centurion, whispering to Chambliss and Baker. Colonel Hotchkiss supervised the removal of the dead logs, underbrush, and trees from the trail. His men lowered the trees to the ground as gingerly as they placed their wives' fine china on the Christmas tablecloth. The path slowly opened.

The next two hours were excruciating. Unable to sit still, Jackson made numerous trips down the path to check on the infantry's progress. Satisfied that the Light Division was pushed up and making good time, he returned to the trailhead and hectored Hotchkiss about the removal of the camouflage. The cartographer assured him that his work party only had a few feet left to uncover, and, per his orders, they were to wait until the infantry was up. Did the general want to change his orders? Jackson didn't.

Once more, he started down the path to check on his divisions.

Stuart stopped him. "You're wearing a new path."

"Hill should have been up by now."

"General Hill is no more than 15 minutes away."

"But the sun will be up soon."

"We have about two hours."

Jackson's watch made another appearance. He was preparing to ride down the path and light a fire under Hill when the object of his wrath rode up and greeted him. "My column is pushed up and awaiting your order. General Early is no more than five minutes behind me."

"Told you," Stuart said with a laugh.

Jackson gave Hotchkiss the order to uncover the trail. By time Early's men came up, without straggling, Smith reported triumphantly, the path was clear of all obstacles. Stuart was the first to step out on the field. With a hand gesture, he sent Williams and Owens to ascertain if Sickles had moved his pickets during the night. The scouts returned with good news. The pickets were still guarding their artillery trains a good three miles away.

Stuart departed the protection of the trees, turned west, and disappeared into the inky blackness. Chambliss' brigade followed. Jackson quickly lost sight of them. He waited 15 minutes. All was quiet, so he ordered the Light Division down into the field. The men moved past him like ghosts, making little sound, holding their canteens next to their bodies to keep them from clanking against their bayonet scabbards. Early's men followed; Hampton's men right behind.

Jackson began to pace again. He checked his watch. The hands refused to budge. The sun peeked its head over the horizon. It was too much to bear. He threw up his hand and began to pray.

A hand on his shoulder and the aroma of coffee penetrated Meade's dreams. He woke up reluctantly, grumpily. In the slate gray darkness of his tent, he saw the shadow of a man hovering over him. "General Williams?" He asked. The silhouette nodded. "What time is it?"

"It's not quite dawn," the adjutant responded. "General Reynolds sent word that he needs to see you right away."

Meade groaned and sat up. Williams handed him a mug of coffee. He drank it as fast as the hot liquid would permit, dropped the cup on the ground, and wrestled on his boots.

"General Reynolds' headquarters is on the turnpike," Williams said.

Meade jerked on his jacket and wrinkled his nose. Both he and the jacket needed a good soaping. "Should I wake the men?" Williams asked as Meade ransacked his desk, searching for his gauntlets.

"No, give them another hour and then get them up. They fought hard yesterday."

He rode off and met a buoyant Doubleday on the road to Hagerstown.

"We might finish it today. Here and at Falling Waters," Doubleday said. "Warren is already in Downsville. There's no way Jackson will be able to hold against both Sickles and Warren."

Doubleday's happy babble was interrupted by a exultant Rebel yell.

Meade whirled about in confusion. *Where did that yell originate?* Gunfire crackled. "It's coming from my flank!" He roared in disbelief. Noise, most of it panic-stricken, drowned out the gunfire. "I'm going back. Inform Reynolds that I believe Jackson is on my flank." Doubleday rammed his spurs into his gelding and sped down the turnpike. Meade wheeled his horse around and raced back toward his corps.

The sun was up when Grant and Reynolds galloped onto the field in front of Lee's defenses. They were greeted by a bevy of activity, none of it organized; a cacophony of confusion. The Fifth Corps' panic had swept through the rest of the army. Companies marched hither and yon with no plan of action. Orders were barked at the top of lungs, but the routed soldiers ignored their offices and run to the right and safety.

A sopping wet Sheridan galloped up "Lee is gone! I pursued the last of his men into the river, but the Reb artillery made it a no go."

"How is that possible?" Grant directed his formidable rage at Reynolds' bland face. "How is it possible for Lee to cross three divisions, and our pickets not hear anything? Where is General Meade? Why doesn't he stop his men from running away like scared women?" He indicated the stampeding soldiers running past him. The artillery belched and drowned out all conversation. "And who is General Hunt shooting at!" Grant hollered when it was quiet again.

"I don't know!" Reynolds did not hide his exasperation.

"Then I suggest you find out," Grant barked. His grand strategy, at first hampered by the rains, then the roads, had finally been undone by the incompetence of a New York politician playing general. "When this is over, Dan Sickles is cashiered! Where are you going?" He shouted at Reynolds.

"I'm going to find General Hunt," Reynolds snapped.

"No, you're not either," Grant contradicted himself. "Sheridan, take your cavalry and drive the Rebels back. We can save the day if we can crush Jackson. But first, stop the men from running."

General Williams rode up. Grant attacked Meade's adjutant before he could speak. "Where is General Meade? Why hasn't he stopped this madness?" Grant gestured wildly, taking in the whole field with the sweep of his hands.

"General Meade is dead," Williams said.

The announcement extinguished Grant's blazing anger. He stared at the adjutant and saw the devastation in his eyes. He also heard the sharp intake of breath and a muttered "oh no" from Reynolds.

"John, I'm sorry." Grant reached out a sympathetic hand, but Reynolds pulled away. "I liked that old curmudgeon very much."

"I'll go and take command," Reynolds said, battling back his emotions.

"Okay." Grant watched him go until Sheridan loomed large in his line of vision. "What are you still doing here? Didn't I give you an order?" He yelled, furious that no one obeyed a single word he uttered.

"I didn't know you were serious," Sheridan replied with a casual shrug. "I just thought you were letting off steam."

"Go!" Grant ordered. "No! Stop!" He countermanded when a rider approached and handed him a message. Grant read it and smiled. Finally, he had caught a break. Warren was three miles from Falling Waters. Gunfire resounded in the east. Sickles was beginning to battle back. If he could reform the men here, he just might trap Jackson between Sickles, Warren, and the rest of the army. He passed the note to Sheridan.

Phil read it. "What do you want me to do?"

"Take command of the Sixth Corps. Exhaust them if you have to. They can rest tomorrow when the war is over."

Sheridan galloped away.

When Lee's cannons fell silent, Jackson knew Pickett was safely across the river. Three divisions away. Two remaining. The Yankees were running. Sickles had not yet mobilized. He couldn't have planned it any better. If he hurried, Early could slip over the river at Williamsport. Chambliss was skirmishing with Union cavalry to keep the way open. Jackson gave the order to retreat and sent Smith to notify Early of the change in plans. Pockets of men began a slow meander back toward the path.

"You need to hurry them," Jackson growled at Hill.

"I've men spread out for a mile. I'm corralling them as fast as I can," Hill growled back.

Jackson glared at the Light Division's commander. "I'm going to check on General Early's progress. When I return, I'll expect to find your entire division ready to march back to the trail."

"It worked splendidly," Early said when Jackson rode up. "Too bad we didn't have more men. It would have been a victory far grander than Chancellorsville."

Jackson was stunned by the little man's nonchalance. "Why aren't you retreating across the river? General Stuart's cavalry can't hold the way open forever."

Early was unaffected by Jackson's temper. "I've ordered the retreat. Gordon and Hays are seeing to it."

Stuart rode up; his face distressed.

Jackson steeled himself. "What?"

"The Sixth Corps is three miles up the road and coming on the double-quick."

This was one contingency Jackson hadn't prepared for. The Army of the Potomac's largest corps bearing down on his scattered men. "Are you sure?"

"Yes, but I'll go check it myself if you want."

"General Stuart! General Stuart!" Fitz dashed up. "I've got to have some help. The Yankees are swarming all over me. Where's General Hill?

He's only sent me 60 men. I must have at least a brigade if I'm to hold the path open."

"General Early, get your men across the river. Now, General!" Jackson shouted at Early, who was still moving a little too casually for his liking. "Fitz, return to the trailhead. I'll have Hill's men to you within the next half hour."

"I can't hold that long!" Fitz protested.

"Fitz, I don't want to hear it," Stuart rebuked his brigade commander. "You'll hold until Hill relieves you. Understood?"

Fitz threw up his hands in surrender and rode off.

"Come with me," Jackson said to Stuart. They found Hill standing in the middle of the field, surrounded by a handful of men. "General, Fitz needs immediate relief."

"Just a few more minutes, General," Hill pleaded, his voice rising.

General Heth rode up with his brigade trailing behind his bay mare.

"General Heth, take command of the defenses until General Hill arrives," Jackson said. "General," this, he directed at Hill, "we have the Sixth Corps coming down that road, no more than 90 minutes away. You must get your division down the rabbit trail and across the river before they arrive. Do I make myself clear?"

A messenger rode up and handed Stuart a note. "From Colonel Chambliss, he needs help, sir."

"What can I have?" Stuart asked Jackson.

"What ever Early has available." Jackson turned to Hill, who was looking about frantically, but little else. "General, I'm not going to tell you again. Please hasten the reformation of your division." Hill swung up on his mare and sprinted away. Jackson heard him hollering at his men to hurry up.

Jackson rendezvoused with Stuart not far from the rabbit trail. The fighting was severe at the trailhead, but for some inexplicable reason, the Yankees were treating the skirmish as a mere diversion. Sickles could have easily taken the defenses if he wanted to. But he hadn't, and Jackson wasn't about to question his good fortune. Nor was he going to question why the Yankees hadn't sent a scouting party into the woods to find out just how the Second Corps had gotten around them this morning. As long as the Yankees remained ignorant of the path, Hill was able to send a steady stream of men through the woods and across the river.

But the situation was deteriorating rapidly. Jackson no longer needed his field glasses to see the Sixth Corps' approach. On his left, the Yankees had regrouped after this morning's rout and closed the escape route at Williamsport. The only avenue to the river was the trailhead, and it was slowly being surrounded.

"General Hill says that Thomas' brigade is on its way down the path," Stuart reported.

"Good, good." That left Lane's brigade. The only difficulty was extricating the Tarheels from their precarious position. If Hill retreated without someone to keep the Yankees occupied, they would just follow the retreating men and trap them in the woods. But Jackson had no one left to take over the defenses. He scratched his forehead. Stuart must have read his mind, for he spoke up.

"I'll relieve Hill. I have the 1st Virginia." He took a drink from his canteen, then offered it to Jackson.

Jackson took a long drink. "How many men will that give you?"

"About 100."

Jackson was appalled at the thought. The Yankees may not be attacking in earnest, but Hill was still scrambling to hold the path's entrance with a brigade. It would be suicide for Stuart to try with 100 men, even if they were armed with repeaters. He said so.

"Fitz is at the fortifications." Without waiting for a reply, Stuart sent McClellan after Fitz.

Jackson didn't like the idea. Fitz's men added firepower but did nothing to alleviate the initial problem. The Yankees would just pursue Stuart down the path and trap him against Lane's retreating men.

"We can hold!" Stuart assured him.

"I know that. It's the retreat that worries me."

"So, I don't go down the path. Colonel Hotchkiss says there's a trace in those woods yonder." He pointed to the woods framing the road on the left. "We'll ride through the gap between the Union forces and make our way down the trace. That should draw the Yankees after us and give Lane time to reach the river unmolested."

It was a good plan, but Jackson still didn't like it. Stuart could just as easily be trapped in the eastern woods. He shook his head. "No, I'll think of another way."

"Once the Light Division is beyond the reach of the Yankees, we'll high-tail it out of there. Remember, I have a very fast horse," Stuart laughed. Jackson started to speak; Stuart stopped him. "Listen to me."

His serious tone brought Jackson up short.

"We've no choice. They have us. We have an hour at the most."

Jackson thought it closer to 45 minutes.

"I'll be away by then."

Jackson started to argue; Stuart held up his hand. "Our duty is to save the army. You know it; and I know it. I'm expendable – Jackson gazed at Stuart with horror – the Light Division isn't. So let's do our duty."

Had it really come to this? Was he about to give the order that might send Stuart to his death? Jackson stared in the path's direction for a long, silent moment. Then without a word, he hugged Stuart close.

"I'll be all right," Stuart whispered in his ear.

Jackson let go. He threw himself up on Little Sorrel and rode off. A few dozen yards away, he turned the Morgan. Stuart was watching and raised his hand. It was such a simple gesture, filled with all the marches, battles, losses, and friendship they had shared in the past three years. It *was* goodbye and was more poignant than any words they could have spoken.

Chapter Thirty Four

Jackson burst from the path and discovered the fortifications almost empty. Surprisingly, all was quiet in his immediate front. From the west, the fierce fighting at the entrance of the rabbit trail resonated through the woods. Jackson spied Rodes in conversation with General Ramseur and headed over to them. Rodes quickly filled him in on the recent developments in the Confederate front. The Yankees had made a feeble attack about an hour ago and then had quit. When it became clear they weren't going to mount another assault, Rodes had ordered all but the oldest cannon sent across the river. Ramseur's Tarheels were crossing now. The Laurel Brigade was guarding the pontoon bridge.

Jackson was more than satisfied. "So, all that's left is Lane's brigade, which should be coming down the path any moment. We need to secure those woods," he pointed to the right, "General Stuart and Fitz's brigade will be using them to retreat…What?"

"Fitz's brigade is already across the river."

For a second, Jackson couldn't comprehend what Rodes had said. "That's not possible." It was an order not to be contradicted.

Rodes stammered that it was true nonetheless. "But I did see Fitz and a handful of troopers disappear up the path no more than ten minutes ago."

Jackson hadn't met the troopers on his way down, so they must have taken the other path. "How many makes a handful?"

Rodes thought for a moment. "Twenty."

Twenty! When Stuart was expecting hundreds! "Mr. Smith, go fetch General Jones." Jackson faced west and listened to the battle. The gunfire was thinning, which meant Hill was pulling out. He took out his field glasses, peered over the breastworks and down the road. The Yankees were milling about, showing no intention of attacking. Good, good. One less thing to worry about. "General Rodes, let's get the rest of the men across the river."

Rodes began to sweep up the stragglers.

Jones rode up. "You needed to see me, sir."

"I need your brigade to ride down the path and assist General Stuart at the trailhead."

"My men are at the river," Jones grumbled in protest.

"I don't care if they're in Richmond!" Jackson bellowed. Jones made a face. "Move!!"

Jones made another face, but went to gather his men.

The first of Lane's men trickled out of the path. Pendleton and Morrison hurried them toward the river. Gunfire ricocheted through the woods. The Yankees were on the path! Jackson's heart thumped. Had Stuart abandoned the fortifications as planned, or had a worst fate ensnared the intrepid cavalry leader and his men?

The gunfight edged closer. More and more men spilled from the paths. Angry shouts and pounding horse hoofs temporarily drowned out the skirmish. Soldiers scattered: somersaulting out of the way of some unseen menace. Colonel Morgan, Hill's adjutant, burst from the path and almost knocked Jackson to the ground. Morgan led Hill's dapple gray mare. Little Powell clung to the mare's mane, doubled over in obvious pain. Before Jackson could help him down, Hill fell out of the saddle and hit the ground with a thud. His face was gray, and blood trickled from his purple lips.

"Fetch Dr. McGuire," Jackson ordered Morrison. He knelt down next to Hill and ripped open Hill's jacket. His red fighting shirt was soaked with blood. Jackson tore the shirt to get a better look at the wound. The bullet had entered mid-chest, and blood spurted out with every beat of Hill's heart.

"Give me your handkerchief," Jackson ordered Hill's adjutant. Morgan thrust a blue bandana in Jackson's hand. He pressed on the wound. The cloth filled with blood and became slippery in his gauntleted hands. Jackson fought his rising panic. Hill was bleeding out before his eyes. Over his shoulder, Pendleton handed him another handkerchief. He threw the bandana on the ground and plunged the fresh one on the wound.

Hill waved a feeble hand. "General Jackson," he murmured, frothy bubbles of blood on his lips. "Just let me go."

Before Jackson could protest, Little Powell slipped away.

Jackson fell back into the dust. He sat with knees bent and elbows on his knees. The bloody handkerchief dropped from his fingers. Jackson started to wipe the sweat from his forehead when he caught sight of his blood-soaked gauntlets. His stomach heaved in protest.

His grand plan to end the war had failed. The army, now severely damaged, was retreating to Virginia where the war would continue. More loss, more death, and more blood on his hands. Jackson peeled off the gauntlets and angrily threw them at the fortifications and the Yankees skulking behind; biding their time; preparing to attack; always attacking; a relentless menace, who didn't quit no matter how many times they were defeated. He had bested them at Manassas, Chancellorsville, Duncannon, and Springville, and still they kept coming. Jackson no longer knew how to stop them. What if they never stopped until the South was ground under their heel, and all he loved destroyed? What kind of life would that be for his wife and daughter? Hatred engulfed his heart. How he wished he had the strength of Samson! He would gladly welcome the opportunity to kill his enemies with his bare hands.

Pendleton reached down to pick up the gauntlets. "Leave them!" Jackson barked savagely. Pendleton backed away, his face stricken at Jackson's tone. Jackson was too angry to care about the young man's feelings.

Colonel Morgan ordered Hill's body taken to the rear. Jackson closed his eyes, unable to bear the sight. Behind him, Lane's brigade continued to flee the paths. The skirmish in the woods petered out. Once more, the Yankees refused to be aggressive, a gift from God but unappreciated at the moment.

"Sir?" It was Lane. "My men are clear. The last of the wounded are being evacuated to the river. I have over 60 dead in the woods."

"Lane," Jackson rudely interrupted his former student. "What can you tell me about General Stuart. Did he get away?"

"I don't know, sir. I was at the front of my column until the shooting started."

Jackson huffed in frustration. No one knew anything. "Get your men to the river. Leave the dead."

"Yes, sir." He backed away and left Jackson alone with his thoughts.

An uneasy feeling swept over Jackson. Something was wrong. *But what was it?* He slowly stood and glanced about him. His uneasiness continued to build. Then it hit him. It was too quiet. If Stuart had safely abandoned the trailhead, the eastern woods should be filled with the sound of horses racing down the trace. But the only horses he heard were those of the Laurel Brigade trotting up from the river. The woods drew him like a magnet. He walked toward them, then began to run. He was six feet away when they exploded with gunfire. Jones didn't hesitate. He ordered his men up the trace and into the woods.

A thick screen of shrubs and bushes hid the path, the troopers, and the skirmish. Jackson fought the urge to plunge through the trees and join the fight.

A sudden, sharp trill of a bugle ascended over the clamor and demanded his attention. Impatiently, Jackson raised his field glasses and peered over the bulwarks. His heart dropped into his stomach. The situation had just gone from bad to worse. The Yankees were preparing to attack. Besides his aides and a few medics assisting Lane's wounded to the river, the fortifications were empty. If the Yankees arrived at the river before Harmon's bridge could be burned, they would simply march across it and continue the battle.

The gunfire ceased. The skirmish was over! Relieved, Jackson ran toward the exit. Horses flowed from the woods. It was the Laurel Brigade, and it was cut to pieces. The horrifying screams from injured horses contrasted sharply with the stoic suffering of the wounded. Medics darted over to offer aid.

A pistol cracked. Jackson flinched. Next to him, a wounded mare had been put out of her misery. Now frantic, he searched for Stuart but couldn't find him.

Jones staggered over. Blood trickled into his eyes from a cut on his forehead. "Sir, the woods are crawling with Yankees." His voice shook from pain and regret. He took out his handkerchief and pressed it against the wound. "We couldn't break through. I'm sorry."

"Infantry?" He hoped to recall Ramseur's Tarheels and send them up the path.

"No, sir." Jones was emphatic. "Like I said, the Yankees have taken over the woods."

"Okay. Report to the river. Cross as soon as practicable and have Doctor McGuire look at that cut."

Jackson stared at the quiet woods. As contradictory as it seemed, he would rather hear the sharp report of gunfire than this eerie silence. Death was in the silence; life in the gunfire. Bullets meant Stuart was still battling his way home.

Like a caged lion, Jackson paced in front of the woods, his lips moving in silent prayer. The skirmish restarted, but it was further away. Stuart must have given up hope of crossing at Falling Waters. He was heading toward the fords further east.

The roll of drums announced the impending attack. Jackson had to go. Pendleton brought Little Sorrel. Jackson's only link with Stuart faded as the battle continued eastward. He swung up on the Morgan and took one more desperate look at the woods. There was nothing more he could do. Stuart was beyond his reach.

The storm raging outside Grant's headquarters was no match for the storm raging inside. Grant angrily strode back and forth in the small den and listened to the wind howl, the thunder crack, and the rain fall. His pursuit of

Jackson had ended at the Potomac. Grant had dispatched an aide with orders to bring up the pontoon bridges, but before the bridges could make their way to the river's edge, the skies had opened up, and the rain had fallen as if poured from a bucket.

His plans to destroy Lee had come to naught. Someone would have to pay for that failure! Grant's rage zeroed in on the one person most responsible: that silly, preening, New York politician dressed up his in fancy uniform, pretending to be a soldier.

At the moment, the object of his wrath was seated in a chair, playing a tune on the chair's arm.

"Dan, we need to know how Jackson got around you. Especially after we warned you he would try." Reynolds shouted over the rain pounding on the roof.

"I don't know what to tell you, John." The tapping on the arm changed into a martial tune.

Grant couldn't abide the casualness in Sickles' tone. He stopped prowling and was about to pounce when Reynolds stopped him with a glare.

"I suggest you tell us something," Reynolds said.

Sickles eyes widened at the iron in Reynolds' voice. His hands fell silent. "Am I in trouble?"

Grant's cry was incoherent, but it physically pushed Sickles back into his chair. Sickles face paled, and his eyes grew enormous.

He's good and scared now, Grant thought, pleased by the fear on Sickles' face.

"It depends on your explanation," Reynolds answered.

"He's Jackson," Sickles shrugged. "I'm not the first general he's managed to flank."

The shrug didn't set well with Grant, and from the flush creeping up in Reynolds' cheeks, it didn't set well with John either.

"That's true, but most of those generals were surprised," Reynolds said. "You were ordered to watch out for your flank, and you didn't. Because of you, the Rebels escaped."

"Then why isn't General Doubleday or General Gibbon here receiving this dressing down with me? How did Lee manage to get his trains, artillery, and men across without being molested? At least I made Jackson bleed before he crossed."

Grant wanted to strangle Sickles. He needed to do something to relieve his boiling anger, or he would commit murder right here in this room. He picked up a small bud vase and hurled it across the room. It broke against the wall; the pieces tinkled to the floor.

"I'm not here to discuss General Doubleday's and General Gibbon's failures, but yours," Reynolds continued calmly, as if there wasn't a madman stalking the room and throwing bric-a-brac against the wall.

"So, you admit they failed?" Sickles questioned combatively.

Reynolds' voice lashed the room. "Dan, unless you're willing to discuss what happened at Falling Waters, this conversation is over."

Sickles addressed Grant. "You didn't see the topography. There was nothing but a massive field to my right and a dense wood to my left. Three miles from Jackson's defenses, another wood came in from the west where it followed the road to the ford."

"Woods have paths," Grant snapped.

"Don't insult my intelligence." The reply was savage. "Of course, woods have paths, and we looked for them. It wasn't until after Jackson retreated that we saw the trail he used. It must have been camouflaged because my scouts and engineers didn't see it and neither did the cavalry."

"Did you post pickets?" Reynolds asked.

"Of course," Sickles spat out.

"Stop!" Grant interrupted the interrogation. "There's only one question here." He rounded on Sickles. "General, you had 20,000 men. Jackson had two divisions. Two divisions!" He shouted. "What were you doing at Falling Waters? Hosting an ice cream social? You should have overrun his defenses yesterday. Two divisions against a Federal corps."

"How many corps did you have at Williamsport?" Coolly, Sickles slid his verbal dagger between Grant's ribs. "The First, the Fifth, and the Ninth. Yet, Lee escaped."

The blade's truth saved Sickles from being cashiered. Exhausted, Grant collapsed in a chair. Thunder crashed and shook the house. He began to laugh. It was this army that was cursed and not him. He had put together a brilliant plan of operation that would have brought any other army to ruin. It wasn't his fault that the universe conspired against him. And how could he, Ulysses S. Grant, a mere mortal, outfight God. It was so clear now. For the last nine days he had kicked against the ox goad, growing more frustrated and angry until he was reduced to throwing vases against walls in a helpless rage. He would stop fighting and surrender to his fate.

"When the rain stops, we'll head back to Washington." Grant reached into his pocket and pulled out a cigar. "General Sickles, you're dismissed."

Sickles bolted from the room.

***

By midnight, the howling wind blew the rain sideways. The river rose to the immense relief of Lee's weary soldiers. For the past nine days, they had prayed that the rain would stop and the river fall. Now, their prayers begged for days of rain and a fast-rising river. The Good Lord probably wished they would make up their minds.

Pendleton was in his tent with Smith and Morrison. The aides were past exhausted, but the storm and their own weariness kept them awake.

Pendleton was terribly worried about Jackson. He had never seen the general so distraught. Since Jackson crossed the river, he had walked many miles from his tent to the edge of the clearing and back again, waiting for news about Stuart. Twice, Jackson had sent Morrison to Camp Deluge to see if there was any news, but Morrison had returned empty-handed.

After supper, a picket had appeared to inform Jackson that the river was over its bank. Jackson calmly thanked the private for his report, but Pendleton saw him tremble at the news.

Unless Stuart was already in Virginia, it would be virtually impossible for the cavalry leader to cross. No matter how strong Centurion was, he would not be able to swim the raging Potomac. Jackson had disappeared inside his tent and that was the last anyone had seen of him.

A horse walked into camp.

"Who do you think it is this time?" Smith asked.

Throughout the night, a steady stream of colonels – Taylor, Marshall, and Long in that order – had come from Lee, seeking news of Stuart.

Thunder rumbled.

"Who wants to go find out?" Pendleton asked.

"I think it's a job for the adjutant, don't you agree, Major Smith," Morrison laughed.

"Yes, I do," Smith said with a wicked smile. "Rank does have its responsibility."

With a groan, Pendleton pulled on his great coat and walked outside.

It was Stuart!

Chapter Thirty Five

"General Jackson! Come quickly! It's General Stuart!" Jackson heard Pendleton yell. Stunned, he sat at his desk with his Bible in his hands unable to move. Then a burst of happiness shot through him like a firework. Praise the Lord, he was back! Alive! Jackson grabbed his rain coat and tugged it on as he ran out of the tent.

"We had almost given up on you," he said joyfully to Stuart, who was hidden in the dark and rain. Jackson could hear Centurion's ragged breath.

Lightning flashed. Jackson beheld the stallion staggering in exhaustion. His coat was lathered with sweat. Stuart swayed in the saddle. He gave Jackson a wan smile.

Another flash of lightning revealed a rip in Stuart's jacket sleeve. The white shirt underneath was bloodstained.

"You're hurt. Come in out of the rain." Jackson motioned toward his tent. "I'll send for Doctor McGuire."

Stuart didn't move. "Am I?" He sounded far away. Then he smiled. "No, I'll return to Camp Deluge. This wonderful horse is very tired." He patted the heaving Centurion. "I hope I haven't ruined him today."

Something was wrong. Jackson moved closer so he could see Stuart's face. "What about you?"

Stuart leaned down. "I'm tired, too," he confided in a whisper. He straightened up.

He was beginning to worry Jackson. "Do you want some supper?"

"I'm not hungry," Stuart said, slurring his words.

It seemed to Jackson that Stuart didn't know where he was or what he was doing. "Come inside," he commanded.

The authority of the order penetrated Stuart's haze. He nodded submissively and dismounted. His legs almost gave way when they hit the ground, but he stiffened. He held onto his saddle and stared at Jackson. Then he let go and slowly crumpled. Jackson caught him before he hit the ground. Smith and Morrison ran from the shelter of Pendleton's tent.

"Mr. Pendleton, go fetch Doctor McGuire."

Pendleton ran toward the corral. Morrison and Smith each grabbed one of Stuart's legs. Jackson wrapped his arms around the wounded man's chest. They carried him into Jackson's tent.

"Let's get these wet things off him before we put him into bed," Jackson said.

Off came cape, gauntlets, fighting jacket, boots, and pants, creating a small, sodden pile on the ground. Jackson peeled Stuart's shirt sleeve away and saw a nasty, jagged cut on his bicep. It was oozing blood, but didn't appear to be serious. There were cuts on his face, bruises on his chest, and a bump on the back of his head.

Jackson pulled the blanket up around Stuart's chest.

"Sir, General Lee will sure want to hear the news," Morrison said, picking clothes off the ground. "He's been most anxious."

Jackson rubbed his jaw. He didn't want to leave Stuart until he knew for sure what was wrong, but Joe was right. Lee needed to be told at once. "Mr. Smith, stay with Stuart until Doctor McGuire comes. Mr. Morrison, get those wet things to Jim and tend to Centurion."

Lee sat at his desk, pen on paper, not writing a word. His thoughts were across the river. His young lieutenant general should have returned to the army by now. Against his will, Lee's mind raced down all sorts of dark paths. Had Stuart surrendered? What if he was wounded? Or dead? Lee couldn't fathom his life without Stuart's sunny smile or infectious laugh.

Lee shook his head to clear it from such ghastly musings and sternly commanded himself not to borrow trouble. Despite the command, he couldn't prevent his mind from imagining the worse. A tear trickled down his cheek, splashed the paper, and ran the ink on the few words he had managed to compose.

Ever since Colonel Long had returned from Jackson's headquarters, practically drowned and with no news, Lee had been reluctant to force his men out in the ferocious storm. So, he had no choice but to wait until Jackson sent word. To keep himself from jumping at every sound in the common area, he decided to write Mary. Two hours later, there were ten words on the page; three of them now smudged beyond comprehension. Surely, if there was news, good or bad, Jackson would send a runner to tell him.

"Sir?" Jackson stood next to him, dripping water everywhere.

Lee hadn't heard him come in. He dropped the pen with a small clatter and dashed a hand across his eyes. "He's dead, then?" He said, giving voice to his fears.

"No, quite the opposite. He rode into my camp about a half hour ago. Doctor McGuire should be with him now."

"How badly is he hurt?" Lee asked, his fears rising anew.

"I don't know." Jackson removed his raincoat. "He collapsed. He has some bruises, and a bullet grazed his arm. He also has a nasty bump on his head." Jackson stepped to the door and shook the raincoat into the night air. Drops of flying water glistened in a lightning flash.

"Can I see him?" Lee didn't intend it as a question. He threw his poncho over his head and organized its folds over his body.

"Of course. He's probably already complaining about how bored he is because no one has come to visit him," Jackson chuckled.

McGuire was still with Stuart, so Lee and Jackson escaped the downpour by crowding into Pendleton's tent. Morrison and Smith sat on Pendleton's bed. Sandie stood in the corner, shirt off, drying his hair with a towel. At the generals' entrance, Jim stopped pacing. He took Jackson's raincoat and hung it on the back of Pendleton's chair.

"How is Centurion, Mr. Morrison?" Jackson accepted the towel from Sandie. Now dry and shirted, Pendleton sat down next to Morrison.

"He has some gashes on his withers, but he ate and drank before going to sleep."

"Have you sent for Jack?" Lee asked Jackson. He removed his poncho and handed it to Jim.

"I will when the storm lets up," Jackson said.

The tent flap opened and McGuire appeared. In the lantern light, Lee searched the doctor's face for some hint of Stuart's condition. Nothing in McGuire's face alerted him of bad news.

McGuire accepted the towel from Jackson and wiped the rain from his face. "Joe, will you ride to cavalry headquarters and ask Major McClellan to come. I need to speak to him."

"What's the diagnosis, Doctor?" Jackson asked.

"He's still unconscious." McGuire folded the towel and laid it over Jackson's raincoat. "His left arm was grazed by a bullet, and he has some broken ribs. The bruises and other cuts are not that serious. But I am concerned about the bump on his head. I can't make a firm diagnosis until I know what happened to him. That's why I've sent for Major McClellan."

Upon hearing McGuire's calm assessment of his patient, most of Lee's anxiousness departed. He asked to see Stuart. McGuire didn't object, so Jackson escorted Lee into his tent. What Lee saw chilled him. Stuart was laying as motionless and peaceful as Fitzhugh had on that horrible morning. "He is so still. I've never known him to be still."

"I think we should enjoy it while it lasts," Jackson laughed. "When he wakes, he'll fill our ears with tales of his heroism. I was forced to listen about his escape from the seminary for a week."

"Somehow, I don't think I'll mind." Lee adjusted the blanket. "Could I impose on your hospitality and have a moment alone with him."

"I'll let you know when Major McClellan arrives."

Lee sat in the chair McGuire had left beside the bed. "You must stop scaring me so. You'll turn these old gray hairs white." He chuckled softly. "While I waited for you to return, I was remembering the first time I met you. It was in my office at West Point. You had been brawling. Oh, Jeb, your eyes were swollen shut, your nose was bleeding, and your lip was cut. Your adversary was twice your size. But you stood toe-to-toe with him and announced that you would fight him again if he found himself unsatisfied by the beating he had just given you. You won my heart that day."

That was rather a bold confession to make! What did he mean by it? Lee was not sure he really knew. What he did know was that for these past hours, he had waited and wept with the same fearful anxiety he would if...if…He grappled for an answer. Why, if it had been one of his sons across the river and in danger of being killed. Lee gasped in self-revelation and stared at Stuart with new eyes. Could it be true? Was his young lieutenant general, with the sunny smile that lit up his world, as dear to him as his own sons?

"Major McClellan has arrived." For the second time tonight, Jackson had come upon him unaware.

"Go ahead and start without me." He waited until Jackson left. "I have to leave for a moment," he whispered to the unconscious Stuart. "If you wake and are frightened, call for me. I'll come right back."

Lee stepped outside. He stared up into the black night and allowed the rain to mingle with the tears coursing down his cheeks. He breathed deeply; his first unencumbered breath since making the decision to turn at Gettysburg. He had been wrong to do so, and, because of that poor decision, thousands of his men were dead on the banks of the Potomac. Five days ago, he had debated whether or not he was up to the job of commanding this army. Now, he knew the answer. He wasn't. The army was only safe because of Jackson's heroics. So, it was time for him to step aside and allow Jackson to carry the torch from here on out. He could no longer bear the crushing burden. This last year had used him up until nothing remained but a tired, sick old man longing for death, ready to join Fitzhugh and his daughter, Annie, who died almost two years ago, in heaven. Once the army was safe behind the Rappahannock, he would send his letter of resignation to President Davis and go home to his wife and daughters. But that was for tomorrow. Tonight, he would allow himself a glimmer of happiness. His young lieutenant general was alive, and he was very grateful to God.

"Centurion was raked by musket fire and fell against the general, knocking him down. The general hit his head against a rock and lost consciousness." Lee managed to catch the tail-end of McClellan's narrative.

"Could that be the source of General Stuart's broken ribs?" McGuire asked.

"Yes, Centurion landed hard on the general's chest. He almost got away. If it wasn't for the quick thinking of Major Mroz, he would have."

"How long was the general unconscious?"

McClellan thought about it for a moment. "About 45 minutes. The Yankees were closing in. We found some outbuildings in the woods. They housed stills, so they were very well hidden. We stowed away in them until the general could ride. When the storm broke, the Yankees gave up the chase. Once General Stuart was awake, we lit out and headed for home. By the time we crossed the river, he seemed like his old self. If I had any idea he was still hurting, I wouldn't have left him."

"Of course not," McGuire said kindly. He addressed the concerns of those in the tent. "It's what I suspected. He has suffered a severe concussion. Which means we'll just have to wait for him to wake up. When he does, he'll have a terrible headache and probably some memory loss, but I predict a full recovery." McGuire put on his coat. "I'm going to check on my patient one last time before I head back to the hospital."

McGuire disappeared into the howling wind. McClellan was the next to go. Lee heard him splashing through the puddles.

"Since Stuart's going to sleep the rest of the night, I suggest we do the same," Jackson told his weary staff. "General Lee, please stay the night."

Lee accepted the invitation. He didn't want to leave until Stuart woke up.

"General Lee, you can have my tent," Pendleton volunteered. "I'll bunk with Joe and Jimmie." He gathered up a few personal items and said goodnight.

Morrison and Smith tramped out after him. Jim went to round up an extra cot to move into Jackson's tent. Jackson made his goodbyes. The wind whistled through the tent at his exit. Another peal of thunder echoed and echoed.

Lee sat heavily on Pendleton's bed and removed his boots. He laid his jacket at the foot of the bed, pulled the thin blanket up around his shoulder, and blew out the candle. Now that he was alone, he wanted to examine the feelings that caused him to confess such a thing to Stuart, but his brain refused to entertain another thought. It demanded rest; he obeyed.

When Jackson woke the rain was still falling. He glanced over at his bunkmate, but Stuart had not moved during the night. Jackson reached for his watch. It was late morning. From the absence of sounds in the common area, his staff must still be asleep.

Stiff muscles from yesterday's exertions assaulted him as he sat up. He stretched, then stopped when his wounded side objected to the abuse. He limped over to Stuart's bed and put a hand on Stuart's forehead.

Stuart opened his eyes, but they were mere slits against the light. "My head hurts," he whimpered, earning a sympathetic smile from Jackson.

"I know it does. But Doctor McGuire says it won't last. How about I fix you one of the powders he left?"

Stuart closed his eyes and nodded. Jackson limped over to the desk, poured a powder into a glass of water, and stirred until the powder disappeared.

"What happened?" Stuart whispered.

"What's the last thing you remember?" Satisfied with the results of his pharmaceutical duties, Jackson returned to the bed.

"Leading the Light Division down into the field."

The long day had been erased from his memory. "How about I tell you later." Jackson held up the glass. "Can you sit up?"

Stuart rose off the pillow and moaned. He grabbed his head and collapsed back on the pillow, palms pressed against his temples.

"It's okay," Jackson said. "I've had plenty of practice giving you medicine." He sat on the edge of the bed and lifted Stuart's head off the pillow. Holding Stuart around the shoulders, Jackson handed him the glass. Stuart drank the medicine. Carefully, Jackson laid him back on his pillow.

Stuart threw an arm over his eyes. "I'm sorry I'm so much trouble."

"Oh, my dear Stuart, you're the kind of trouble I love having around."

Stuart almost grinned.

There was a knock on the tent flap. Jackson gave permission; Doctor McGuire entered. “Good morning, General Jackson. How’s our patient?”

Stuart removed the arm from his eyes. “I have a headache, an upset stomach,” he raised the blanket and peered down into the darkness, “and no clothes on but my summer drawers.”

“I see you’re back to your old self,” McGuire laughed.

Chapter Thirty Six

Manassas Gap, Virginia
Last week of August 1864

Across the Potomac, thirty-five miles from Washington, Bull Run Creek meandered through the hilly Virginia countryside. Once green and lush, the hills and forests now bore deep scars from the two ferocious battles fought along the creek's banks. Both Southern victories. Both routs. To the west of the creek, a series of rolling hills, Matthews Hill and Henry House Hill, to name two, overlooked the creek. It was on Henry House Hill that Jackson forever became known as Stonewall. Now these hills bristled with Colonel Crutchfield's guns.

Lee cantered down the bank of the creek, still very much in command of the army. As he had promised himself outside Jackson's tent, he had sent his resignation to the Cabinet one week after the army was safely entrenched behind the Rappahannock. His letter had set off an immediate firestorm. President Davis and Secretary of War, James Seddon, had telegraphed him and beseeched him to reconsider. Lee had refused. The change in command needed to occur before those people marched from Washington City.

Three days later, on the morning train from Richmond, Davis had arrived at Lee's headquarters. Over breakfast, the president had bombarded his commanding general with words like duty, honor, and the Cause, but Lee had held firm. He was ill, and that infirmity was interfering with his ability to lead the army. It would be better to turn command over to Jackson.

At the mention of Jackson, Davis had held up his hands. Command would devolve on the senior Johnston and not Jackson. Lee had argued against such a suicidal course of action, but Davis had stubbornly stuck to his guns. Johnston would be given the army.

Lee had hesitated. Joe was not a fighter. He believed in waging a campaign of retreat, giving up territory he fully expected to win back in victory. Except Joe never put his troops to battle. When his opponent was the cautious McClellan, who hated to fight almost as much as Joe did, a strategy of retreat might have carried the day. But Grant was not McClellan. He would chase Joe to the gates of Richmond and throw his superior numbers against the Army of Northern Virginia. With their backs to the wall, how could his men fight? How could they win? No, Lee couldn't abandon them to such a fate.

Feeling manipulated, Lee had informed a relieved Davis that he would stay. After the president left, he had refused to come out of his tent the rest of the day.

Lee found Jackson standing under the remains of a once mighty oak. "If you want to make a dash toward the Valley, I won't stop you." He gestured to his left down the Warrenton Turnpike.

Jackson laughed. "Don't tempt me."

A rider galloped up and handed Lee a message. He scanned it and handed it to Jackson. Sheridan was riding through the Valley, destroying crops, confiscating livestock, and burning homes. Defeated at Winchester, General Breckenridge was in full retreat up the Valley. Sheridan had evacuated Winchester and burned it to the ground. Nothing remained but foundation stones and ash.

"I must return to the Valley," Jackson declared. "I'll take Rodes and the Light Division and…"

Lee interrupted his enraged Second Corps Commander. "That's what General Grant's hoping I'll do. Those people are in the Valley to divert our strength and cause a breakthrough here. Colonel Taylor, please find General Stuart for me on the double."

"You're going to send Stuart?" Lee heard the disapproval in Jackson's voice. "No, I should be the one who goes."

Lee put a hand on Jackson's shoulder. "If I could spare you, I'd send your whole corps into the Valley to teach those people a lesson, but I need you here."

Stuart rode up with his entourage of aides.

"General Stuart, I haven't seen you all day," Lee admonished, though his smile softened his words.

Ever since his confession at Stuart's bedside, Lee had spent many sleepless nights wondering what he should do. He loved his young lieutenant general like a son and probably had since West Point. Though he desired to tell Stuart the truth, in the end, he hesitated yet again. What if he pressed the point, and Jeb, embarrassed and uncomfortable, declined? Then what? To go through the rest of the war in mortified awkwardness? Lee couldn't risk that. Having Stuart near and being the recipient of that sunny smile would have to suffice. And, for now, it did.

Lee quickly explained the situation in the Valley. "I need you to ride and put a stop to it."

Stuart swiftly made his decisions. "I'll leave you Baker and Chambliss. I'll take Fitz and the Laurel Brigade." Stuart's aides scattered to round up the brigades he mentioned. “Don’t worry, sir, I’ll drive them from the Valley.”

The artillery on Henry House Hill began to bark. Pendleton approached with a message for Jackson. “If you gentlemen will excuse me,” Jackson said. "Stuart, you be careful.”

“I’m always careful.”

Jackson swung up on Little Sorrel. “Is that so? How’s your head?”

“Touché,” he laughed.

With a wave, Jackson rode off, followed by Pendleton and Morrison.

“Let me echo General Jackson’s sentiment,” Lee said. “You be careful.” He was surprised to find tears pricking his eyes.

“Don’t you worry, sir. I’ll come back.”

“General Reynolds! Come, have a cup of water.” Grant held up a mug. His jacket was off, his shirt sleeves were rolled up, and the habitual cigar was clenched between his teeth.

“Don’t mind if I do.” Reynolds wearily fell into a chair. He took off his hat and wiped beads of sweat from his forehead.

Grant handed him a mug. It was cold in his hand. He pressed it against his forehead.

“Long afternoon,” Grant said.

Reynolds grunted his agreement.

“For a time, I thought we had them…” Grant trailed off. “I guess we try again tomorrow.”

Reynolds held out his cup.

From the bucket between his feet, Grant produced a dipper and sloppily poured water into the cup. Water splashed them both. “Casualties?”

Reynolds wiped water from his pants. “I don’t have the preliminaries yet. I’ll forward them when I do.”

Grant dropped the dipper back into the bucket. “What brings you out here, John?”

“Sheridan. He marched everyone out of Winchester and burned it to the ground.” Grant smoked in silence. “You don’t seem surprised by the news.”

“I told Phil to obliterate the Valley. The crops and livestock must be kept out of Lee’s hands.”

“I agree, but he’s doing more than destroying crops and livestock. He’s burning down homes and destituting women and children.” Reynolds paused and waited for some kind of reaction, but Grant continued to smoke his cigar. "I can't condone such a barbarous act in my army. I will not." On this, he was firm.

Grant blew out a long stream of smoke. "Well, John, actually, it's my army."

Reynolds' laugh was bitter. "Yes, I know. And I'd be okay with that, if I wasn't the one Congress continually interrogated about the decisions you make in the field. So, please excuse me, if I feel somewhat responsible for what this army does. And what Sheridan is doing is beyond the pale."

"I'm trying to win this war. If destroying Winchester helps me achieve victory, then you should view it as a positive thing," Grant lectured.

How he hated that patronizing tone! "If I believed destroying Winchester helped the war effort, I'd have sent Sheridan into the Valley with a fistful of matches."

"Well, I think it does." Grant blew a smoke ring.

Reynolds sipped his water. "I don't think you've thought this strategy through. When we win this war…"

"Well, it's good to hear you finally admit it."

Reynolds' eyes flashed in anger. "I challenge you to tell me when I said we would lose." He poured out the water and gestured with the cup for Grant to tell him of such an occasion.

The moments dragged by. Silent. Uncomfortable. "Go on with your thought, John," Grant said dismissively.

Reynolds dropped his head and rested his chin on his chest. Why should he be the lone voice crying in the wilderness? He pulled on his hat and started to leave, but memories of Win, Buford, of grumpy old George Meade, and Couch stopped him. Hancock wouldn't have condoned such behavior from Sheridan. He would have busted the cavalry leader to private 20 minutes after meeting the surly little man. "You haven't thought one day past the war's end." Reynolds raised his head but refused to look at Grant.

"My job is to win the war." Grant threw his cigar on the ground and stamped out the ash. "What happens after that is up to the politicians. Once the South is whipped, I'm confident they'll let her up easy."

"It's either naïve or arrogant to think that the South would forgive her rapist just because he suddenly grew magnanimous and offered to forget all about the brutal assault."

Grant jerked back in his chair. "That's a bit harsh, John," he said in distaste.

"It's probably not harsh enough," Reynolds retorted. He took a deep breath. "Sheridan is sowing the seeds of a hatred that may never die. He's degrading the good people of the Valley, subjecting them to a power that is not merciful, but vindictive and petty."

Grant lit another cigar. "Where's your anger at Jeb Stuart for the raids he conducted last winter in your backyard? I don't think the citizens of Harrisburg will be too pleased to hear your concern for the Rebs after being kicked out of their homes for an entire winter."

"When the Rebs evacuated Harrisburg, the good people found their homes standing and their possessions intact. Stuart paid for most of the things he requisitioned, which is a nice way of saying stole," Reynolds conceded. "But there was nothing vindictive in what the Rebs did. Unlike Sheridan. And I won't be a party to it." He reached into his pocket, pulled out a letter, and handed it to Grant.

Grant stared at the paper like it was a snake ready to strike. "What's this?"

"It's my resignation."

Grant angrily ripped the letter into pieces.

"I don't think you can keep me from resigning."

"I don't want you to resign." Grant poured himself another cup of water. "I may disagree with you about what is being done in the Valley, but I'll have it stopped. I'll order Sheridan to only destroy what contributes to the Confederate war effort."

"But can you enforce the order?" Reynolds asked. He believed Sheridan would continue his rampage no matter what Grant commanded.

Grant smiled. "I have my ways."

In the hot August sun, Reynolds was slowly turning into a puddle. All the liquid in his body was oozing out his pores. He loosened his tie and removed his jacket. When that failed to bring him relief, he unbuttoned his vest, then discarded it in a fit of heat-produced pique.

For the past hour, a steady stream of sweaty, dust painted runners had descended on his field-quarters, bringing the same message: no breakthrough, ammunition running low, men exhausted from the heat, can they retreat? He had sent back the same reply to his generals: one more push! When the Rebels refused to budge, the runners began their treks all over again, except they were sweatier, dirtier, and, if possible, smellier. Well, I'm no rose myself, he thought after catching a whiff of Doubleday's courier.

Grant rode up, puffing vigorously on a cigar. "Are we going to do it?"

"Not today."

Grant absorbed the news. "I just heard from Sheridan." He wiped his sweaty brow on the corner of his jacket. "He was turned back at Edinburg."

A runner appeared from Warren. There was no breakthrough, ammunition was running low, men exhausted from the heat, can they please retreat? *The please was new.* Reynolds glanced at Grant to see if he wanted to opine on the battle. Grant just puffed away on his cigar. Reynolds sent the runner back to tell Warren to try again.

"So not today?" Grant asked.

"No."

Grant examined his cigar. "Sound the retreat. If Sheridan is turned back tomorrow, we'll return to Washington and rethink our strategy."

When the runners returned, they were told to pull back.

Chapter Thirty Seven

Washington City
Early October 1864

Grant and Reynolds waited in the hall outside Lincoln's office. They were not alone. Six men sat with them, waiting for John Hay to interview them for a position in the Bureau of Indian Affairs. Lincoln stepped out of his office. As one, the applicants rose, waved their resumes, and clambered for Lincoln's attention. Lincoln beat a hasty retreat into his office and slammed the door. When all was quiet again, the door cracked open and his large hand poked through. He gestured invitingly. Once more the applicants rushed the door. Grant and Reynolds shoved their way through the clamor. Reynolds managed to shut the door, but not before a job seeker thrust his qualifications into his hand.

Lincoln settled into a chair, which was conveniently placed in front of the fireplace. The week had produced unseasonably cold weather. An autumn rain drummed against the window panes. "Does this rain mean there won't be any further attempts to get after Lee until spring?" Lincoln hoped that wasn't the case. Lee might be safely bottled up in Virginia and Sherman slowly marching through Georgia, but the war was far from being won.

"I think it depends on whether we get a long Indian summer," Grant said, taking a cigar from his jacket pocket. "If we do, I'll try to break through at Manassas Gap again. I'd much rather spend the winter on the Rappahannock than in Washington."

The answer satisfied Lincoln. "So, General Grant, what do you think of General Lee now?" He asked, smiling mischievously.

Grant laughed but didn't answer.

Lincoln rubbed his hands together. "Well, gentlemen, besides the setback at Manassas, I must say that I'm very pleased with the whole campaign." He picked up a folder nestled between his body and the arm of the chair. "Except for one thing." He opened the folder; a pencil slid out. He caught the pencil before it hit the floor. Once the file was settled in his lap, he took his spectacles from his breast pocket and perused the report as if he couldn't quite believe what he was reading. "I asked you here because I'm very concerned about the heavy losses you sustained. Over 12,000 dead, 23,000 wounded, and 3,000 missing." He put the report down and stared reproachfully at the generals over the rim of his spectacles.

"Not to make light of the numbers," Reynolds remarked, "but only one-third of the wounded are seriously so. The rest will return to their regiments at some point."

Lincoln made a note on his report and re-added the figures. "Still, you've lost over a quarter of your fighting force. These are numbers I'll have a hard time explaining to Congress and even a harder time replacing. Is there any way you could go about this without so much death?"

"I have two advantages Lee doesn't," Grant said. "I have supplies, which, now that he is out of Pennsylvania, he'll have a hard time replenishing, and manpower. Lee can't replace the men he loses in battle. I can."

"Do you think I'm growing soldiers out back in the garden along with the peas and cucumbers?" Lincoln asked, amazed at Grant's blasé attitude toward his losses.

Grant shifted in his chair – first to the right then back to the left. "No, sir," he said hurriedly, "but the North has plenty of men who should be in uniform and aren't. Lee can only get weaker while my strength remains the same or increases. He might have turned me back at Bull Run Creek, but what I have planned next will finish him." Grant reached into his portfolio and handed Lincoln a sheaf of papers.

Lincoln took his time and read over the plans. With each turn of the page he grew more encouraged. Grant didn't lack for aggression, and Lincoln always found that refreshing.

"As you can see, sir," Grant said when Lincoln turned the last page, "four armies will converge on Richmond from different directions and force Lee into the extensive breastworks around the city. We'll starve him out."

From Reynolds came a loud exclamation. "You don't agree, General?" Lincoln asked, surprised by Reynolds' disapproval.

"I haven't seen General Grant's plans," Reynolds backpedaled, shrinking into his chair.

Grant waved his cigar in irritation. "Speak freely, John."

"I just don't believe it'll be that easy to drive Lee into the Richmond trenches. It removes the one weapon we don't have an answer for: Jackson's maneuverability. When he gets loose, we usually get routed."

"What about it?" Lincoln asked his lieutenant general.

Grant shrugged. "Sheridan in the Valley will break Jackson off from Lee."

Reynolds leaned forward. "It didn't work in August."

Grant took a short breath and blew it out angrily. "That's because the force Sheridan commanded was too small. I'll not make that mistake again. This time, the force I send down the Valley will demand Jackson's full attention."

Reynolds yielded, but Lincoln observed that the Pennsylvanian was not convinced.

"When do you think the Army of the Cumberland will arrive?" Lincoln asked, concerned about the approaching winter.

Grant handed Lincoln a telegram. It was from General Thomas. The Army of the Cumberland was already on the move. "If the weather stays nice, it will take Thomas about five weeks to reach the Virginia border," Grant explained.

Lincoln didn't hide his disappointment. Thomas wouldn't arrive until the middle of November, which didn't leave much time for campaigning. "Can I keep this?" Lincoln indicated the papers. "Good. Now, I have one more topic to discuss, then I'll let you get back to running the war. What do you propose to do about General McClellan?"

"I haven't forgotten about my prisoner." Grant stubbed out his cigar in the spittoon by his chair. "Just this morning, I sent him a telegram and outlined his options. He could be out of prison this evening if he chooses."

Lincoln raised a quizzical eyebrow. "You're not going to allow me a say in the matter?"

"Of course," Grant deferred. "But I would advise against it. If you intervened, the matter would just become politicized."

"Then I'll stay out of it." Lincoln stood. "I want to invite you both to dinner. Perhaps next week?" He walked toward the door.

"That depends entirely on the weather, sir." Grant shook the President's hand and followed Reynolds out the door.

"Telegram for you, General," the guard shouted through the small barred window in the heavy iron door. A slip of paper skidded into the cell.

McClellan picked the scrap from off the cold stone floor. He couldn't read it in the dim light, so he dragged his chair over to the high window and climbed upon it. The telegram was from Grant. His successor was willing to set him free if he resigned his commission in the army.

McClellan wadded up the thin piece of paper and hurled it across the cell. When that didn't assuage his anger, he picked up the chair and threw it against the wall. It clattered to the ground intact. He stormed over and heaved it above his head. Crash! A leg broke away and a splinter cut his cheek. Crash! Crash! All that was left in his hands was the backrest. Exhausted, he tossed it to the ground and threw himself upon the wooden plank that masqueraded as his mattress. He wouldn't give Lincoln the satisfaction of resigning.

"Hear that!" His voice bounced all around the cell. "I won't give you the satisfaction."

When he had first been arrested, he had waited patiently for his legion of fans to storm Fort Hamilton as the French peasants had done the Bastille. He had waited in vain. Lee had retreated, and Grant had caught up with the Rebels, first at Gettysburg, and then again at the Potomac where the Confederate dead numbered in the thousands. In their relief, the citizens no longer cared that Lincoln had run roughshod over their constitutional rights. Nothing mattered but Lee was going and then was gone.

As the months passed by, the people's silence didn't shake McClellan's faith that God had great plans for his life. This cell was a crucible, a testing ground, to qualify him for leadership. The longer the silence; the more convinced he became. Now, God was tempting him with escape. This was his Gethsemane moment. Two choices lay before him. He could resign and be rid of this torment, or he could wait upon God and allow God to vindicate him.

He preferred the latter. Despite what the headlines declared, he had not called for Lincoln's assassination in his impromptu speech on the front porch. He had been very careful not to do so. For the newspapers to suggest otherwise was a bold-face lie. For Grant to arrest him on such a flimsy charge was a travesty of justice. To be jailed like a common criminal was an indignity. But to be forgotten by the very people who had screamed his name only five months ago, well, it was his cross to bear. He would participate in Lincoln's show trial and prove his innocence. When he was acquitted, the people, his people, would demand that he rule over them.

His attorney, on the other hand, the brilliant and expensive Richard Bayne was certain McClellan would be found guilty. After all, the newspapers had winnowed down his speech to one damning statement: *Shall we slay the tyrant just as Brutus slew the tyrant?* The very next line, when McClellan had shouted that he wouldn't join his name to the likes of Brutus or Judas Iscariot, had gone unreported and had been quickly forgotten by the crowd who stood on his front lawn. They all suffered from collective amnesia and it put McClellan in a tight spot.

The rusty hinges of his cell door squealed. Bayne strode into the cell. "Good afternoon, General."

McClellan didn't get up. "Richard."

"Before I left my office, I received a copy of General Grant's telegram."

"He shouldn't have bothered!" McClellan bolted to his feet. Bayne groaned; McClellan heard it. "I didn't call for the death of the president!" He declared hotly.

"No, you didn't," Bayne replied with understated patience. "But it is impossible to prove that now."

"Truth has no place in a court of law?" In agitation, McClellan paced the narrow cell. Seven steps up and seven steps back.

"Not when lies have become part of the public consciousness." McClellan stopped pacing. "I'm sorry, General, but the prosecutor will be able to supply a long line of witnesses who heard you say that the president should be assassinated."

McClellan threw himself back on his mattress. "But if I resign my commission, I'll lose any chance to recover my political aspirations."

"Even if your name was cleared in court, you'll not be named the Democratic candidate for president. It's over, General. The crowd has turned against you."

That was true enough for the present. The people had proven to be very fickle. But, McClellan didn't consider it the liability his attorney apparently did. After all, the chief characteristic of any crowd was its fickleness. It never knew what it wanted until someone told it. "The crowd can be recaptured," he said. "Look at how they holler Lincoln's name."

"That's because Lincoln is winning." Bayne cleared his throat. "And to be honest, that is something you didn't do."

Oh, what he wouldn't give for his sword. He would gladly run the lawyer through for suggesting that he was at fault for what happened on the Virginia peninsula. "That is because that great ape wouldn't give me the necessary manpower," McClellan educated the lawyer. "He was too worried about Jackson. How many telegrams did I have to endure, warning me about that ragtag army in the Valley? He cost me my glory!" McClellan sat up and punched the stone wall in anger. Bayne shook his head in frustration. "What?" He yelled, shaking his stinging fist in an attempt to alleviate the pain.

"I'd need to put you on the stand. How can I do that with your deep-seated anger toward Lincoln?"

"I can control my temper!" He shouted, proving just the opposite.

"It's time to realize that your dreams have slipped through your fingers. You can't retrieve them. Not in today's political climate. Lincoln could reinstate the election tomorrow and be re-elected. He is close to winning the war. To sit in this damp cell and martyr yourself for some delusion of grandeur is a fool's errand. And I've never known you to be a fool. Take the deal, and let's go home." McClellan lay back down. "I've been hesitant to tell you, but no one remembers you. They don't discuss you in their parlors or in their men's clubs except to joke about you. That's what you've become, a national punch line."

A stab of anguish pierced McClellan's heart. He turned his face to the wall. He closed his eyes and prayed for a sign.

"If you're ready, General, I can have you released today."

The word *ready* ricocheted through his soul like the very voice of God. In a split second, everything was explained: his arrest, his imprisonment, even the cruel reality Bayne had just laid out. The people were simply not ready to receive him as their savior. Just as the people had not been ready to receive the blessed Savior when He had come. They had rejected Him, too. McClellan wanted to laugh as fear gave way to relief. And just like the Savior, his rejection was temporary also. When the people were ready to repent of their sins, they would beg him to save them. And he would.

He sat up and smiled. He had passed the test. "Call the commandant. I'll resign my commission."

Chapter Thirty Eight

The Rappahannock River
December 24, 1864

The common area around Lee's headquarters was empty except for the dried leaves the arctic wind swept from one side of the clearing to the other. Lee's aides had retreated into the relative warmth of their tents. The remnants of this morning's snow flurries clung to the bottom of barren trees. The yellow sun in the slate gray sky seemed disinterested in warming the small camp. Stuart dismounted; his nose reddened by the cold. He blew on his gauntleted hands, pulled two presents out of his saddlebags, and barged into Lee's tent unannounced.

"Merry Christmas!" He boomed.

Startled, Lee turned toward him. He held a letter in his hand. Tears streamed down his face.

"General Lee, what's wrong?"

Lee handed him the letter. Mary had written from Richmond. Charlotte, Rooney's wife, was dead.

"I have nothing left of him now," Lee said softly.

Stuart crouched down and stared up into Lee's wounded eyes. "I'm so sorry."

Lee retrieved the letter. "I loved them like one person." He read the painful words again.

The loss of Charlotte was already stirring up the old sadness over Rooney's death. Stuart didn't want to leave Lee alone in his grief. And he wouldn't! "General Lee, I insist you come and spend the holidays with me."

Lee's smile was heartrending. "No, you go and be with your family."

"I don't think I'm going to take no for an answer." He rose and walked in a small circle to relieve his cramping thighs.

"Jeb," Lee protested feebly, "you haven't seen your family for almost two years."

Stuart didn't reply. He gathered up Lee's shaving kit and laid it on the neatly made bed. Gauntlets and great coat were added to the growing pile.

"What of Flora?" Lee tried again. "She's not prepared to receive a guest."

"Flora won't mind." He put his hands on his hips and looked around the tent. "Now, where are your saddlebags? Let's get you packed."

Lee pointed under his bed. Stuart dragged out the bags. He shoved things into them in rapid succession. Lee reached into one of the desk's many cubbyholes and pulled out a wrapped package. "Pack this, too."

Stuart's eyes gleamed with curiosity. He turned the package over and examined it carefully. He held it next to his ear and shook it. Nothing rattled.

"You can open it on Christmas and not a minute before," Lee admonished with a laugh. "So put it in my bag before you break it."

Stuart shook it again. "What is it?"

"In my bag, General!"

With one more shake, Stuart thrust the present in one of the saddlebags. "Well, I think that's everything. Just let me go inform Mr. Taylor where you'll be."

"Tell him I'll be back the day after Christmas." Lee held up his hand to stop Stuart's loud objections. "I'll spend Christmas with you, but I want you to have time alone with your family."

Because he had no other choice, Stuart consented. He slung the saddlebags over his shoulders and went to find Taylor.

It was almost dark when Lee and Stuart rode down the main street of Trimmer's Crossing, a village on the Alexandria and Orange Railroad. Up ahead, Lee spied a small, dark haired boy wearing a large plumed hat. He was swinging back and forth on the wrought-iron gate that guarded the walk of a large brick house. The use of the house was a gift from one of Major McClellan's relative's friend-of-a-friend. Lee couldn't follow Stuart's winding trail of who was related to whom and to what degree, or how exactly Major McClellan wound up with an invitation to use the house over Christmas. Lee was just happy that McClellan was spending Christmas in Richmond and had offered Stuart the house in his place. Stuart jumped at the chance and inveigled a second invitation for Jackson. Stuart's leave would end the day after the New Year. Jackson would arrive the next day and stay for ten.

The gate swung forward. This time the boy's patience was rewarded. He saw the horses, hitched up his pants, and ran into the house. The generals rode up to the gate. The front door opened. A pretty, young woman, dressed in a plain green dress, stepped outside, followed by the young boy, who was jumping up and down. When Lee and Stuart reached the bottom of the steps, the child suddenly dashed across the porch and leapt into Stuart's arms.

Stuart caught him with a loud oomph and staggered backward under the boy's weight.

"Pa!" Jimmie Stuart released his pent-up excitement in one exclamation. "Pa, I missed you so much!" He squeezed Stuart's neck and gave him a big kiss.

"Who are you?" Stuart asked, perplexed.

The boy's eyes grew large. "I'm your little boy." Stuart said nothing. "Jimmie." He prompted.

Stuart shook his head. "No, no, you're too big to be my Jimmie. Last time I saw him, he was knee high to a grasshopper. Why, you're almost a man."

"That's 'cause I was almost three when you left for the North. Now, I'm four and a half, and I done growed."

"That must be it," Stuart laughed. He tickled the boy, who shrieked with delight. "Now, let me say hello to your mother." Stuart switched the boy to his back. "Are you set back there?"

"Yes, Pa." He blew Stuart's plumes. They tickled his nose and he giggled.

Stuart climbed the stairs. He hesitated at the top but only for a moment. Lee smiled. Stuart wasn't reticent by nature.

"Oh, my darling Flora." Stuart picked her up in a bear hug and swung her around and around. "I can't believe it, but you've gotten prettier." He kissed her. He tried to set her down, but she clung to him. He kissed her again. They put their foreheads together and whispered things Lee was glad he couldn't hear, for such sentiments weren't meant for a stranger's ears. Another kiss. When Stuart finally released her, Flora was breathless and discomfited. Tears on her cheeks announced her great happiness. When Stuart stepped away, she grabbed his hand. "General Lee, this is my Flora." He gave her hand a tender squeeze.

"I'm pleased to meet you, General Lee." With her free hand, Flora pushed her dark hair back in place. A flush grew over her contented face.

"I hope I'm not intruding."

"Not at all." The free hand now fanned her hot face. "Oh, it appears we have a guest." Flora turned their attention to the gate. An older man walked toward them. He had a basket slung over his arm.

He stopped at the bottom of the stairs and addressed Lee. "Sir, my son serves in the Second Corps with General Jackson. I wanted to bring you something for your Christmas dinner." He took a pie from the basket and held it out. "My wife made it. She's famous for her mincemeat pie."

Lee accepted the gift. "This is very kind of you."

"Thank you for taking such good care of my boy. Now, I'll not be disturbing you any more tonight. Merry Christmas."

"Merry Christmas," Lee returned.

"Did he just give you a whole pie?" Jimmie asked in amazement.

Lee winked at the boy "He did, and, after dinner, if it's alright with your Mama, I'll cut you a big piece."

Jimmie climbed down to get a closer look at the pie.

"Flora, where's Ginny?" Stuart asked.

"She's taking a nap, but I'll fetch her." Flora led him into the house.

"How would you like to carry the pie into the kitchen for me?" Lee asked the boy.

"Yes, sir." Jimmie took the pie and walked, oh, so carefully, down the hall.

Lee joined Stuart in the living room. Stuart removed his hat and gauntlets and laid them on the table by the door. He crossed the room to the large fireplace. A mirror hung over the mantle. He smoothed his hair and raked his fingers through his red beard. He saw Lee staring at him in the mirror's reflection. Stuart grinned then straightened his tie. "I've been waiting for this moment a long time."

He didn't have to wait any longer. Flora came into the room. Lee faded into the background. Like the whispered endearments on the porch, this moment didn't call for a witness, but deep down, he was glad he was here. What made his young lieutenant general happy, Lee was discovering, made him equally happy.

Virginia was dressed in a white linen nightgown. Her blond curls were in disarray and her blue eyes were still brushed with sleep. "My darling," Flora announced, "this is Virginia Pelham."

Tears filled Stuart's eyes. His hand brushed a gold spun curl. "Oh, Flora," he whispered, "she's beautiful." A finger caressed the baby's cheek. "I've a little girl again." He took her in his arms. "Hello, my darling. Do you know who I am? I'm your Pa."

There was a knock at the door. Jimmie ran down the hall. "I'll get it!" He shouted.

"I know I've been gone a long time, but I want you to know that I've held you every night in my dreams." Ginny laid her head on his shoulder. In typical Stuart fashion, she fell asleep the moment her eyes closed. Stuart gathered Flora to him and wept.

"General Lee, come quick!" Jimmie cried from the hallway. "There's a lady here, and she's got a pie and a cake!"

The house was quiet. The children were asleep, and Stuart and Flora had retired to their room. Lee laid his Bible in his lap and pondered the fact that for an entire evening, he had not been bowed down with the overwhelming devastation of his losses. For so long, he had struggled against an unrelenting melancholy that made him feel as if he was living under a glass jar. Each morning, he woke, disappointed that death had not come in the night to relieve him of his sorrow. But this evening, life had returned as suddenly as spring to the winter landscape. He could think of Fitzhugh, Annie, and even dear Charlotte without drowning in sadness. Perhaps he had finally reached that place Joe Johnston spoke about the morning after dear Fitzhugh's death – where the anguish lifts and all that remains is the joy their lives had brought. And there was so much joy to remember!

From the Bible, he reverently read the words that marked the season. He held the small, worn book close to his chest for a brief moment then placed it on the table next to the bed. He blew out the candle and lay down. The mended linens smelled of lavender. After sleeping in his camp-bed for the better part of year, he didn't know if he could sleep in such feathery comfort.

A hand shook his shoulder. Lee came awake with a start. *Were those people attacking?* He smelled the lavender and remembered that he was not along the Rappahannock, but in the library of Major McClellan's relative's friend-of-a-friend. His shoulder was shaken again. He turned over. In the glow of the firelight, he found himself staring into inquiring blue eyes.

"Do you want to be my grandpa?" Jimmie asked.

Not expecting such a question, Lee sat up.

Jimmie flopped his elbows down on the bed and gazed up at him. "My best friend Billy Miller has a grandpa, and his grandpa takes him fishin' and to the store to buy him candy and all sorts of fun stuff. I wanted to go fishin' with 'em, but Billy Miller told me to get my own grandpa. Well, that just made me mad, so I hit him. Ma made me sit in the corner for an hour 'til I was sorry. I ain't sorry, though," he confided.

"You have a pa to take you fishing and buy you candy. Yes, that's a job for a father," Lee counseled gently.

"No, it ain't." Jimmie sat down on the edge of the bed. "Billy Miller's father is at home. He got wounded marchin' with ole Stonewall. Wish I could march with ole Stonewall," this was said with wistful yearning, "now, he just sits on the front porch with his wooden leg. He don't do nuttin' with Billy. Billy's grandpa is the one who takes him to the fishin' hole. Do you got any other grandkids?"

"I had two, but they died." They were Fitzhugh's children dead in infancy.

"So did my sister, Flora. That made Ma and Pa sad. Now, I got me another sister, Ginny. She don't do much. Girls are borin'." The tiny oracle sighed in weary wisdom and plucked at the comforter.

"I have four daughters. I think girls are wonderful."

Jimmie pondered that for a moment. "Well, they don't like fishin' or nuttin' like that. If you were my grandpa, we would go fishin' right?" He raised and lowered his eyebrows in rapid succession. The cajoling smile erupted into a tiny replica of Stuart's sunny one.

Lee was captured by the son just as he had been captured by the father. "I couldn't take you fishing until after the war."

Jimmie kicked his slippered feet while he considered Lee's statement. "That's okay, providin' you promise now to take me fishin' and buy me candy. Then when Billy Miller says I ain't got no grandpa, I can say yes I do too. And I won't be mean like Billy Miller and not share my grandpa. He can come fishin' with us if he wants to. But you must sit next to me and make a fuss over me. Okay?"

Lee bit his lip to keep from laughing. "Well, Jimmie, we'll have to ask your pa's permission."

"He'll say yes. He always does," Jimmie said confidently. "I can read, you know. Want me to read you sump'em?"

Lee didn't want the evening to end, so he agreed. Jimmie sprang off the bed, ran out of the room, and scampered up the stairs. When he reached the top, Stuart's door opened. "Jimmie, why aren't you in bed?" Stuart asked his son. "Santa Claus won't come if you're not asleep. Now, scoot."

"I'm goin'."

Lee laughed. There would be no further talk of grandfathers or reading demonstrations tonight. He lay back down, enveloped in lavender and feathers. Upstairs a door creaked followed by a squeak of stairs. A moment later, Jimmie ran into the room, carrying a large book.

Lee sat back up. "I believe your pa told you to get in bed," he scolded.

Without another word, Jimmie climbed into the bed and snuggled next to Lee. "I am in bed," he cackled, quite pleased at coming up with such a clever solution. He opened the book. "Can you light a candle or sump'em so I can see? I ain't allowed to play with matches."

Lee lit the candle. Jimmie turned to the first page. He pointed at a big letter *A* in the center of the page. "A, is for apple…ant…"

Lee listened until Jimmie fell asleep around *K* is for kites. He picked up the boy and placed him on the couch in front of the fireplace. He covered him with the worn comforter and stoked the fire to warm the room. He blew out the candle. With a laugh, he went back to sleep.

Chapter Thirty Nine

Lee opened his bedroom door. "Jimmie's in here."

"What's he doing in there?" Flora asked. She had just come down the hall from the kitchen in response to Stuart's announcement that Jimmie wasn't in his room, and, no, he didn't know where the little boy had gotten to.

"He came to read to me last night."

She blushed. "I'm sorry, sir."

"He reads quite well," Lee said to relieve her of her embarrassment.

She beamed with pride. "Jeb," she called up the steps, "he's in General Lee's room."

Stuart came down the stairs carrying Virginia. He peeked past Lee and saw his son still asleep on the couch. "Jimmie, Santa Claus came during the night. Don't you want to look at all your presents?"

Jimmie's eyes flew open.

"Just his stocking before church," Flora said, before returning to the kitchen.

Jimmie climbed off the sofa. "Grandpa, want to look at my presents with me?" Stuart's eyes widened in surprise as Jimmie pulled on Lee's hand, insisting grandpa come and look at his presents.

"You go ahead, Jimmie." The little boy dashed out of the room. Lee began a rapid explanation. "He visited me last night and asked me to be his grandfather. His little friend has one, so he wants one, too. I said we needed to get your permission first."

Stuart was stunned. "You'd do that for my son?"

"I'd be delighted. But only if it were okay with you and Flora," he added quickly.

Gasps of wonder and happiness emanated from the living room.

A gasp of wonder emanated from Stuart also. "It would be an answer to our prayers. Since Flora's father betrayed us by staying with the Union, the children have only had my mother close by. And…" He stopped and blushed scarlet.

Lee observed his reddening cheeks. "And what?"

"After the war…I mean…when we win…well, it would give us a strong reason to stay in contact. A reason to visit each other, I mean."

Lee gave Stuart's face a thorough study. "Why would you want to stay in touch with an old man like me?"

"Why, General Lee, I I…" Stuart choked on his words. Unable to meet Lee's eyes, he fiddled with the trim on Virginia's dress.

Lee watched Stuart intently. A glimmer of hope sparked. Was Stuart going to confess his love? Perhaps this fine young man, blushing profusely at the moment, would welcome the idea of Lee being a father to him. He was about to press the point when Flora stepped into the hall and announced breakfast was ready.

"Coming!" Stuart darted down the hall, leaving a disappointed Lee alone in the doorway.

Lee threw his great coat across his arm and walked into the living room. Stuart was seated on the worn brocade couch. His Bible was open, and he was reading psalms to a sleepy Ginny.

"So, you're leaving us already?" Stuart asked.

Lee was warmed by the unhappiness in his voice. Since Stuart's aborted confession, he had covertly observed his young lieutenant general but had been unable to gain any more insight into his feelings. "I should have left two days ago." Ginny held out her arms. Lee set down his gauntlets and scooped her up. "You're such a pretty little girl." He gave her a peck on the forehead and handed her to Stuart. "Now, where is that new grandson of mine?"

"Out on the front porch. He thinks your admirers have come to see him," Stuart laughed.

"I've already kissed Flora goodbye and thanked her for her hospitality." He pulled on his coat and picked up the gauntlets. "No, no, don't get up. I'll say goodbye to Jimmie, and then I'll be off. Thank you for these last few days, Jeb. They've been a tonic for my weary soul."

He left the parlor and stepped out onto the porch. His appearance was greeted with claps of joy from the gaggle of gawkers that stood sentinel at the gate day and night. The men waved and the women fluttered their handkerchiefs at him.

Jimmie waved back. He was decked out in his new Christmas finery: a red silk-lined cape, fighting jacket with plenty of braid, a yellow silk sash, and new plumes for his hat. He had spent the morning pretending the porch railing was Centurion. Throughout breakfast, the adults had been treated to his high-pitched voice calling "boots and saddles, boys," "let's go 'turion," and singing the ever ready *Jine the Cavalry* to the extreme pleasure of his father.

Lee sat next to the little boy. "I have to leave now, Jimmie."

Jimmie wrapped his arms around the sleeve of Lee's great coat and rested his cheek against the rough wool. "You gotta go back to the war?"

"Yes, I do."

"Are you takin' all them presents with you?" Jimmie referred to the continuous stream of baked and canned goods that had entered the house since Lee's arrival.

"I'm taking some. The rest I've left with your Pa and Ma."

"How come no one gave you any candy?" Jimmie turned somber eyes up at him.

"I wondered the very same thing," Lee confided to Jimmie's approval. "But there was a candy cane in your stocking."

"I already ate it." Jimmie untangled his arms, put his chin in his hand, and sighed dramatically in disappointment.

Lee smothered a smile. "Jimmie, I was thinking of taking some candy back to headquarters. Would you like to come to the store and help me pick out some?"

"Can I get some, too?"

"If your Pa says you can."

Jimmie sprang to his feet and ran inside. The door banged after him. "Pa! Pa!"

"Jimmie! Quiet! You'll wake your sister!"

Jimmie ran into the living room and threw himself on the couch. Ginny lay asleep in a low crib at Stuart's feet. "Grandpa's gonna to the store to get some candy. Can I get some, too?"

Stuart put down his Bible and gave his son a piercing stare. "Candy cost money. Do you have any?"

Jimmie stood and dug into his pant pocket. He pulled out the three shiny pennies he had found in his Christmas stocking.

"Why, you're a regular Midas!"

He didn't know what a Midas was, but it sounded good, so he smiled in pleasure.

"But I'm thinking you might need more candy than those three pennies can buy, so..." Stuart produced his coin purse and handed his son a dime.

Jimmie stared at the shiny silver coin with reverence. "Thank you, Pa!"

"You obey your Grandfather Lee, you hear me," Stuart commanded.

"Yes, sir," he saluted.

"Do you have anything for me?" Jimmie threw his arms around Stuart's neck and kissed him. Stuart tickled his belly and produced a peal of laughter. "Sshhh! You'll wake your sister."

"But you were ticklin' me!" Jimmie protested his scolding.

"I'll tickle you again, if you don't get going."

The front door's bang announced his departure.

"General Lee!" The storeowner declared with a mixture of surprise and awe when Lee walked in with Jimmie. He put down the barrels of flour he was carrying and quickly unrolled his shirtsleeves over his large forearms. "Welcome to my store. My name is Ryne." He gestured proudly at the half-empty shelves. The store was spotless and the windows sparkled in the winter sun. Ryne shook Lee's hand then looked down at Jimmie. "And who might this be?"

"I'm General Stuart, Junior," Jimmie said with a salute.

"We've come to buy some candy," Lee announced.

"Of course. My selection's not what it was before the war, but I believe you'll find something to satisfy." He gestured for them to follow him down the center aisle.

Jimmie stopped dead in his tracks. "Grandpa! Look!" He pointed at a display of fishing rods.

"Just a moment," Lee called to Ryne.

"I can't reach it. Can you get it for me?" Jimmie asked. He clapped his hands in anticipation as Lee pulled a pole down from the shelf. "Oh, this one is much better than Billy Miller's pole," he said, after examining the pole carefully.

"How much is it?" Lee asked the storekeeper.

"Three dollars."

"I can buy it," Jimmie said. "I'm rich." He handed the pole to Lee, dug in his pocket, and produced the dime and three pennies.

"You are rich!" Lee exclaimed. "Not only can you buy the pole, but you'll have enough left over to buy some candy, too."

The storekeeper pried the rod from Jimmie's grasp. "I'll wrap this up for you. The candy is over there." He pointed to a small display next to the register.

Lee stood before the candy counter and waited while the little boy analyzed the contents of each jar. "Well?" Lee winked at Ryne, who stood poised to obey Jimmie's command.

"I want one of those and one of those and one of those and five of those and five of those." Jimmie pointed at the glass jars filled with sugary sweets.

"Is that all?" Ryne grinned at Lee.

Jimmie pointed at a large container of licorice whips. "And six of those."

"Give him what he wants," Lee said.

The storekeeper filled a large bag full of candy and handed it over the counter to Jimmie.

"We have to pay now," Lee said. "I'll need your money." Jimmie gave Lee the coins. "How much do I owe?" Lee picked up the pole and handed it to Jimmie. "Can you carry all that?"

"Yeah!" He held the rod in one hand and his haul of candy in the other.

"You owe me nothing."

Lee demurred. "I can't just take them."

"Sir, your money is no good here. I have two sons with General Pickett. If they found out, if their mother found out, that I was ill-mannered enough to charge you for your purchase, I'd never hear the end of it. You carry the hope of us all on your shoulders. It's we, who are in your debt. God bless you, sir!"

Touched, Lee thanked the man for his generosity. Ryne handed him a small bag filled with hooks, bobbins, and line for the pole. Lee thanked him again and dropped the bag into Jimmie's outstretched hand. They made their goodbyes to Ryne and exited the store.

At Lee's appearance on the front step, his fan club clapped and cheered.

"Why do all these people keep clappin' for me?" Jimmie asked in bewilderment.

"Because they love you." Lee waved. Jimmie imitated him. Lee shook hands and spoke kindly to those gathered around Traveller. He swung up on the gray gelding, grabbed Jimmie by the coat collar, and lifted the little boy up on the saddle.

Lee addressed the crowd. "I don't have to tell you that we still have plenty of hard fighting left. Please continue to pray for us." He waved a final time and cantered down the street. He let Jimmie down in front of the house.

"Grandpa, you didn't buy no candy for yourself."

"You're right. I guess I forget."

"Do you want some of mine?" He held up the bag of candy.

"Well, maybe a piece of licorice." Jimmie opened the bag and handed Lee a long licorice whip. "Thank you. Now run into the house, so your Pa will know you have returned safe."

Lee waited until the door closed behind the boy. He urged Traveller forward and started the journey to the Rappahannock, no longer a prisoner of grief or despair. The blush on Stuart's face when he choked off his confession was the best Christmas present Lee could have hoped to receive. More dear than Stuart's actual gift: the volumes his father, Light-Horse Henry Lee, had authored on his campaigns during the Revolution. Stuart's blush gave him hope that his young lieutenant general might be open to a father/son relationship. When Stuart returned from leave, Lee would watch, wait for an opening, and attack with all the alacrity he was famous for. He was so happy that he burst into a rendition of *Jine the Cavalry*.

Chapter Forty

Trimmers Crossing had barely recovered from the whirlwind visit of Lee and Stuart before it braced itself for the arrival of the great Stonewall Jackson. In the brief calm, the town's ladies baked and arranged their wares in beautiful baskets to present to the hero of the Valley, Chancellorsville, and Falling Waters. Yesterday morning, the general's wife and daughter had arrived from Richmond. Then, in the evening, a wagon had pulled up and packages and foodstuffs had been carried into the house for the most scandalous amount of time.

At dawn, the children gathered at the edge of town and competed to be the first to announce the news of Stonewall's arrival. They waited long into the afternoon. Impatient squabbles over why Stonewall was late broke out between the freezing sentinels. But all the disagreements were forgotten when two soldiers were spotted on the road south of town. Miniature Paul Reveres ran through the streets, shouting at the top of their lungs: "Stonewall is coming!" "Stonewall is coming!"

Clothed in their Sunday best, the citizens swarmed their porches to catch a glimpse of the gallant knight on his faithful charger. They could not have been more disillusioned at the reality: Jackson, astride Little Sorrel, dressed in his black raincoat and weather-stained kepi. Jim had given the coat a thorough cleaning, but it was still in bad shape; especially when compared to the color and excitement of Jeb Stuart's finery. Once they recovered from their disappointment, they greeted him warmly.

Jackson returned their hellos by lifting his hat, embarrassed, as usual, by all the fuss. Joe Morrison rode along side, waving and helloing enthusiastically. The two men went up the walk, waved one last time from the porch, and disappeared inside the house.

Anna ran down the hallway to greet them. "Merry Christmas, darling." She rushed into Jackson's waiting arms. The cold clung to his coat, and she shivered in his embrace. He tried to release her, but she wouldn't let him. Jackson was cognizant of Morrison standing behind him, watching the tender reunion. He felt as self-conscious as a teenager in the throes of first love. "Merry Christmas." He gave her a quick peck, but she refused to accept such a meager offering. Her arms went around his neck, and she pulled his head down to her. He kissed her.

Anna stroked his cheek before greeting her younger brother. "Joe, let me look at you. You're so thin! Didn't Tom feed you in Pennsylvania?"

Morrison laughed and kissed her. "Merry Christmas."

Jackson took off his coat and hat and handed them to his brother-in-law. He began a systematic search of the rooms for Julia. He spied her sitting on the couch, looking at a book. She was dressed in a bright blue dress. Her blonde curls fell around her face. Pretty as a picture! His little girl! He marched into the living room and fought the urge to swoop her up in his arms as he had done that long ago morning when he said goodbye.

Anna came and stood next to him. “Julia,” she called softly. Julia looked up from her book. Jackson’s breath left in a rush. She looked just like him, down to the blue-gray eyes. “Here is your Papa, come home from the war.”

Jackson knelt down next to the couch. “Hello, Julia.”

She dropped the book and edged away from him until she was next to Anna. Then, she bolted off the couch and hid behind her mother’s skirts.

Her rejection was a mortal wound. Throughout their time apart, during the long marches and sleepless nights, he had dreamt of this reunion, playing it over and over in his mind. She was supposed to run into his arms, not away from him in terror. He tried not to let his disappointment show, but Anna knew him too well. She advised him to give Julia time to get use to the idea of having her Papa home.

To distract him, Anna gestured at the ornate Christmas tree that consumed the corner of the room. Presents spilled out from underneath. “I can’t believe you have so many packages for us.”

“Where did you get the tree?” Joe asked. He plopped down in a chair by the window and waved to a clump of children standing at the gate and calling for Stonewall to come out and play.

“It was a present from General Stuart. Julia and I decorated it yesterday.”

“You did, why that’s wonderful,” Jackson said to Julia, who had appeared from behind Anna to stare at him. At the sound of his voice, she disappeared once more into the skirt’s folds.

Among the many presents was a small table and four chairs. On top of the table sat a box with a large red bow. This was Julia’s main gift from her father: a china tea set.

While in Harrisburg, Jackson had asked Stuart what little girls liked to play with. Stuart, preparing to leave on his first raid since being declared fit to return to active duty, had smiled and winked. Two weeks later he returned, and, pleased as Jack Horner, held up a box.

“What do you have there, Stuart?” Jackson asked from behind the big desk; commentaries on Isaiah stacked up around him.

"Come, see!" Stuart placed the box on a side table. With a flourish, he opened it and took out a tiny teapot. "This, my friend, will give you many hours of enjoyment." Stuart handed the teapot to Jackson.

Jackson was afraid his large hand would crush the delicate china. "I don't know what to say." Gingerly, he set the teapot down.

"You will. Nothing compares with sipping imaginary tea from a tiny teacup, poured by your daughter while she mimics her mother with complete accuracy." He took out one of the tiny teacups. "For a father, it's heaven on earth. Flora loved having them, and even though I had to share her attention with her three favorite dollies, I never missed them."

"Do you think Julia will be too young?" Jackson placed a tiny cup on a tiny saucer. Even his pinkie was too fat for the cup's handle.

"Not forever." Stuart emptied the box of the rest of the dishes and, like a merchant, displayed them on the coffee table. "I'm not through, either. The carpenter owes me a favor, so he's making you a table and four chairs."

"I'll pay him," Jackson insisted.

"Oh, no, you won't either. He owes me. Believe you me, having him make you the furniture is letting him off easy." Stuart playfully poured tea into Jackson's cup.

"What did you do? Save his life."

"Something like that!" Stuart laughed.

Anna pointed to the few packages she had brought from Richmond. "I was hard pressed to find anything suitable. When the ships came in from England, I did manage to get you a few things. You too, Joe."

"This is all I want." Jackson hugged her close.

The late morning sun poked its rays through the mended curtains and cast a fiery glow on the skein of red yarn Morrison held between his hands. As Anna rolled the yarn into a tight ball, she related the utter devastation the Yankees had wrought on Lincoln County and Cottage Home. The house and crops had been burned, the livestock had been stolen, and the slaves had run off with the Yankees. The Morrison clan was now scattered to the far corners of the Confederacy. Anna and Julia were staying in Richmond, at the home of Reverend Moses Hoge and his wife, Susan.

Jackson wasn't listening. Instead, he was strategizing on how to win the affections of his daughter. Five days of his leave had flown by, and Julia was no warmer. True, her eyes no longer rounded in terror whenever he entered the room and her possessive need for her mother's skirt had eased.

True, too, she played with the doll and blocks he had bought her, but the tea set was ignored, and so was he. Anna explained that Julia was just playing hard to get, and he should be flattered. He wasn't. All he knew was women were a complete mystery, even at the age of two.

All yesterday afternoon, Julia had played contently at his feet, which he interpreted as a sign of acceptance. When Jim announced dinner, Jackson picked her up to take her into the dining room. Without warning, she stiffened in his arms, arched her body away from him, and screamed bloody murder for her Uncle Joe to save her. Hastily, Jackson set her down, then watched as his daughter hurled herself into Morrison's protective arms. Which begged another question: why had Julia accepted her Uncle Joe without reservation? It was Uncle Joe's hand she grabbed when it was time to go to bed. Uncle Joe to whom she brought her books. Unable to contain his jealously, Jackson had snapped and growled at Joe the entire evening.

Julia burst into the room, a living doll in a new plaid dress. She ran to the couch, grabbed Jackson's hand, and pulled and pulled. "Tea party, Papa!" She demanded. "Tea party!"

"Tea party, Papa," Anna said with an encouraging smile.

Jackson allowed himself to be pulled from the couch. He followed his daughter as she ran across the room, up the steps, and into the nursery. The tea set had been unpacked, and a plate of cookies cooled on the small table. Seated on one of the chairs was the doll Jackson had given her for Christmas. Opposite the doll was an older, more ragged doll that had been Anna's favorite when she was a little girl.

"Sit, Papa!" Julia ordered.

It took some maneuvering, but he managed to perch himself on the small chair. He prayed it was sound enough to bear his weight. Julia sat down next to him.

"Would you like some tea?" She held up the tiny, flowered teapot.

"Yes, I would," Jackson responded, still in shock over his sudden reversal of fortune.

She poured invisible tea into his cup. "One lump or two." She picked up the sugar bowl and waited.

"One, please."

The tiny tongs pinged against the cup.

Jackson pointed at the older doll. "Who is this?"

"Betsey."

"And this one?" He pointed at the doll he had bought.

"Mary."

"Who am I?"

"Papa," she laughed.

He could wait no longer. "Can your Papa have a hug?"

She climbed out of her chair and wrapped her arms around his neck. With a swoop, he placed her on his lap. She snuggled against him. "Would you like to help me eat a cookie?" He asked.

"Yes!"

He drank countless cups of tea until Julia fell asleep in his arms. He laid her in her bed and drew up the covers. As he pulled the door closed, he saw the china pot glistening like a precious jewel in a sunbeam. Stuart was right. Heaven on earth!

Chapter Forty One

Rappahannock River
Near Fredericksburg
February 1865

The small potbelly stove in the corner of Lee's tent could not overcome the cold snap that gripped Virginia in its unrelenting grip. Lee poked at the fire and watched the flame blaze before it gave up and died. He shivered and sacrificed the rest of his kindling and a few sheets of stationary. Thus fueled, the fire roared to life. Satisfied with the stove's output, Lee returned to his desk. He stared down at the letter he was composing. It was another desperate plea to the Commissary Department to forward immediately any and all supplies to his starving men. Since the New Year, he had been forced to cut rations twice. His men were eating every third day, and, then, not enough to keep them alive. How could they march or fight in such condition?

Lee wadded up the letter and fed it to the fire. It was not Colonel Northrup's fault there was no food to send. Atlanta had fallen two weeks ago. It was a blow. A mortal blow, perhaps. All supplies moving from Georgia, Alabama, Florida, and those being shipped in from Europe had simply ceased. With the Army of the Cumberland wintering in North Carolina, another vital supply line had been cut. Virginia was fast becoming an island. The good people along the Rappahannock and Rapidan shared what they could with the army, but in these lean times, Virginia's citizens faced the difficult decision between feeding the army or their children. Only the farmers in the Valley sent a regular stream of foodstuffs. Not enough, though, to feed over 50,000 men.

Lee's hands were icicles. Perhaps another cup of coffee would chase away the cold. He rose and felt a sharp pain, like a small knife, pierce his heart. The tent began to spin. He staggered to his bed and lay down. He held tightly to the cot's side; the only stable thing in his whirling world. The pain intensified. His left arm tingled. "Walter! Walter! Please come here. I need you."

It was his heart, and this episode was far worse than the ones he had previously suffered. Not taking any chances, Doctor McGuire restricted Lee to total bed rest. Once his patient was tucked in, McGuire went straight to

Johnston and Jackson and bluntly told the two corps commanders that unless Lee's workload was reduced, the resulting stress would kill him. Johnston agreed to take over supplies and logistics. This left the planning of the spring campaign to Jackson. Walter Taylor joined the conspiracy and forbade any talk of the war around Lee.

For three weeks, Lee read, caught up on his personal correspondence, and then climbed the tent walls out of sheer boredom. The first seven days of his forced invalidity had been tolerable because Stuart had come to visit every afternoon. He brought Sweeney with him for hours of singing and entertainment. But, then, Jackson sent Stuart to North Carolina to spy out the Union army in Greensboro. It was a lonely and irritable Lee who growled at his staff for any infraction of the rules and took to eating in his tent.

This morning, Doctor McGuire had finally released him from house arrest with the admonishment to take it easy. Immediate orders were given for Traveller to be brought around. The winter air was biting, but Lee didn't care. He gave Traveller his head, and the Grey pounded down the road leading to the First Corps.

Once seated in Johnston's tent, Lee asked his First Corps Commander a series of questions to discern the state of his army. As serious as a parson, Johnston showed him the reams of correspondence between First Corps' headquarters and Davis, the War Department, and the Commissary Department. Bottom line: Richmond had nothing to send. The few supplies trickling down the Alexandria and Orange Railroad were all that could be hoped for. Johnston was issuing another order to cut rations, starting the day after tomorrow. Lee buried his head in his hands. His poor men! How much longer could he ask them to starve by his side? He made his goodbyes and rode to Jackson's headquarters.

"Hello!" He called. The common area was empty, but the aroma of roasting turkey floated from the kitchen. His stomach growled in appreciation. The first real sign of appetite he had experienced since he fell ill.

Smith came out of Jackson's tent. "Good afternoon, General Lee."

"Does General Jackson have a moment to see me?" He gave Traveller's reins to the aide.

"I always have time for you," Jackson shouted from inside. Lee entered and was enveloped in a cloud of heat. In the corner, a small stove puffed and smoked. Maps were strewn over Jackson's desk and bed and on the ground between. Lee saw maps of the Valley, southern Virginia, and North

Carolina. Jackson cleared off a chair. "Here, sit, sit. I'm glad to see you up and about. You look like your old self again."

"Almost."

Jackson made a concerned face. "Is your heart still troubling you? What does Doctor McGuire say?" He rose, added some kindling to the fire in the stove, and stoked the fire impatiently. It obeyed and emitted more warmth to the sweltering tent.

"Doctor McGuire is very tactful, but he can't disguise the fact that I'm wearing out." Lee examined one of the maps. It was filled with mileage and marching times. "I must confess that I feel like a shirker. I lay in bed all day, leaving you to do the hard work of planning the spring campaign." He gave Jackson a reproving stare. "But my convalescence wasn't helped when you sent General Stuart away. Or the fact that he took my nephew and Rob with him. Not helped at all."

Jackson's face turned red. "I'm sorry my sending Stuart away has displeased you," he spluttered. "I assure you he was the best man for the job. Colonel Hotchkiss is in the Valley, or I would have sent him. Time was of the essence."

"I was teasing you," Lee said with a fond smile. It amused him that after all these years, Jackson still didn't realize when he was being teased. "Of course, Jeb is the best man for the job. I miss him that's all. If I'm truly to recover my health, I need plenty of youth and laughter around me."

"Well, you're welcome to Mr. Smith and Mr. Morrison anytime you want, providing their work is done," Jackson volunteered.

Lee indicated the papers and map. "It seems to be a lot of work. Am I allowed to know what you're planning?"

"I'm still in the preliminary stages and won't have solid answers until Mr. Hotchkiss and Stuart return. But…" Jackson gestured to one of the maps. Lee drew his chair closer. "I don't think the Yankee strategy is all that hard to figure out. They plan to surround us." For the next few minutes, he expanded on his plan.

"Of course, I approve. But I don't know how we can expect the men to march such long distances if all they have to eat is a few strips of moldy bacon and two bites of cornbread every other day. If we can't figure out a way to re-victual this army, it will dissolve out from underneath us. Tomorrow morning, General Johnston will issue another order to cut rations." His face was pained. "My men are starving, and I can't do anything about it. Nothing!"

In helpless frustration, he pounded a fist on the desk then passed a weary hand over his eyes. "So great is my concern for what's coming in the next few weeks, I can't sleep. I spend my nights praying for some way to win." He choked back his tears. "Another fear has arisen. I think of Rob and my nephew. Now, Custis has joined the ranks. Then, there's you and General Stuart. Should I needlessly risk lives, fighting a war we are destined to lose because the nation is bankrupt and can't provide enough oats to feed the horses?

"These are selfish thoughts. I know they are. But I don't want to live whatever years I have left without Jeb's laughter. The more desperate the situation becomes, the greater the chance of his…" Once more Lee stopped to fight back his tears. He couldn't stand to think of Stuart dead and Centurion's saddle empty. "I can prevent it. All I have to do is go see General Grant."

"First of all," Jackson said with a mixture of compassion and sternness, "you don't risk anything. I'm here because I choose to be. The same is true with every soldier that remains. Whether you commanded us or not, we would still be here. So, you must not take that responsibility on yourself. It's wrecking you. Second, if the good Lord decides Stuart's days on this earth are finished, He will call Stuart home to be with Him. You have no say in that."

Despite his efforts, a tear slipped down Lee's face.

All sternness fled. "Sir, you have to know that you're not alone. I'm here to help you. Not because I'm your subordinate, but because I'm your friend, Robert."

Lee began to weep. "You're my right arm, Thomas. I rely on you more than I rely on any other man. But I need your friendship. I do."

"You have it." Jackson reached out his hand.

Lee seized it and thought back to the exhausted man he had first met on the Virginia peninsula. He had almost misjudged him. Now, Lee understood how fatigue and illness could overwhelm you and prevent you from doing your best. How thankful he was that when he reorganized the army, he decided to take another chance on the shy and taciturn man from the Valley. It was one of the best decisions of his life.

"Do you think we should surrender?" Suddenly afraid to meet Jackson's eyes, Lee gazed down at the desk. Jackson squeezed his hand. Lee looked up and saw the blue-gray eyes burning with the light of battle.

"I don't think that time has come. Yet. There's still an opportunity to do the Yankees great harm."

"And if we don't?"

"Whatever you decide, I'll be by your side," he said with quiet conviction. "And so will Stuart and General Johnston."

Lee retrieved his hand and pulled out a handkerchief to wipe his eyes. Jim appeared in the door.

"Dinner's ready, General," he said. "Good evenin', General Lee. I sure hope you'se hungry. Mister Joe done kilt that fat old turkey he's been trackin' for days, and I cooked it up nice and tender."

Lee smiled at Jackson. "Suddenly, I'm famished."

Full of turkey and good cheer, Lee led Traveller past his dining tent. His aides were inside, drinking coffee and devouring a cake Colonel Long had received in the mail. Lee waved, rounded the corner, and paused to take off his gauntlets.

"The only thing Jeb Stuart wants to hear from General Lee is 'call me father.'" He heard Taylor say. Spellbound, he riveted his attention on the mud splattered tent.

"You shouldn't speak so harshly of Stuart," Long rebuked. "He loves the general very much and saved him after Rooney's death."

"I wasn't being critical," Taylor explained. "It's touching to see General Stuart dance in attendance. I just don't think he'll get what he wants. Not this time."

Lee realized he was eavesdropping. He pulled off his gauntlets and hurried Traveller to the corral. His mind whirled about in a fever. He unsaddled the gelding and turned him lose. Hungry, Traveller nuzzled him. Lee opened the feed bin. He closed his eyes to ward off another painful memory. Last summer, this bin had teemed with treats. Now, it contained two shriveled apples. More proof that his army was starving out from underneath him.

He held the apples out for Traveller. The gelding didn't mind their condition and ate them noisily. Lee stroked the velvet nose and replayed the moment in the hall when Stuart stopped speaking and flushed red.

A slow smile broke out on his face. He had been right. Stuart was going to confess his love. Of this, he was now positive. Suddenly, everything was brought into sharp focus. The cups of coffee Stuart had prepared for him on cold winter days; the visits when he was confined to the sickbed; the presents brought back from raids. The smiles! And the laughter! Hours and hours of laughter that came from Stuart's efforts to entertain. An explosion of all the small kindnesses ripped through Lee's heart until it culminated in a kiss on the cheek the day Fitzhugh died. He remembered how Stuart allowed him to cling to his hand that tragic day, how he sat outside Fitzhugh's tent and guarded a grieving father's privacy. These weren't the actions of a junior officer. Only a son would care so much. A son! When Stuart returned from North Carolina, Lee would reveal his desire to be a father to his young lieutenant general. In his joy, he only saw Stuart's acceptance.

"You wanted to see me, General Lee." Stuart stood in Lee's doorway; a gift in his hand.

"I do," Lee smiled. "Please have a seat."

Stuart entered the tent and looked around for a chair. Not seeing one, he perched on the edge of Lee's camp-bed so not to muss the perfectly arranged covers. "I brought you a little something." He held up the package.

"In a moment. I want to ask you a question, if I may?" Lee rooted through his desk and pulled out a yellowing letter. He passed it over to Stuart. "Do you remember this?"

Stuart slid the letter from the envelope and recognized his handwriting. He scanned it. "I do." The letter brought back a rather embarrassing moment. In the early days of Lee's command, the newspapers had dragged him over the coals for not attacking McClellan's army and driving it back down the peninsula. Instead, Lee had ordered the army to dig trenches around the Confederate capitol. Old Granny and King of Spades the headlines screamed. So, Stuart had written a letter filled with advice on how best to attack the Army of the Potomac. As if Lee needed his advice!

"I want to know why you wrote it."

Perplexed by the query, Stuart stared at Lee. "Because I thought the newspapers were being unfair to you," he finally said.

"Why would it matter?"

Lee watched Stuart flutter for an answer. "It just did." Was all he would confess before beginning a careful inspection of his sash. Lee recognized the sudden scrutiny of the yellow silk as Stuart's way of avoiding the question.

"Then perhaps you can answer me another question. When you told me about Fitzhugh, you kissed my cheek. Why?"

Stuart jerked his head up and stared at Lee. "B...be...because..." He faltered under Lee's questioning gaze.

Lee rose from the chair and sat down next to him. “Don’t be afraid to answer, Jeb.” His smile was meant to encourage, but it only increased Stuart’s confusion.

“Because you were suffering,” Stuart said, pleased with his answer because it didn’t give too much away.

“Wrong,” Lee corrected as if Stuart had answered mistakenly on a West Point exam.

“I didn’t think about why I did it.” Stuart looked down at the ground and moved dirt around with the toe of his boot. “I just did.”

Lee’s heart sank in disappointment. He had been wrong about the kiss on the cheek, the flush in the hallway, all of it. He returned to his desk. “Okay, you can go.”

Stuart groaned in misery. He was a coward. A miserable, lowly Yankee coward, and unless he summoned his courage, he may never get another opportunity to tell Lee how he felt. “You’re the greatest man known to me,” he sobbed. He refused to look at Lee. “I wanted you to know that I’d take care of you.”

“I know.” Lee returned to the bed.

Stuart was flabbergasted. “You do?”

“Yes, though it took me a while to realize that’s why you did it.” Stuart didn’t respond. “Oh, my young lieutenant general, what kindness of God has brought you into my life.”

Stuart heard pleasure in Lee’s voice.

“Well, here you are. Now, what am I to do with you? I have an idea, if you’ll hear me.”

“What?” Stuart wiped his nose with the back his hand.

“I…” Lee paused in nervousness. He swallowed and continued. “Since West Point, I have loved you as a son. I don’t want to hide those feelings any longer. If you would allow me this joy, I’ll love you as dearly as any father ever loved a son.”

He watched the impact of his words turn Stuart into all sunshine and joy. The tears were gone, replaced by the smile of a delighted boy. Stuart nodded. Lee threw his arm around Stuart’s shoulders, drew him near to his breast, and kissed his forehead.

“Do you…Could I…I mean…” Stuart whispered, afraid that his next request would bring the ruin of his dreams.

“Don’t be afraid to ask me anything.”

Stuart untangled himself and searched Lee’s face. Lee’s brown eyes radiated love. “Do you think I could call you father.” He spoke very rapidly, expecting Lee to cut him off. "I mean not in front of the men or anything like that. I would be very careful about that…"

"Hush, Jeb. Why not try it first and see if you like it."

Heartened by all that had passed between them, Stuart took the final plunge. He opened wide his heart to Lee. "I love you." A brief pause. "Father."

Touched beyond words, Lee felt tears slip down his cheek. "I love you too, my son."

Then they both laughed and wiped away their tears.

Chapter Forty Two

"Oh, good! You're just the person I need to see," Stuart said when Jackson came into his tent. He spun around in his chair and held out two fists. "Pick a hand."

Jackson picked the left. Stuart turned it over and revealed a small toy soldier dressed in a red uniform. "That means I'm Napoleon." He spun back around to his desk and emptied his other hand. A blue-uniformed soldier tumbled onto a pile of toy soldiers. "And you're Wellington. But don't think for a minute that you're gonna get the better of me this time."

"What do you have there, Stuart?"

Stuart busily sorted the soldiers. "Jimmie's birthday present. I picked them up in a store in North Carolina." With the main sorting complete, Stuart concentrated on assembling his army.

Jackson sat down and picked through his men. "There's no cavalry."

"Can you believe it?" Stuart was outraged. "Two hundred soldiers and not a dragoon in the bunch. The only ones on horseback are Napoleon and Wellington." He moved a pile of papers to make room for his left flank. "How are the roads?"

"Recovering nicely considering all the rain we had over the last two weeks." Jackson had watched Stuart prepare his line long enough. He began to fill in his own.

"The rains did keep the Yankees in Washington."

"That it did. Can I move these papers?" Stuart nodded and Jackson laid them on the bed. "What does your spy in the War Department tell you?"

"He says Grant is chomping at the bit to get at us by the end of April." Stuart glanced at Jackson's line and began to shift men from one side of his line to the other. "I had five men desert last night."

Jackson chewed on his lip. "I had 23."

"Any news about supplies?" The toy Napoleon rode the entire length of his line to shouts of *vive l'Empereur.* The Emperor must have been displeased by what he saw, for Stuart fiddled with his soldiers, returning most to their original position.

Jackson moved his troops to match Stuart's new deployment. "We're supposed to get a shipment of flour later this afternoon. It'll be enough to last the boys a couple of days. After that, it's in God's hands."

"I really don't blame the men for deserting."

Jackson shook his head in amazement. He firmly believed that desertion was the worst offense a soldier could commit. And to hear Stuart defend the criminals! It angered him, and he said so.

"If I thought they were being cowardly or couldn't bear starving anymore, then maybe," Stuart said swiftly. "But I don't know what I'd do if I received a tearful letter from Flora, begging me to come home and save my family from starvation. The Yankees have picked the Cotton States clean as a bone. At least Flora can get meat, flour, and milk."

Jackson slammed a tiny infantry man on the desk in disgust. "You wouldn't slink away in the middle of the night like a coward."

"No, I wouldn't."

Mollified by Stuart's answer, Jackson dropped the subject. "I got a letter from Anna today." He tapped the pocket where the letter resided.

Stuart began his troops on a circling motion around Jackson's flank. "What does the beautiful Mrs. Stonewall have to say?"

"She sent me a drawing from Julia."

Stuart smile was mischievous. "What of?"

Jackson blushed. "I don't know. Does it make me a bad father if I can't cipher what my two-year old has drawn?"

"If it did, then I would be a charter member of the bad father club. Once, La Petite drew me a picture and proudly presented it to me. I was quite enthusiastic in my praise for her accurate rendition of a cow until she burst into tears. It wasn't a cow, but me on Skylark. She cried for an hour."

"What did you do?"

"I bought her a doll. But Flora solved the problem. She writes what the picture is supposed to be on the back." He began to search his desk.

"I'll tell Anna to do that."

He found what he was looking for and pulled a piece of paper from one of the cubbyholes. He handed it to Jackson. "Here's Jimmie's latest masterpiece. What do you think it is?"

Jackson turned it every direction. "I have no idea."

"Turn it over."

He did and read Flora's handwriting: *Jimmie playing Stonewall and flanking the Yankees.* He turned the picture back over. "Oh, yes, now I see." He returned the drawing. "Why is Jimmie playing me and not you?"

With a laugh, Stuart slid the picture back into the cubbyhole. "Because my son thinks that ole Stonewall is the finest soldier in the land. When his little friends get together and play army, he usually does play me. But if the opportunity presents itself, he trades up. Flora writes on the days that he gets to play you, the supper table is filled with non-stop chatter about all your fine qualities." Stuart advanced two soldiers across the desk.

Jackson picked up a soldier and fiddled with it. He hadn't come to Stuart's headquarters to discuss his daughter's artistic ability, but, now, he was unsure if he should share the joyful news the letter contained. Why he was nervous all of a sudden, he didn't understand, but he was. Stuart's cough brought him from his thoughts.

Jackson placed the soldier on the desk and moved more soldiers up to join the lone infantryman. "There was other news in Anna's letter."

"What kind?" Stuart pulled men from his center to oppose Jackson's assault.

"I'm going to be a father again." Jackson flushed with both pride and pleasure.

"Congratulations!" Stuart slapped Jackson on the back. "This calls for a celebration. All I have to offer is water, but it's cold."

Jackson held up his hands and refused. "What I want is for you to be the godfather."

"Of course, I will. But I'm still the uncle, right?"

It pleased Jackson to hear Stuart use that word. "Yes, you'll be both uncle and godfather. You'll pray that the pregnancy will go smoothly."

"Every night."

Jackson picked up another soldier and toyed with it. "I need to talk to you, my dear Stuart."

"Are you trying to divert me now that I'm on the verge of victory?"

"Look at your left flank."

Stuart glanced at his shabbily defended line. All his soldiers were on his right.

"Now, my right flank." It bristled with soldiers.

"When did that happen?" Stuart cried in defeat. He reached over to his trunk and picked up his scabbard. With a deft movement, his French sword was unsheathed and surrendered. Jackson received the sword and, with a quick snap of his fingers, was in possession of the scabbard.

Jackson slid the sword back into the scabbard and laid it on the ground. Stuart poured the soldiers into their velvet bag. "Stuart, have you thought about what might happen if we're unable to extricate ourselves from the trap the Yankees are preparing to spring."

"What do you mean?" Stuart opened his trunk and placed the bag inside.

"We might not win…"

"No! I don't want to hear anymore!" The lid slammed down. "I don't want to live if we lose!"

"No, Jeb, put that thought from your mind," Jackson rebuked. "I used to think the same, but we have more reasons to live than not."

Stuart violently shook his head. "The Yankees aren't just going to forgive and forget. I saw what they did to Winchester."

"If that's true, then we can't abandon our families to make their way alone in such a world, can we? What kind of men would that make us?" He received no answer. "Stuart, I want you to come to Lexington." Stuart's eyes flew open. "I know you have your heart set on returning to Patrick County, but I'm asking you to come to the Valley instead."

"What would I do in the Valley?"

"The same thing you'd do in Patrick Country, I reckon."

"No." The quickness in which he answered dismayed Jackson. "My family is in Patrick County."

"I'm your family also, Stuart," Jackson reminded him.

"Not really." Stuart began to return the papers to his desk. "I mean, we joke about it…"

Joke! Is that what Stuart thought?

"And it's been great fun, but that's all it's been." He waved his hand to brush away the seriousness of the conversation and took great pains to make sure the paper piles on his desk were perfectly aligned.

Jackson's face flushed in mortification. He stammered wordlessly as a sharp pain burst in his heart. *A joke!*

Stuart slammed a pile of papers onto his desk. "Oh, come on now," he said testily. "Surely, you didn't think that conversation on the porch in Harrisburg made us family, did you?"

Jackson jerked to his feet and swept his gauntlets and kepi from the bed. He whirled about and faced Stuart, who was straightening a pile of reports. Jackson wanted nothing more than to shout angry words but couldn't summon any that would hurt Stuart as much as Stuart had just hurt him. Instead he bolted from the tent and called for Little Sorrel.

The tent flap opened, and Jackson saw Stuart standing in the doorway. He took one step into the tent and paused. He swept off his hat and held it in his hands. His shoulders were slumped; his face a pale study of misery. Jackson gave him a cold stare before returning his attention to the map he was analyzing. Stuart didn't say anything. He just stood there, slowly spinning his hat between his hands.

Jackson set down his pencil. "What can I do for you, General?"

Stuart winced at the formal tone and took a small step backwards. "I didn't like the way we left things this afternoon."

"I don't have time for such nonsense." Jackson knew by the stricken look on Stuart's face that he was being cruel, but he couldn't stop himself.

"I'm sorry to have wasted your time," Stuart said softly. "It won't happen again." He bowed and put on his hat, but faltered when he reached the door. "Do you think any of this is easy for me? I feel just like a sheep-killing dog!"

"I don't care," Jackson said acidly. He picked up his pencil. "I think we're through here, don't you?"

"Why won't you let me explain?" Stuart implored. He took a tentative step toward the desk. Jackson folded his arms against his chest and glared at the young man, who took another step back toward the door. "I can't go to the Valley with you…"

Jackson cut him off with a sharp gesture. "You made that perfectly clear this afternoon, General."

"Stop calling me that!" Stuart cried. "Let me explain. Please!" He stepped forward again, his arms open in supplication. Jackson waved an angry hand in permission. "At Duncannon, after my wounding, you sort of took me over. Made all types of decisions for me. You even determined that I would recover in your headquarters. You never asked me if that's what I wanted." He rubbed his head as if stricken by a sudden pain.

Jackson twirled the pencil through his fingers. Stuart was right. The decisions he made in the aftermath of the cavalry leader's wounding were all done without Stuart's consent. He gestured, less angrily this time, for Stuart to continue.

"It's been almost two years since my wounding. Two years of you and me in each other's lives like we have a right to be. Never asking if we wanted it to be so. I always expected it to end when we won. You would go your way. I would go mine."

The end of the pencil tapped a sharp tattoo on the desk. "What you do after the war makes little difference to me."

To his credit, Stuart ignored the cutting remark. "When I was injured at the Potomac, I knew something was wrong. I couldn't remember where I was, or what I was supposed to be doing. I didn't even know my men." This revelation caught Jackson by surprise. Stuart never mentioned that he had recovered his memory. "I didn't dismiss my men when we crossed the river. I just left them. I had to find something." He stopped speaking.

"What?" Jackson prompted, his tone still sharp and abrupt.

"Someplace safe," Stuart answered.

Jackson reeled under the impact of Stuart's confession. "But you came to me."

"I know." He nervously tugged on his beard. "How many times have I come looking for you in the night? How many times have I laid my problems at your feet, expecting you to handle them? What have I given you in return?" He shook his head to indicate nothing. "We have a perfect give and take relationship, you and I. You give and I take, and for that I'm very ashamed. That's why I can't go to the Valley. How can I take any more from you?" He was breathing heavy, and his face was the color of chalk.

"My dear Stuart." The familiar endearment received a bittersweet smile from the tormented man. "I don't understand."

"I don't have much left to my name, and I don't have any prospects either. My only career has been the army, so I'm not sure how I'll make a living when the war is over. I don't even know how I'll feed my family or provide a roof over their head. My brother…Alick…has promised to help me." He left nothing hidden.

"You can take his help but not mine?" Jackson was compassionate. He had never witnessed Stuart so despairing, so defeated.

"Because he's my family," he choked out.

"I'm your family, Stuart." Jackson waited for a reaction, but Stuart just flushed red before turning paper white. "If we lose, our country will be in ruins and our money worthless. I'll be in the same boat as you. But if we stick together, we can support each other in the hard times ahead." Stuart nodded appreciatively. "Furthermore, we don't have a perfect give and take relationship. Can't you see, I've been just as selfish with you."

"When?" Stuart gasped.

"You've already said. I didn't ask if you wanted to convalesce in my headquarters. You did so because it's what I wanted. And every moment since then. Why just this afternoon, I barged into your tent to share my news with the one person I couldn't wait to tell." He held up his hands. "You don't have to worry whether or not the relationship is lopsided. It's not." He took a breath. "Whatever you decide, I'll understand because, well, whether you choose to believe it or not, I'm your brother."

Stuart's shoulders heaved and tears welled up in his eyes. Then a smile erupted on his face. In the light of that sunny smile, as General Lee so aptly named it, Jackson's anger turned to ash. Stuart edged his way down the bed and perched on the corner. "I do have Centurion and Virginia, so I'm not exactly destitute. I'm going to start a horse farm. Alick is going to help me."

"That's wonderful." Jackson said, envious of Alick's role in Stuart's life.

"I think so, too." He gazed hopefully at Jackson. "But I could easily start it in Lexington."

"Yes, you could," Jackson agreed. A flicker of hope stirred in the pit of his stomach.

"I lied."

"About what?" Jackson asked, confused by the sudden shift in topic.

"When I said that we joked about being family. It was a lie. I've never considered it a joke."

"Then why say it?"

"I was ashamed to tell you the real reason I couldn't accept your invitation."

"I see." Jackson leaned back in his chair. He should be angry that Stuart had lied to him, but all he felt was relief that Stuart hadn't meant the cruel words.

"I'll come to Lexington with you."

"No, I don't want you to come because you feel guilty."

"I don't."

"Stuart…" The object of his unfinished sentence suddenly fell back on the bed, convulsed in laughter. "What?" Jackson laughed; the hurt forgiven and forgotten.

"I was just thinking what Jimmie will do when he hears the news that ole Stonewall is going to be his neighbor. Flora will have to scrape him off the ceiling."

Chapter Forty Three

The first battle of the spring campaign was fought in Richmond against Jefferson Davis' stubborn insistence that the Army of Northern Virginia's main objective was the defense of Richmond. Lee, patiently, and Jackson, a little less so, argued that Grant's strategy was to surround the army, force it into the trenches, then batter and starve it into defeat. Davis' edict played straight into the Yankees' hands. The only chance the army had to win was to remain between the converging armies and try to beat them in detail. Davis disagreed. Lee's orders remained unchanged. Defend Richmond!

In a rare display of defiance, Lee, with Jackson in tow, headed straight for Secretary Seddon's office. The Secretary proved to be a sympathetic listener. He mounted a second assault on Davis' diktat only to be rudely turned back. Unbowed, Seddon brought the issue up at the next Cabinet meeting. After an acrimonious and bitter argument, the Cabinet overrode Davis' strenuous objections and appeals to constitutional authority. Lee's strategy was approved.

At the end of April, Stuart's spy in the War Department sent word. Sheridan was preparing to invade the Valley via Thorofare Gap. Jackson decamped from his winter quarters along the Rappahannock and marched to Culpepper. When Sheridan turned south up the Valley, Jackson's foot cavalry met him at Front Royal.

Once Jackson evacuated Culpepper, Johnston marched his corps into the city to either support Jackson in his struggle against Sheridan or to oppose Grant when he marched toward Manassas Gap.

Four days later, Reynolds led the Army of the Potomac, 110,000 strong, from Washington. Johnston hurried to Bull Run Creek. Reynolds halted at Centreville to await the battle's outcome in the Valley. Jackson sent Sheridan reeling back through Thorofare Gap. Reynolds set his army in motion with the hope of crushing Johnston between his two forces. He arrived at the creek's bank to discover Johnston had flown the coop. During the night, the First Corps had slipped back to Culpepper to rendezvous with Jackson.

Grant now expected Lee to head east to Richmond. When word reached him that Lee was marching south toward Charlottesville, Grant froze in indecision. From Charlottesville, Jackson could return to the Valley via Staunton and march on Washington. To coerce Lee into the Richmond trenches, Grant sent a dispatch to General Benjamin Butler at Norfolk. The next day, 35,000 Yankees marched up the peninsula to seize the railroads at Petersburg and cut Richmond's last supply line. Lee refused to take the bait.

Davis summoned Custis Lee and removed him from command of the Richmond homeguard. Standing behind Davis was the homeguard's new commanding general, the hero of Sumter, Pierre Gustave Toutant de Beauregard. The reasons for the change in command had nothing to do with Custis' ability, Davis assured Lee's oldest son. He just believed that the Confederacy should take advantage of Beauregard's vast experience in these difficult times. Custis wasn't fooled. Beauregard had been given command because he agreed with Davis that Richmond's safety was paramount.

When word came from Lee for the homeguard to head down the Richmond-Danville Railroad and rendezvous with the army, Beauregard belayed the order. The Yankees were sitting in Culpepper. Until Grant chose to chase Lee, Beauregard didn't see the necessity of uncovering Richmond.

In response to Beauregard's refusal to obey orders, Lee sent a testy telegram to Davis. Lee needed Beauregard's men sent to him immediately. The army was leaking manpower. On the march from Culpepper to Charlottesville, over 4,000 men had sat down on the side of the road and refused orders to keep moving. Each night, hundreds more slipped away. Unless the homeguard marched without delay, Lee would have no choice but to surrender the army. The threat did the trick. The small command left Richmond.

Outside Charlottesville, on the wide, green lawns of a large mansion, Lee met with Jackson, Stuart, and Colonel Hotchkiss. A map was spread out on a table. Stuart wasn't paying attention to Hotchkiss' description of the roads west of Amherst. He was leaning against a tree, trying to determine if Lee's hair was whiter than it had been this time last year. He was about to reach a conclusion when Lee glanced up from the map. Caught staring, Stuart tried to avert his eyes, but it was too late. Lee gave a small smile then inclined his head toward the map. Stuart pushed off from the tree and studied the map with renewed interest.

A courier, dressed in a ragged gray uniform, rode up. "Where's General Lee?"

He sat on a skeleton of a horse that had been so misused that it angered Stuart. While Lee identified himself and received the rider's message, Stuart petted the shivering animal. He could feel its ribs through its mangy coat. "Major, are all your horses in this condition?"

The major didn't answer. Incensed at the courier's treatment of his inquiry and the animal, Stuart was about to lay into him when Lee suddenly swept the table clean of all maps and papers. The horse shied. Stuart caught the reins and soothed it.

"The entire homeguard!" Stuart heard Lee's ragged voice.

"Yes, sir," the courier said. "It was a terrific slaughter. Over half our men are either dead or wounded. General Beauregard had no choice."

"My son, General Lee." Lee could not continue. He sagged weakly against the table.

Stuart's heart sank. Not Custis, too! He dropped the reins and rushed to Lee.

"He was fine the last time I saw him," the courier said.

Lee swallowed hard. "And that was?"

"When General Beauregard was preparing to surrender. The fighting was all but over."

Lee nodded once and stepped away from the table. He gestured for Stuart not to follow. Stuart obliged but kept a watchful eye on the pacing, angry Lee.

The courier addressed Jackson. "Sir, it's been two days since I had anything to eat. Can you spare a scrap of bread?"

"Mr. Taylor!" Jackson called. "Let's get the major some supper."

"Colonel Taylor, have this poor animal sent to Jack," Stuart ordered, as Taylor led the major toward the cook tent. "Tell him to do what he can."

Lee continued to pace; his face red with rage. He beat a fist into an open palm and muttered under his breath about the stupidity of politicians. "How far is the Army of the Cumberland from Danville?" He asked Stuart when his steps brought him back to the table.

"Two days."

"And Grant has advanced to Orange Courthouse?" This was directed to Jackson, who confirmed the news. "We need to go. General Grant revealed himself to be a most determined pursuer in Pennsylvania." Lee mopped his forehead with his sleeve. "Perhaps we'll find food in Amherst. General Stuart, please send the wagons this evening and bring us whatever can be foraged." It was a dismissal. Without another word, Lee left them. He stalked over to the campfire and sat down heavily in a chair.

Stuart wasn't ready to be dismissed. Not until he was certain Lee was okay. He motioned for Jackson to join him, then marched over to the fire. He knelt down next to Lee. "If you want, I'll go to General Reynolds under a white flag and see if there is news about Custis."

"I wouldn't recommend it," Jackson advised with a frown. "The Yankees might not realize they have Custis in custody."

But Stuart had caught the relieved expression on Lee's face. "You went under a white flag to General Grant to remove that little man's bounty off my head. Why is this different?"

"How do you know what I did?" Jackson asked, stunned.

Stuart gave Jackson a puzzled look. "I'm surprised you still have to ask. I'm the eyes and ears of this army."

"Did Pendleton or Morrison say anything to you?"

"No, they'd never do that. Well, when Mr. Pendleton first took over as your adjutant, he was a fount of unintended information. But he caught on to my ways and has been very loyal to you ever since." Stuart saw his answer didn't satisfy Jackson. "Well, if you must know, it was General Harvey Hill's aide. A very talkative man. Hard to shut him up once he gets going."

"You shouldn't get him going at all," Jackson declared from behind a thunderous face and a pointing finger that Stuart dodged so not to be poked in the nose.

"I can't help it if people want to volunteer things up to me," Stuart shrugged, but his eyes told a different story.

"I think you can help it. You just don't want to."

"Boys! Do I have to send you to your rooms?" Lee's rebuke was fatherly.

The adversaries stared at each other for a long moment, Jackson angrily and Stuart unrepentantly, then both burst into laughter at the absurdity of such an argument at such a time.

"Jeb, thank you for the offer, but General Jackson is correct. We shouldn't call attention to Custis. General Jackson, can I turn over the movements of the army to you. I want to be on the road by dawn."

"Yes, sir."

Lee rubbed his eyes. "How far can we get?"

"I think that will be up to the men and the horses."

"Jeb, you'll get those wagons out?"

"The moment I get back to my headquarters."

"That will be all then."

With a jerk of his head, Jackson indicated to Stuart to do as Lee requested. Reluctantly, Stuart followed. He had only taken a few steps when he glanced back at Lee. The suffering man tore at his heart. "I can't leave him!" He didn't wait for Jackson to answer. He hurried back to the fire and sat at Lee's feet. Lee didn't acknowledge him.

Stuart reached up, took Lee's hand, and massaged it in silence. "Give me your other hand." Lee did. "Father, I know you're worried about Custis."

"I'm worried about all my men," Lee's voice shook. In the deepening shadows, he reminded Stuart of the vulnerable Lee, in those first horrible moments when he had heard the news that his beloved Fitzhugh was dead. He had never really recovered from that blow. Stuart could see all the pain and anguish rising once more to the surface.

Lee retrieved his hand and lifted Stuart's chin. "You're my Benjamin, Jeb. My Benjamin." He leaned forward and kissed Stuart on the temple.

Stuart was touched by the gesture even if he didn't quite understand it. He knew of Benjamin from the Bible, youngest son of Jacob and all that, but not why Lee would consider him such. He would have to ask Jackson.

"Now, go get those wagons out."

Stuart stood and brushed grass from his pants. "Do you want me to come back?"

"No."

Stuart returned to Centurion and fed the stallion sugar lumps as he contemplated what to do. General Johnston rode up. "I am so glad to see you," Stuart told the First Corps Commander. "The homeguard has surrendered near Jetersville." Johnston gasped. "General Lee is afraid for Custis."

"What have you heard?" In the campfire's light, Johnston saw Lee sitting in a chair, staring out into space.

"Custis is alive. And there's no reason to suspect otherwise. But I'm afraid the old sadness is overtaking him."

"Then perhaps I can remind him of happier times."

"Thank you," Stuart said gratefully. He threw himself up on Centurion, and, with one more desperate look back at Lee, rode off to get the wagons out.

Johnston dragged a chair close to Lee's. "Good evening, Robert."

"Joe."

"I wonder what General Scott would do to get us out of this predicament." Johnston put a hand on Lee's arm. Lee clasped it.

"He would have a plan."

"His plans were usually yours. You were the true hero of that war, Robert."

"No." Johnston felt Lee tighten his grip. "Those people have my boy, Joe. They have my boy."

"God will keep him safe for you."

Lee nodded but didn't say anything.

In the golden firelight, Johnston gazed at the noble face, now lined with worry and anguish. How different it looked from the Lee of Mexico. The young lion was gone. In his place sat a weary soldier worn down by worry and death.

"I got a letter from Lydia before we moved out to Manassas," Johnston said. "She wrote about a dinner party you attended. She remarked how unencumbered that night was of the cares of this present time and wondered if we will ever have those carefree days again." Johnston's tone was lighter than his heart.

Lee didn't speak. He gripped Johnston's hand tighter.

"Do you think we will?" Johnston asked.

Lee shrugged.

Johnston interpreted the shrug as another, more important query. Was it even possible with all that lay between them? Johnston placed his other hand over Lee's. Lee turned and faced him; the question now in his eyes.

Johnston's heart lurched in sorrow. "Robert, I want to apologize for my resentment over the ranking list and command of the army." He found it difficult to continue under Lee's unwavering gaze. "I've carried around so much bitterness that it poisoned everything I touched. But you never allowed it to touch our friendship. Even after I was replaced by Longstreet, you saved me." Tears welled up in his eyes, but didn't fall. They remained dammed up, waiting for Lee to speak; to forgive him.

Lee turned his attention to the fire. "I didn't seek the army, but I'll admit I was envious of you. You were in the field, and I was confined to my desk in Richmond. When I was given command, I jumped at the chance. I was just happy to feel useful again. But I never undermined you. And if so ordered, I would have relinquished command upon your return."

"I know," Johnston acknowledged. His tears began to flow. He removed his handkerchief from his pocket and wiped his eyes. "I didn't realize just how out of control my wounded vanity had become until I demanded the army the day Fitzhugh died. It was so important that I had it. To prove to my detractors how wrong they were to treat me so. And what happened? God knocked me off my high-horse, literally." He began to laugh. "And General Jackson won the battle." He sobered. "If someone would have told me that I could be so cruel, I would have challenged him to a duel to defend my honor. But I was *that* cruel. I'm so sorry. I know it doesn't erase what transpired, but if I could have just one hour to live over again, it would be that one."

"I have a few of those hours, too."

Johnston knew he didn't deserve such mercy, and it almost broke him. But then Lee smiled, and the old man sitting next to him was transformed into the lion of memory.

"Let's say no more about it." Lee squeezed his hand again. "You'll have to refresh my memory about the dinner party. What brought it to Lydia's remembrance?"

Laughing through his tears, Johnston unfurled his story.

Chapter Forty Four

The army was up by dawn, and, with no breakfast to eat, on the road not much later. The ranks were thinning. Twelve hundred men had disappeared in the night. By midmorning, the columns' pace had slowed to little more than a mile an hour. Jackson rode up and down the line, urging the men to press on. They stepped lively for Old Jack, but when he rode past; they hung their heads and trudged on. At noon, Jackson called a halt and gave the army a two hour rest.

Sheridan's cavalry lunged forward, nipping at Jackson's flank, endeavoring to separate Rodes' division from the long, weary column. Stuart hurled Baker and Chambliss at the Union troopers and pushed Sheridan back on his haunches. Stuart couldn't pursue the retreating Yankees. Virginia wobbled under him; her sides heaving from exertion. Sheridan sensed the weakness and remained nearby: prowling, waiting, watching for another opportunity to spring forward and maul the laboring troops.

"General Jackson," Colonel Crutchfield hailed as Jackson rode by. "The mules are exhausted. Over 60 of them are down and won't get back up."

A frown creased Jackson's face. "What do you suggest?"

"We leave some of the older guns behind."

"How many?"

"Thirty."

Jackson blenched. What would the Yankees think when they discovered he was abandoning artillery.

"Sir?" Crutchfield asked.

"Do it!" He exclaimed in anguish.

Sheridan led Grant and Reynolds to a small collection of cannon scattered in a clearing; spiked and ruined. Mules lay all around, gasping for breath. A few of the animals nibbled at the spring grass, but the majority lay on their sides waiting to die. Overhead, buzzards circled in the clear blue sky. On the side of the road sat a handful of Rebs, heads hung low, staring at the dirt and not at the Union soldiers gloating over them.

"Sheridan, get in front of them," Grant ordered. "Cut them off! General Reynolds..." But Reynolds was talking to the exhausted men, now prisoners.

"What division?" Reynolds asked.

"Early's division, sir." Came the muffled reply.

"What can I do for you?" Reynolds was kind.

"Do you have anything to eat?" One Virginian asked, tears in his eyes.

"Colonel Rosengarten, take these men to the rear and get them something to eat."

"When is the last time you ate?" Grant asked. They didn't answer but continued to stare down at the ground. He patted the nearest one on the back. "It's okay. It's almost over." The Confederates nodded in defeat and trudged after Rosengarten.

At North Garden, Sheridan slammed into Pickett's Virginians. Chambliss' brigade was Pickett's first line of defense, but Chambliss was killed in the opening moments of the skirmish. His men, desperate and outnumbered, fled to the back, leaving Pickett exposed and vulnerable.

Sheridan dismounted Gregg's division and sliced Kemper's brigade from the column. Armistead turned back to help only to find the blue troopers of Gamble's brigade strung out along the road; an impenetrable wall. Kemper fought until his men ran out of ammunition, then he surrendered his brigade.

Without mercy, Sheridan ordered Gregg to join Gamble's assault on Armistead. Garnett came up fighting and Hampton's brigade joined in. Between them, they managed to push back the Yankees. Sheridan quickly reformed and charged. The Virginians were thrown to the ground. Snarling, Sheridan ripped and tore until Fitz Lee's brigade emerged from the trees and inflicted enough damage to chase Sheridan off.

The Confederate wounded overwhelmed the hospital trains. Johnston had no choice but to abandon them to the Yankees.

Undaunted, Sheridan rode north and cut Jackson's column in two. Jackson hurried the Light Division to the desperate fight. Hill's former division stood like a stone wall until the rest of the corps could make its escape. Sheridan retreated into the lengthening shadows. The Light Division clutched rifles in trembling hands and waited for the attack to be renewed. But Sheridan was gone. Jackson ordered the men to push on to Covesville – two miles away.

The columns straggled into the town, a shadow of their former selves. No longer were they the smart and jaunty men marching down Pennsylvania roads. Now, they were scarecrows in ragged and filthy uniforms. Most of them were shoeless. They dragged their rifles in the dust. Jackson sent a wagon back down the road to pick up weapons and the other items tossed aside by men too weak to bear the weight of an empty canteen.

Lee greeted them. The men roused themselves for Marse Robert and, for a moment, they recaptured their glorious past. Hats and the rebel yell were enthusiastically raised. But the illusion shattered when they begged Lee for something, anything, to eat. Lee had nothing to give. Stuart's teamsters had reported the cupboard bare in Amherst. The men drank their fill of cold water and fell into a dreamless sleep.

Under a star-filled sky, Stuart's pickets brought in three Yankees bearing a white flag and a message from Grant. Stuart left the Yankees with the pickets and hurried the message to Lee, who was with Jackson and Johnston.

9:00 p.m.
May 29, 1865

General Lee,
Let's end this without further bloodshed. I'm willing to meet you to discuss the surrender of the Army of Northern Virginia. Can it not be over?

U.S. Grant

Lee passed the note to Johnston. "What of Pickett?"

"He lost over half his force."

Lee wilted at the news. "Well?" He asked the impassive Jackson.

Jackson drained his canteen. "What do you want to do?"

"General Stuart!"

"You're not going to surrender, are you?" Stuart cried. He knew the army had incurred a terrible licking today, but surrender?

"Not yet," Lee snapped, his face angry. "I'd like you to take a message to General Grant and ask what terms he would extend my men."

Stuart sat frozen on Centurion.

"Stuart," Jackson prompted.

"Of course," Stuart said swiftly.

"Give me just a minute," Lee snapped again. Johnston lit a candle and held it up while Lee scratched out a note.

With alarmed eyes, Stuart watched Lee. "Has it come to this?" He whispered to Jackson.

"It's in God's hands."

Stuart felt a chill race down his spine. Surrender! Even though Jackson had tried to warn him that this day was a very real possibility, he thought

Stonewall was just being overly cautious. He never conceived it could actually happen. Not with Lee and Jackson in command. They had accomplished the impossible so many times, Stuart believed they would continue to work their magic and find a way out of the Yankees' trap.

Lee came over to Stuart and handed up the note. "I'll wait for you here." Without another word, he stomped off.

On the main road to Charlottesville, Stuart and Colonel McClellan ran into Sheridan's pickets. Stuart asked to see General Grant, but an hour later, Sheridan rode up. "What do you want?" He demanded.

"I have a message for General Grant." Stuart took the note from his pocket and held it out. Sheridan snatched it from his hand. "I'm to wait for a reply."

Sheridan wasn't listening. He broke the seal and read the message. A triumphant smile erupted on his face. He sent an aide off with the letter.

Stuart dismounted to allow a weary Centurion the chance to graze. McClellan patterned his behavior after his surprisingly subdued chief. The adjutant glanced around and beheld a sea of campfires. An impressive display of the strength and power of the army now bearing down on the worn-out Confederates. The scent of roasting beef filled the breeze. Beside him, Stuart's stomach growled. It had been two days since the cavalry leader and his adjutant had shared the last of the cornbread.

The Yankees kept up a constant stream of vulgar comments about the Southern cavalry and Stuart in particular. Sheridan didn't contribute to the coarse insults, but neither did he order his men to stop. From beneath the brim of his hat, McClellan furtively watched Stuart and prayed his chief would ignore the rude jibes. The last thing he wanted was Stuart to resort to fisticuffs to defend his honor. Thankfully, Stuart ignored the vile slurs, though his jaw was clenched in anger and the knuckles grasping Centurion's reins were white with rage. *Just keep ignoring them, General.* Stuart didn't.

"I was sorry to hear that your recent stay at Front Royal was unpleasant," Stuart said breezily to Sheridan. "Is it true you lost a large portion of your baggage when you fled from Jackson in terror?" He chuckled.

Sheridan spluttered wordlessly, but Stuart had timed his rejoinder perfectly. Grant and Reynolds rode up.

"General Stuart!" Reynolds jumped off his horse and hurried over to shake Stuart's hand.

Grant scattered Sheridan's hooligans with a wave of his hand.

"General Grant, what would you have me tell General Lee?" Stuart asked the Union chief.

"Convince him of the folly of continuing," Grant said.

Stuart stiffened. "No, sir, that's not my place."

Grant sighed. "I'm trying to avoid more bloodshed." It was an appeal, but Stuart remained unmoved. "The only terms I can offer is unconditional surrender." Exasperation tinged his voice.

"I'll tell him." Stuart turned to Reynolds and spoke in a low voice. "General Lee's son, Custis, was captured at Jetersville. Could you check on him and send word? I'd be obliged." He gathered up Centurion's reins.

"I'll inquire immediately."

"Thank you."

"Unconditional surrender!" Devastated, Lee fell back in his chair.

Utterly spent, Stuart threw himself at Lee's feet. "General Reynolds said he would find out about Custis and send word."

"Thank you." Lee's voice had lost its previous irritation.

"I reckon already being there and all was not the same as going under a white flag to ask. So, technically, I didn't disobey any order."

"I applaud your initiative." There was a long silence. "I snapped at your earlier. I'm sorry."

Stuart sat up. "I do understand the decision you must make tomorrow if the battle goes against us." Lee reached out a hand and Stuart took it. "McClellan, Pope, Burnside, Hooker, Hancock, Reynolds, and Grant. They never out generaled you. We're only in this fix because they've out supplied us. And that was beyond your control. I know if the men had food in their bellies, and the horses could eat their fill of oats, we would whip them again."

"I believe you're right." Lee's smile was tired.

"Father, when's the last time you slept?"

"I'll sleep when General Jackson returns."

"No, you'll sleep now," Stuart said.

Lee's eyebrows shot up in amusement at the command in Stuart's voice. A grin tugged at his lips, but he didn't argue. Stuart laid out some blankets and made a pillow from his cape. Lee stretched out. He closed his eyes and fell asleep.

Stuart sat down in Lee's vacated chair and kept watch over the sleeping man until Jackson returned, trailed by his aides. Too exhausted to say their usual hellos, the young men unstrapped their bedrolls and lay down around the fire. They fell asleep the moment their heads hit the ground. Gentle snoring filled the night. Jackson poured himself a cup of coffee and offered some to Stuart. He refused. That bitter brew of roots and yams and whatever else the cooks concocted to pass as coffee made him ill.

"What did General Grant say?" Jackson asked.

"Unconditional surrender."

Jackson grimaced, but Stuart didn't know if it was from the coffee or the news. Jackson took another sip and poured what was left in the cup on the ground. "That's some terrible tasting coffee," he remarked.

"I don't know how you can drink it."

Jackson chuckled. He took out his watch. "Dawn will be here in about three hours. How about we grab some sleep." He crawled beneath his blanket.

"Is General Jackson back?" Lee asked, when Stuart lay down next to him.

"He just went to sleep." Stuart drew his blanket up around his shoulders.

"How are the men?"

"General Jackson says the Yankees will find the men in a feisty mood tomorrow."

Chapter Forty Five

Covesville, Virginia
May 30, 1865

The men *were* in a feisty mood as Grant soon discovered when he foolishly believed he could roll up Lee's army in a light charge consisting of the Second and Fifth Corps. The field in front of the Confederate defenses quickly filled with the dead and wounded. A triumphant Rebel yell chased his men back across the clearing. Grant called up the First Corps and sent his men back to work.

This time, the hammer he had been swinging since the Susquehanna shattered the Army of Northern Virginia. The center splintered and the blue troops poured through the breach, pushing the exhausted Confederates back against their defenses.

"It's over," Grant said with immense relief. He turned to Reynolds. "How long until the Sixth Corps can be brought up?"

"Thirty minutes."

"Then let's end it."

Reynolds sent orders to Warren.

"How easily I could be rid of this and be at rest," Lee murmured, watching as McLaws and Early gave way. "I have only to ride along the line and all will be over!"

At Lee's words, Stuart's heart fluttered madly. For a stunned moment, he couldn't speak but resisted the urge to grab Traveller's bridle. "I never told you about my last letter from Flora," he chattered in an attempt to distract Lee from his suicidal thoughts. "Jimmie caught a catfish with that fishing pole you bought him at Christmas. Remember? Father?"

Lee didn't answer. He just stared at the retreating Yankees.

Frightened, Stuart blurted out: "Papa!"

Lee turned his sad face to Stuart. "Was it a big one?" The words contained no emotion.

"Two feet, and he landed it himself." Stuart talked just for the sake of talking. "Flora wrote that he marched into the kitchen, held it up, and announced that he'd like catfish for dinner."

"He's a good boy."

"He can't wait to go fishing with you, Father." Stuart held his breath and waited for Lee to respond. Another long moment of silence passed. Stuart's heart raced into his throat. *Please talk to me.*

"I prefer Papa," Lee said. His brief smile was wintry. Stuart's heart wobbled back into his chest. He stared at Lee, but the older man hid his emotions behind bland brown eyes and an expressionless face.

"Now, let's go see General Jackson." Lee nudged Traveller and headed toward the shattered center.

Stuart urged Centurion forward and caught up with Traveller. He kept a sharp eye on Lee as they rode the shipwrecked line to where Jackson and Johnston, along with Hood, Early, and Rodes conversed in low but emotional tones. Couriers came in and out of the group with great speed. Lee and Stuart joined them.

"What's the situation, General Jackson?" Lee asked.

Jackson turned toward them. Stuart's heart sank. It was over. The light of battle, which had always burned in Jackson's eyes, had gone out. Stuart had never seen the blue-gray eyes so remote and distance. If God was merciful, the ground would open up and swallow him whole.

"Ah, I see." Lee's voice was calm. "General Johnston?"

All Johnston could utter was no.

"Then it's time for me to see General Grant." From across the field, bugles and drums called Grant's army to assembly. "Those people are preparing to charge again. At least, let's spare our men that. What do you suggest, General Jackson?"

The end came quickly. Under a white flag, Pendleton and Morrison rode out from the decimated center. They were met by five Yankees. A Union captain practically ripped the letter from Pendleton's hand. Waving swords and screaming huzzahs and hurrahs, the soldiers galloped back to the Union lines, which erupted into shouts of victory.

From all around him, Stuart heard a storm of catcalls. The army still wanted to fight. So did he.

Lee, Jackson, Stuart, and Pendleton rode up the half-mile, tree lined driveway of Kilkenny Gardens, a small plantation three miles west of Covesville. They were re-splendid in formal coats, sashes reaching to boot tops, and glistening swords and spurs. Jim, with tears dripping off his chin, had brushed Traveller, Little Sorrel, and Centurion until their coats shone.

As they neared the large farmhouse, the front door opened. A tall, white-haired gentleman came out on the porch. Pendleton dashed ahead and, with a low bow, introduced himself to Mr. Charles Waterman. The adjutant explained the circumstances that brought the Confederate generals to his home.

"Oh, no!" The elderly man cried. "Of course, of course. You're welcome here."

The men dismounted.

"Henry! Jacob!" Waterman called into the house. Two teenage boys spilled out of the door. "Take the horses round back and give them some feed and water. We don't have much, but what we have is yours," he said to Lee.

"Your kindness is appreciated," Lee assured him.

They followed Waterman up the stairs and into the dark, cool hallway.

"You can use the library." Waterman pointed to their right. The room was dimly lit; the far wall covered with bookshelves. Jackson gestured for Pendleton to go first.

"General Grant should be here at 11:30," Lee informed his host. Stuart headed toward the windows. "He won't be alone. Do you have a safe place you can retire to when those people arrive?"

"My grandsons and I should be safe enough in the kitchen. Do you need anything before I leave?"

Lee shook his head. Waterman slid the large oak doors together; they were alone.

Stuart opened the blue velvet curtains shrouding two large windows that overlooked the yard. The morning sunlight poured in, and the room came alive in brilliant shades of blue. An empty fireplace framed one wall. There was a large desk, a couch of sky blue silk, several chairs upholstered in royal blue velvet, and polished mahogany tables scattered throughout the room. The shelves glistened in a rainbow of books bound in various colors.

The volumes drew Jackson like a moth to the flame. Pendleton plopped down on the high-back couch and began a methodical search of his haversack. Stuart paced between the windows and peered out at the front lawn every time his circuit took him past a pane of glass. The sound of his jangling gold spurs filled the room. His watchcase opened and closed every few minutes.

Lee prowled about, not wanting to sit, not wanting to think. His fingers ran over the polished desk, and, despite his best efforts, he was back at

Arlington, in a home that would never be his again. *Why had they fought? Oh, Fitzhugh!*

With a tiny exclamation, Jackson found a book that interested him and joined Pendleton on the couch. He eagerly opened the small red volume and began to read. Stuart kept quiet watch between the two windows. Lee completed his circuit of the room. He finally settled into the velvet chair next to Jackson.

The small mantle clock rang the half hour. All looked up expectantly. Stuart stared out the window, but the driveway remained empty. One-by-one, they returned to their tasks. The minutes dragged by. The clock chimed noon. There was no sign of Grant. Stuart loudly sighed in exasperation.

"Stuart, sit down!" Jackson's voice filled the tense room like an artillery barrage.

Stuart did so. He fidgeted and squirmed in impatience. "I think it shows an immense lack of breeding to be late to a surrendering!" He declared, vexed.

Lee laughed until tears sprang up in his eyes. Since the New Year, he had been terrified of this hour. How he had wept and prayed to be spared its moment of testing. The fear had almost broken his will to live, for now he realized that if Stuart hadn't been with him, he might have acted on his desire to be spared this test. He didn't know when the hour had lost its ability to terrorize, but he knew why. There were three reasons. He glanced at Jackson absorbed in the book, murmuring his agreement with whatever the author had written. Stonewall, his right arm. "I'm your friend, Robert," Jackson had assured him when Lee was at his lowest. Never were truer words spoken, unless they were spoken by his young lieutenant general when, in fear, Stuart revealed the depths of his feelings by calling him "papa." And young Mr. Pendleton examining his haversack yet again. No matter what happened when those people arrived, whether he was taken prisoner or paroled, he knew he could endure the uncertain future. Not because he was suddenly brave or strong, but because he was not alone. "I don't know how I could have done this difficult thing without you," Lee smiled, first at Stuart and then at Jackson.

"You'd have found a way, sir," Pendleton said when Lee's glance fell upon him. "I've no doubt."

The sound of horses thundered up the drive. Stuart sprang to the window. "The yard is filled with Yankee generals. Thick as fleas. There must be at least 30."

"We're a little outnumbered," Lee quipped.

"We've never let that bother us in the past." Jackson returned the book to its place on the shelf and came to stand behind Lee's chair. Pendleton joined him.

Stuart slid open the doors and took his place along side Jackson. The front door creaked. The sound of boots in the hall. As Grant, Reynolds, Sheridan, and a host of other generals flooded the library, Lee stood and welcomed them as if they were his guests at Arlington.

Grant removed his hat. "I apologize for being late."

"It doesn't matter, you're here now." Lee returned to his seat. "I've reserved the desk for your use."

Grant sat down behind it. The rest of the generals crowded around him. Those who couldn't fit between the desk and the fireplace had to settle for standing in the doorway or in the hall.

"I've come to arrange the surrender of my army," Lee said, not wishing to prolong the ordeal.

Grant nodded. "The only terms I can offer is unconditional surrender. The men will be paroled and allowed to return home. All weapons and army property will be surrendered. As for you and Generals Jackson, Stuart, and Johnston, I have telegraphed President Lincoln to see if he desires your arrests. I was hoping to have an answer before I came. That's why I'm late."

Lee was careful not to reveal any emotion. Behind him, the three men were still as statues. "General Johnston is with the army."

Grant spoke low to one of the generals, who left the room. "I've sent for him," he informed the Confederate generals.

"Are we to be your prisoners, then?" Lee's voice was even.

"Until I hear from the president, yes."

"I see." He tugged on his sleeve cuff. "Well, if you'll write up the terms you've proposed, I'll see that my men act upon them."

Grant opened his order book. He took out a cigar and lit it. He puffed furiously while he pondered and wrote. The room was deathly still. No one spoke; no one moved. The only sound was Grant's pen scratching against paper. The mantle clocked chimed the half hour; its small musical notes loud in the quiet.

Grant dashed his cigar in the cut crystal ashtray on the desk. With a small slap, he closed his order book and handed it to Reynolds, who brought it to Lee.

Lee opened the book and flipped to the last entry. From his pocket, he drew his spectacles. He read the document several times. His face gave away nothing. When finished, he handed the book, opened to the surrender terms, to Jackson. The Second Corps Commander frowned as he read them. As he returned the book to Lee, Stuart stuck out his hand. Jackson hesitated, but after a nod from Lee, he surrendered the book to Stuart.

Stuart read a few lines and shook his head in disbelief. He addressed Grant. "Sir, unlike your army, my cavalry and the artillery personnel own their horses. I believe their animals should be exempt from being classified as captured army property."

Grant lit another cigar. "The terms are as stated."

"I had no idea your men owned their own horses," Reynolds interjected. He ignored the stare from Grant. "We don't have to change the terms. I'll just advise my men to allow the soldiers to return home with their animals."

Grant glared at Reynolds, but he acquiesced.

"Mr. Pendleton, please copy the terms," Lee said.

Pendleton sat down on the couch, took out Jackson's order book, and furiously copied the surrender terms.

"General Lee, do you need anything?" Reynolds asked.

Lee saw the concern in Reynolds' eyes. "Food for the men and forage for the animals. Whatever you can provide."

"Would 30,000 rations be enough?"

"What do you think, General Jackson?" Jackson agreed. "Thank you. That will be more than sufficient." He smiled at Reynolds.

"Colonel Rosengarten, beef, salt, hardtack, coffee, sugar, whatever you can lay your hands on," Reynolds ordered his adjutant. Rosengarten rounded up several of the Union officers and exited the room.

Pendleton finished his secretarial duties. He brought both order books, pen, inkbottle, and blotter to Lee. Lee quickly signed the surrender terms in Grant's book. Reynolds took the books to Grant. The Union chief examined both documents, was satisfied by what he read, and signed his name to the document contained within Jackson's book. Reynolds returned it to Pendleton.

Lee stood. "Since we're your prisoners, where would you like us to wait until you hear from Mr. Lincoln?" He asked Grant.

"There's a clearing with some nice shade trees across the road from the driveway. I believe you'll be comfortable there. It won't be for long. While you wait, I'll have some lunch brought to you."

"Mr. Pendleton, could you please have the horses brought around?" Lee asked.

Pendleton hastened from the room.

"If there's nothing else, we'll retire to the clearing to await the verdict." Lee headed out of the room. He paused at the front door to don his gauntlets. Jackson fidgeted impatiently beside him. Where was Jeb? A quick glance discovered him talking to Reynolds. Stuart thanked the Union general and joined them. Jackson pushed open the front door and stepped outside.

"General Reynolds just informed me that Custis is safe and on his way home," Stuart said.

Relief rather than happiness poured through Lee at the news. His sons were safe and war could no longer claim their lives. He offered up a grateful prayer to the Savior. Pendleton arrived with the horses. Wanting nothing more than to be away from this place, Lee hurried down the stairs, leaving Stuart to catch up. He took Traveller's reins from the adjutant.

"Sir, we've got trouble." Jackson pointed up to the porch. Sheridan had blocked Stuart's way and would not let him past.

"Do you find yourself unsatisfied on some account?" Stuart's voice, hard and edged with steel, floated down to them. "Because I'll be happy to oblige you right here and now. Surrender or no. Just say the word."

"STUART!" Jackson bellowed, angrier than Lee had ever seen him.

Stuart stepped around Sheridan and skipped down the stairs. Jackson collared him at the bottom and gave him a lecture complete with admonishing finger. Sheridan stared down at Stuart, murder in his face.

A chastened Stuart walked over to Lee. "The war is over, my dear boy," Lee laughed and handed his young lieutenant general Centurion's reins.

"Yes, Father."

"I much prefer papa," Lee said with an affectionate smile. He swung up on Traveller and saluted Grant and Reynolds as they came out on the porch. The Union generals returned the salute. Lee turned and cantered down the driveway. Jackson, Stuart, and Pendleton saluted and followed their commanding general.

Chapter Forty Six

Jackson watched his weathered-stained canvas home fall to the ground for the last time. His wagon was already packed with his trunks and papers – all that remained of the Second Corps of the Army of Northern Virginia. In his pocket was his parole, signed by Grant and Reynolds, guaranteeing his freedom so long as he didn't take up arms against the United States Government. At the surrender ceremony yesterday each soldier received a similar parole.

"General Jackson!"

He turned and saw Early dismounting.

"I've come to say goodbye."

Jackson smiled at the gruff little man. "What are your plans?"

"Home and after that, I don't know. I just wanted to say…" Tears trickled down his weathered cheeks. "Oh, the hell with it…" He hugged a surprised Jackson. "It's been an honor, General. An honor." Without another word, he remounted and disappeared down the path.

A rush of tears stung Jackson's eyes. He took out his watch to give himself something else to concentrate on. He opened the case, but couldn't read the numbers. An appreciated distraction drew near: Pendleton and Smith, leading horses. Jackson closed his watch and slipped it back into his pocket. "So you're off!"

"Yes, sir. I told my father we'd arrive at his camp before breakfast," Pendleton said.

Smith pulled the cinch tight on his saddle. "I'll go to Richmond if you want," he said to Jackson.

"That's not necessary. Do you have the key to my house?" Smith nodded. "I talked to Doctor McGuire last night. He'll be staying with you once he ships the last of the wounded to the hospital in Washington City. So, you should expect him by the end of next week. Now, both you boys will look after Jim on the trip."

At the mention of his name, Jim came around the last falling tent. He carried a cup of coffee. "You don't have to worry none about me, sir. I'se have your house ready when you and Mrs. Anna comes home." He handed the mug to Jackson.

"Don't neglect yourself, Jim." Jackson sipped the rich coffee. Since the surrender, there had been plenty of real coffee and food enough to fill the stomach. "When I arrive, I'll expect to see a sturdy bed with a soft mattress in your room."

Jim's eyes glowed warmly at Jackson's fussing. "Yes, sir," he said and saluted. He took the reins of a bay mare from Pendleton.

"If you're going to meet General Pendleton, then you best be on your way. If you need anything, send word for me at the Hoges."

"Bye, Joe!" The three men shouted at Morrison, who appeared from the direction of the corral; Little Sorrel poking his pocket in search of a treat. The dust settled and Jackson and Morrison were alone.

Jackson swung up on Little Sorrel. "Let's go home, Joe."

When the Yankees marched over Bull Run Creek, Richmond emptied. The roads south spilled over with refugees. Then Butler marched north from Norfolk and south was no longer a safe destination. The refugees headed west toward Lee and the army. Where Lee was, there was safety. Flora Stuart and her children were among the human flood seeking a safe haven. After days of walking, she managed to rent a small house in Perkinsville.

It was to this house, the weary travelers headed. Two days after Lee, Jackson, and Stuart made their final farewells to the men who had followed them faithfully for four years, they trotted down the street and found the small wooden structure with its sagging porch, broken windows, and desperate need of paint.

Stuart stared at the dwelling and shuddered. Would this dilapidated house be the best he could provide for his family? He became aware of Jackson watching him. He turned his head so Jackson wouldn't see his fears.

"Together, we'll make it," Jackson murmured.

Stuart tried to smile but failed.

The front gate refused to open, so Stuart gave it a swift kick. The gate flew off its hinges and blocked the gravel path. Another kick sent it into the weed-infested yard. Overhead, mockingbirds screeched and screamed. An empty nest lay abandoned in a half-dead tree. The corpsmen unhitched the mules from the wagons and led the braying animals around back. Across the street, a widow appeared on a wooden stoop.

"Why are you all making such a racket?" She demanded angrily. "My children have the croup and need their sleep."

Lee offered apologies. With another glare at the noisy interlopers, she disappeared into a decrepit hovel.

Flora came out onto the porch, such a pretty picture in a blue dress, she stole Stuart's breath away. He ran up the steps, careful to sidestep the holes in the stairs, and caught her in his arms. She playfully pushed at him and cried: “Don’t!” Stuart ignored her protests, pulled her to him, and gave her a hearty kiss.

“You let me go!” She ordered, laughing.

“One more kiss, Honeypot, and I will.”

Flora kissed him on the nose, wriggled free, and greeted Lee.

“Daughter, I don’t know how you manage it, but you grow prettier every time I see you.” Lee kissed her cheek.

Stuart bounced up and down in excitement. “Flora, this is General Jackson,” he announced grandly.

Jackson blushed and climbed the steps.

“General Jackson, I’ve heard so much about you that I feel like I already know you,” Flora said, fighting off Stuart’s attempt to kiss her again.

“I feel the same way, Mrs. Stuart,” Jackson replied with a small bow.

“It’s Flora.”

“Then I’m Tom,” he smiled shyly. He turned his attention to the bottom of the steps and motioned Morrison onto the porch. “This is my brother-in-law, Joseph Morrison.”

“Joe, ma’am.” Morrison took off his hat and bowed at the waist.

Ginny toddled onto the porch. Behind her, she dragged a quacking toy duck on wheels. She took one look at all the men, pivoted, and toddled right back into the house.

“That was my Ginny,” Stuart laughed, when the quacking faded. “Flora, you remember Colonel McClellan.” The adjutant waved from the yard.

“Of course I do. I’m very glad to see you again.” She addressed the men. “Unfortunately, the butcher correctly guessed why I ordered a large roast this morning. He has proven to be a most excellent town-crier. Tributes have been arriving for you all day. So, we’ve plenty of cakes and pies and cold lemonade to drink.”

“Flora, where’s Jimmie?” Stuart questioned. “I want him to meet ole Stonewall.”

She frowned and pointed in the direction of the side porch.

“Jimmie!” Stuart rubbed his hands in anticipation. He rounded the corner and beheld the little boy sitting on the steps. His arms were crossed on his knees, and his face was buried in his arms. His small body heaved in silent sobs. “Jimmie?” Stuart sat down next to his weeping son. “What’s the matter?”

Jimmie looked up at his father, his little face blotchy and tear stained. "Is it true? Are we 'rendered?"

"I'm sorry, Jimmie…" Stuart got no further. Jimmie buried his head in his arms and, with a large yowl, began his sobs anew. Stuart scooped him up and held him close.

"I don't like being 'rendered." He wailed into Stuart's chest.

"That's because you haven't thought of all the fun things that come from being surrendered."

Jimmie's tears stopped as if someone turned off a faucet. "What things?" He gazed expectantly at his father.

"Your pa never has to leave you again," Lee said, sitting down next to Stuart. "And you and I can finally go fishing." He poked the boy in his stomach.

"And buy candy?" Jimmie asked eagerly.

"That's the deal we made at Christmas."

Jimmie flashed his grandfather a huge smile.

"And I'm going to buy you a pony and teach you to ride," Stuart said.

"My very own…" Jimmie fell silent. Jackson had come around the side of the house.

"Jimmie, this is General Jackson." Stuart winked at Lee.

Jimmie ducked his head against Stuart's chest. Then he pulled his father's head down and whispered in his ear. Stuart nodded. Jimmie ducked his head again. When he dared to peek at Jackson again, his eyes were as round as silver dollars. "Are you really ole Stonewall?"

Jackson sat down on the other side of Stuart. Jimmie's eyes never left him. "People call me that, but I'd like you to call me Uncle Tom."

Jimmie giggled and ducked his head against Stuart's chest.

"Gentlemen, come and get something to eat," Flora called from the kitchen door. "Jimmie, there's gingerbread."

Jimmie pulled on Jackson's sleeve. "Do you like gingerbread?" He whispered.

"I do," Jackson replied with a kind smile. He reached over and plucked the boy off Stuart's lap and placed him on his own.

Jimmie stared rapturously at his hero. "You know, when I played army," he gushed, "I got to flank the Yankees and everythin'. Oh, it was so much fun." His face fell and his lower lip trembled. "I guess with us 'rendered, you won't be flankin' the Yankees no more."

"That's true," Jackson acknowledged. "But sitting here with you, your father, and grandfather is a whole lot more fun than flanking the Yankees. I'm hungry for some gingerbread. How about you?"

Jimmie's head bobbed up and down. Jackson set the boy on his feet and followed him into the house.

"You go ahead, Father," Stuart said to Lee. "I'll be there in a moment."

"Are you sure?" Stuart nodded. With a tired groan, Lee stood. "Jeb." Stuart looked up. "I do prefer papa." Lee went into the house.

Stuart felt a wave of happiness sweep through him. Through the window, he could hear the voices of Lee, Jackson, Morrison, and McClellan intermingled with Flora's soft drawl, Jimmie's high-pitched laughter, and Ginny's happy chattering. These were the sounds of his life now. How he preferred them over the boom of artillery, the rattle of musketry, and the shout of orders. He raised his eyes to Heaven and thanked God for not only bringing him safely through the war but filling his life with a multitude of loved ones.

"Pa?" Jimmie stood in front of the door. He held out a plate of gingerbread.

"Come here." Jimmie hurried over. Once more, Stuart sat him on his lap. "Do you know how much I love you? No? Let me show you." Stuart tickled him until he squealed with laughter.

The first stars had just appeared in the dark blue sky when the small wagon train halted in front of the Lee home in Richmond. The house was ablaze with light. A face appeared in the window. Lee recognized his youngest daughter; his "precious life." The door opened. Custis appeared on the porch, holding a lantern. Behind him, came Lee's daughters; their excited voices drifting down the walk.

"General Jackson, you're welcome to come in," Lee invited.

Jackson shifted in his saddle. "Sir, I'm four blocks from my family. I think Joe and I will press on."

"Of course. Why don't I come and visit your family the day after tomorrow, if that is acceptable."

"More than acceptable," Jackson agreed.

"Are you coming, Jeb?" Lee opened the gate and waited for Stuart.

"In a moment," Stuart said. He bent and twisted in a myriad of positions, working out the kinks in his body.

Lee waved goodbye and hurried up the walk. His girls could wait no longer. They ran down the steps and into his waiting arms.

"Will I see you in the morning?" Jackson asked Stuart.

Before Stuart could answer, a small group of Union soldiers walked past. He watched them go down the sidewalk. "I'll never get used to Yankees in Richmond. I can't believe the war is over."

"It won't be for me until I kiss my wife."

"Go on. I'll see you in the morning!" Stuart gave Little Sorrel a pat.

Jackson nudged the small Morgan and cantered down the road.

Jackson took the steps two at a time and the wide porch in four long strides. Before he could knock on the door, it flung open. Anna threw herself in his arms, crying incoherently. Jackson wrapped his arms around her and kissed her.

"I can't believe you're home to stay!" She declared.

Jackson placed his large hand over her stomach. "How's the baby?"

"Everything's fine," Anna reported dutifully. "I had a doctor's appointment yesterday and received a clean bill of health. Oh, Joe!"

Morrison came upon the porch laden down the saddlebags. "Drop those bags and give your sister a hug." The moment the bags landed on the porch, she hugged him close. "I'm never letting either of you out of my sight again. Now, come," she slipped her arm through Jackson's. "Your daughter has been waiting all day for you."

They went into the house.

"Papa! Papa! Papa!" Jackson heard Julia's chirping as Hetty, her nurse, carried her down the large staircase. He took her from Hetty and was stunned by the changes. Julia was taller, and her face wasn't as babyish, but the blue-gray eyes were still his own.

She squeezed his neck. "Tea party, Papa!"

"Oh, not tonight, darling. It's bedtime," Anna said.

"'Morrow?" She squeezed Jackson's neck again.

"Tomorrow and every day afterwards." Jackson reached over, pulled Anna close, and thanked God for His blessings.

Chapter Forty Seven

"It's amazing what victory will do," Lincoln said to Grant with a chuckle. For the past hour, he had stood in the White House's Red Room, shaking hands with the recently converted. Four years of scorn, ridicule, and revilement past the point of decency wiped away at Covesville. Hail to the Chief! Hail to the Victor! Now, his former enemies confided, with straight faces and sincere voices, that his stubborn determination to see the war through had been the right course all along. How glad his new friends were that they had joined him in the trenches to lift up his fatigued arms so the fighting could continue.

Grant glowered. He didn't like public spectacles, and, since his return to Washington, he had become one. He stood in his formal uniform and stiff collar, shaking hands until his own hand was bruised and swollen. What was worse, Mary Todd Lincoln had forbidden smoking in the receiving line. He was desperate for a cigar. He glanced out the wide double doors of the red wallpapered room and saw the line twisting and snaking down the hall. He groaned. If everyone continued to greet him like long-lost relations, he would never smoke a cigar again.

Reynolds didn't like the attention any better than Grant. He stood with an unnatural rigidity and pumped each hand once before passing the admirer on to Grant. Sheridan, on the other hand, had stood in line for a whole fifteen minutes before he huffed in exasperation and departed. Not even a nasty glare from Mrs. Lincoln could bring him back. With a sullen sneer on his face, he stood at the punch bowl and drank glass after glass of the sugary concoction. The cavalry leader would have fled altogether, but Stanton and Secretary of State Seward had cornered him and proceeded to pepper him with a thousand questions about the march from Manassas to Covesville. Grant laughed. It seemed rude didn't deter politicians.

"Shall we make a break for it," Grant whispered to Reynolds, who pumped another hand and shoved the young wife of an old senator toward him.

"I'd like nothing better," Reynolds replied, ignoring the praises from the old senator.

"Only if you take me with you," Lincoln stage whispered. "I can't believe what standing in your victorious shadows has done for my popularity."

"Sir, we're military men. We're not used to such public displays," Grant complained.

"There's dancing after the supper buffet." Grant deflated in defeat. "You might as well get use to it, General Grant. You, too, General Reynolds. You're the men of the hour. Even those who hated us, now fall prostrate at our feet."

Grant pointed to a dark haired man with a dark mustache. "That's a familiar face. He has as many eyes on him as we do," he said to Reynolds.

Reynolds strained his neck to get a better view. "I believe that's John Wilkes Booth, the actor. Good news! I think I see the end of the line."

"Don't tease me, John. I haven't had a cigar for ages."

Reynolds shook Booth's hand and introduced him to Grant.

"General Grant, I'm honored to meet you." Booth's voice was silky with sincerity.

"Mr. Booth, I saw your Hamlet. It was a magnificent portrayal. Top notch! May I present to you my wife. Julia, this is John Wilkes Booth."

Julia, freshly arrived from the salon, greeted the actor and enthused over his Hamlet.

"You're too kind, Mrs. Grant. Too kind indeed." Booth stuck his hand in his pocket.

"Is this your first time in the White House?" Julia asked.

Booth removed his hand from his pocket and something silver flashed. He raised his arm. A loud pop; the acrid smell of gunpowder filled the room. The President fell backward onto the floor. The concussion of the shot echoed loudly before it faded into silence. Booth raised his arm again. A bullet ripped into Grant's temple. Grant collapsed; Reynolds caught him.

Booth threw down a derringer and ran toward the double doors. Another burst of gunfire sent the guests cowering behind tables, couches, and chairs. Reynolds looked up from his kneeling position and saw Booth lying dead at the feet of two soldiers.

The room thawed into pandemonium. A keening scream rose high above the confusion. Hysterical, Mary Lincoln fell prostrate across her husband and begged him to wake up. Blood flowed across the red carpet. Lincoln was dead.

Julia pressed her lace handkerchief against Grant's temple. She spoke softly to him. His mumbled responses were coherent.

Sheridan tore the crowd away and threw himself down next to his fallen chief. "General Grant…" He choked out.

"Sheridan, I think I…" Grant fell silent.

"Let's get him upstairs into one of the bedrooms," Reynolds said. "Sergeant!" He had to yell to be heard over the high-pitch wailing.

Four soldiers sprang forward. They lifted Grant from the floor – "Gently!" Sheridan commanded – and carried him out of the room and away from the horrible screams ripping through the Red Room.

The soldiers entered the first bedroom they came to. They laid Grant on a large four-poster bed. Blood seeped from his temple, staining the white linen pillowcase. The doctors moved in. From the doorway, Reynolds saw Lincoln's body being borne down the hall. Mrs. Lincoln stumbled after her husband. She was still shrieking, out of her mind with fear and grief.

Stanton burst into the room. "General Reynolds, General Sheridan, come with me!"

It was an order, so with one more look at the fallen Grant, the two generals followed the Secretary of War down the hall and into the Cabinet Room. Stanton lit a lamp. Reynolds sat down at the long table. Sheridan sat opposite him. Through the windows, Reynolds could see the streets filling with people: angry, combustible, demanding retribution against the South. They were one incendiary speech away from turning into a lawless mob.

"There has been an attempt on the lives of both the Vice President and the Chief Justice," Stanton announced grimly.

"When?" Reynolds asked.

The murderous shouts from the street intensified.

"The same time the president was murdered. We've no idea how far the conspiracy goes. I do know it has a Rebel stench all over it." Stanton clawed his goatee in agitation. "Booth had a letter in his pocket where he confessed he killed the president…" Stanton's voice broke. He swallowed and dabbed at his eyes with a large handkerchief. "To avenge the South's defeat. He urges Lee to retake the field and keep fighting. To prevent that from happening, I want you to arrest Lee and any other Confederate general you can lay your hands on."

Reynolds recoiled. "On what grounds?"

"Treason!" Stanton slammed his hand down on the table, shaking the lamp. Their shadows jumped and danced on the wall.

"Do you have any proof linking Lee to Booth?"

"Proof!" Stanton's arms made wide gestures of indignation; the handkerchief whirling about. "The President is dead. General Grant is dying. They were murdered by a Southern. That's all the proof I need."

It appeared to Reynolds that Stanton was well on his way to becoming his own lawless mob. "That may well be…"

"General Reynolds, I gave you an order," Stanton shouted. His face turned a deep purple. He rammed the handkerchief into his suit pocket and glared at the truculent general.

"General Grant and I gave those men our word…"

"Are you refusing a direct order?" Stanton bellowed incredulously.

"I'll arrest them," Sheridan volunteered. He stood and silently appealed to Stanton to give him permission.

"Sit down, Phil!" Reynolds yelled.

Sheridan returned to his seat but remained coiled, waiting for Stanton to give him permission to strike.

"The army won't be used to settle such an obvious political score," Reynolds stated coolly.

"Even if ordered by the commander-in-chief?" Stanton barked, apoplectic at Reynolds' refusal.

"When last I checked, you weren't him."

Furious, Stanton glared at him. Then he stomped from the room and slammed the door behind him. Once more shadows danced on the walls.

"I always thought you loved those Rebs a little too much," Sheridan sneered.

Enraged, Reynolds lunged across the table at Sheridan. Lucky for Phil, he couldn't reach him, or he would have thrashed the cavalry leader within an inch of his life. He sat back in his chair. "You best clear out of my sight, Phil," he ground out between clenched teeth, "before I have you arrested and thrown into the foulest cell I can find."

With the same murderous glare Reynolds had seen countless times in the past two years, Sheridan bolted the room.

Reynolds walked over to the window and threw it open. He stuck his head out and breathed in the cool night breeze. Below, the crowds seethed and boiled. The cries for vengeance escalated. It wouldn't be long before he would have to send soldiers into the streets to keep order.

The angry voices followed Reynolds out of the room and down the hall. He halted at the bedroom door and steeled himself for what he would find inside. He tiptoed in. The atmosphere was thick with hopelessness, like fog in a river valley. The doctors were losing the battle. Reynolds stood at the headboard and stared down at Grant's waxen face until a doctor elbowed him roughly out the way.

Reynolds glanced around for a place to stand. He saw Julia Grant huddled in a wing-back chair. He joined her. "How is he?" He didn't know why he asked such a foolish question. He knew the answer.

She was very pale, but composed. She grasped the bloodstained handkerchief in her hand. "He's dying," she whispered.

A drop splashed; Reynolds' cup overflowed.

Unable to withstand Seward's cold analytical assessment of the emergency or Stanton's bellowings, Vice President, now President Hamlin signed his first executive order and commanded Reynolds to arrest Lee, Jackson, Stuart, and Johnston for treason. Stanton returned to the White House and re-summoned Reynolds and Sheridan to the Cabinet Room. With unconcealed triumph, he flourished Hamlin's edict. Reynolds ripped it in shreds and fed it into the lamp's flame.

Stanton handed Sheridan a duplicate set of orders. "General Sheridan, you'll take command." Sheridan raced from the room.

"You're breaking the promise General Grant made to those men," Reynolds said.

"General Grant was wrong to make it," Stanton retorted.

"So you're leaving?" Lee asked, startling Stuart in the dark quiet of the house. Lee lit a candle next to the bed and illuminated his young lieutenant general standing in the doorway, saddlebags thrown carelessly over his shoulders. He motioned for Stuart to enter.

Stuart laid the bags in the hall, walked over to the bed, and plopped down on the end. "I told Flora I'd be home today."

Lee cleared his throat. "Oh, Jeb." He took Stuart's hand. "I've been steeling myself for this moment since the war ended, but I find I can't do it. I can't tell you goodbye. It's too soon."

"Well, I've come up with the perfect solution to that problem," Stuart said merrily. "Come to Lexington with me and General Jackson. We'll raise horses and children together."

" Jeb…"

"Papa," Stuart interrupted. "Have I ever asked you for anything?"

"No, you've only wanted me to be happy."

"Then come to Lexington, and I'll look after your happiness forever."

He couldn't love Jeb Stuart more than he did at this moment. He squeezed Stuart's hand. "What if I travel with General Jackson to Lexington next week. Just to see what my options are. Oh, how I love that sunny smile, but I can't be swayed by it. I have responsibilities and obligations that must come first. I mean it, Jeb."

"It's enough that you're coming." Stuart gave Lee a stern glare. "I give you fair warning. I plan to wage an arduous campaign to convince you to stay."

"I quake for my future," Lee said with mock terror. "Now, I must insist on a kiss before you go."

Stuart kissed Lee's cheek and allowed Lee to kiss his.

"You must think me an old woman with all my kissing and pawing," Lee half-apologized in embarrassment.

"I think you're the greatest man I've ever known." He kissed Lee's cheek again. "Now, I must be going. Flora's waiting."

Lee walked him to the door. Stuart hurried down the stairs and walk.

"Goodbye, Papa!" Stuart called from Centurion.

"Goodbye, my son!"

Centurion's hoofs clattered in the street. Lee shut the door and went back to bed. He blew out the candle. Lexington! What opportunities were there for an old soldier in Jackson's beloved Valley? He was almost asleep when he heard someone pounding on the door as if to knock it off its hinges.

Chapter Forty Eight

Reverend Hoge rushed downstairs. Someone was pounding on his front door. He moved through the foyer, avoiding the windows that fronted the porch. He stepped to one side of the door and peeped out a window. He immediately drew back into the shadows. "Yankees!" He hissed up the stairs to where Jackson stood.

"You better let them in before they knock the door down," Jackson said.

Hoge chanced another look. This time, he was spotted. A Yankee captain shouted something and gestured for Hoge to open the door. Taking his time, the reverend unlocked the door and cracked it. The door was thrust open, knocking him against the wall. Hoge banged his head and was momentarily stunned.

"Is Thomas Jackson here? Well?" The captain barked when Hoge didn't answer fast enough.

Hoge glanced up the steps; Jackson had disappeared. He nodded.

"Get him! I have a warrant for his arrest."

"What for!" Hoge blurted out, more from surprise than curiosity.

"That is none of your business. Now, are you going to get him, or do we tear the place apart looking for him?"

From upstairs, a door opened then closed. The sound of boots echoed on the wooden floor. Jackson came down the steps fully dressed. "I'm General Jackson."

"I have a warrant for your arrest."

"What are the charges, Captain?"

"Conspiracy to commit treason against the United States Government."

Jackson reached into his pocket and pulled out his parole. "I have my parole signed by General Grant…"

"You Rebs should have thought about that before you murdered him," one of the sergeants hissed from the door.

Hoge gasped, but Jackson received the blow without expression. "Then I insist on speaking with General Reynolds." He returned the paper to the safety of his pocket.

"General Reynolds has been relieved of duty. General Sheridan is in command." The captain motioned to his men.

A fat corporal stepped forward. "Hold out your hands!"

Jackson did as he was told. Snickering, the corporal clasped heavy manacles around his wrists and shackled his feet. "Come on, you Reb trash." He pushed Jackson forward.

Jackson lost his balance and crashed against the door jamb. Indignant, Hoge tried to interfere only to receive a backhand across the face. Jackson protested, but quickly quieted when the corporal thrust a bayonet against his throat.

"Move!" The captain barked at Jackson.

Jackson hobbled out the door and into the night. The streets were deserted. The steps he had run up only four days ago now proved a daunting challenge. The shackles' chain only stretched far enough to allow his feet to graze each step. When he arrived at the bottom in one piece, Jackson thanked God for His small mercies.

He was pushed over to a covered wagon and half-lifted, half-tossed into the back. He rolled over and sat up, but fell against the wagon's side when it lurched forward and started down the street. The wagon turned. He tried to lift up the cover to see where the Yankees were taking him, but the canvas was lashed tight and wouldn't give. The wagon halted and spilled him forward.

The soldiers dismounted. A few minutes later, Jackson heard them pounding on a door. Custis Lee's voice filled the night, then General Lee's. The door closed. Suddenly, it was quiet.

Jackson sat up. The wind of doom swept through him. Grant dead! Reynolds relieved! Sheridan in command! Their paroles worthless! Arrested secretly in the night! From the street, Jackson could hear the stamping of feet as soldiers prowled beside the wagon, making sure their prisoner stayed put. Gusseted like a Christmas goose, how could he escape?

A fearful premonition seized his heart. Anna's face, pale with fear as she clutched at him in the bedroom, swam before his eyes. He would never hold her or Julia again! He began to pray: a rush of words that made little sense. He kept praying until the fear subsided, and he could breathe again.

The front door opened. Footsteps hurried down the walk. A gate squeaked and the steps came closer. The canvas flap was thrown back and the tailgate was lowered. A body was thrown in. It was Lee! The soldiers reversed the process, and Jackson was plunged in darkness.

"Here, General Lee! Let me help you." Jackson maneuvered and half-dragged, half-jerked Lee into a sitting position. "Didn't they want Stuart?" He whispered.

"Yes, but he was already gone. He has about a 15-minute head start. Custis was able to convince those people that Stuart was headed toward Patrick County."

The wagon came to a sudden stop. Lee and Jackson tossed and tumbled into each other. The Yankees departed, and, after the now routine pounding on the door, there was silence.

Quiet footsteps approached the wagon.

"General Jackson!" Jackson recognized his brother-in-law's terrified voice. "What can I do?"

"Stuart is on his way to Perkinsville," Jackson whispered. "Find him and warn him."

"Is there anything else?"

The premonition assaulted him again and stole away his speech. He fought back his fear. "Watch after my family, Joe." A moment's hesitation. "Until I return home," he added. It was a mustard seed of faith, and Jackson prayed it would be enough.

"I will. I have to go. The Yankees are coming."

They heard him steal away from the wagon. The tailgate was lowered and another body was thrown in. Groans of pain revealed it to be Johnston. He had argued his innocence a little too vigorously and paid for it with a rifle butt to the head.

"Captain," Lee said before the flap was closed. "Where are you taking us?"

"Fort McNair, Washington City." The flap came down. The wagon plodded down the empty streets.

Eight weary days and nights later, the wagon halted inside Fort NcNair. An armed guard waited; rifles and bayonets at the ready. Jackson laughed in disbelief. What danger did this bedraggled, exhausted, and chained threesome present? With shoves from rifle butts, the Confederate generals were marched into the bowels of the fort. In the murky light, Jackson saw a long hall lined with cells. At the end of the hall, two armed sentries stood and watched the procession.

Johnston was shoved headfirst into the first cell on the right. The heavy door slammed and keys rattled in the dark. Jackson and Lee were propelled, by bayonet, down the hall toward the door guarded by the sentries. At their approach, the sentinels snapped to attention.

The fat corporal swung the door open and first Jackson, then Lee, were pushed into the dank room. Jackson stumbled but managed to keep his feet. Behind him, Lee crashed heavily to the floor. Jackson reached down his hand to help, but the fat corporal slammed a rifle butt into his shoulder. Tired of being pushed, prodded, and abused, Jackson fired up and challenged the corporal. With a quick shake of the head, Lee ordered Jackson to stand down. It was the hardest order Jackson ever obeyed, but obey it he did. Lee managed to find his feet. His jacket was covered with the same slime that carpeted the stone floor.

Jackson glanced around. From the barred window opposite the door, a foul order wafted into the cell. Each side wall had an iron bed frame pressed against it. Drops of water dripped on the moldy, rat eaten mattresses and the stiff, mildewed blankets. At the end of the beds, close to the window, stood a rickety table and two spindly chairs. The angry squeals of rats protested this intrusion of their home. A large rat ran over Jackson's boots.

"Turn around Reb," the corporal ordered Jackson. Roughly, the soldier removed the shackles. Jackson wanted to stretch his arms wide to relieve his cramping muscles, but he wasn't given the chance. "Over here!" The corporal barked. He gestured for Jackson to join him at the end of the bed.

Jackson saw an iron ring attached to the wall and a rusty chain attached to the ring. At the end of the chain was a shackle.

"Do you mean to chain me to the wall?" Jackson asked incredulously.

"Can't have you Rebs escaping after what it cost us to defeat all of you."

"All of us?" Lee asked. His shackles were off, and he was rubbing his wrists.

"Sherman finally ran Longstreet to ground. He surrendered two days ago. Sheridan ordered his arrest, so you can look forward to company all the way from Georgia."

Jackson was ordered to take off his boots. He sat down on the bed and did as ordered. Water from the floor soaked his thin socks. The shackle went around his left ankle and was secured by a small lock. Another click confirmed Lee was shackled as well.

"I hope you like your new home," the corporal jeered. He slammed the door behind him.

Jackson pulled on the ring; it didn't budge. Three more pulls failed to dislodge it. He slipped toward the window only to be halted by the chain a good five feet from his goal. A hostile rat stared at him from the table. He chased it away. The rodent crawled up the stone wall and disappeared out the window. Jackson crossed to the bed, peeled back the stiff and filthy blanket, and sat down on the mattress. Straws poked him like tens of sharp needles. He leaned against the wall, but straightened up when he discovered the walls were as wet as the floor. He moved the bed away from the wall then collapsed back on it.

"How are you, sir?" He asked Lee.

Lee was examining the shackle around his ankle. "All I can think of is that I could sleep for a month."

"Well, why don't we start with that," Jackson said, coiling the long chain at the foot of the bed. He lay down and fell asleep.

Chapter Forty Nine

The knock on the door was so soft that, at first, Charles Waterman thought he imagined it. He looked up from the book he was reading and listened intently. Silence. He returned to the novel. No, he didn't imagine the small tap, for there it was again. Waterman set the book down on the table, went into the foyer, and heard another soft knock, more insistent than the other two.

"Who's there?" He asked through the heavy door.

"General Stuart."

Jeb Stuart? Puzzled as to why the South's Beau Saber would return to Kilkenny Gardens, Waterman opened the door and observed the haggard cavalry commander standing next to a younger man, who was peering about like he expected Yankees to jump out of the bushes. "General, this is a surprise."

"May I come in?" Stuart's request was urgent.

"Of course." Waterman stepped aside. Stuart and the young man slipped by.

"I'm sorry, sir, to come so suddenly upon you." Stuart stripped off his gauntlets and hat. "This is Captain Morrison." He gestured at Morrison, who bowed. "He's General Jackson's brother-in-law."

Waterman sized up the disheveled men. Both appeared not to have slept for a week. They were filthy; their uniforms covered with dried mud and dust. Their eyes darted here and there; they jumped at every sound. Waterman thought back to the surrender and Stuart in his cape and plumes; his uniform glittering with braid. He couldn't image what had occurred to reduce Stuart to such a state.

Waterman gestured toward the library. "Come and have a seat."

"Sir, do you think your grandsons could tend to our horses. I have money." Stuart reached into his jacket and pulled out a worn leather wallet.

"General Stuart, your money is no good here," Waterman said with a kind smile. "Henry! Jacob!"

The teenagers rambled down the stairs. "Could you see to our guests' horses? Thank you, boys," he called after them as they trooped out the door.

Waterman ushered his guests into the library. He sat down in his chair. "Now, General Stuart, who is after you?"

Stuart didn't deny the charge. He took up position next to the window and peered out at the lawn and driveway. "You haven't heard the news?"

"Well, yes," Waterman replied, mystified by the question and Stuart's behavior, not to mention Captain Morrison standing guard at the library's entrance. "I know that both Mr. Lincoln and General Grant have been assassinated."

"General Lee and General Jackson have been arrested for those murders." Stuart left the window and collapsed on the couch.

"That's absurd!" Waterman scoffed.

"There's a warrant for my arrest, too," Stuart informed his host. "I need a place to stay, while I think about my next step."

There it was. Stuart had come to Kilkenny Gardens to hide. "You're more than welcome to stay."

"Thank you." Stuart slumped against the back of the couch.

Waterman gazed at the exhausted men. "General Stuart, when was the last time you ate?" He didn't wait for a reply. "Supper should be ready in about an hour." He stood. "Why don't I show you to your room? You can wash up and have a good rest. I'll call you when dinner is on the table."

"Do you have a plan?" Morrison asked Stuart after Waterman departed.

"At the moment, no."

Morrison plunked down on the bed. He was wildly disappointed in Stuart. Ever since he had caught up with the cavalry leader on the road to Perkinsville, he had waited for Stuart to launch a raid to free Jackson and Lee. Instead, Stuart had wandered the Virginia countryside like a man who had suddenly lost his equilibrium. Morrison was seriously considering leaving Stuart to his ramblings and heading to the Valley to round up Sandie, Smith, and maybe General Rodes or General Early. Those brave men would do anything to free their beloved Old Jack from a Yankee prison.

Stuart poured water in a bowl and splashed some on his face. "I believe the Yankees mean to hang General Lee and General Jackson." He dried his face on a snowy white towel.

"You can't let that happen!"

Stuart stripped off his boots and stretched out on the bed. He was silent for a long moment. Suddenly, he sat up and pointed a defiant finger at Morrison. "No, I'll not let that happen. Even if it means I restart the war." He lay back down. "Even if it costs me my life."

Morrison smiled in relief. Finally, Stuart sounded like his old self.

***

The key rattled in the lock. Surprised by the sound, Jackson and Lee sat up and turned toward the door. Usually the cell door only opened twice a day: once at dawn for breakfast and again at twilight for supper. Other than that, they were left alone to navigate the circumference of their chains. Once a week, they were allowed to bathe. Their laundry was also done on the same day. While they waited for their clothes to dry, they wrapped themselves in their filthy blankets. This morning, with breakfast, two new blankets had been delivered. Jackson had proclaimed it a miracle.

The door banged open. “Attention!” The guard shouted. Jackson and Lee came to their feet, but not to attention.

John Reynolds strode into the cell. His eyes began to water from the putrid smell seeping in through the window. The breeze must be blowing in the stench from the Washington Channel. Reynolds took in the scene before him: the wet walls and floors, the rickety table and chairs, and the two men, drawn and weary, their uniforms fraying, and their linen graying.

“That will be all, Lieutenant,” Reynolds told the sentinel when it appeared that the officer was going to remain in the cell and eavesdrop on their conversation.

“Yes, General.” The lieutenant closed the door behind him.

“General Reynolds,” Lee greeted him coolly.

“I’ve been delayed,” Reynolds apologized, then worried that his apology might sound insincere. After all, it had been six weeks since their arrest. He was getting ready to explain about the loss of command and Sheridan’s insistence that the prisoners’ location be kept a secret when he heard the rattle of chains. He glanced around and saw a rusty chain extending from the wall to Lee’s bloody and chafed ankle. Jackson’s ankle was bound as well. “How long have you been chained?” He asked, horrified.

“Since we were arrested,” Jackson said.

“I’m sorry I was unable to prevent that from happening. I just found out where you were this morning.”

“We heard you were relieved of command.” Lee’s words were cut off by a cough. He doubled over and fought for air.

“General Lee, are you ill?”

The coughing eased and Lee took some deep breaths. “It’s just a cough.” He sat wearily on his bed. Jackson remained standing.

“May I sit?” Reynolds gestured to one of the spindly chairs.

"Of course, where are my manners?" Lee coughed again. His face turned red, and his body convulsed in agony.

"Have you seen a doctor?" Reynolds asked.

"We've seen no one except the guards," Jackson answered. He sat on the bed. "Do you know what's going to happen to us?"

"There'll be a trial." They must have expected the news because their faces revealed no surprise. "Secretary Stanton has gathered witnesses from some of the riff-raff that deserted your army during the last days of the war. They will testify, for drinking money I'm sorry to say, that John Wilkes Booth shot President Lincoln and General Grant on your orders." He shook his head to indicate his disgust at what was happening to them. "You and Generals Johnston and Longstreet will be found guilty and executed. Probably before the summer is over."

Another coughing jag hit Lee. Reynolds searched the room for a water pitcher, but didn't find one. He strode to the door and threw it open. He surprised the lieutenant with his ear pressed against the door.

"Bring me a pitcher of cold water and three mugs," Reynolds snapped. "And fetch a doctor."

The lieutenant patiently explained that the prisoners were only allowed water with their meals. Tired of being stonewalled and spied on, Reynolds unleashed a tirade that blistered the young man's ears and sent him scurrying down the hall. Satisfied that his orders were finally being obeyed, Reynolds closed the door and returned to his chair.

"Thank you," Lee said between gasps. He passed a dirty handkerchief over his mouth.

Reynolds was mortified. He was being thanked! It was almost too much to bear. Somehow, he needed to give the prisoners some hope to hold on to as the days ticked nearer to their probable execution. He chuckled suddenly. He knew just the thing. "I do have some good news."

"Please share." This plea came from Jackson.

"There was a raid at Harpers Ferry last week and a cache of weapons were stolen. I managed to sneak a peek at the report. It had General Stuart's fingerprints all over it."

"You don't know that for sure," Jackson said defensively.

"Ah, General," Reynolds confided with a knowing smile, "I would recognize a Stuart operation, even if the leader hadn't been riding a fast black stallion and wearing plumes in his hat. Just like I know that Fitz Lee has gone and captured two wagon trains. Colonel Mosby and his guerillas are active again. Sheridan is fit to be tied. I rather enjoy that part," he laughed.

The door opened and the lieutenant entered. He handed Reynolds a pitcher of cold water and the right number of cups. "The doctor is coming," he announced. He saluted and exited.

Reynolds poured the water and handed each man a tin cup. He was ashamed when they drank greedily and held out their cups for more. "I'll do what I can to improve your condition. Get you out of the stench and rats," he remarked after a fat one popped its head through the barred window. He clapped his hands, and the rat had somewhere else to be.

Jackson set his cup down on the bed. "General, if you could manage it, I'd like a Bible."

"That's an easy request." Reynolds tried to make it a joke, but in the depressing atmosphere, the joke fell flat. "If you'd like, I could send a message to your families."

The anxiety in Jackson's face eased, adding to Reynolds' guilt. "I'd like that very much. My wife's expecting a baby in the fall."

Reynolds couldn't meet Jackson's eyes. If he didn't find a way to stop this farce, Jackson would be dead long before his baby was born. "Of course." His reply was muffled. The doctor entered. "Well, I'll be going. I'm sorry I'm unable to do any more for you at the moment."

"You've done enough," Lee said. Reynolds was aware that the Confederate chief was no longer cool toward him. Lee removed his jacket and shirt so the doctor could listen to his chest.

Jackson offered his hand. "Thank you, General Reynolds, for the blankets."

Reynolds nodded in acknowledgement and shook Jackson's hand. "I'll get you Bibles and paper and pencils right away." With a wave, he disappeared into the hall. The door slammed behind him.

"General, there's someone here to see you," McClellan announced.

Stuart looked up from the map of Fort Monroe he was studying. Gathered around the table with him were Fitz, Jedidiah Hotchkiss, and Colonel John Mosby, whose guerillas had terrorized the Yankees with raids deep behind Union lines. "Do I know him?" Stuart asked warily.

"No, sir. He won't give his name," McClellan replied.

Stuart frowned. Since his decision at Kilkenny Gardens, he had moved rapidly to organize a rescue mission. So far, he had enjoyed immeasurable success raiding Union storehouses for arms and other needed supplies. But each victory brought the wrath of Phil Sheridan closer to his tent door. If an unknown stranger had found his headquarters, perhaps it was time to move deeper into the Blue Ridge Mountains.

The stranger said something to McClellan.

"He says to tell you he was a general in Longstreet's command," the adjutant relayed.

This was a surprise. Since Longstreet's surrender, only a trickle of soldiers had traveled from Georgia to Virginia. This was the first officer and a general to boot.

"Well, show him in," Stuart said.

McClellan waved the man into the tent. He strode to the table and waited to be addressed. He was a tall man; thin and wiry. His eyes blazed fire, and his long black goatee quivered, for he was laughing at some private joke. A long scar marred his cheek. "See you're plannin' a little raid," he said, pointing at the map on the table. "I got me 400 men across the border just itchin' to help out."

Stuart didn't know whether to be amused or annoyed by the man's familiarity. "Have we met?"

"No, General Stuart, we ain't. But your reputation is known throughout the Confederacy. I'm Lieutenant General Nathan Bedford Forrest."

Stuart gasped in surprise. "General Forrest, your exploits are known to the soldiers of the Army of Northern Virginia as well." Stuart stretched out his hand. Longstreet's cavalry leader grasped it and gave it a couple of pumps. "Please join us." Stuart shooed Mosby out his seat.

Forrest spun the chair around and sat.

Stuart made a quick introduction of those at the table. "And your escort was my adjutant, Colonel McClellan." Stuart retook his seat. "Tell me, General Forrest, are your men armed?"

Forrest cackled like a hen. "It ain't my fault if the Yankees in Tennessee just leave their weapons sittin' around ripe for the pluckin.'"

Stuart laughed. "We've had the exact same problem here in Virginia. In fact, Colonel Mosby's in the process of plotting a raid to pinch a cannon or two."

"That a fact," Forrest cackled again.

"I'm hoping for a battery," Mosby said with a wide grin on his face.

There was a pitcher of lemonade on the table. Forrest pointed at it. "Do you mind? I have a powerful thirst." Stuart didn't; Forrest poured a glass. "How many men do you have, General?"

"Right now, a little over 2,500. More coming every day."

"All under arms?"

"Not yet," Stuart admitted. "But hopefully our raid on Fort Monroe will correct that deficiency."

Forrest drained his glass. "If you don't mind me askin', how do you manage to hide from the Yankees? You being on their most wanted list and all."

"I move my camp every three or four days. That keeps me out of the Yankees' reach. I've also divided the men into small groups, independent of each other, and under the command of our finest generals. It makes it easier to decamp, scatter, and hide, if necessary. And the folks in the Valley aren't too keen on giving us up either. That helps a lot."

Forrest nodded. "So, let's raid a fort!" He rubbed his hands together in anticipation. "What can my men do?"

"Colonel Hotchkiss." Stuart gave the cartographer the floor.

Chapter Fifty

Grant's Office
War Department
August 1865

Sheridan poured himself into a chair in front of Grant's old desk.

"What's wrong, Sheridan?" General William Tecumseh Sherman, the victor of Atlanta and Savannah, asked. "You got your guilty verdicts. I thought that's what you wanted."

Sheridan grunted and scowled. "Did you hear about the raid at Fort Monroe?"

"I did." Sherman signed his name to a report and placed it on a growing pile. "Lost six cannon."

"Stuart!" Sheridan sneered. "He's behind it."

"Not according to our intelligence. It was Fitz Lee and John Mosby." Sherman signed his name and laid another report on the pile.

Sheridan's scowl deepened. "That may be, but Stuart is the ringleader. I'd bet my last dollar on it. Without him on the scaffold, it's an empty victory. Empty!" He slammed his hand on the desk and jostled the reports.

"Don't mess up my piles," Sherman warned, pointing an angry pen at him. "Sam left this desk a mess, and I finally got it organized." Sheridan grimaced at the rebuke. "It's an empty victory anyhow, considering those men didn't do anything wrong. I happen to agree with Reynolds on this. If Sam were alive, he'd have never allowed this travesty to take place. Our witnesses were so drunk, they could barely put two coherent words together."

Sheridan didn't reply. He slept just fine at night. "When will the Rebs hang?"

"Two weeks." Sherman leaned back in his chair. "We're telling the newspapers that the execution will occur in three weeks. It's my hope that once Stuart finds out his men are dead, he can be convinced to disband his force without further bloodshed."

"Why not hang them tomorrow and set a trap to catch Stuart?"

"Simple answer. Congress isn't in session. Too many of them want to witness the event. It'll be as close to a Reb most of them will get," Sherman laughed derisively. "Stanton's allowing them two weeks to make their way to Washington. He's planning quite the spectacle."

"So, you're just going to let Stuart go?" Sheridan asked, perplexed at this part of the strategy.

Sherman set down his pen. "Okay, I have to ask. What did Stuart do to put such a big burr under your saddle?"

Sheridan thought back to the moment he first laid eyes on Stuart: riding out of the woods along the Susquehanna, singing at the top of his lungs, mocking him, and holding him in such contempt that even at the last, he had skipped down the steps at Kilkenny Gardens, making sure those damnable plumes danced in insult. "It's personal." He left it at that.

Sherman laughed. "Too bad you don't have any leverage to make Stuart come in of his own volition."

Sheridan perked up. "What do you mean?"

"I think my meaning's plain enough. Do we have anything in our possession that Stuart would surrender to obtain?" He raised his eyebrows and gave Sheridan a pointed look.

"He'll come in for Lee," Sheridan said, his memory alive with all the times Lee's affection for the peacock had been on display.

"I hear Lee's very sick." Sherman picked up his pen and signed another report.

Sheridan nodded eagerly. "Do I have your permission? To make the trade. If I can find Stuart?"

Sherman leaned back in his chair again. "You'd be willing to give up Lee for Stuart?"

"I'd give them all up for Stuart."

Sherman considered the proposal. "If you could find Stuart, yes. But Stuart alone wouldn't be enough. He must also promise to disband his irregulars and return all the weapons he has stolen. If you can get him to agree to that, then I would allow it. But just Lee. That way, we keep the politicians happy."

"You don't care how I find him?" Sheridan asked.

"You can set the Valley ablaze if you have to. Anything to save us from restarting the war." Sherman sat up and took another report off another pile. "Now, leave me in peace, so I can get through all this paperwork."

Sheridan bolted into the cell and scattered the rats Jackson no longer bothered to chase away. At his entrance, Jackson hid his Bible under the blanket. He cast a fearful eye on the water pitcher and mugs sitting on the table. He grimaced. Lee's medicine sat next to the mugs. What if Sheridan confiscated them. Or worse, what if he countermanded Reynolds' order that the prisoners were to have fresh water three times a day? Jackson murmured a quick prayer.

Sheridan only had eyes for Lee. He stopped in front of Lee's bed, reached into his jacket pocket, and produced a piece of paper. "Copy and sign that." He thrust the paper at Lee.

Lee shot a look at Jackson before reading the paper. Anger burned his face. He shook his head and handed it back to Sheridan. The little man refused to take it, so Lee dropped it. The paper fluttered to the floor.

Sheridan glared at Lee. He kicked the paper over to Jackson's bed. "Pick it up and copy it."

Lee shook his head, but Jackson pretended not to see. He picked up the paper and read it. He went rigid with rage. Sheridan was trying to coerce Stuart into surrendering. The scheme would work because Stuart would do anything for Lee. Even die in his place. He shoved the paper at Sheridan.

If it were possible, Sheridan's glare turned even more murderous. He tore the paper from Jackson. "We can either do this hard or easy, but either way, I'm going to have Stuart on that scaffold."

Jackson was careful to keep his face neutral, free from the hatred rising up and threatening to overtake him. He could do bodily harm to Sheridan, and the ferocity of his anger scared him.

"I may not know where Stuart and his merry band are hiding, but I do know they're in the Valley. General Sherman has given me a free hand to do whatever I must in order to find them."

Jackson didn't like the term "a free hand." The blackened foundation stones of Winchester rushed to his mind. He knew he shouldn't give Sheridan the satisfaction, but he had to know. "What do you plan to do?"

Sheridan smile was predatory. A chill raced up Jackson's spine. "I'm going to rip it apart, starting with Lexington. I'll burn the city and VMI to the ground if I have to. Then I'll work my way down the Valley until either Stuart surrenders or someone gives him up."

"It won't work," Jackson said, more confident than he felt.

"Well, we'll just have to see about that, won't we?" He rounded on Lee. "Copy the document."

"No."

He wadded up the paper and threw it at Jackson. "The destruction of the Valley is on your heads. Guard!"

The door clanged shut behind him.

***

Two soldiers entered with blazing torches, blinding Lee in the sudden illumination of the cell. Slowly, his eyes became accustomed to the light. He beheld Sheridan standing at the foot of his bed, a look of demonic triumph on his face.

"You're free to go." Sheridan unshackled the chain that had kept Lee tethered to the wall these past months.

The guards shoved another man forward and removed his manacles. The prisoner was free, but that freedom was illusionary. The chain that had imprisoned Lee was now wrapped around the unfortunate man's ankle. Lee tried to see who the prisoner was, but he was only a shadow hidden behind the torches. He was tall, yet, not bulky enough to be Longstreet. Earlier this evening, the guards had removed Jackson from the cell. Maybe they were returning him.

"Sheridan, a moment to say goodbye."

Lee cried out. It was his young lieutenant general.

"I'll give you five minutes." Sheridan exited. The guards and torches went with him. A faint stream of moonlight trickled through the bars. It left enough light for Lee to confirm the awful, terrible news.

"Jeb." It wasn't really a word but a moan of deepest agony. "What are you doing here?"

Stuart collapsed on the bed and buried his face in his hands. "Sheridan terrorized the Valley. He burned crops and homes. My small force tried to fight back, but we were betrayed by a friend." His voice shook. "So many dead." He looked at Lee, his face bleak and his eyes tortured. "How will I tell General Jackson that I killed Sandie Pendleton and Joe Morrison?"

Lee wrapped his arm around Stuart and tried to pull him near, but Stuart pulled away. "I'm sorry I couldn't rescue you. I was ready to flee…"

"You should have kept running." Lee wiped a tear from Stuart's cheek.

"I couldn't. Not when General Reynolds came under a white flag and informed me that you were ill."

"What does that have to do with anything?" Lee asked, unable to make sense of what Stuart was saying.

Stuart smiled faintly. "I promised that I would never leave you."

Without another word, Lee pulled Stuart to his chest and wrapped his arms around his dear boy.

The cell door opened. "Time's up!" Sheridan announced.

"Go on, Papa." Stuart's voice was muffled in Lee's breast. "Teach my Jimmie to be an honorable man."

"Like his father."

Stuart sat up. "Like his grandfather. Take care of Flora and Ginny for me."

"I will. I promise."

"Come on!" Sheridan barked.

"I love you, Jeb." Lee took Stuart's arm and walked with him until they reached the end of the chain. Lee embraced him. Stuart's body convulsed in sobs. "You're my darling boy. My favorite child." Lee didn't want to let go, but neither did he want Sheridan to rip Stuart from his arms. He raised Stuart's chin with a gentle hand. "A sunny smile before I leave." Stuart smiled; his father was pleased. Lee turned and walked out the door. When it slammed behind him, Lee went to pieces.

"Sir, sir." A hand shook his shoulder. "Wake-up, General, you're dreaming."

Lee opened his eyes and, in the pale light of day, saw Jackson standing over him. "It was just a dream!" He exclaimed. Tears of relief sprang to his eyes. Stuart was still out there, somewhere.

"I think that one qualified as a nightmare from all the moaning you were doing."

Lee started to cough. Jackson walked to the table and poured a powder into a tin mug. Lee laughed, still half-terrorized. The dream had seemed so real. He could still picture Stuart's final smile. Not sunny, but bittersweet.

"Here." Jackson handed him the mug.

Lee drank down the mixture. "I'm sorry if I disturbed you." He handed the mug back.

"General Lee…"

"It's our last morning together. Call me Robert. Okay, Tom?"

Jackson set the mug on the table. "Of course, Robert."

Lee walked to the edge of his chain and stared out the bars. The breeze was blowing in the other direction, so the cool air seeping in through the window was pleasant. "How long has the sun been up?"

"For about an hour."

"Oh." Lee was disappointed. "I thought Jeb would have come in the early dawn."

"No." Jackson returned to his Bible. "If he's coming, he'll try to arrive closer to the actual time of our execution. That way, he won't have to waste time or lives ransacking the fort to find which cells are ours." Jackson chuckled. "Though, he has always been able to find spies in the most surprising places. Perhaps he has one here."

If Jeb didn't come, then this was his final morning on earth. A thought that didn't trouble him overly much. The Savior was waiting, and Lee had long desire to see Him. He went and sat down next to Jackson. "What is the Scripture today, Tom?"

"The 23rd Psalm." Jackson pointed at the page. *"Yeah, though I walk through the valley of the shadow of death..."*

"I will fear no evil, for Thou art with me," Lee finished the verse. "Death is but a shadow."

Jackson set the Bible down. "We'll go through that valley together."

Lee was silent for a moment. "After all the trials we've endured, I think it's only fitting that we should make this final journey together."

"What we've shared these last three years is deep and impenetrable, like the depths of the ocean. It has bound us together." Jackson intertwined his fingers together. "Forever." He tried to pull his fingers apart, but they remained intertwined. "It will take more than a scaffold to rip us apart."

"I have appreciated your friendship, and I have thanked God for it every night. Thanked Him for those times when I stood at the defenses and feared all was lost. All I had to do was look in your eyes to know that victory was ours."

Jackson blushed at Lee's words.

They were silent for a moment. The room turned gold in the morning sun.

"Is there anything we could have done differently?" Lee asked. It was a question that had haunted him since Gettysburg.

Jackson shook his head. "The duty was ours; the consequences were God's."

Tears pooled in Lee's eyes. He battled them, not wanting to give in to the emotions that were surfacing even in Jackson. Lee could hear the struggle in Jackson's voice; see it in his face.

"We always knew it could end like this if we lost," Jackson continued. "And we knew the odds were stacked against us from the beginning."

"I'm very weak," Lee confessed. "Will you help me mount the scaffold? I don't want to appear fearful."

"Of course."

Lee lost the battle. A tear slipped down his cheek. "Be my right arm one last time."

Jackson didn't stop his own tears. "I consider being your right arm the great honor of my life."

"You are more than my lieutenant. In these last years, you've become my closest friend."

"Who'd have thought in the madness of war, we would have found the blessings of God. I know that you lost a son, but you also gained one. And Stuart gained a father, and I, a brother. Then there are Sandie and Joe, Smith and Jim, and even Dr. McGuire. They're a part of my family as much as Anna and Julia. They have claim to my heart, and I know I have claim to theirs."

"And me?" Lee asked. Where did he fit into Jackson's extended family?

"You're the best of us. Stuart's right. You're the greatest man any of us have ever known. We're all the richer because you have led us."

Lee drew Jackson into an embrace. "Thank you," he whispered.

"No, thank you," Jackson whispered back.

In the hall, they could hear the guards coming to fetch them.

"Well, it's time," Lee said, releasing Jackson.

"I am the Resurrection and the Life, saith the Lord. He that believeth in Me, though he were dead, yet shall he live: And whosoever liveth and believeth in Me shall never die," Jackson recited.

The cell door opened. They stood and put on their coats. Two guards entered and released them from their chains. They sat down on their beds and pulled on their boots; the left one rubbing against the sores on their ankles.

Jackson offered Lee his right arm. "Take my arm, Robert." Lee slipped his hand through. Jackson grasped it. They followed the guards into the hall and found Longstreet and Johnston waiting.

"No talking!" A guard barked before anyone could speak. They made due with smiles and nods. Lee noted how gray Johnston appeared. And Longstreet had lost so much weight. Lee wondered how he looked. Sickly? Frail?

"Let's go!" The fat corporal shouted. He thumped Longstreet on the back with his rifle butt. Longstreet refused to move. Lee smiled at the small act of rebellion. Good ole Pete! He would move when he was ready. And now it appeared he was ready. They started down the long hall. Through an open door, the sunlight beckoned them.

"Do you think he's coming?" Lee whispered to Jackson.

"What do you think?"

"I think he's coming."

Jackson squeezed Lee's hand in agreement.

They stepped out into the bright sunlight and breathed deeply the fresh air.

Forrest approached Stuart at the mess table. His eyes swept over Stuart's cape, thigh high boots, plumed hat, sash, sword, and the many other falderals Stuart wore. *Well, dressing like a dandy didn't diminish Stuart's abilities, and they were keen as any soldier he had ever met.* "Are you sure about this?" Forrest asked. "The Yankee papers say the hangin' won't take place for another week or so."

Stuart sipped a cup of coffee. "It's a ruse to prevent us from rescuing our men. Once they're dead, the Yankees will offer another parole if we peacefully return to our homes."

"Your source told you this?" Forrest was skeptical. He would feel a whole lot better if Stuart would share more information. He had heard from Longstreet that Jackson was always tightlipped with his plans. It seems Stuart had learned to do the same.

Stuart handed Forrest a letter. "From my source."

Forrest sat down at the table and held the letter up to the lantern. "And you're certain we can trust this General Reynolds?"

Stuart poured another cup of coffee. "I know him to be an honorable man."

Since there was nothing he could say to affect the situation one way or another, Forrest handed the letter back to Stuart, who fed it into the lantern's flame. It flared and turned to ash. Morrison walked up, leading Centurion.

"Is it time?" Stuart asked.

"Yes, sir."

Stuart threw the remains of his coffee on the ground. Taking the reins, he swung up on the great black stallion. "Boots and saddles, boys! Boots and saddles!" His clear trumpet voice echoed in the night. With a wave of his hand, he spurred Centurion forward into the dark Virginia countryside. The long column followed in his wake.

To be continued...

Historical Notes
After Chancellorsville:

John Buford played a pivotal role during the first day of the Battle of Gettysburg. His division held off Heth's division of A.P. Hill's Third Corps until the rest of the Union army could arrive. Buford died of typhoid fever in December, 1863.

Darius Couch was wounded at Chancellorsville. After quarrelling with Joseph Hooker, he requested a transfer. He commanded the Department of the Susquehanna and defended Harrisburg during the Gettysburg campaign. Couch died in 1897 at the age of 75.

George Armstrong Custer was appointed commander of the 7th Cavalry and served in the Indian Wars. In 1876, Custer lost his life along the Little Bighorn.

In 1864, **Jubal Early** led the Army of the Valley against Sheridan and was soundly defeated. After the surrender, he fled to Canada. He returned to Virginia five years later and resumed his law practice. Early died at the age of 77 after falling down a flight of stairs.

After Jackson's death, **Richard Ewell** was given command of the Second Corps. At the end of the war, he moved to Tennessee and became a farmer. Ewell died of pneumonia at the age of 55.

Ulysses S. Grant capitalized on his fame by running for president in 1868. After his post-war fortune was stolen by his business partner, he wrote his memoirs to provide for his family. He completed them a few days before he died. Grant was 63.

After Stuart's death at Yellow Tavern in May 1864, Lee promoted **Wade Hampton** to lead the Army of Northern Virginia's cavalry. After the war, he entered politics and served South Carolina as both governor and senator. Hampton died in 1902 at the age of 84.

Winfield Scott Hancock remained in the army after the war and served out west. He replaced George Meade at the head of the Department of the Atlantic. In 1880, he ran for president but lost to John Garfield. Hancock died in 1886 at the age of 62.

In Lee's reorganization of the army, **Ambrose Powell Hill** was promoted to command the Third Corps. Little Powell was killed in battle on April 2, 1865.

John Bell Hood was wounded at Gettysburg and again at the Battle of Chickamauga. When Joe Johnston was removed from command during the

Atlanta campaign, Hood was given the army. He was unable to prevent Atlanta's fall. After the war, he moved to Louisiana where he married and had eleven children. Hood succumbed to yellow fever at the age of 48.

Anna Morrison Jackson never remarried and wore mourning for the rest of her life. She lived out her life in her native North Carolina and raised her two grandchildren after Julia's premature death. Anna died in 1915 at the age of 84.

Julia Jackson married William E. Christian in 1885 and had two children: a daughter, Julia Jackson Christian and a son, Thomas Jonathan Jackson Christian. Julia died of typhoid fever in 1889. She was 26.

Thomas "Stonewall" Jackson was severely wounded at Chancellorsville. He developed pneumonia and died on May 10, 1863. Jackson's last words were, "let us cross over the river and rest under the shade of the trees."

After recovering from the wounds sustained during the Peninsula campaign, **Joseph Johnston** took command of the Department of the Mississippi. He opposed Sherman during the long march through Georgia and was replaced by John Bell Hood during the Atlanta campaign. In the last days of the war, Lee requested Johnston be returned to command. Johnston died of pneumonia at the age of 84.

After the war, **Fitzhugh Lee** took up farming. He served as Virginia's governor. In 1896, he was appointed as consul-general in Havana. When the Spanish-America war broke out, Fitz re-entered the army and was commissioned a major general of volunteers. He saw no action. Fitz died in 1905 at the age of 69.

On April 9, 1865, **Robert E. Lee** surrendered the Army of Northern Virginia at Appomattox Court House. After the war, he served as president of Washington College in Lexington. He died of heart failure in 1870. Lee was 63 years old.

William Fitzhugh "Rooney" Lee survived the war. He married Mary Tab Bolling and had two sons. Rooney died in 1891 at the age of 54.

The historical record is split on whether **Jim Lewis** was a slave. After Jackson's death, Lewis became Sandie Pendleton's servant. When Pendleton died at Fisher's Hill, Lewis was overcome with grief. Lexington's *Gazette and Banner* recorded his last words: "De dear ole General's gone and Marse Sandie too, it's Jim's time next."

Abraham Lincoln was re-elected for a second term. Less than a week after Lee surrendered at Appomattox, Lincoln was assassinated by John Wilkes Booth.

George B. McClellan lost the 1864 election to Lincoln. He used his biography, *McClellan's Own Story*, to justify his war record. It was published posthumously. McClellan died suddenly in 1885.

Hunter Holmes McGuire had an exemplary post war career. He served as president of both the American Medical and American Surgical Associations. A monument in his honor was placed in Richmond's Capitol Square.

The defeat at Chancellorsville caused Lincoln to make a change in leadership. He selected Pennsylvanian **George G. Meade** to command the Army of the Potomac. Meade's post-war career was distinguished. He served as head of the Military Division of the Atlantic, the Department of the East, and the Department of the South. Meade died in 1872 at the age of 56.

After Jackson's death, **Joseph Morrison** transferred to the 57th North Carolina and suffered a wound that resulted in the amputation of his foot. After the war, he spent four years in California before returning to his native North Carolina to run the Mariposa Cotton Mill. Upon the death of his father, he inherited Cottage Home. Joe died in 1906 at the age of 64.

Alexander Swift "Sandie" Pendleton continued to serve as assistant adjutant general for the Second Corps. He married Kate Corbin on December 28, 1863. He was wounded at the Battle of Fisher's Hill. Sandie died on September 23, 1864, five days shy of his 25th birthday.

After Chancellorsville, **John Fulton Reynolds** was offered command of the Army of the Potomac, which he turned down because of Lincoln's penchant for meddling. Reynolds commanded the First Corps during the Gettysburg campaign. Reynolds was killed on the first day of battle.

Robert Rodes remained a division commander in the Second Corps. He fought with Jubal Early in the Valley and was killed during the Battle of Winchester. Rodes was 35.

Phillip Sheridan was promoted to lieutenant general in 1869. Two months after sending his memoirs to his publisher, he suffered a massive heart attack. Sheridan is buried at Arlington in front of the Custis-Lee Mansion.

After the war, **James Power Smith** returned to Union Seminary and was ordained as a Presbyterian minister. Smith died in 1923 at the age of 86.

Flora Cooke Stuart survived her husband by 60 years. She served as the headmistress of the Virginia Female Institute in Staunton, which was renamed "Stuart Hall" in her honor. Flora never remarried.

James Ewell Brown Stuart was wounded at Yellow Tavern on May 11, 1864. He died the next day in Richmond. Stuart was 31 years old. Lee wept bitterly when he heard the news.

James Ewell Brown Stuart, Jr. married Josephine Phillips and fathered five children, including a son, James Ewell Brown Stuart III. Jimmie died in 1930 at the age of 70.

Virginia Pelham Stuart married Robert Waller in 1887. She had three children. Ginny died in 1898, a month shy of her 35th birthday.

The saga continues in…

Let Us Fight It Out

Chancellorsville Chronicles
Volume 2

The story shifts west as General James Longstreet assumes command of the Department of the Mississippi. His mission: Stop the fall of Vicksburg and prevent the Confederacy from being split in two. His opponent is none other than his old friend, Sam Grant. But when President Lincoln summons Grant to assume command of the war in the east, a new and dangerous nemesis arises in his place: ***Sherman***! Now Longstreet must gather all the fighting men he can to oppose Sherman's massive army as it sweeps through Georgia.

LaVergne, TN USA
07 July 2010

188616LV00003B/56/P